S0-AGJ-497

More...

Take a Chance on Me

"Comic sharpness . . . the humorous interactions among Thomas, Emma, and Emma's quirky family give the book a golden warmth as earthy as its rural Maryland setting. But there are also enough explicit erotic interludes to please readers who like their romances spicy."

—*Publishers Weekly*

"Donovan blends humor and compassion in this opposites-attract story. Sexy and masculine, Thomas fills the bill for the man of your dreams. Emma and Thomas deserve a chance at true love. Delightfully entertaining, *Take a Chance on Me* is a guaranteed good time."

—*Old Book Barn Gazette*

"Full of humor, sensuality, and emotion with excellent protagonists and supporting characters . . . a wonderful tale. Don't be afraid to take a chance on this one. You'll love it."

—*Affaire de Coeur*

"Impossible to put down . . . Susan Donovan is an absolute riot. You're reading a paragraph that is so sexually charged you can literally feel the air snapping with electricity and the next second one of the characters has a thought that is so absurd . . . that you are laughing out loud. Susan Donovan has a very unique, off-the-wall style that should keep her around for many books to come. Do NOT pass this one up."

—*Romance Junkie Review*

"Susan Donovan has created a vastly entertaining romance in her latest book *Take a Chance on Me*. The book has an ideal cast of characters . . . a very amusing, pleasurable read . . . all the right ingredients are there, and Ms. Donovan has charmingly dished up an absolutely fast, fun, and sexy read!"

—*Road to Romance*

"Contemporary romances don't get much better than *Take a Chance on Me* . . . such wonderful characters! You want sexual tension? This book drips with it. How about a love scene that is everything that a love scene should be? There's humor, a touch of angst, and delightful dialogue . . . *Take a Chance on Me* is going to end up very, very high on my list of best romances for 2003."

—*All About Romance*

Knock Me Off My Feet

"Spicy debut . . . [A] surprise ending and lots of playfully erotic love scenes will keep readers entertained."

—*Publishers Weekly*

"Donovan's blend of romance and mystery is thrilling."

—*Booklist*

"*Knock Me Off My Feet* will knock you off your feet . . . Ms. Donovan crafts an excellent mixture to intrigue you and delight you. You'll sigh as you experience the growing love between Autumn and Quinn and giggle over their dialogue. And you'll be surprised as the story unfolds. I highly recommend this wonderfully entertaining story."

—*Old Book Barn Gazette*

"From the beginning I was hooked by the author's fast-paced writing and funny situations . . . I highly recommend this debut book by Susan Donovan. You'll just have to ignore the ironing and vacuuming and order pizza for the family until you've finished being knocked off *your* feet by this saucy, sexy romp."

—*A Romance Review*

"Hilarious . . . full of sass and sizzle."

—Julie Ortolon,
USA Today bestselling author of *Don't Tempt Me*

The
KEPT
WOMAN

Susan Donovan

St. Martin's Paperbacks

This is a work of fiction. All of the characters, organizations and events portrayed in this novel are either products of the author's imagination or are used fictitiously.

THE KEPT WOMAN

Copyright © 2006 by Susan Donovan.

For information address St. Martin's Press, 175 Fifth Avenue, New York, NY 10010.

ISBN: 978-0-312-36609-4

Printed in the United States of America

St. Martin's Paperbacks edition / July 2006

St. Martin's Paperbacks are published by St. Martin's Press, 175 Fifth Avenue, New York, NY 10010.

10 9 8 7

For Conor and Kathleen, the only people in the
world who can call me Mom

Acknowledgments

The author would like to thank many people who helped in the creation of this book.

First, a big, sloppy thanks to Richard Sullivan, proprietor of Busview Acres of Indianapolis, Home for Wayward Gentlemen and Itinerant Romance Authors. (Yo, Rich—I still have your house key and have considered selling it on eBay.)

Also, thanks to Jon Schwantes, Ann DeLaney, and Jim Shella for answering questions about Indiana politics from both the candidate's view and the media's perspective.

Thanks to Jorgi Kane of Maryland's Tranquility Salon and Spa for answering questions about hairstyling and life.

Thanks to Judy and Allen Ditto for placing the winning bid at the 2004 Maryland Symphony Orchestra Ball and Silent Auction, allowing me to name a fictional character after Allen.

Thanks to my agent, Irene Goodman, for her insight and savvy.

Thanks to my editor, Monique Patterson, who is so sweet and fabulous that it hardly bothers me that she's RIGHT all the time.

Thanks to Arleen for being my Anam Cara.

Thanks to Steven for dreaming with me.

Just a reminder that this book is fiction and all the people in it are products of my imagination. Any resemblance between fictional characters and actual people is a coincidence.

1

The low hum of music and laughter droned in Samantha Monroe's ears, and she began to feel woozy. Maybe it was the two margaritas. Maybe it was the hellish week she'd just put in at the salon. Maybe it was the latest threatening letter from Wee Ones Academy beginning with the ominous sentence: *"Due to your child's unresolved toileting issues, we must ask you to find other daycare arrangements within two weeks."*

". . . and then, you're not going to believe this!" Sam's best friend, Monté, continued entertaining the table with her blow-by-blow of last Saturday's date with the Mad Unzipper. Since Sam was quite familiar with the tale, she let her eyes wander through the happy-hour crowd at the Lizard Lounge, noticing the group of young, carefree women at the bar, enjoying life, and she had to wonder . . . had she ever looked that happy? Had she ever felt as wild and sexy as those girls clearly did? Did she ever wear spike heels that high? Was she ever that *young*? Should she call Lily again to make sure Dakota ate his fish sticks and that Greg didn't indulge in more than an hour of PlayStation?

". . . and the man just stands his ass up from the couch, unzips, and says, 'Monté baby, I got your python right here!' "

The explosion of laughter made Sam smile to herself, and she returned her attention to her friends. She loved each woman at that table, even if their behavior was bordering on obnoxious. That was the whole point of their Drinks & Depression Nights, anyway. The last Friday of every month, they'd have a couple drinks, bitch about work, life, love (or the lack thereof), and laugh a lot. Then make plans for the next time.

Sam looked past the zebra-striped upholstered lounge chairs and out the picture window. It was a wet and cold early November evening, and the season's first snow was spitting down on the streets of Indianapolis. It was nearly pitch-dark by six o'clock these days. The holidays were just around the corner. No wonder tonight's group consisted of only the most hard-core D & D Night attendees.

Sam glanced to her right to watch Monté McQueen tell her story, her black braids swinging with the rhythm of her words. Monté had been her coworker for thirteen long years at Le Cirque. She was a damn fine stylist and the most steadfast friend Sam had ever had. When Mitchell left three years ago, Monté had held Sam's hand and advised her that a woman with kids didn't have the luxury of giving up. Monté certainly knew of what she spoke.

To Sam's left was Kara DeMarinis, one of her most loyal clients, looking fabulous and powerful in her usual fabulous power suit yet managing to be one of the most down-to-earth people around. Also at the table were Le Cirque owner and general business goddess Marcia Fishbacher and veteran salon patrons Denny and Wanda Winston, identical twin sisters with wildly divergent lifestyles.

And every one of these women was howling with laughter and smacking her palms on the tabletop at Monté's story. Every one but Sam. She knew she should force herself to be more cheerful tonight, because these get-togethers were her therapy. Unfortunately, she was too damn tired for cheerful. She was too tired for therapy. In fact, Sam knew that if the most gorgeous man-babe in the world were to saunter through the front door of the Lizard Lounge at that very instant, partially clothed and completely raring to go, she'd be too tired for him, too.

With a sigh, Sam managed to use her last bit of energy to order an unheard-of third margarita, and when it arrived, she ran the tip of her numb tongue along the freezing cold glass, scooping up a few coarse grains of salt. As she swallowed what would be her only solid food of the evening, a variety of concerns wafted through her weary, tequila-soaked brain. Rent was due in three days, but Mr. Westerkamp hadn't fixed the garbage disposal as promised—so would she face eviction if she refused to pay? Lily was still gunning to go to France with her class next year, but where the hell was Sam going to get an extra three thousand dollars to send her there? And Greg refused to get back into speech therapy, deciding the stutter itself was less painful than the teasing his classmates gave him for going to a "special" class.

Sam took another sip—a gulp, really—and felt her insides wash with the heat of the alcohol. Her mouth began to move. "I never did understand what is so wrong with being a kept woman," she muttered. "If I could find a way to do it without damaging the kids, I'd gladly live in a penthouse with a chauffeur and a maid and a chef in exchange for giving some old geezer a little nooky every once in a while. I mean, where's the harm in that?"

Dead quiet settled over the table, and Sam realized she'd uttered those rambling thoughts *out loud*. Kara gripped Sam's upper arm and stared at her with big, brown eyes.

"If he's not too old or geezery, of course," Sam added as clarification.

"Well, sure." Marcia rolled her eyes. "A girl's gotta have her standards."

"Tell me if the old coot has a brother," Denny said. "I could use a sugar daddy myself, and it certainly wouldn't hurt if he was partial to lesbians."

"I don't think lesbians have sugar daddies," Wanda told her sister.

"I'm cuttin' you off, Sam." Monté pried the stem of the margarita glass from Sam's tingling fingers. "And I'm drivin' you home and puttin' you to bed. We have a wedding party coming in for updos and makeup at nine tomorrow and you need your rest."

"God. I just *haaaate* weddings," Sam moaned. "I

hate brides. I hate updos. I hate all those damn hairpins and all that freakin' happiness, and at nine in the morning! It's just not natural! I want to grab those brides by their shoulders and shout, '*Don't do it! Run away! Run before it's too late!*' "

Marcia blinked in concern, and Sam was making a mental note to never again have more than two drinks in the presence of her boss when Monté scooped her from her chair and stood her on her feet. "C'mon, Cinderella. Time to take a ride in the carriage before it turns into a big, fat pumpkin."

Kara DeMarinis leaned back in the leather armchair and studied Jack Tolliver at leisure, aware there wasn't a woman in the world who would classify the man as *geezery*. Oh, she'd heard him called a few other choice things over the years, such as misogynist asshole, arrogant dickhead, and booty-call bastard, but never *geezer*. So at least that was one hurdle she'd already cleared.

Jack finished laughing and relaxed his long athlete's body against the antique cherry desk that once had belonged to his father, the late, great Indiana governor Gordon Tolliver. Jack shook his dark head and wiped his eyes. Apparently, Kara's suggestion had made him laugh so hard he'd cried.

"I've always loved the way you think outside the box, but Kara, babes, you're thinking outside the known *universe* with this one."

"It's doable, Jack. Remember when Errol Binder borrowed a neighbor's golden retriever for his publicity shots? The man hated pets. And how about when Charleton Manheimer used his press secretary's kids to stand in for his own grandchildren in that thirty-second public education spot? The grandkids were in boarding school in Vermont."

Jack blinked. "No way."

"Yes. So there's some precedent for this. And I've known Samantha Monroe for twelve years. She's great. She's hardworking and responsible and middle-class—everything you're not. And she deserves a break. She's perfect."

Jack raised an eyebrow and quirked those infamous lips of his. "You cannot be implying that I'm an irresponsible trust-fund slacker."

Kara smiled back at him cheerfully. "Well, you are."

"Fine, but if we're being blunt, then let me just remind you that no woman is perfect, especially the ones that you can buy."

"She's not for sale. She would be more of a rental."

Jack produced another hearty laugh. "Good God, Kara! I will not rent a fake fiancée! It is immoral and reprehensible, not to mention pathetic!"

Jack raked his large hands through his waves of dark hair, pushed himself up from the desk, and turned his back to Kara. He began to pace through the office as he thought aloud. "Besides, if I want to benefit from her strengths, I'll have to eat her weaknesses, won't I? Does she have a criminal record? Speeding tickets? How about her credit rating? Is she even registered to vote?"

Kara smiled to herself, watching the sway of Jack's muscular bottom as he paced, the way the wide ledge of his shoulders rolled with each step. She knew there was no man less in need of dating intervention than Juicy Jack Tolliver. But Kara also knew that at this crucial point in his political career the emphasis needed to be on the quality of the women in his life, not the quantity, and Jack's tendency to focus on the latter had suddenly become a bigger liability than ever.

"I've already started opposition research on Samantha—anything and everything your challengers could come up with I've got covered. So far, a spotty credit rating after her divorce is all I'm seeing, and that's understandable. Makes her more sympathetic even."

Jack shook his head, still facing away from Kara. He spoke so softly she could barely hear him. "What about Tina? Damn. She was a redhead. You know how I love redheads."

"You've only been dating her a month."

"It's been a real good month."

"She's a twenty-five-year-old belly dancer, Jack, which may be entertaining to you personally but won't exactly send the right message to voters. Besides, I don't think she's a natural redhead."

"The color might be from a bottle, but it looks good on her. And for the record, Tina is a pediatric nurse who only moonlights as a belly dancer. And she's incredibly flexible."

"Good. Then she'll recover nicely when you break up with her."

"No one's going to believe I'm engaged anyway." Jack chuckled, staring up in exasperation at the room's ornate pressed-tin ceiling. "I'm just supposed to wake up one day and *bam!*—I'm suddenly overcome with the urge to commit? Please. Who's going to believe that crap?"

"People change, Jack. The voters would accept that you've matured, that you found the right woman and decided to settle down. It happens to men all the time."

He glanced over his shoulder, one eyebrow arched, a green eye narrowed at her in doubt.

"And there's plenty of time before the primary," Kara continued. "A dinner here, a basketball game there, an anonymous tip to the *Star*'s city desk, and pretty soon you've got a blossoming romance in place before the February filing deadline. It doesn't look rushed. And you're golden."

"Or I'm dead meat." Jack whipped around. "Surely you realize I'd be nailing down my own coffin lid if someone discovers this little business transaction? Maybe, I don't know, someone like *Christy Schoen*?"

Kara had anticipated this concern, and she nodded crisply. "I will micromanage the hell out of the media. I will personally keep Christy on a short leash."

Jack roared. "Careful. That little bitch will yank your arm right out of its socket sniffing out a lead story for *Capitol Update*."

Kara smiled. She'd been a guest on Christy's Sunday TV show more times than she could count, and she knew all about the journalist's pathological disdain for Jack. Kara couldn't exactly blame her—no woman likes to get kicked to the curb in public. "You really were a real ass to Christy, you know."

"Yes, I was. But pardon me if I feel the time for apologizing is long gone."

"Well, we'll handle Christy, because we have to," Kara said. "As for the rest of the media, the secret will be a light touch. A little public exposure will go a long way with this. And you can always explain that Samantha and the children treasure their privacy."

"Children?" Jack's eyes went huge. "This rental woman comes with *children*?"

Kara shrugged good-naturedly. She knew this part would be the hardest for Jack, but it was also the piece that was going to appeal most to voters. "Three kids. I know them. They're great. Her baby, Dakota, is the cutest little—"

"Stop right there." Jack began laughing again, and this time his chortle had an edge of madness to it. "Sure, I'd like to be the newest senator from Indiana. I'd like that just fine. But Kara, there will be no *babies* rented in order to get me there. No kids. This is insane."

Kara waved a manicured finger in the air. "Think about it, Jack. What would scream *reformed* more than having a hardworking divorced hairstylist and her three kids at your side? You can play it down. Let the voters make their own inferences. I'm telling you. It will work fabulously."

"Absolutely not." Jack shoved his hands down into the front pockets of his chinos and glared at her. "And I would think that after four campaigns and twenty years you'd know me better than that."

Kara tilted her head and paused for a moment, then sighed. "That's just it, Jack. As your longtime campaign manager and dear friend, I can tell you the truth, and the truth is that you've just been handed your last shot. Allen Ditto's decision not to run for the Senate again is a *gift,* and if you don't make it happen now, you never will."

"That's just one possible scenario."

"It is the only one." Kara eased out of her chair and walked to where he stood by the wall of bookcases. She gave him a friendly pat on the shoulder. "Look, Jack, it's been four years since you ended your lieutenant governor gig and two years since Christy helped the voters decide you were a punkass, sexist pig not fit for the Seventh District congressional seat."

Jack winced.

"Every focus group and poll we've commissioned has said the same thing—voters want to support you, but they can't get over your reputation as a player, especially women voters. That's all that's keeping you from winning, Jack. The money is there—the Tolliver name still opens checkbooks—and we're already well on our way to the three million it will take for this campaign. But honestly, I don't think there's enough money in Fort Knox to get you elected unless you make a gesture of the grandest kind."

Jack squeezed his eyes shut and let out a hiss of disgust. Kara was pretty sure it was self-directed.

"You've got to show voters that you're not the same man who was caught ogling a speaker's booty at a teachers' convention two years ago! They have to see that you've changed. That you have a new perspective on life and family and can better represent hardworking Hoosiers in our nation's capital." Kara paused, making sure Jack was following along. He seemed less pissed, so she continued.

"It's creative campaign strategy. It's a business arrangement. It's a way to tweak your private life into shape on incredibly short notice."

"Oh my God," Jack mumbled.

Kara smiled big. "Let's say Sam Monroe and her kids hang around for six months or so, then after the primary you can have a quiet, amicable breakup and, once again, ask that the public respect her privacy. No one gets hurt."

"And how could we be sure she wouldn't talk?"

"A simple nondisclosure clause. If she talks, she has to give back the money, and she'll want that money. Trust me."

"Uh-huh."

"And think about it! Remember how Manheimer droned on at that homeless roundtable about how the Tollivers were too rich to identify with those in need and even owned a mansion that no one even lived in? Hey—Sam and the kids could move in here. It would be seen as an act of compassion and generosity. Am I a genius or what?"

Kara watched Jack chew his lip. She watched his fiercely intelligent green eyes scan his surroundings, calculating the truth of her observations, weighing the risks of her plan, and plotting his next move. Kara had known Jack since their freshman year in Bloomington. Jack was sharp. He was a man who could think on his feet, keep a clear view of what was critically important, and make his move right in the nick of time. It's what had once made him the NFL's hottest quarterback. It's what made him a natural politician, like his father and his father before him.

Kara waited for Jack to say something—anything. Finally, after what seemed like an eternity, Jack's bright green eyes flashed and he gave her a decisive nod, exhibiting the kind of clarity of purpose he'd need to pull this off. At that moment, Kara felt truly proud of Jack the politician—and Jack the man—and waited for his pronouncement.

"By any chance, is this woman a redhead?"

Sam eased her two o'clock client under the heat lamp with a cup of chamomile tea and a copy of *People* magazine, set the timer for twenty minutes, greeted her two-thirty client with a smile and sent her off with an apprentice for a shampoo, then ran to the kitchen at the back of the salon. At the most, she had ten minutes to eat something and call the evil Mrs. Brashears, administrator of Wee Ones Academy.

Sam hopped up on a countertop, grabbed the cordless phone, and took a bite out of her now-cold Taco Bell chicken-stuffed burrito.

"Mrs. Brashears?"

"Well, hello, Ms. Monroe. I was wondering when we were going to hear from you."

Sam wiped her mouth on a napkin, realizing that though a week had passed since she received the note, she still hadn't decided how to deal with this latest threat from the Montessori Mafia. Begging had worked in the past, but she had a feeling she'd used up all her sympathy points. And legal action was probably not an option because, as far as she knew, there was no such thing as discrimination against the potty challenged.

"Dakota is showing little or no progress," Mrs. Brashears said, her voice dripping with concern. "Have you found other arrangements for him?"

Sam swallowed a bite of burrito and felt her heart being swallowed along with it. "I've tried every approach out there," she said, hearing herself default to the sympathy tactic again. "I tried the star chart on the bathroom door, forced him to wear big-boy underwear, gave him a quarter for each successful potty, applauded every time—oh God! Look, Mrs. Brashears, my other two kids did the potty-training thing so naturally, I just don't understand this!"

"Ms. Monroe—"

"I even promised him we'd get another dog if he could only—"

"Bribery will never build a child's independence or encourage creative problem solving, and I certainly don't think adding another dog to the mix will help your family dynamics in any way, shape, or form."

"Right." Sam took a swig of Diet Pepsi and checked her watch. If she left her two o'clock under the heat lamp too long her foil would fry.

"And if I may say so, Ms. Monroe, it appears to me that you are having some difficulty being present for your children lately. You might want to consider a more flexible work schedule, perhaps going part-time until—"

"Until *what*? Until my ex-husband surfaces and

pays all his back child support?" Sam jumped off the counter and stood in the middle of the salon's little kitchen, staring blankly out the small fogged-up window over the clothes dryer, calling to God or somebody to give her patience enough to survive this phone call—this day—without completely losing it.

"All I'm suggesting is—"

"And just an FYI, Mrs. Brashears: I've been up to my *butt cheeks* in independence and creative problem solving for the last three years! How *dare* you imply that I'm not taking care of my kids!"

Sam heard an offended gasp on the other end of the phone. Though it would mean the end of Dakota's private school experience forever, Sam couldn't help herself. It was time for a Montessori smack down.

"My determination to take good care of my kids is the only reason I've let your ridiculously uppity school hold me hostage for the last six months—it's kept me sane to know Dakota was safe and nurtured while I work. But Wee Ones has more rules and regulations than the IRS!"

"Ms. Monroe. Really—"

"I work incredibly hard to keep a roof over Dakota's head, along with the heads of his brother and sister, which makes a total of three heads, unless you count the dog, and that would make four heads! And if you add my own head, we're talking five! Five heads on one hairstylist's salary! Now how's that for *family-fuckin'-dynamics*?"

After a moment of stunned silence, Mrs. Brashears cleared her throat and said, "There are many other Wee Ones mothers in your position, Ms. Monroe, and I can assure you that their three-year-olds have successfully navigated sphincter management."

"Sphincter management?" Sam burst into laughter. "Oh jeez, I've heard it all now."

At that moment, the salon's apprentice poked her head into the kitchen and hissed, "Your two o'-clock's gonna burst into flames."

Sam put her hand over the receiver. "Take her out from under the lamp. I'll be right there."

"You have one week, Ms. Monroe."

Sam sighed. "Yeah. OK. Look, I'm sorry for saying the 'f-word,' but if you could just give me just a little more—"

"One week." Mrs. Brashears hung up, and Sam stood in the middle of the salon kitchen, a barely touched chicken burrito clutched in one fist and the cordless phone in the other, and she let the tears flow.

For two whole minutes, Sam let her shoulders shake and her spine soften, and she cried. Then she hung up the phone, threw away her lunch, blew her nose, and went back into the salon. She strolled through the clary sage–scented rooms color-washed in a Sonoma green, where the sounds of New Age flute and wolf calls floated through Marcia Fishbacher's vision of a southwestern oasis in the heart of downtown Indianapolis. Sam held up her chin, straightened her back, and knew that though everything in her life was falling apart, she'd still be expected to smile and work her soothing magic on her appointment book full of stressed-out clients, giving them that mix of technical skill, artistry, and pampering for which Le Cirque was famous, and for which they were willing to pay obscene amounts of money.

Monté opened the back door to Sam's house without knocking. Her son, Simon, ducked under her arm and ran ahead inside, calling for his best friend, Greg. Monté kicked the door closed with her boot and headed to the dinette set between the tiny kitchen and living room of the Arsenal Street bungalow.

"Dinner is served!" she called out, tossing three large pizza boxes on the table. "Best get in here before I eat it all!"

Lily sauntered into the dining room first, a quizzical look on her pale baby-woman face, followed by Dale, the family's raggedy little mutt. "'Sup, Monté?"

"Hi, sweet pea. How was school today? Where's your mama?"

Lily shrugged her narrow shoulders and ripped open the first pizza box. A straight waterfall of reddish-blond hair covered her face as she peered under the lid. "Did you get a vegetarian?"

"Bottom one." Monté hooked her purse on the back of a chair and threw her leather coat over it, then plopped herself down, looking at Lily in amazement. It seemed like only last week the child had been wearing that pink fleece coverall with bunny ears, riding around, her little cheeks like shiny apples, in that earth-mother backpack thing Sam used for all three kids.

Maybe it was just that Monté could see the changes better in Sam's kids than in her own tall and strong thirteen-year-old, but it seemed time raced by so fast it was a shock to the system.

"So where's your mama?"

"Chasing Dakota. Trying to get him to wear Batman underwear." Lily took the few steps necessary to reach the kitchen cabinets and reached for a stack of plates. Monté checked her out from tip to toe and shook her head—the girl was all long legs and long hair and an all-wrong application of dark brown eyeliner that made her look like a blue-eyed raccoon.

"Should I open a bag of salad?"

"Sure!" Monté hoped her cheerfulness didn't sound too forced. "Let's make this a well-rounded culinary experience!"

Lily smiled a bit, and Monté breathed easier. It wasn't good news when a fourteen-year-old girl couldn't muster up a smile on pizza night. "So? You didn't say. How was your day?"

Lily returned with the plates and shrugged, helping herself to two slices. She was about to say something when Greg and Simon raced in, and the room was suddenly rocking with loud kid voices and laughter and Dale's high-pitched barking and then Sam arrived with Dakota in her arms, the little red-headed angel-boy pressing his cheek against her shoulder, his eyes lighting up at the sight of Monté.

She reached out for Dakota and the baby fell into her lap, wrapped his arms around her neck, and gave her a sloppy toddler kiss.

"Auntie Monté," he cooed, and Montés eyes locked with Sam's in the middle of the chaos, and they smiled at each other. Monté knew exactly what was conveyed in that wordless greeting: *Who needs men to have a good time?*

By nine o'clock, Dakota was deeply asleep, Sam had rustled the older kids to bed, and Monté had washed the dishes. The two women sprawled out on the couch and shared a bottle of Chardonnay.

"If I drink more than one glass of this, Simon won't be the only sleepover guest tonight," Monté said, folding her legs under her.

"The more the merrier," Sam said with a sigh. "Oh, I forgot to tell you—Kara's on her way over. She said she wanted to discuss something with me."

"Kara? What in the world? On a Monday night?"

Sam shrugged. "She just said it was important and that she needed to see me right away. I told her to come over after the kids were in bed."

Monté frowned. It wasn't that she didn't like Kara DeMarinis—Sam had been cutting her hair for a decade and had brought her into the D & D club six years ago. It was just that Kara seemed a little distant at times. Snooty even. She was some kind of big-shot political consultant with an office in one of the new downtown buildings, an attorney who ended up on Sunday afternoon TV talk shows, arguing about laws and the politicians who made them. Monté knew that Kara leaned way too far to the right for her tastes, but she had to admit Kara was smart. And both she and Denny Winston had done some free legal work for Sam a couple years ago, trying to help her track down Mitch after the divorce went through. That had been nice.

It was just odd that Kara was coming over to Sam's on a school night.

"Did you screw up the woman's color or something?"

Sam laughed. "You and I both know that that's never gonna happen. She said it was something to do with her job."

This was getting stranger by the minute. "*Her* job?"

"You're off tomorrow, right?" Sam asked absently, as if she didn't even realize she'd changed the subject.

"Yep." Monté studied her friend. Sam was looking more washed-out than usual. Monté wanted to come right out and ask her if there was something wrong—or something *newly* wrong—but the slight slump in Sam's shoulders told her to go easy tonight.

It sometimes amazed Monté that Sam had held it together as well as she had these last three years. She'd remained strong when Mitchell announced he was gay and left town. She'd juggled the demands of raising three kids while standing on her feet sixty hours a week at the salon. Monté knew that if Sam had finally reached her breaking point, the girl was entitled to have it.

"So, what do you think of the salon renovation?" Monté waited for Sam to respond, but her friend looked far away in thought. "As long as I got enough natural light at my station, Marcia could do up the place in early train wreck for all I care, but if you ask me, she's taking the desert thing too far—a big ole cactus in downtown Indianapolis? Puh-leeze. Next thing you know she'll be bringin' in Gila monsters or some shit and makin' us wear turquoise, and you know I don't look good in anything green."

Sam finally giggled and looked up at her friend. "Early train wreck has always been my preferred period, obviously." She waved her hand around like a game show hostess. "How'd I do?"

Monté quickly scanned the living room and grinned. The small space featured an indestructible microfiber couch and love seat in a stain-camouflaging beige, an inexpensive entertainment center in an oak finish, an oval coffee table, and a couple floor lamps. All of it was accented with the by-products of family life—various book bags, a stray sock or two, clumps of dog hair, Greg's comic books, CDs that belonged to Lily, and little Thomas the Tank Engine pieces strewn all over the carpet.

"Mmm-hmm." Monté nodded with approval. "You did a bang-up job, girl."

Sam sighed, and Monté watched quietly as her friend began her ritual. She would stare at each of the eight paintings that hung on the off-white living room walls. She would allot three seconds to each painting, making a silent evaluation of her art and her life, then move on to the next, until she'd reviewed them all.

Monté didn't need to look along with Sam—she knew each of her friend's brush strokes by heart, even the ones Sam hid in the basement, covered by a drop cloth and years of dust. The combination of tiny dots and broad sweeping arcs defined all of Sam's oil paintings. The colors were so bold and rich it didn't seem possible that they'd come out of the petite, pretty, auburn-haired mommy sitting on that couch. But they had. And Monté knew those paintings were as much a product of Sam as her children were.

"You'll be able to paint again someday. I know you will."

Sam took a sip of wine and offered Monté a weak smile. "I'll start painting the day you get up onstage and belt one out like the old days."

Monté laughed. "Lord, that's not fair, and you know it! I couldn't squeeze into one of my stage dresses if my life depended on it."

"Then buy a few new ones."

"Hmmph. I think I'd be better off going to night school for my degree and maybe one day I can get off my feet."

The doorbell rang, and Sam pushed herself up off the couch and went to answer it, ushering in Kara along with a cold blast of wind. Monté watched the women hug briefly, and Sam draped Kara's expensive shawl-collared dress coat on one of the dinette chairs.

"Hey, Monté!"

Despite the friendly greeting, Monté could tell Kara wasn't pleased to find her there. Now she was certain something was up. She could smell it. There was no way she was leaving now. "Hey, Kara," she said. "We were having a glass of wine. Would you like to join us?"

Kara looked nervously around the room, like she was trying to make the decision to bolt or stay. "That would be nice," she said, just as Sam returned with an extra glass. Kara sat on the love seat and immediately let out a squeak and reached under her bottom.

"Sorry," Sam said, holding out her hand for the small plastic figure. "Seems you sat on Bob the Builder."

"Hope it was as good for Bob as it was for me," Kara commented drily, and everyone laughed.

"So what's up, Kara? Is there something wrong?" Sam leaned her elbows on her knees and stared at the new arrival, clearly as perplexed as Monté was.

Kara's eyes darted toward Monté, which prompted Sam to say, "Whatever we need to talk about, I'm sure Monté won't mind listening."

Kara chuckled and put her untouched wine on the coffee table. She brushed the sleeve of her suit jacket. "Well, it's a legal matter. A personal legal matter."

Sam and Monté snapped to attention.

"You suing Le Cirque?" Monté asked, appalled.

"*What?*" Sam gasped, just as Dale loped into the living room and jumped up on Kara's blended-wool pencil skirt.

"No! God, no! Are you kidding?" Kara laughed, placing the dog back on the floor without missing a beat. "Thanks to you, no one in this town knows I went gray at twenty-six. This has nothing to do with the salon. I love you guys."

Monté sat up even straighter. Wild dogs couldn't drag her ass out of there now. *Hell* no.

"I don't understand," Sam said, shaking her head.

"*Diaper change me, Mommy, and don't forget to use the wipes.*"

Dakota had suddenly appeared in the living room. He stood next to the couch in only a T-shirt, which hit just above his little knob of a belly button. A heavy training diaper sagged from his hand, and his little baby parts dangled in the breeze.

Sam sighed. "Sweetie, if you'd use the big-boy potty, you wouldn't be uncomfortable every time you tinkled in your pull-ups."

"No. Nuh-uh. I don't like the big potty. Change me now." Dakota held out the soggy lump of plastic.

Monté shook her head, watching this familiar but futile exchange between mother and son. Dakota looked like a redheaded cherub, but he was a devil child when it came to his bodily functions, no doubt about it.

"How about we go on in and sit on the big potty just to see—"

"No, Mommy! No. No. No! Change me now! Use the wipes!"

Monté and Kara stared at each other with raised eyebrows, not saying a word, until Sam returned a few moments later and collapsed on the couch. She sighed deeply. "At this rate, he'll be wearing pull-ups when he goes up onstage to receive his diploma— and I'm talking the one from *college*."

Kara cleared her throat. "Speaking of college—"

"Oh my God!" Sam sat straight up and smacked her palms on her denim-covered knees. "Does this have something to do with Mitch? Did you come here to tell me they found him?"

"Oh, sweetie, no." Kara tilted her head and groaned. "Look, Sam. I have a proposition for you, an offer that could change your life and your kids' lives. It's a little off-the-wall, but I figure I can at least throw it out there for your consideration."

Sam grew very still and said, "OooK."

Kara cleared her throat. "Do you remember what you said last Friday at the Lizard Lounge? About how there was nothing wrong with being a kept woman?"

Sam blinked. "I said *what*?"

"Sure she remembers," Monté said, uncurling her legs and placing her feet square on the floor. "Go on."

Sam glared at her. "I do?"

"Sure you do. You said if there was a way to swing it without damaging the kids you'd do it in a heartbeat."

Sam frowned, then dragged her gaze back to Kara. "Obviously, Jose Cuervo was doing the talking last Friday, not me." Then she laughed. "Why? Did you go out over the weekend and find some loser who wants to be my sugar daddy?"

Kara folded her hands in her lap and bit the inside of her cheek to keep a straight face. "Actually," she said, noting how Sam's grin was slowly melting into something akin to horror, "I was hoping you might help him be a winner."

2

Jack hadn't been this nervous since his first and only Super Bowl appearance, at the end of his first and only year as an NFL starting quarterback, when he realized the TV cameras were going to be as unforgiving as the fans. His hands had been so sweaty that he fumbled the first snap, dread coursing through him as the textured leather of the ball slid right through his fingers and bounced on the AstroTurf. His fingers were nearly that wet now, and no matter how many times he jerked at his tie, he couldn't seem to get rid of the nagging feeling that he was choking.

He couldn't fumble this. Kara had been right. This was his last shot at an elected office on the national level. In his heart, he knew it.

"The hard stuff is over, Jack. Relax. This is a formality."

Jack chortled, twirling a felt-tip pen in the fingers of his damp right hand and ignoring Stuart.

"That little lady was quite a negotiator, too, let me

tell you." Stuart walked over to the miniblinds at the windows and pulled them shut, casting the sixteenth-floor conference room in muted light. "A signing bonus, private school tuition, college trust funds, monthly stipend . . . I haven't worked that hard to hammer out a contract since the labor dispute at the kosher meatpacking house back in '99."

Jack looked up at his lawyer accusingly. "I hope you're not implying that I'm being led to slaughter."

Stuart smiled. "Of course not. Did you read the opposition research we did on her?"

"Yeah. Nice work." Jack shook his head in amazement. Kara and Stuart had done such a complete background check on the Monroe woman that Jack almost felt guilty—she'd be walking in that room in a moment and he'd already know everything about her, from her shoe size to her credit score.

Sam Monroe's health was excellent—no current prescriptions; allergic to codeine; hospitalized for childbirth only. No complications. Minor carpal tunnel from her job. Four ceramic fillings in her molars. She saw a counselor during and after the divorce and was treated for mild depression for six months.

She made forty-five thousand dollars in commission last year, not counting tips. She still owed a few thousand on her student loan, but her 1997 Toyota minivan was paid for. She rented a house for nine hundred dollars a month and she was often late with the rent. Her Visa and Discover cards were maxed out.

She'd graduated from Valparaiso public schools and earned a respectable B average at Hanover, a college for artsy-fartsy brainiacs.

Her divorce had become final a little over three years ago. Prosecutor's office records showed her ex-husband, Mitchell James Bergen, no known address, was currently fifty-four thousand dollars in arrears in child support payments. She had no history of felony charges or convictions, but her DMV records showed three speeding tickets in the last fifteen years and a warning for a broken taillight. Her registration and auto emissions inspections were current, and her children had no juvenile truancy or criminal issues.

Her job history was flawless. She'd been at the salon for thirteen years and was loved by her clients and boss. Apparently, she used to paint. Kara said that she was talented and had sold some pieces, but her stuff was too abstract for most people's tastes.

Her parents and a married younger brother still lived in Valpo, though they weren't particularly close. Sam was attached by the hip to a fellow stylist named Monté McQueen, a never-married mother of one who paid for cosmetology school by singing in a now-defunct Indianapolis R&B band. It seemed the drummer's sperm donation was the only thing he'd ever done for their son, Simon, and the two women and their kids acted as a de facto man-free family unit.

Jack figured that, in contrast, Samantha Monroe probably knew just the standard things about him—the knee injury and the teachers' convention debacle. Of course, she also knew he was pathetic enough to pay someone to pretend to adore him.

"They're late, right? I bet she's changed her mind."

Stuart checked his watch. "They are not late and I doubt it. I think Samantha Monroe is anxious to sign on the dotted line."

"Am I actually doing this?" Jack pushed back from the conference table, stood, and sent his leather chair rolling halfway across the room. He headed to the wet bar, his mind racing.

Allen Ditto had pulled the rug out from under Hoosier politics with his surprise announcement that he would not seek another term. He was seventy-nine years old and had served for nearly three decades but was still sharp as ever. Most everyone, Jack included, assumed that Ditto would serve until he died. But the old man shocked everyone at home and in Washington with his announcement that he was done.

"*I never intended to serve so long that I'd have to be carried out of here,*" Ditto had said in his press conference. "*I prefer to leave on a high note, giving Indiana voters an opportunity to think long and hard about my replacement.*"

Yeah, well, the old fucker could have at least given Jack a heads-up—Ditto had been one of his father's best friends.

"Could you grab me a bottled water while you're over there?" Stuart asked.

"Sure." Jack sighed. If only he'd seen Ditto's move coming, he could have been more prepared for this. It was Ditto's fault he had to rent a fiancée.

Jack brought the bottled water to the conference table and leaned his palms flat on its surface. He hung his head and laughed at himself. Hell! He didn't even *want* a fiancée. If he'd wanted one, he would have gone out and found one on his own! It wasn't like he was actively avoiding finding a bride; it's just that he'd never encountered one he could envision in that role, let alone the rest-of-your-life that followed.

And now here he was, about to enter into a legal agreement with a female he'd never met, who'd be paid to pose as the woman who'd finally gotten badass Jack Tolliver to settle down.

His mother was going to shit a brick when she found out what he was up to.

Jack laughed out loud.

"What's so funny?"

He looked up. "It just dawned on me that Samantha Monroe and I will be admitting in advance and in writing that we're using each other. How refreshing." Jack smiled and stood up tall, patting his friend on the shoulder. "Stuart, this might very well turn out to be the most honest relationship I'll ever have with a woman in my life."

Just then, the conference room door opened, and Stuart's secretary ushered in Jack's last resort. She looked taller and wider than her pictures, and her hair was blond and spiky instead of the soft auburn curls he'd expected, and her face—holy hell! Her face was far more severe than he remembered and Jack was just about to slap himself when the defensive end of a woman moved into the room to reveal Kara, followed by the woman he'd been waiting for.

Jack went completely still. Samantha Monroe was cute. Real damn cute. She looked wholesome, just like the photos Kara had shown him. She seemed nervous, and he couldn't blame her. Her eyes were huge and blue and they scanned the room, seeking him out, and when her gaze clicked with his he swore it made a noise that everyone could hear.

It reminded him of the sound of an air lock being sealed, and he suddenly had trouble breathing.

Samantha Monroe lowered her chin and gave him a nod accompanied by what might have been the most disarming smile he'd ever seen. It conveyed embarrassment, humor, and cunning. As Stuart introduced everyone, Jack reached over the conference table to awkwardly grab Samantha Monroe's cute little hand. That's when he started to buzz all over. He was still buzzing as he lowered his body into his seat, realizing a nanosecond too late that his seat was still somewhere across the room.

Jack rebounded from the floor, easing into the chair Stuart had kindly wheeled back into place. His knee hurt like hell. He saw Kara roll her eyes. He heard the Amazonian attorney snicker. And he looked over to see Samantha Monroe gaze at him with pity, like she was about to reach in her purse, pull out a Band-Aid, and apply it to his boo-boo.

Dear God. He wasn't sure getting elected to the U.S. Senate was worth this.

"Shall we get started?" Jack asked, like the graceful statesman he was.

Sam decided not to panic. So what if Jack Tolliver was a goof? He wouldn't be her *real* fiancé. And she sure wasn't going to laugh, because there was nothing funny about being in a conference room full of lawyers who were about to deposit a huge honking wad of cash into her gasping checking account. She was taking all of this quite seriously.

Tolliver looked exactly like his pictures; she'd give him that. He wore an expensive, perfectly tailored charcoal gray suit. He had the presence of a movie star, complete with a long, muscular frame, big shoulders, thick, well-cut dark hair that would need a trim in two weeks. He had a high, strong nose, forest green eyes, and a wickedly attractive set of lips. Sam and the kids had spent hours researching this guy on the Internet. According to Greg, if it hadn't been for the career-ending knee injury in the third quarter of the Super Bowl, Jack Tolliver could have been one of the game's greatest. According to Lily, anyone that tall, dark, rich, and hot had to be a complete jerk, and she'd shown Sam the articles about the national teachers' convention scandal to prove it.

Sam pursed her lips, remembering that video clip they'd all watched. It was about a half hour before the event began. Jack had apparently thought no one was paying any attention to him as he placed his notes on the podium. His eyes had strayed to the sight of one of the conference presenters, bent at the waist, retrieving a dropped pen. It was like he couldn't stop himself. He smiled and said, *"I'd gladly stay after school to get me a piece of that."* A week later he lost his bid for Congress. Exit polls showed he got less than 20 percent of the female vote. The press called him everything from a cad to a sex addict.

But looking at Jack now, as he tried to recover

from literally falling on his ass, Sam didn't know what to think of the man.

He began to talk, and Sam heard the deep resonance of the voice more than she heard the specific words. He had an orator's voice. A politician's voice. An actor's voice. Jack Tolliver's voice was mellow but precise, and he used his hands when he made a point. His hands were large, masculine, and well manicured. She'd seen many photos of him cradling a football, his arm cocked, ready to shoot it off into space. She remembered the way his big, smooth hand had cradled hers just moments ago.

Denny cleared her throat. "Sam?" Her attorney scowled down at her.

"Yes. Right. The living arrangements." Sam smiled, pleased that she'd apparently been listening subconsciously while allowing her mind to wander, a skill she'd perfected as a mother and a hairstylist. "I've already told Mr. Foster that we'd prefer a home of our own."

"Please call me Stuart," Jack's lawyer said with a friendly smile. "As I explained to you previously, and as my client was just reiterating, we can't do that for you. It's either your children's private schooling through high school accompanied by the college trust fund or a home. Not both. Like everyone, Mr. Tolliver's resources are finite."

Sam smiled to herself, aware that Jack Tolliver's definition of "finite" might be a bit different from her own. Things were so damn finite at her place that just last week she'd had to choose between new rear tires and Greg's birthday dinner. She would make it up to him. She always had.

"Of course," Sam replied.

"Your family will have use of the Sunset Lane estate for the duration of your agreement, which will end fourteen days after the primary, so that would be May 23." Stuart flipped through some documents and continued. "We agree that you will not formally engage the services of a real estate agent in your search for your own home prior to May 31, correct?"

Sam shrugged. "If that's absolutely necessary."

"It is," Stuart said, his eyes serious but kind. "The press could easily find out you were house hunting, and the homes in your price range would not corroborate the story of you and Jack planning a permanent union."

"But I can look for a house on my own if I do it discreetly, right?"

"Only if you're very discreet." Stuart looked at his copy of the agreement again. "And, as we have agreed, Jack will continue to reside at his condo on the canal downtown but use the office at the estate when necessary. You do agree to that, Samantha?"

"Well, sure! It's his house. Of course he can use it." She looked over at Jack. He sat quietly, studying her, and his expression had softened some. He'd dropped the politician's mask, and for just an instant Sam saw something very appealing in that face. For a brief moment, Jack Tolliver looked almost sweet.

"The dog has to stay outside," he said.

"How about an enclosed porch? You have one of those?"

Jack nodded. "Fine. But you will be held accountable for any damages to the Sunset Lane house, and any repair costs will be taken directly from your monthly stipend."

OK, so he wasn't sweet.

Denny piped in. "Aside from normal wear and tear and maintenance, of course. My client can't be held responsible if one of the outdoor shutters were to come loose, for example."

"Unless the kids were swinging from it at the time," Jack said.

Sam cocked her head and blinked at him. OK—maybe he wasn't even decent. Maybe Lily had been right about him being a complete jerk. "My kids don't swing from shutters, Mr. Tolliver."

"How about chandeliers?"

Sam smiled sweetly. "How about you just take your chandeliers and shove them—" Denny stomped on Sam's toes under the table. "Into storage for the next six months?"

Stuart inhaled sharply. Kara groaned. Denny placed her hand over Sam's. But it was Jack who had Sam's attention, those deep, dark, green eyes boring into hers, shining with surprise and maybe even amusement. Then his mouth hitched up. He smiled at her.

"Excuse us." He stood. "Ms. Monroe and I are going to grab a quick bite of lunch."

"We are?"

"Yes." Jack arrived at Sam's side and touched her elbow. "I think we need to have a chat before anybody signs anything."

"I agree completely." Sam grabbed her purse and followed Jack Tolliver out the conference room door. She looked over her shoulder at Denny. "If I'm not back in an hour, call the police."

"A girl could really get used to this kind of five-star dining," Sam said, sucking soda through a plastic straw. "Do you bring all your fiancées here?"

Jack took another bite of his sinfully good cheeseburger—as always, crispy on the outside and juicy on the inside—and felt a big glob of mustard drop on his chin. Before he could reach toward the dispenser at the table, Sam had snagged a napkin and wiped it off for him.

"Why are you doing this, Samantha?"

Sam looked around at the lunch crowd at the Workingman's Friend diner and shrugged. "I figured if you're running for Congress people shouldn't see you with mustard on your face."

"Technically, I haven't declared yet, and I brought you here because, in case you haven't noticed, this place has the best burgers in town. Besides, that's not what I was asking you and you know it."

Jack set down his overloaded bun and leaned toward her. Sam was obviously a resourceful woman. A survivor. Her husband had been some flaky artist type who hit the road right after their third kid was born, the kid named for one of the fifty contiguous states, Montana or Nevada, he couldn't remember which. And though she had a degree from Hanover in medieval art history or something equally useless, she'd found a way to make ends meet.

"Why did you agree to this," Jack lowered his voice to a whisper, "this make-believe relationship?"

"For my kids' future."

"Fair enough, but—"

"Look, Jack. I've done nothing but think about Kara's proposition for two weeks straight, turning it over in my brain and looking at it from every possible angle, and it always seems to boil down to this— if my children and I can play a part for six months, we can reap the benefits for the rest of our lives. When will an opportunity like this come again? My two older kids understand what is expected of them, and why we're doing this."

Jack leaned over the table and whispered, "They can't tell *anyone*—not even their best friends, or the deal is off."

"They know that."

"Same goes for you, Samantha."

She nodded, and Jack got to watch as she smoothed a hand through the loose red curls that framed her angelic face. Sam was thirty-six, but she could have easily passed for twenty-nine. Her skin was peachy and smooth and devoid of makeup, except for a clear sheen of lip gloss and maybe some mascara. She was wearing a very soft-looking pale blue sweater with tiny satin-covered buttons down the front, which made him frown. Unbuttoning all those suckers would be a time-consuming affair.

"Too late for that, Jack," she said. "My best friend already knows. Her name is Monté McQueen, and she works with me at the salon, and she was there the night Kara came over. Her son, Simon, knows too. And then my lawyer, Denny Winston, whom you've met."

"Indeed."

"How about you? Who knows on your end?"

"Stuart and Kara, of course, and my mother will have to be informed eventually."

Samantha blinked. "Right. Your mother. I read about her. She's this society bigwig, right? When will you tell her?"

The choking feeling was upon him again, and Jack yanked at his tie. Marguerite Dickinson Tolliver was going to go postal when she heard about this—no doubt about it. The great disappointment of her existence was that at the age of thirty-eight her only child had yet to select a beautiful woman of status and grace with whom to procreate, naming the whole lot of them Something Dickinson Tollivers.

Though Jack had successfully kept encounters with MDT to a minimum over the last two decades, there was no way she wouldn't find out about him cavorting around town with a hairstylist, and there was no way he wouldn't hear MDT's opinion about it. She had ways of knowing what went on in Indianapolis, even from a thousand miles away.

"I thought it would be best to wait until everything was a done deal," Jack said matter-of-factly. "My mother spends the winters in Florida, so she's out of town for the time being. It can wait."

Samantha nodded.

"Tolliver? Hey, stranger!" A heavy hand smacked down on Jack's right shoulder just as he took another bite of heaven. He looked up into the glistening red face of Brandon Miliewski, a gambling-industry lobbyist with whom Jack had wasted many evenings as lieutenant governor. "I heard you might throw your hat into the ring for Ditto's seat? Is that true? And who is your lovely lunch companion?"

Jack swallowed his mouthful and motioned toward Samantha, who was already shaking hands with Miliewski. "This is a friend of mine, Samantha Monroe."

"A pleasure," the lobbyist said to Sam. His gaze flew back to Jack. "So, is it true?"

Miliewski was jangling the change in his trouser pockets and seemed in no hurry to move on, and Jack knew that whatever answer he gave to this man would be echoing throughout the State House in a matter of hours. "I've heard that rumor, too, Brandon. It's an intriguing possibility, I must admit."

He laughed. "An intriguing possibility? Come on now, Jack! Since Ditto dropped the bomb that he's not running again, all anyone's been talking about is whether you're stepping up to the plate. You're the sexiest thing the party's got to offer—by a long shot!"

"Well, thank you." Jack looked at Samantha's wide-eyed stare. "He meant 'sexy' in the political context, Sam. As in I'm young, have some charisma, and happen to have a recognizable name."

"But only if the voters can forgive you for—" Brandon's eyes darted toward Samantha, who was now munching on a French fry, a frown marring her cute face. Miliewski cleared his throat. "Well, Jack, this was nice. Let us know when we can host a little shindig for you." With a wink, the lobbyist walked away from their table, chuckling to himself.

"I'm afraid I missed some of the finer points in that conversation." Sam dabbed at her lips with a napkin and took a quick sip from her straw. "I've never followed politics all that closely."

Jack smiled. "You'll probably live a longer and happier life."

"Don't you like it? Politics, I mean?" She looked so earnest sitting across the table from him, her face attentive and open, her back straight against the ancient red vinyl chair. "Why are you running for the Senate if you don't love politics?"

There it was—out of the mouth of a babe. The question he tried not to ask himself. Jack chuckled and decided he'd give her the abridged version of his dilemma.

"I'm a Tolliver," Jack said, keeping one eye on Miliewski, who was placing his to-go order at the counter. "And historically, Tolliver men have done two things well—football and politics. I blew out my knee, so I went straight to the politics."

Samantha scowled at him, leaned back into her chair, and crossed her arms over her cute chest. He wished he'd stop thinking that everything about the woman was cute, but it was. Her breasts were adorable—sweet rounded handfuls that would look mighty fine in a 34C demi bra, if he wasn't mistaken.

"Look, Jack," she said, her crisp voice jarring him from all thoughts of flimsy lingerie. "It's obvious that if it weren't for Kara's scheme, you and I would never have met, let alone been friendly. And—I'm just being honest here—I'm not even sure I like you very much."

"Really now?" Jack was trying not to smile, but there was something about this feisty, cute, C-cupped rental woman that made him want to grin.

"Really. I think you're a phony. I think you're a spoiled rich boy who's never had to work for a damn thing in his life, and if I weren't completely exhausted and drowning in debt I would never, ever agree to this farce. But I'm desperate. I just wanted you to understand that upfront."

Jack let those remarks stew for a moment, then smiled. "Samantha Monroe—desperate hairstylist. That has a mighty nice ring to it."

Unfortunately, Sam didn't appreciate his witticism. She grabbed her purse and stood up, clearly ready to end their lunch. Jack stood with her, helped her with her coat, and escorted her out the glass door of the diner and onto a chilly Belmont Avenue. He felt the eyes of Brandon Miliewski boring into his back and, just to get a rise out of him, reached for Sam's hand and hooked it around the sleeve of his overcoat as they approached the corner.

Jack glanced back to find Brandon's chubby face peering at them in blatant fascination from the inside of the burger joint.

"Are we starting already?" Sam glanced down at Jack's hand covering hers, then peered up at him. Her lovely blue eyes narrowed with uncertainty and those cute cheeks began to blush pink, from the cold or the contact, he didn't know which.

"We sure are." Jack lowered his lips toward her forehead, where he intended to deliver a chaste kiss for Miliewski's benefit. But something made him dip his head a few inches lower. Maybe it was the warm, spicy scent of her hair or the way her plump lips separated in surprise. But he wanted more than a dry peck, and he used one finger to lift her adorable little chin, and his mouth was suddenly on hers. The kiss lasted all of three seconds, but the buzz he'd felt back at Stuart's office had returned, only this time he was also buzzing below the belt—big-time.

Samantha Monroe was as warm and moist and soft as she looked, and she let out the tiniest little mewl of shock as his lips covered hers. It was three seconds of buzzing bliss.

Sam jerked back like she'd been seared by a hot brand. "Money first, then nooky," was all she said.

Jack laughed and pressed her arm tighter to his side. He was relieved to see Sam smiling, and the two of them grinned all the way back to Stuart's office. Later, as Jack watched Samantha Monroe sign on the dotted line, the memory of that kiss sent a tingle to his lips and additional buzzing to his boxers.

For a brief, thoroughly insane moment, Jack hoped Sam might have enjoyed the kiss, too, even a little bit, and even though it was only politics.

3

"Shut *up,* or what? This place is humongous!"

Lily was first to jump out of the van, and she stood stock still, her hands on her hips and her mouth hanging open dramatically.

Greg soon tumbled out of the backseat and stood with his sister in the circular gravel driveway. "J-j-jeesh. Is that an indoor pool back there? And a greenhouse? No way!"

Simon was right behind. He put a hand on Greg's shoulder and shook his head in slow appreciation. "Son," he whispered. "This could be Kobe's joint or somethin'."

"You sure got the right address?" Monté took very slow steps to stand behind the kids. She blinked a few times in amazement. "'Cause this place looks like Buckingham Palace. You've even got yourself some turrets, girl."

"Of course it's the right house, or the key card wouldn't have worked in the gate!" Sam listened to the "oohs" and "ahhs" as she tried to extricate a fidgety Dakota from his car seat, noting with annoyance that in the twenty-minute drive the child had managed to spill the entire contents of his juice box down his front and clumps of white dog fur now stuck to his jacket, creating an attractive mangy parka look.

Sam sighed, knowing that this was no way to make a good first impression—not that she necessarily wanted to impress Jack Tolliver. But what was wrong with putting her little family in the best light possible? After all, that was the job she'd just signed up for—to improve Jack Tolliver's image. And she was going to be paid quite well for it.

Dale barked and squeezed between Sam's legs, and as soon as Dakota's little feet hit the drive, he went running after him. Sam shut the van door and finally got a leisurely look at their new digs.

"Holy f——." She slapped a hand over her mouth and stared at the looming limestone structure. Denny had mentioned that the estate was as imposing as houses got in Indianapolis, but Sam really had no idea it was *this* imposing. Sam wasn't aware that normal people lived in houses like this. Maybe that was the whole point—the Tollivers weren't normal people. They were abnormally rich people.

She'd probably driven by this hidden lane a hundred times over the years and never even took note. It was studded by a dozen or so estates tucked behind woods, privacy walls, and strategically placed shrubs. People who lived in these houses obviously didn't want the riffraff to know what was back here.

"Well? Do we go in the front door?" Lily was nearly jumping with excitement, and Sam couldn't remember the last time she'd seen her daughter jump. It was before puberty; that much she was sure of.

Sam patted the front right pocket of her coat for the house key, just as the huge mahogany front door creaked open and the studly politician stood framed in its archway.

She watched a warm smile spread across Jack Tolliver's face, and she couldn't help but think about how unexpectedly hot the man's kiss had been, and how it took every bit of self-control she had not to jump him on the sidewalk, wrap her legs around his waist, and beg for it. Of course, that was not the kind of public display his campaign would benefit from. But it was just plain cruel for him to kiss her like that, when she hadn't had any for going on eighteen months.

Samantha snapped back to the present. Jack's smile had frozen on his face as he observed the collection of people on his driveway. Maybe Sam should have mentioned that Monté and Simon were helping them get settled, but she didn't think it was a big deal.

She noticed how Jack seamlessly recovered from his surprise and descended the limestone steps leading to the walkway. He wore pressed khakis and a crisp white dress shirt with the sleeves rolled up. A navy and burgundy Argyle sweater was tossed casually over his shoulders. If it weren't for her beat-up Toyota van in the drive, the vision of this man and this house would have looked like a living, breathing Ralph Lauren magazine ad.

Sam thought she saw a slight limp in Jack's gait, but it was gone as soon as it appeared. He had moved to within a few feet of Lily, Greg, and Simon and had extended his hand in greeting when a noise caught his attention. Jack turned his head and . . .

"Lord have mercy," Monté sighed.

Perhaps Stuart had hidden a loophole somewhere in the body of the contract, an escape clause to be used in an emergency. That's the thought Jack clung to as he set out seven mugs and made seven cups of hot cocoa and engaged in small talk with these seven people. Because clearly, this was not going to work.

The littlest kid had been naked from the waist down. Right out on his front lawn. In *December*. With dog hair stuck all over the front of his little coat!

Meanwhile, the source of the dog hair had been merrily taking a dump on said lawn.

Now seated at the breakfast bar in the kitchen were three silent, wide-eyed adolescents, who looked like they were afraid to breathe the wrong way. It was obvious that the brown-haired boy, Greg, had a wicked stutter. The girl, Lily, was sickly pale, skinny, and wore so much eye makeup she looked like someone had given her two shiners. The African-American kid, Simon, kept his arms crossed over his chest and his lips tightly sealed.

And Sam's friend Monté had been scanning the house from top to bottom and making little humming noises of approval when she saw something she liked. Such as the powder room off the foyer. And the front staircase. And the media room, the pool and fitness center, and the built-in Sub-Zero refrigerator. Jack felt strangely violated when Monté turned that same assessing gaze on his person, her eyes taking him in from tip to toe, a deep "*mmmm, mmmm, mmmm*" vibrating in her throat.

Then there was Sam. She had obviously been embarrassed by what happened in the front yard, and she'd chased after little Arizona and put his clothes back on him, apologizing all the while, rambling on about potty training, a subject Jack believed should only be broached on a need-to-know basis, and he sure as hell didn't need to know anything about potty training and never would.

At that moment, Sam held the squirming red-haired kid like she feared he'd run away or touch something or take off his pants again. The scruffy white dog was barking his head off and clawing at the glass door of the Florida room.

Jack blinked, recalling that Kara had used the word "perfect" when describing Sam and her entourage. What had the woman been *thinking*? The only votes this crowd would bring him would be sympathy votes.

"I think now that I can take a leave of absence from the salon and be home with him every day, he'll get the hang of it real quick."

Jack nodded at Sam's comment, vaguely aware she must once again be referring to Utah's potty-training problems, and realizing that when she said the word "home" she meant this house, the house built by his grandfather Wilson Milford Tolliver in 1927, now home for Sam and her brood for the next six months.

Jack chatted with Sam about the real estate market, the specifics of the kids' school transfer, and the hours usually kept by Mr. and Mrs. Dyson, the handyman and the housekeeper. All the while he tried to keep his mind and his eyes off of Samantha Monroe's curvy little shape. She'd worn a pair of snug jeans today and another little sweater thing, and though the clothes were simple, she looked unbelievably gorgeous in them. It pained him to admit that Sam's butt was just as cute as the rest of her. It pained him further that he couldn't seem to forget that kiss outside the restaurant.

There had to be a loophole somewhere.

The kids sipped their hot cocoa in silence as Jack calculated how much time it would take to get all their stuff back out of the house. The movers had arrived earlier that morning with boxes of clothes and toys and books and CDs, mentioning that most of Sam's furniture and belongings went into a big storage facility on West Tenth Street out near the Speedway. As the movers carried several large boxes and a few wardrobes up to Sam's suite, Jack couldn't help but be curious about what Sam had decided she couldn't live without for six months.

Six long months.

"I'd like to get my room set up if that would be OK." Lily's request came out in a tentative voice, and Jack found himself trying to look past the smudged eye pencil to see the girl beneath. She had blue eyes just like her mom, but her mouth was pinched and thin, not plump and cute like Sam's. Jack gave her a polite smile, thinking that the girl had just moved into a stranger's house and was supposed to start at Park Tudor School on Monday, transferring from the inner-city Tech High. All of this couldn't be easy for her, either.

"Sure. No problem. I'll give you all a tour of your upstairs wing."

It became very quiet. Sam cleared her throat.

"I've never lived in a place with wings before," she said with a smile, trying to engage the surly teenagers in small talk. "Greg knows that all I've ever wanted was an attached garage."

Monté nodded. "Hmm-hmm. Only wings I've ever experienced are the chicken kind."

The two women let loose with a guffaw, and the kids started to snicker—even Simon—and Jack found himself comforted by the thought that as soon as everyone was settled in their rooms he'd be on the phone with Stuart.

Sam let her head sink back into the sea of down pillows and tried to slow her breathing and calm her pulse. It struck her as ironic that her heart had apparently chosen that evening to pound out the rhythm of three years' worth of doubt and sadness and worry—now that everything was going to be fine. Maybe it was just an adrenaline letdown. Maybe it was just that she finally had a little time to breathe. To think. To *feel*.

Unfortunately, most of what she was feeling didn't feel so good.

It helped to look down at Dakota's peaceful face beside her, his little bow of a mouth open in blissful dream-sleep, his cheeks flushed, his baby eyelashes fluttering from the images only he could see. He'd lasted about five minutes in his new room next door, too scared to be alone. Sam knew that poor Greg had to be loving the peace of having a bedroom of his own after all these years, so she'd welcomed the little one into her suite. Sam had turned out all the lights but the one over the sink in the adjoining bathroom and had tucked Dakota into the down comforter.

She studied his cherubic face and let her fingers play in his curls. Dakota certainly had inherited her hair, but the rest of him looked just like Mitchell. Sometimes, Sam was caught off guard by the resemblance and before she could even think about protecting herself the pain would have already sliced her into pieces. Sure, it hurt that she'd apparently done such a bang-up job at being a wife that her husband decided he was gay and filed for divorce—all while she was pregnant. But what killed her was that once Dakota was born, Mitchell just left—he left his kids—and no one knew where he was or even if he was alive. That's the kind of hurt that never heals, Sam knew. It was the kind of pain you just had to find a way to live around, like how tree roots bust up through the sidewalk in order to survive. Life has to go on.

Sam closed her eyes and listened to the sounds of this strange, huge house. She heard the mechanical hum of the furnace, the chimes from the grandfather clock in the foyer—and she felt her heartbeat settle and her pulse return to normal.

The most important thing was that they were all together and everyone was healthy. The happiness would come in six months, when they'd fulfilled the terms of the contract. By then, they'd have found their own cozy little house. When Sam eventually went back to the salon, she could afford to hire a nanny for Dakota until he started school. Lily could go to France or anywhere else she wanted to travel. Greg would be getting the best—and most private—speech therapy available in Indianapolis. And all three of her kids would be encouraged to dream big, to apply to the most exclusive colleges in the country—and it would all be taken care of.

That was why she was doing this. *That* was why she and her kids were here.

Sam opened her eyes again. Even in shadow, this room looked like a set from an old Hepburn and Tracy movie. Yards of pale satin flowed like waterfalls from elaborate wrought-iron drapery rods on high windows, puddling onto the plush off-white carpeting. The same satin adorned the two sofas in front of the white marble fireplace mantel. The walls were covered in a rich, velvety cream-on-white fleur-de-lis wallpaper. Every stick of furniture in the place looked like expensive antique stuff, and maybe even French, but Sam couldn't be sure. A mixed bouquet of fresh flowers spilled its colors from a huge cut-glass vase on the round marble coffee table, and Sam wondered if Mrs. Dyson had put them there and what it would be like to have a housekeeper.

The bathroom was bigger than the living and dining rooms of her old house combined. It was a retreat of solid white marble, spotless glass, and gleaming stainless steel. There was a shower with six showerheads, big enough for . . . well . . . she'd allow herself to contemplate the possibilities some other time. Plus there was a sunken Jacuzzi tub, heated towel racks, a heated floor, and stacks of fluffy, clean-smelling, pristine white towels of every size.

But it was the bed upon which she and Dakota now floated that was the most extravagant thing in the suite. It was a king-sized four-poster yacht with a diaphanous canopy overhead. The coverlet was a satin cream and rose stripe, fringed all along its edge in tiny white hand-tied tassels, topped with what looked like two dozen accent pillows of varying sizes, shapes, and fabrics. The sheets were the finest quality Sam had ever felt against her skin. And the cumulative effect was a deeply satisfying luxuriousness that bordered on sinful. She couldn't help but compare all this splendor to her simple double bed at the house on Arsenal Street, where she'd lived in her former life.

Sam felt a smile curl on her lips, recalling the last conversation she'd had with her landlord, Skeeter Westerkamp. Yes, they were breaking the lease and moving out. Yes, she would gladly forfeit their damage deposit. And *hell yes,* he'd been a cheap horse's ass and she wished Skeeter good riddance. That's when they'd piled in the van and left behind the broken garbage disposal, the leaking bathtub, the cracked window in the boys' room, and the not-quite-reliable furnace and driven through the gates of the Tolliver mansion.

The theme song from the old *Beverly Hillbillies* TV show wafted through Sam's mind, and she chuckled to herself. At least they hadn't pulled up with kitchen chairs and steamer trunks tied to the luggage rack.

Sam's eyes traveled across the room, to the huge walk-in closet and the cardboard wardrobes that held her paintings. Maybe in addition to breathing, thinking, and feeling she'd find some time to paint in the next six months. She only hoped she remembered how and that there was still something inside her worth painting.

Her thoughts meandered to Jack, and she felt a little surge of heat course through her belly. She blamed it on that kiss, that wholly unfair kiss on the sidewalk that day, the one she hadn't been able to shoo from her mind. It hadn't lasted long and it was all part of her assignment, but that kiss had done some serious damage. It was like Jack Tolliver had opened the pop-top to her can of loneliness—the same can she'd been shaking around for three years—and left her with a big mess to clean up. Sam was going to have to find a way to compartmentalize Jack's kisses, she knew. She'd have to find a way to see them for what they were—business. And maybe with all this time on her hands, she'd think about finding a real man to date, someone she could really kiss and really touch and maybe even really love.

Besides, Jack Tolliver was not her type. He was so handsome he was almost otherworldly, and he was obviously an egomaniac. He had no outlet for creative self-expression that she could see, and that was a red flag in her book. All that said, Sam remembered the brief flash of realness she'd seen in his face at his lawyer's office, after he'd gotten up from the floor. And the sound of his laugh after that kiss, and the sense she had about him while they sat together at the diner, a sense that there was some kind of war being waged inside of Jack, a war between a the person he really was and the person the world expected him to be. . . .

"Mommy?" A soft voice carried through the room and Sam saw the double doors of the suite slowly open. Lily poked her head inside and smiled sheepishly.

"Hi, sweet pea."

"I can't sleep. It's too weird being here. Can I come in with you?"

Sam reached for the coverlet and pulled it back, patting the firm bed for Lily. Her daughter giggled as she ran across the room and jumped in.

"Easy," Sam whispered, nodding to Dakota.

"Oh. Didn't know he was here." Lily propped herself up on an elbow. "We're only missing Greg and Dale now. Should I go get them?"

Sam chuckled. "Dale is banished to that room with indoor-outdoor carpeting for the duration, I'm afraid."

Lily sighed. "That is just so heinous. I mean, we have a maid, right, so what's the big deal? It's like His Excellency doesn't trust us to keep an eye on our own dog or something. I mean, dude! Dale isn't a Great Dane or anything. He's a fifteen-pound *marshmallow,* for Christ's sake."

Sam closed her eyes tight, wondering which issue needed addressing first—Lily's insulting nickname for Jack, her apparent plans to lead a life of leisure, or the use of language she'd rather not hear coming from her fourteen-year-old daughter. "Listen, Lily—"

"Yeah. OK. Sorry. I'll never call him that to his face and I know I shouldn't use the Lord's name in vain, but it's not like we go to *church* or anything, Mother, and Dale is just a little harmless puppy."

Sam smiled at Lily. "Jack is not used to being around dogs and kids. We're going to have to clean up after ourselves and be religious about following Dale around with the scooper, you know?" Sam stroked her daughter's smooth hair. "Maybe we should just be religious all around and start going to church every weekend. Just for the hell of it. What do you think?"

Lily's eyes popped wide. "God, Mother! You're not going born-again on me, are you?"

Sam laughed softly. "No, but I'm going to be the best, most attentive, loving, wonderful mom I can be for the next six months. I want to enjoy you kids—enjoy every minute I get to spend with you."

Lily arched one eyebrow. "OK—you are really starting to skeeve me out now."

Dakota stirred, and the two of them giggled and shushed each other. Sam took hold of Lily's hand. "Remember, sweet pea," she whispered. "We're not really rich people. We're just playing them on TV."

There was a faint knock on the door.

"Mom?" Greg whispered. "It's too quiet in my room to sleep." He walked over to the edge of the bed and frowned when he saw that his sister and brother had beat him to the punch.

"Move over, Bones," he said to Lily.

"No," she grumbled. "And stop calling me that, Sped."

"Come over here, big guy." Sam pulled the comforter away from the other side of the bed and made a spot for Greg, who snuggled in next to Dakota. She stroked Greg's smooth cheek and smiled at her oldest son. Getting him into private school and away from the unforgiving city kids would be a godsend. She expected to see him blossom in a place where a smart kid who happened to need speech therapy wouldn't be labeled a dork or sped, that unkind abbreviation for "special ed."

"There's plenty of room for all of us in here, and I think now would be a really great time for the two of you to stop calling each other names." Sam looked to each of her older kids. "We have to be on top of our game for the next six months. We've got to work together. We've discussed how important this is."

"I know," Lily muttered.

"OK," Greg sighed.

"We have a meeting tomorrow with Mr. Tolliver, his attorney, and Kara. We're going over the basic

rules and our schedule for the next week. I'm counting on you guys to be civil to each other."

"Yeah," Greg said.

"Whatever," Lily said.

"How about I sing us all a lullaby?" Sam asked.

Lily's sigh was full of angst. "We are not toddlers
anymore."

A sharp stab of regret hit Sam in the chest. Oh,
how she knew that! She was painfully aware that the
years had whizzed by in a blur of hair and bills and
diapers and take-out pizza and collapsing marriages
and not enough sleep and she planned to use this
next six months to make up for all of it.

Sam cleared her throat and began to sing a slow,
soft tune to her children. *"This is a story 'bout a man
named Jed . . ."*

She and the kids giggled themselves to sleep.

"This had better be good," Christy Schoen repeated to
herself for the third time in as many minutes. She'd
never liked Brandon Miliewski, and she certainly
didn't appreciate waiting for anyone, especially
someone she didn't like. She would give him exactly
two more minutes, and that was only because she was
an optimist and there was always an outside chance
that one of the sleazy lobbyist's tips might be worth
hearing.

A chubby guy in a casual windbreaker burst
through the door of the Chatterbox Tavern, looking
to his left and right like somebody would recognize
or care that he was there. Good God. She and the
bartender were the only living souls in the hole-in-

the-wall establishment. It was four o'clock on a Sunday afternoon. Normal people were home with their families, relaxing and discussing matters of public import just featured on that afternoon's *Capitol Update with Christy Schoen*.

Today's show had been all about Ditto's surprise announcement that he would not seek another term, the flood of candidacies it had spawned, and the impact that a change in representation would have on the state. Of course, Jack Tolliver, that bastard, was stirring up the most interest by simply not bothering to announce. He got publicity by doing *nothing*. She hated that about him more than anything else. OK— maybe not as much as she hated the way he treated women. Like they were disposable. Like they were interchangeable. Like the world was just chock-full of women as smart, beautiful, and fabulous as she was. As if!

Christy took a calming breath. One day, he'd see what a giant mistake he'd made the night he dumped her. One day, he'd come back to her.

Brandon made his way to Christy's table and bent down in an attempt to kiss her cheek. She prevented actual contact with a flat palm to his chest. "Have a seat," she said.

"You look gorgeous, as usual." Brandon's beady eyes lit up his flushed face.

"You look good, too," she said, hoping it didn't sound like the lie it was, because Brandon didn't look good. He looked like the porky geek of a former state legislator from bum-fuck Madison, Indiana, that he was. "I'm having coffee. Want one?"

"No thanks. I'd rather share a bottle of wine with you."

She scrunched up her nose like she smelled something unpleasant and said, "Maybe some other time."

As Brandon slowly removed his jacket, Christy felt his eyes roam all over her. She was used to this, of course, and she sighed softly. Sometimes it was a burden to be beautiful in the sleek, blond, and photogenic kind of way that she was.

"I mean, wow. You look *really* good, Christy."

She folded her hands on the tabletop and smiled at him. "You have exactly five minutes."

"Hey! Great! Fabulous!"

Brandon fidgeted in the chair and tried to pretend he wasn't just shot down. She hated men who retreated like that, without a fight. Even if Brandon were the hottest man alive, she'd not respect the guy—a wimp if there ever was one. "Let's have it, Miliewski."

"It's about Jack Tolliver."

Hello. Christy pretended to be only marginally interested. "Let me guess—he's seriously considering a run for Ditto's Senate seat. Everyone within five hundred miles of the State House has heard that rumor."

Brandon chuckled, cutting her off with a dismissive wave of his hand. "I started that rumor, baby," he said proudly. "But there's more. Something I was saving just for you."

The gleam in Miliewski's little eyes told Christy to sit there and listen and not be too appalled that he'd just called her baby. *Baby!* Maybe she should have answered one of his eleven voice mails from last week, if this was about Jack.

"He's dating someone new. Someone a little out of the ordinary."

The expectant tension Christy had been holding in her shoulders released, and she groaned. "Is that all? Everyone in town knows he's been seeing the belly dancer bimbo for the last month or so."

"No way!" Brandon shook his head. "Tina is a nurse at Riley children's hospital! My sister works with her!"

"A nurse who happens to moonlight in harem pants every weekend at Santorini's."

Miliewski's eyes shot open. "No kidding?" He licked his lips. "That is so hot."

Christy reached for her purse and started to stand up.

"Well, anyway, this is a different woman," Brandon said, nodding with certainty. "Way different."

Christy planted her butt right back in the booth. "OK. Who is she?"

"Her name is Samantha Monroe."

"Samantha *who*?" Christy wracked her brain—she'd heard that name somewhere but couldn't place it. "Who is she?"

Miliewski shrugged. "He took her to lunch at Workingman's Friend the other day. She's a cute red-head with a nice set of real ones."

Christy shook her head in disgust. "You are pure class, Miliewski." She sighed and gathered up her purse again. "That's it? Just a name? You dragged me out on a Sunday to tell me the name of some big-boobed chickie Jack took out for a burger?"

He frowned. "They weren't big, just nice. And you're the one who said you didn't have any time but today to see me and—"

"Fine. Thanks, Brandon. Good luck trying to get the video poker bill out of committee." In a flash, she was on her feet, coat on, car keys in hand.

"But there's something different about this one," Brandon said, looking past Christy, a pensive smile on his face. "She seems kind of sweet. She's older than the standard twenty-somethings he's usually boinking. She looked nice and normal and he was talking to her softly, like he really cared what she was saying. Like they had important things to discuss."

Christy was listening.

"And then I saw him kiss her out on the sidewalk. It was one of those kisses that didn't last a real long time but got the message across, you know? And Tolliver laughed afterward—a big laugh—and she smiled like a cat who'd swallowed the canary."

When Brandon brought his dreamy gaze back to Christy, he jerked in surprise, and Christy tried to shake off the shock that must have been plastered all over her face.

"You OK, Christy?"

"I'm just fine." She pursed her lips and blinked. "Thanks for the tip, Brandon, and for coming out today. I do appreciate it, but Jack's love life is really none of my business, and it's certainly not news." She brushed past him on her way to the door but stopped when she heard Miliewski's nasty laugh behind her.

"You are so full of shit," he whispered.

Christy spun around, her mouth open in astonishment.

Brandon stood up and walked toward her, savoring Christy's surprise. "Anything that man does is news in this town—at the *Star,* the *Business Journal,* at all three affiliates *plus* Fox and even the local access channels, and you know it." He cocked his head at her and grinned. "You helped make it that way, Christy."

She didn't know what to say. His aggressiveness had caught her attention. She found it strangely exciting. Her heart began to beat a little too fast.

"And you and I both know that if Samantha Monroe happens to be Jack's babe du jour at the time he declares his candidacy—and he will declare, of course—the woman's life is going to be a living hell. You'll see to that, too. It's what you do."

Maybe it was the lighting, or lack thereof, in the Chatterbox, but Brandon Miliewski appeared vaguely attractive standing there, the assertive smirk helping his face appear broad and strong instead of merely chubby.

Brandon reached behind him and pulled out the chair Christy had been sitting in. "Now. How about that bottle of wine?"

Christy nodded. The confidence in his voice, along with his obvious appreciation of her talents, seemed to soothe her. "I suppose just a glass wouldn't hurt," she said.

4

Stuart bent forward at the waist and braced his palms on his knees, sucking air. Jack watched the sweat stream off the ledge of his friend's chin and puddle onto the hardwood floor of the racquetball court.

"Damn, Jack," Stuart panted. "Don't take it out on me. I'm not the one who got you into this. Kara should face this punishment. Not me."

"Kara can't return my serve."

Stuart looked up from his crouched position, blinking behind clear plastic safety goggles. "Like I can?" He straightened and put a hand to his lower back. "I gotta get some water."

Jack watched Stuart stagger out of the racquetball court and into the hallway and take a big gulp from his bottled water. Jack followed, knowing he had to ask just once more to make sure. "So you're absolutely positive there's no way we can back out of this?"

Stuart squirted some water onto his forehead and patted his face with a towel. "Sure you can, Jack. But then she walks away with everything—every dime she negotiated for, her monthly stipends and the trust fund—and you get nothing. Is that what you want? I mean, it's been exactly three days. What could the woman have done in three days to scare you like this?"

Jack laughed off the question. Sam Monroe didn't scare him . . . exactly. "It's a comfort level thing, Stu. It's too much, that's all. The kids. The friend. The friend's kid. The diapers. The dog. It's just not my style."

Stuart nodded, a sly smile moving across his face. "You know they aren't real, right, Jack?"

Jack chuckled at Stu's bluntness. "Of course they're real! I've been staring at them for days on end, and I'm telling you, Samantha is packin' only what God gave her. I know the difference."

Stuart stared at him with his mouth hanging open, then shook his head. "I'm not talking about the woman's ta-tas, Jack. Jesus! I meant *they* as in all the *people* you just mentioned."

Jack adjusted the Ace wrap around his knee and nodded. "Of course. I knew that."

"Anyway." Stuart took another chug. "What I'm saying is that Samantha Monroe isn't really your fiancée. She and her kids are just props. So if they annoy you, just go home to your condo and forget them. Don't let the situation get you down. Has Kara been running some numbers by you?"

"Yeah. Looks like Preston-Norwich is in to the limit in both corporate and private contributions, and so is Gerring Pharmaceuticals. But Charlie Manheimer's got a boatload of family values money, Stu. It's got me a little worried—those religious right organizations have a ton of cash to play with."

Stuart shrugged. "Manheimer can talk the talk all he wants, but you, my boy, are going to be walking the walk, right in front of the voters. I think the less of a deal you make of Sam and the kids the more impact it's going to have."

"That's what Kara said."

"So you ready for the Pacers game?"

Jack sighed. Tomorrow night was supposed to be his first official public outing with Sam. Their first date, so to speak. They had courtside seats to watch Indiana annihilate Milwaukee. Kara had planned everything down to what they should both wear and how he was to whisper in Sam's ear at least twice a quarter to ensure the photographers would catch it. He had been instructed to kiss Sam's cheek and buy her popcorn. He had been reminded to drape his arm around her shoulders protectively as they walked out of Conseco Fieldhouse. Like he needed to be told how to date a woman! He could practically write the field guide! "Yeah. I'm ready."

Stuart tossed the water bottle into his gym bag and glared at Jack through his goggles. "Is there something else you're not telling me? What's going on?"

Jack shook his head. He sure as hell wasn't going to tell Stuart that he'd lost sleep several nights in a row thinking of Sam and the way her lips felt just damn perfect under his. He wouldn't dare tell Stuart that he'd already decided that the first gift he'd buy her would be a flaming red bra and thong set, something to accentuate her pale flesh and warm curls.

"Nothing," Jack said.

"No way, Jack." Stuart laughed. "Anything but that." He shook his head in disdain. "Look, it's just six months. You can go without the kitty for six months. You have to. You're clear on this, right?"

Jack rolled his eyes.

"No. Really, Tolliver. You want to be U.S. senator? Then keep Mr. Man in your pants for the next six months. Think about it. Let's say Christy or any lucky city desk reporter sees you stepping out on your new 'fiancée.' You think they'd keep that little secret to themselves? Maybe back in your dad's day, but not now, dude. You think getting caught cheating on your intended is gonna win back the hearts of the voters? I sure as hell don't."

Jack took a quick glance around the hallway of the Columbia Club just to make sure no one could overhear this little chat. The place was crawling with politicos, journalists, lawyers, and captains of industry and commerce. "Keep your voice down, Stu."

"And even worse—if you even *think* about messing with Samantha Monroe, it's gonna get really complicated really fast. This is business, Jack. She is a prop—keep reminding yourself that—*prop, prop, prop.* She's pretty and sharp, but she's a prop nonetheless."

Jack nodded silently.

"Repeat after me." Stuart got right in his face, and Jack had to laugh at how goofy he looked lecturing

him in those ridiculous goggles. He resembled a
pissed-off frog. "Samantha Monroe is not real. She
is a prop. Say it."

"Sam Monroe is not real," Jack whispered, feeling
fairly foolish. "She is a prop."

"Good." Stuart slapped Jack in the upper right
forearm and nudged him back into the racquetball
court. "Now finish kicking my ass so I can get back
to the office."

"You gotta get me out of that hellhole." Lily slammed
her Army surplus knap sack onto the kitchen table
and stared at her mother with real panic. "I'm serious. That place is completely fucked up."

Before Sam could gasp at her daughter's language, Lily had already started apologizing.

"I'm sorry, but it's true. I refuse to go to school
with a bunch of rich-kid suck-ups and phonies. So
far, the only difference I can see is that private
schoolies are better at hiding shit than the kids in
public school. Whoops—I meant to say 'stuff.'
Sorry."

Sam stood stock still with the plate of homemade
cookies in her hands. This wasn't turning out to be
the after-school Kodak moment she'd planned. She
wanted this afternoon to be special—perfect. But her
chest felt heavy and her stomach churned with a sudden anger. The language pouring out of her daughter's innocent mouth! Amazing! Where the hell did a
ninth-grade girl learn to talk like that?

Oh shit.

"I'm gonna get some milk to go with those," Lily

said, marching across the kitchen, her tartan uniform skirt swaying at the backs of her skinny, pale thighs. Sam hadn't noticed that her daughter had accented her ensemble that morning with a pair of gray wool socks and hiking boots with thick treads and Day-Glo orange laces. It also looked like she'd rolled up the skirt's waistband at least twice, because it was markedly shorter than it was when she'd left the house.

"Those cookies look good, Mom. Did you really bake them? What are they?"

"Chocolate chip with pecans," Sam managed, still unable to move.

Greg's hand scooped three from the plate before Sam could place it on the table. She hadn't even seen him come into the kitchen. "And how about you, Greg? How was your second day?"

Greg shrugged, munching on a cookie. "These are great," he said with his mouth full. "Real good, Mom. Thanks."

Sam collapsed into a chair.

"Where's diaper boy?" Lily plopped down across from Sam and reached for the plate of cookies.

"He should be getting up from his nap in a minute."

"Any miraculous breakthroughs today?" Lily asked with a grin.

Sam sighed. "Well, he sat on the potty for about a half hour with *Goodnight Moon*. I think he taught himself to read, but that's about it."

"You could've gotten me some milk while you were up," Greg said, frowning at his sister. "You never think of anyone b-b-but yours-s-self."

Lily laughed, a few cookie crumbles spilling from her mouth onto her standard-issue navy blue cardigan, which Sam noticed was buttoned once at her navel, barely covering a Nine Inch Nails T-shirt. Sam marveled at the fact that Lily had been at Park Tudor School exactly two days and was already pushing the envelope on the dress code. Where did the girl get her nerve?

"You lost the use of your limbs now, too?" Lily asked Greg. "You need occupational therapy now in addition to speech therapy?"

"S-s-screw you, Lily."

"Bite me, weasel."

"Stop it!" Sam felt her entire body vibrate with regret. When did her beautiful little children become so caustic? When had they started hating each other? She remembered the two of them—just a year apart—playing Fisher-Price farm together, taking baths together, sleeping together. Until he was seven, the ultimate reward for Greg was the right to snuggle next to his sister in her double bed, where the two of them would laugh and talk until they drifted off to sleep. Sam had often checked on the two of them before she went to bed herself, observing how Lily's hand draped protectively over her little brother's forearm, their faces slack with the deep sleep of innocence.

Her two oldest kids didn't look so innocent at the moment. They looked angry. They looked tired. They looked unsure. And she couldn't exactly blame them.

"It's going to be all right, guys," Sam said, reaching across the table to touch them. "All I ask is that

you give Park Tudor one grading period, and if by
the spring you don't like it, I won't force you to go.
I'll even send you back to Tech if you like, or anywhere else you want. We can even buy a house in the
district you prefer."

Lily blinked. "Seriously?"

"Yes. I want you to be happy. But I also want you
to have the best opportunities—art, drama, music,
foreign language, you name it—and you have more
of a say at Park Tudor than at Tech. You have more
control over what you do. But if you're not happy,
what's the point?"

Lily and Greg looked at each other, then at Sam.
Greg narrowed his eyes. "Is this child psychology or
something?" Sam watched him get up from the
table, open one of the kitchen's glass-front cabinets,
and pull out a cut-crystal drinking glass like he'd
lived here forever.

She smiled. "It's not psychology. I just love you
guys and want the best for you. It's that simple."

"Gotcha," Lily said.

"There's one nice kid I met," Greg volunteered.
"He seems OK. He's into chess."

"Sounds like a keeper," Lily muttered.

"How about you, Lil? Any potential friends on the
horizon?"

Lily reached for another cookie before she answered her mother. "Not really. Everybody's in established little cliques. One loser dude keeps
bugging me, though. He's in my AP English class
and he calls me 'Goth Girl.' So original."

"But how would we go back to Tech, Mom?"

Greg sat back down with his milk. "Now that we've got some money, why would we move back to the East End?"

Lily made a face. "We could live on some fancy cul-de-sac in Carmel and Jack could get us in Tech if we wanted. Look at the way he pulled strings to get us into Park Tudor at the end of the grading period. Guess it comes in handy to have that much clout."

Sam smiled. "We will never take advantage of that."

"I bet he could get us into anything," Greg said, not bothering to hide his excitement. "I'd like to sit at the f-f-fifty-yard line to watch the Colts play, then go down on the field for autographs. I know he could do that!"

"I'd like front-row seats at the Green Day concert." Lily said, her eyes lighting up. "With a limo ride and backstage passes."

Sam laughed. She was about to explain that Jack Tolliver was not their own personal gravy train but realized that would sound ridiculous. Because that's exactly what he was.

The game had definitely started, Jack noted, because Samantha Monroe was now seated next to him looking dutifully datelike. He hoped she'd loosen up some and be quick about it, since the Indiana versus Milwaukee contest had started, too, and all around them were the usual suspects tucked into their prime courtside seats—the Marion County prosecutor, the U.S. Attorney, the president of Indiana University–

Purdue University Indianapolis, the mayor, the managing editor of the *Star,* and assorted wives, kids, lobbyists, trial attorneys, legislators, professional athletes, and trophy bimbos, including three women Jack was fairly certain he'd dated at some point, especially the brunette who had not stopped scowling at him.

That any one of them had failed to notice Jack with Samantha was a near impossibility. He'd already exchanged greetings with most, including the brunette, whose name he thought might be Amanada. Or Amelia. He chuckled a little to himself, realizing that for a politician he was pretty damn awful with names.

He looked over at Sam again. There was no way that any of these people could see Sam over here and think, *Love-struck fiancée.* Descriptive phrases like "nervous wreck" and "fish out of water" were far more likely. Jack wished Sam would stop bouncing her leg up and down like that.

He smiled at Sam and she offered up a pained and brief smile in response. Jack sighed. Kara had instructed both of them to dress down for the evening as evidence they were attempting to be low-key about the relationship. She'd suggested they both wear jeans and casual shoes and tops. She told Sam to go light on the makeup (which seemed silly, considering that Jack had hardly seen her in anything other than lip gloss) and to minimize jewelry. She told Jack to wear a ball cap as if he were trying to hide from the press.

"Need anything else, Sam?" He felt ridiculous and knew that she did, too. Sam had hardly said ten words to him that evening, and her leg kept shaking like there was a swarm of fire ants crawling up the curve of her lovely left calf. Jack checked her out again from head to toe, noting that Sam had opted for a simple scoop neck black T-shirt obviously made of some sort of cotton-Spandex blend, because, even untucked, it clung to her curves like a coat of shellac. She wore simple black leather boots with a two-and-a-half-inch heel. Jack had been unable to determine whether they were the ankle-high or the knee-high variety. Thigh-high seemed too much to hope for and probably wouldn't work with such close-fitting jeans anyway. As icing on the cake, Sam had chosen a pair of simple silver hoop earrings—not so small that they were invisible, but not so big as to be gaudy. Her hair fell in soft waves to her shoulders.

The lady could do casual just fine.

"Nope. I'm good," she said, staring out at the basketball court.

"Enjoying yourself?"

Sam tilted her head and raised her blue eyes, peering up beneath the brim of Jack's ball cap. The look on her face spoke volumes. Enjoyment apparently was not her primary sensation at that moment.

"Do you even like basketball?" Since she was already looking at him and he was already bending down toward her, he decided to use the opportunity to get in one of his required whispers of the first quarter. The instant he brought his lips to her curls, he felt her tense up. "Relax, Sam," he soothed. "Pretend like you're having the time of your life, that I'm Prince-Freakin'-Charming."

That got a little chuckle out of her, and Jack felt surprisingly proud of himself.

"I'm a little out of practice with the whole dating thing, and I've never really cared for basketball." Sam made this admission with a whisper.

Jack feigned horror. "And you call yourself a Hoosier? My God—the next thing I know you're going to tell me you don't like car racing! Or country music!"

Sam made a little humming sound deep in her throat that caused the hairs on Jack's forearms to spike to attention. It had been such a sexual sound, though unintentionally so. He wondered how she made that sound and how he could get her to make it again.

"The truth? I don't like either. Never have. I think car racing is noisy and stupid and country music gives me reflux. Sorry."

Jack blinked. "That's treason, babe." His lips brushed against her hair as he spoke. "Downright sedition. If anyone gets wind of this I'll lose the election for sure."

Sam turned her face toward him, and this time her eyes sparkled. Blue eyes like hers were lethal enough without the sparkle. He felt that buzzing sensation again.

"Maybe you should have checked me out before you brought me on board as the future Mrs. Jack Tolliver."

He grinned. Oh, he'd been checking out Sam all right, and he wasn't referring to the detailed reports he'd been given from Kara and Stu.

"But football isn't bad, I guess," Sam continued, a faint curl at the edge of her lips.

"Oh yeah? Ever see me play?"

She shook her head. "Unfortunately, your years with the Colts coincided with the years I spent breast-feeding and working overtime. Didn't have a lot of room in my life for sports back then."

Oh, damn. Now he wouldn't be able to stop staring at her breasts. It seemed Sam wasn't at all shy discussing bodily functions. Maybe motherhood did that to a woman. Not his own mother, of course. MDT made a point of avoiding a variety of topics, especially anything unduly earthy or real.

He wondered if sex was one of the bodily functions Sam didn't mind discussing.

"How did you manage to nurse babies while working overtime?" Jack surprised himself by asking but figured it was a way to keep Sam's breasts at the center of their conversation.

"I didn't have much choice." Sam's gaze strayed to the action at midcourt. "I was supporting all of us while Mitch tried to get his glass studio going. Mitch is my ex-husband. He was a glassblower." She looked at Jack again, a tiny frown between her neat auburn eyebrows. "Well, I guess he still is—it's not like he's dead or anything. At least not that I know."

It was all Jack could do not to make the observation that apparently, from what Kara had told him, glass had not been the only thing Mitchell was blowing back then.

Sam tilted her head to the side and smiled wistfully. "Anyway. I used a breast pump. Ever heard of those?"

Damn, damn, damn. Jack was thoroughly enjoying this conversation. "Of course."

"I did that for all my kids, but Dakota didn't want to stop. I was still nursing him in the morning and at night when he was over a year old."

So the kid was a boob man—Jack had something in common with the little streeker after all. "Seems he has his own timetable for everything."

Interesting. He hadn't really expected this, but Sam was now smiling at him in a way that nearly knocked the wind from his lungs. It was a combination of sparkling eyes, white teeth, dimples, tiny little crow's-feet, and joy that shocked the hell out of him. She was responding to him. Her shoulders had relaxed. Her leg had stopped bouncing. And she'd just made another one of those soft humming sounds he liked so much.

And all he had to do was feign interest in her children.

She nodded. "Dakota is definitely his own person."

Without warning the vision appeared to him—Sam stretched out on the guest bed's white sheets, her compact femaleness bursting the seams of that red thong and demi bra set he was going to purchase as soon as humanly possible. She would bend a knee and slide a bare foot up along the sheet, tuck it up near that cute butt, stretch her arms out over her head, and give him that full-force smile. Her curls would spill out on the pillow. He'd start his ministrations just behind her ear—the barest of kisses on the most tender spot of flesh. He'd let his tongue lick inside the hollow of her throat. He'd kiss down her sternum, letting his lips linger over those creamy mounds of flesh plumped up inside their prisons of crimson lace.

Sam had stopped talking and was obviously waiting for him to respond to her last comment. Unfortunately, he'd been too busy thinking about licking her to have heard what she'd said, but he figured it was a safe bet that it had something to do with potty training, so he took it from there.

"Well, truth be told, I'd be crapping my pants, too, if my parents had named me Dakota."

Jack froze. He hadn't wanted to say that *aloud*. What was wrong with him?

"Pardon me?"

"I'm saying that Dakota is an unusual name. Maybe it contributes to his unique personality."

Sam shrugged. "Yeah, well, Mitchell insisted on it. Some celebrity named their baby Dakota and he thought it was cool. So there you go."

Yes, and celebrities also name their kids after fruits and vegetables. Jack managed to keep that observation to himself. "So what's his middle name?"

Sam sighed. "Benjamin."

"Now that's a normal, dignified name. Maybe if you called him Ben he'd feel a little less antisocial."

Sam frowned. "What?"

"Just a thought."

Sam laughed. She laughed with such gusto that Jack noted that several people swiveled their heads from the action on the boards to the sound of Sam's amusement. He laughed right along with her, just as a series of camera flashes went off near them.

"And exactly how much experience do you have in child rearing, Jack?"

He grinned down at her, knowing this was the absolute perfect time for the night's first kiss on the cheek. "No experience whatsoever," he said, bringing his lips to the soft, smooth side of her face. She smelled good enough to eat. Devour, really.

Flash. Flash. Flash.

"So, Sam. Getting back to something you said earlier . . . exactly how long has it been since your last date?" Jack already knew the answer—eighteen months. He even knew who it was—the architect Sam's boss hired to renovate the salon. They went out twice. Dinner the first time. His place the second.

Sam blinked, her laughter coming to an abrupt halt. "Let's just say I've been out of circulation," she said.

Jack knew he wasn't pacing himself well, but he couldn't help it. Samantha Monroe was just too delicious. He leaned in for his second required kiss of the night and made sure the corner of her mouth touched his, which caused her to gasp.

"Popcorn?" Jack asked.

If it weren't for the new receptionist—a girl who'd just moved to Indiana for God's sake and didn't even know who she was—Christy was certain this would have been less of a hassle. Yes, she was a week early for her touch-up, but she'd been one of Le Cirque's most loyal and high-profile clients for six years now and expected to be squeezed into Marcia Fishbacher's schedule if and when necessary.

Marcia seemed a bit flustered today, juggling three clients at once, and Christy looked around the salon straining to catch a glimpse of that Samantha Monroe woman. Christy had nearly given herself a forehead slap that morning when she'd seen the photo in the *Star.* Of course that's where she'd heard that name before—she'd only been staring at the woman once every four weeks for six years. Samantha Monroe worked for Marcia! And although Christy hadn't said three words to Samantha in all that time, she recognized her immediately when she opened the morning paper.

"Now let's see how we're progressing here, shall we?" Marcia opened a neat fold of foil attached to a hunk of hair near Christy's face, peeling it back to check the progress of the bleach. In the mirror, Christy saw the same trim, neat, and preserved brunette she'd always seen, and once again wondered if Marcia was forty or sixty. It was impossible to tell. "I think we're good to go. Let's do a wash and then squeeze in a quick trim."

Before Christy could respond, her stylist was halfway across the salon, instructing a young apprentice to meet Christy at the shampoo station toward the back. Clearly, it was so busy in here today that if she wanted any information out of Marcia, she'd have to just dispense with the small talk and get right to it.

A few moments later Christy was perched in the chair at Marcia's station. Christy's wet locks hung straight from a center part at the top of her head, looking almost brown in the mirror. She wondered for an instant if she should go brunette but laughed it off. Christy Schoen—journalist, political analyst, TV personality—was a blonde. It was as simple as that. So why would she allow her hair to return to its natural lackluster mop? Why mess with excellence?

"All right. This is looking lovely. Just lovely." Marcia finished inspecting the lightened strands and reached for her scissors. "How have you been, Christy? Something unexpected come up? An event or something?"

As Marcia snipped proficiently, removing microscopic portions of hair around her face and at the ends, Christy spun a tale about having a last-minute assignment that interfered with her regularly scheduled appointment. Like she'd ever allow that to happen! She wasn't ashamed to admit that she built her work schedule around hair, nail, and eyebrow-shaping appointments. It was the nature of the TV beast.

"Well, I do apologize that we're a little rushed in here today. It's been crazy trying to juggle clients since one of our busiest stylists took some time off. I'm telling you, we've been running around like chickens without heads lately."

"Oh? Which stylist was that?"

"Samantha Monroe. Do you know her?" Marcia pointed across the room with her scissors, then resumed trimming. "Her station is over there, next to Monté."

Christy smiled into the mirror. Things came so easily to her sometimes it was scary. She looked over at the tidy—and clearly empty—styling station near a large window. There were no pictures tucked into the edges of the mirror. No tubes or bottles placed on the counter. No indication she'd be back anytime soon.

"I see. Did she have a baby or something?"

Marcia laughed and shook her head. "She's already done her service to mankind—three times over. Sam asked for a leave of absence to work on a new relationship and spend time with her kids. Apparently she's so serious about this man that she's moved into his house. I had to let her do it, even if it meant us being shorthanded."

Christy felt her body start to hum with the oddest mishmash of emotions—shock and anger chief among them. This had to be a mistake. The caption under the photo this morning was something cutesy about how Jack Tolliver may be keeping mum about his candidacy but wasn't the least bit shy about the way he felt about Samantha Monroe, his date for the Pacers game. The photo showed Jack leaning close to give the Monroe woman a kiss on the cheek. The kiss was obviously mid-laugh for both of them, and Samantha's head was tilted back at a slight angle, her eyes bright. Christy could tell by the way the muscles in Jack's neck strained that he was laughing, too.

The kiss looked spontaneous. It looked real. It looked intimate.

That bitch was *living* with Jack?

"You don't say?" Christy smiled bravely, then swallowed. "Come to think of it, I did see her picture in the paper this morning with the former lieutenant governor. Is that the man she's moved in with?"

Marcia stopped snipping, and Christy watched the woman's glance slide over to the opposite end of the room, toward the stylist named Monté. It almost looked like Marcia didn't want the woman to overhear this conversation.

"Sam's trying to keep it low-profile," Marcia said in a whisper. "Apparently, it's happened pretty fast and she's really crazy about this guy. I think he has his own apartment and is just letting her live in his family's house or something. Honestly, I'm trying to respect her wishes, but I swear to God I'm so happy for Sam I could bust! I can't keep my mouth shut about it! After everything she's been through these last few years, Sam deserves to have a little happiness. I swear, I cried when she told me about him. It's like a fairy tale. We're all thrilled."

While Marcia had been talking, Christy witnessed the transformation of her own expression reflected in the mirror. She looked thoroughly disgusted. She needed to get her act together.

Marcia looked into the mirror to catch Christy's eye. "Oh no. I've done it now, haven't I?"

Christy smiled sweetly. "This is a real dilemma for me, as you can appreciate."

Marcia let out a groan, just as Monté sauntered by.

The woman nodded at Christy, her dark eyes quickly scanning her over as she passed. The encounter wasn't exactly lovey-dovey.

Christy lowered her voice to a whisper, too. "You've given me some really good stuff in the past, Marcia. I've never revealed you as a source and I won't do it now. Please don't be concerned."

The stylist shook her head. "It's not that, Christy. It's just that this is so important to Sam and I'm so pleased for her. I don't want anything to screw up this chance at happiness for her and the kids."

Christy was about to respond, but Marcia had already grabbed the blow-dryer and round brush. So she endured the noise and the heat of the dryer and thought this through.

When had Jack Tolliver ever dated anyone over thirty?

Not ever.

When had Jack Tolliver ever dated anyone with kids?

Puh-leeze!

When had Jack Tolliver ever asked a woman to move into what Christy could only assume was the family estate on Sunset Lane? Especially if this woman brought along three children?

Not in this lifetime!

This was such a crock of shit. This was, beyond a doubt, connected somehow to his campaign and just might be the hottest scoop Christy had come across in her entire career. Jack was up to something. She could smell it. And whatever it was, she already knew it was going to make the teachers' convention scandal look like a tiny little misunderstanding.

Christy waited patiently for the dryer to stop. She smiled at Marcia in the mirror and told her she'd done a fabulous job, as usual, and left her a hefty tip.

5

Marguerite Dickinson Tolliver held the delicate Wedgwood china cup between thumb and index finger, took a sip of her morning coffee, and nearly spit it out.

There on her laptop screen was a black-and-white photo of her only child at a basketball game with some plain little redhead. The two of them were laughing like kids. And the bile began to rise in Marguerite's throat.

She sat the cup down into its saucer and pursed her lips, taking her eyes away from the computer and looking instead at the controlled lushness of her backyard. Nestor, the new gardener, certainly had talent. The edging between the flower beds and the lawn itself was razor sharp, the way she liked it. Not a single weed could be seen poking its intrusive little head through the dark cocoa-hued mulch. The blossoms of the cape honeysuckle and the wild alla-manda were healthy and full, twisting along the south trellis. The koi pond positively shimmered with cleanliness.

Her son, on the other hand, was a mess. His personal life had the makings of a cheesy made-for-TV movie. His career was in shambles. And he hadn't returned any of her phone calls.

At least Allen Ditto had been kind enough to listen to her troubles. She'd called the old rooster three times since he tossed his concrete block into the windshield of Indiana politics with that poorly timed announcement. He claimed he'd simply forgotten to notify Jack in advance that he'd decided not to seek another term. He also claimed his decision had nothing to do with anything except that he was tired of Washington and needed to go home. Marguerite knew that was horse hockey on both counts. It was no secret that Allen didn't think Jack worthy of the U.S. Senate, and she'd certainly heard all about Allen's decidedly untired social life of late.

Since Carla's passing two years before, the man had been downright sprightly. Widower status seemed to suit him. Not that Marguerite could blame Allen, because his wife had been crazier than a hoot owl. Her phobias had gotten worse with each year in Washington, and Allen hadn't taken her anywhere since the aluminum foil incident at the White House in 1991.

Marguerite had seen the whole fiasco with own eyes, her beloved Gordon at her side, his health by that time in rapid decline. Some nitwit server came through the dining room with a single shiny sheet of foil, to do what no one ever really knew, and Carla saw it, heard it crinkle, and disintegrated in front of the president, the First Lady, a smattering of visiting dignitaries, some famous Hollywood producer and his wife, along with much of the Senate Foreign Relations Committee.

It was a shame, a real shame, to see Allen lead Carla out of the State Dining Room as she shrieked incoherently, spittle rolling off her chin onto the bodice of her lovely Dior creation.

Too many years in politics could do that to a person. Marguerite had, in fact, seen worse.

She folded her hands and stared at the fountain at the center of her in-ground pool. The board of directors of the Naples Garden Club was due for lunch that afternoon. The caterers were on top of the menu preparation. She'd already selected what she would wear—that melon orange suit with the pastel Chanel scarf that matched so nicely. So she had ample time for a chat.

Marguerite picked up the cordless telephone that sat just to her right, beside her laptop computer and the stack of newspapers on the breakfast table, and called her son.

Of course she got his voice mail. He was avoiding her. He'd been avoiding her for twenty years.

"Jack, this is your mother, Marguerite. You may remember me. I gave you the gift of life." She paused for effect. "I do not have the foggiest idea what you think you're doing, but you must realize that you need to declare soon, and that your campaign would benefit greatly if you managed to avoid being photographed with cheap-looking waitresses and the like."

She sighed.

"I love you, darling boy. Please call me soon. If you don't, I'll be forced to get my answers from Kara and Stuart and I might even decide to join you at the Sunset Lane house for the holidays. I can't think of anything more lovely than a family Christmas, just like we used to have."

"You sure that swim diaper is gonna hold?"

Sam had been wondering the same thing and scooted forward on the lounge chair to study Dakota. He was bobbing along in the ornate indoor swimming pool near Lily, buoyed by a bright yellow swim bubble and a pair of water wings, looking thrilled to be alive. So far, it seemed the waistband was holding. The leg openings were still snug. Diaper engineering had come a long way since Greg was a baby. At least Sam prayed it had.

" 'Cause I don't think ole boyfriend is gonna be too happy if Dakota decides this is the potty he's been waitin' for."

Sam gave Monté a sideways glance. "Jack is not my boyfriend."

"Mmm-hmmm. Sure looked like it in that picture."

Sam snorted in surprise. "Gimme a break, Monté! I'm doing my job. You know Kara had that all planned out, down to the number of times he was supposed to hold my hand. Don't be ridiculous."

"And don't get all huffy on me."

"Anyway, this is just the beginning, so get over it. I didn't even enjoy it much. It was awkward."

A piercing scream from Lily drew their attention back to the pool. The boys were on either side of her, splashing like they meant to drown her.

"Stop it *right now*!" Monté stood as she yelled, and her usually resonant voice ricocheted around the pool house like the voice of God herself. She pointed a red-tipped finger at Simon. "Boy, you gang up on Lily like that one more time and I'm tellin' you, this will be the last time your black behind gets anywhere near this pool! And Greg? You leave your sister be! You hear me?"

The quiet was so profound that Sam decided they could've heard a fly rub its wings together.

Monté eased back into her lounge chair and tugged on her knit top so that it covered some of her ample cleavage, then continued her commentary without missing a beat. "This is me you're talkin' to, Sammy, and if what you were doin' in that picture was work, then girl, I'm ready for a career change."

Sam laughed, then sighed deeply. "All right. Fine. There were parts I enjoyed."

"You *know* you got that right." Monté tossed her braids for emphasis. "Jack Tolliver *is* fine—one fine-ass white man, and I bet I know exactly what *parts* you enjoyed, 'cause they're probably the same parts I enjoy every time I lay eyes on him. He's got a behind on him that could make a woman damn near pass out." She took a long drink of her iced tea, like she was close to doing just that.

"Oh, really?" Sam asked, trying not to agree with her out loud. "Why don't you date him, then?"

Monté roared with laughter, and she had to place her drink on the table before it spilled. "I'm not sure Indiana has evolved enough for that kind of crazy mess, Sammy."

"Good afternoon, everyone."

Sam and Monté startled, turning to see Jack poised in the pool house doorway. Sam immediately wondered just how long he'd been listening. His face—his handsome politician's face—was set in that plastic mold of pleasantness that was really beginning to annoy her.

"Everyone having a good time?"

"You bet," Monté said, patting her cleavage like she was having heart palpitations.

"Good. Excellent."

"We're officially an item now, it seems." Sam smiled at Jack in an attempt to distract him, concerned he may have overheard Monté talking about him being a fine-assed white man.

And really, she wasn't lying. At that very moment, Jack was looking delicious in a pair of gray tweed pleated trousers and a black cashmere henley sweater. Everything the man had to offer—his big shoulders and arms, tapered waist, long and strong legs—was simultaneously showcased yet tastefully hidden. The dark sweater only highlighted his dark hair and contrasted with those sinful green eyes. Sam had to hand it to him. Jack Tolliver knew just what he was doing. Maybe being the sexiest thing your party had to offer was not just due to charisma and name recognition. Maybe raw, potent maleness and excellent taste in clothing played a small part as well.

Hell. She'd vote for him.

Jack smiled at Monté, then locked his eyes on Sam. "Yes, we're a hit. Reporters have been calling all day. Kara's doing the 'no comment' thing for the time being, which will only make them hotter for the story."

Sam drew her gaze away from Jack to check on the kids. Dakota was hanging on to the side of the pool, as he splashed with his little feet, watching Jack with fierce concentration. The big kids were treading water at the other end.

"How long will she keep saying, 'No comment'?" Sam asked.

Jack waved amiably to the teenagers down at the deep end. They waved back and called out their hellos.

"The filing deadline is the first of February. Kara and I think that for maximum fund-raising impact, I need to declare by the beginning of January, in about two weeks. I'm scheduled to appear at the grand opening for the zoo's new dolphin aquarium, and we thought it would be good if you and the kids were there with me."

"Now, how about that?" Monté pushed herself up off the lounge and busied herself folding towels and lining up the kids' gym shoes, humming to herself. Sam knew all too well that when Monté piddled around and hummed, it meant she was biting her tongue. Sam had seen her do it a thousand times at the salon. *Just keep on biting*, she pleaded silently.

"So, you got a ring?"

Sam shut her eyes in embarrassment at Monté's question. When she opened them, it appeared that Jack and her friend were in the middle of some kind of staring contest.

"A ring." Jack chuckled softly and ran a hand through his hair.

"There ain't no ring," Monté whispered to Sam, giving her neck a series of sassy back-and-forths.

Sam was just about to offer Monté cash money to keep her comments to herself when Monté moved her accusatory stare back to Jack.

"How's a woman supposed to convince the world that she's engaged if there's no rock on her finger? You know that a man in your position would be giving his woman something real big and real sparkly, and we're not talking no Diamonique."

Jack moved to the edge of a poolside dining table and leaned against it with casual grace, sending Sam a guilty smile.

Monté started up again. "Now, what's that rule of thumb? A man should spend two months' salary on the engagement ring?" She patted the neatly arranged stack of towels, clearly enjoying the hell out of herself.

Jack's laugh surprised Sam. It was deep and warm and most definitely not the response Sam was expecting. With relief, she laughed right along with him.

"Thanks for that suggestion, Ms. McQueen." Jack's deep green eyes shimmered with amusement. "But seeing that I'm currently unemployed and not earning a salary of any kind whatsoever, I'm not sure that works to Sam's benefit."

"You know that's not right," Monté replied.

"We'll come up with something." Jack straightened and walked toward the shallow end of the pool, where he knelt near Dakota, who looked up at him with wet curls and a big smile.

"Hi, Mr. Jack."

"Hey, little guy. How's the water?"

"It's good in here! I can swim! Wanna see me swim?" Before Jack could answer, Dakota was flailing his limbs wildly, his diaper-encased bottom bobbing to the surface as he splashed water all over Jack.

"Oh jeesh! Sorry!" Sam was out of her lounge chair and at poolside in a flash, handing Jack a towel. She watched him wipe off his face, surprisingly unperturbed. He stayed kneeling.

"That's some powerful swim stroke you got there, Dakota Benjamin."

Dakota clung to the pool edge again, breathing like he'd just completed an Olympic event. He beamed up at Jack. "I'm a good swimmer. Did you see?"

"I did see." Jack stood with a wince of pain. He looked down at Sam and gave her a small smile. "Thanks for the towel."

She stood with her bare feet riveted to the slip-proof flooring, staring up into Jack's gaze. The agitated water reflected upon his green irises, making it appear that he was sparkling from the inside. She took the towel from him, and the tips of his fingers grazed her hand.

Did his knee still bother him? For the first time, it dawned on Sam that Jack might still be in pain from his football injury. Greg had said that it had been nasty and footage of that fateful sack still showed up on sports highlight shows every now and then. Greg said it took six surgeries and four years before Jack could walk without a brace.

"Kara says she wants us to go out for dinner tonight. Do you think everyone will be OK by themselves for a few hours?"

"Oh, I'll be happy to stick around," Monté interjected, though no one was talking to her. "You two kids go on out and enjoy yourselves."

Sam shot her a warning glance, hoping to God that Monté saw she meant business. "Absolutely, Jack," she said brightly. "Where are we going? What does Kara want me to wear?"

Unless Sam was mistaken, Jack's eyes suddenly flashed with a sparkle that had nothing to do with the reflection from the pool. Then he dragged his gaze from her neck down to her toes and back up again before looking her in the eye. She'd just felt that gaze on every inch of her skin. She felt her cheeks burn, but there was nothing she could do to stop the blush.

"St. Elmo Steak House. So something dressy casual would be fine."

"Great. I haven't been there in years."

"Hmmph," Monté said from behind them. "I never did understand what 'dressy casual' is supposed to mean. You supposed to wear flip-flops with your evening gown or something?"

Sam blinked, plotting exactly how she'd strangle Monté the first chance she got. "Sounds fine, Jack. What time would you like me to be ready?"

"Seven, if that works for you."

Sam was still recovering from the obvious way he'd been checking her out, and her voice might have been a little too chipper when she said, "I work for you, so seven works for me!"

Sam watched, fascinated, as a brief frown of confusion marred Jack's otherwise agreeable expression. He then lowered his gaze to his shoes and shoved his hands in his pockets before he looked up at her again. The frown—and whatever thought had caused it—had passed.

"See you at seven, then. And remind me to dig up a ring in the next couple weeks, OK?"

Sam was wondering how a man goes about "digging up" an engagement ring when she noticed the pool had become silent. All four kids were lined up near the shallow-end steps, listening intently.

Jack noticed the audience, too, and turned on the charm. "How's Park Tudor treating you?"

"It's pretty g-g-good," Greg said.

"Great." Jack looked expectantly at Lily, and Sam hoped her daughter would at least be civil. She watched the girl's dark-rimmed eyes tighten before she smiled. "It's OK, thanks," she said with a shrug. "Some of the kids are real snobs, though."

Jack chuckled. "Everywhere's got its share of snobs, Lily, but you have every right to be there, so don't give them the satisfaction of making you uncomfortable."

"Yeah, I guess," Lily said, then she brightened. "Hey, Jack? You ever go to concerts at the Fieldhouse?"

Sam tried to end this line of questioning. *"Lily . . ."*

"On occasion. I saw Pearl Jam there a few years ago."

"No way!" Lily's mouth hung open.

"I hear 50 Cent is coming in the spring. Would you guys like to go?"

"I could roll with that," Simon said, trying to look as nonchalant as possible while his eyes widened.

"I'll see what I can do about tickets. In the meantime, I'm on my way to a meeting."

Jack said his good-byes to Monté and the kids, and Sam walked him to the doorway. Sam heard Simon in the background saying, "Naw! He can't get those tickets! The man's fooling with us!"

Sam watched him stroll down the hallway that connected the pool house to the rest of the mansion, noting that he was tall and dark and smooth and impossible to stop staring at.

Jack glanced over his shoulder and said, "Oh, and no flip-flops—and no damn-near passing out."

It had been a long day, and Christy retreated to her office in the Channel 10 studios and shut the door. She groaned with relief as she unzipped her snakeskin boots and yanked her feet from their stylish prisons. She wiggled her toes and tried to get the circulation back in her legs, realizing her wisdom teeth were bugging her again. Someday, she knew, she'd have to have them taken out, but where was the time?

She checked her e-mails. The prosecutor's office

hadn't bothered to get back to her about their repeated attempts to locate one Mitchell J. Bergen, the
former husband of that beautician Jack was parading
around with. It was no wonder they hadn't responded
to her inquiries. It must be embarrassing that an entire task force couldn't locate one measly no-talent
glassblower.

Christy laughed to herself, thinking how entertaining it would be when she'd get around to doing
their job for them, in a spare afternoon.

The details of Samantha Monroe's life were coming quite easily. A single trip to the Marion County
Clerk's office managed to unearth Samantha's marriage license and divorce decree, a visit to the state
health department's Web site revealed she had a
valid cosmetologist license, and a five-minute call to
the Indiana Bureau of Vital Statistics rounded up the
birth records of her three children. The rest of the
Monroe woman's life story Christy got from Marcia
Fishbacher, who said Samantha's husband had been
a deadbeat who'd lived off his wife's flair with a pair
of scissors until he skipped town. The reverence in
Marcia's voice indicated she thought Samantha
Monroe was a combination of Vidal Sassoon and
Mother Teresa, or some nonsense.

"She's been through the wringer," Marcia had
said. "I know her new boyfriend is running for office,
but Christy, please don't do anything to hurt her. She
deserves any joy she can find."

Yeah? And who doesn't? With gusto, Christy
deleted at least a dozen spam e-mails from that assumed she was an impotent man in dire need of a

home loan, remembering the night Jack made a fool of her in front of her peers.

She'd been up for an Associated Press Excellence in Broadcast Journalism award. She eventually lost to Al Gilligan over at Channel 3, but that wasn't the point. The point was that she and Jack had been dating for about three months and she really thought they'd go all the way to the altar. She was in love and assumed he was, too. Technically, he never actually said the words, but she could see it in his eyes. And her parents were thrilled with Jack. Marguerite simply adored her, even inviting her on a girls' shopping day to Chicago—which never happened, because Jack obviously suffered from some kind of hormonal disorder that prevented him from forming any kind of deep bond with a woman!

That night at the awards banquet, he just couldn't seem to resist dragging a Fox associate producer into the bank of pay phones and nibbling on her neck.

Had Christy been the one to witness this indiscretion, she could have dumped him with her pride intact. But no—her boss and four of her coworkers on their way to the men's room saw everything and, with glee, relayed the details to all at the Channel 10 table. When Jack returned to his seat a few moments later, looking refreshed and at peace with the world, no one could keep a straight face. When Jack reached for Christy's hand as it lay on her lap, she snapped. She twisted his index finger with all her might and hissed at him, "You disgusting pig!"

It was the highlight of everyone's evening, of course. Christy left the banquet without a little gold statue and without a date to her cousin's wedding that next weekend. But what galled Christy the most was how awful everything had gone on a night when she'd looked so great. Marcia had done her hair in an elegant upswept twist, and the cute little pink satin strapless dress she'd found on sale at the Circle City Nordstrom fit so perfectly it hadn't even needed alterations!

That should have been her night!

Jack should have been her man!

They looked so perfect together!

Christy sighed, returning her attention to the task at hand, and slogged through e-mails from viewers, coworkers, sources, and, of course, Brandon Miliewski.

She yawned with abandon and propped her stocking-clad feet upon the desk. As mind-numblingly bizarre as it seemed, that sebaceous hick Miliewski had sent her six e-mails in one day. It was rather sad that he'd been flirting with her for years now. Sadder still was the fact that he clearly thought buying her one glass of cheap Zinfandel made her the future Mrs. Video Poker.

"Sorry, big guy." With a few clicks, Christy deleted Brandon's request that she join him and his colleagues at St. Elmo that night for dinner, and an additional five e-mails, which she didn't bother to read. What had she been thinking the day at the Chatterbox Tavern? Miliewski wasn't assertive or attractive—he was a fat ferret. Getting the scoop on Jack's latest bimbo must have left her light-headed.

Christy clicked off her computer and slipped on a

pair of flats for the walk out to the parking lot, thinking to herself that the teacher convention thing was soon to become a mere hors d'oeuvre on her buffet table of revenge.

She got into her little yellow Nissan 350Z and shook her head in regret. She'd never been able to wear that gorgeous pink dress again—it held too many bad memories.

"Her name was Tina. And things were already coming to an end before you and I signed our agreement."

"Do you miss her?" Sam was immediately embarrassed by the intimate nature of her question. She had no right to be talking to Jack Tolliver like this—and that's exactly what made this arrangement so strange. He was her date but not really; she was starting to like him, but she didn't know why; she thought he was funny and sweet and a prick at the same time; her panties got damp whenever he glanced her way, which was just plain disconcerting.

"Truthfully, I do miss aspects of that relationship," Jack answered. As he sipped his wine, the sparkle in his eyes indicated he amused himself.

"I imagine she had aspects out the wazoo." Sam turned to look out the window onto Meridian Street. They'd gotten the best table at St. Elmo, which shouldn't have surprised her, but it was a little thrill nonetheless. She'd only been in this venerable old downtown steak house once in her life—when Mitchell took her here for their tenth anniversary. It had been such an unexpected splurge at the time, and she remembered how she'd struggled to enjoy herself while wondering how the hell they could afford thirty-dollar steaks and a forty-dollar bottle of wine, even on their anniversary.

Mitch had reassured her. Told her to relax. Then their waiter had delivered a dozen long-stemmed red roses to their table and Mitch took her hands in his and said, "Happy anniversary." He leaned across the table to kiss her hand and they talked about how big Greg and Lily were getting. Mitch told her about his latest glass projects, and for the first time in a long time she'd felt a sweet excitement being in his company. She allowed herself to believe things might be getting better between them, that Mitch might be turning some kind of corner as a husband and an artist.

Sam sighed softly, blinking at the city lights outside the window, remembering how her husband had taken her home that night and made love to her.

Within three weeks she found herself spending the first waking hour of every day on her knees, suffering from morning sickness the likes of which she'd never experienced with Greg or Lily. One Tuesday morning, Mitch appeared behind her in the bathroom door. She could have sworn he was saying something about their marriage being a sham and that he'd discovered he was gay, but it was hard to hear when her ears were ringing from the retching. Mitch moved out the next week, the same day the mailman delivered the Visa bill for their anniversary meal. It became one of many shared debts her husband never got around to helping her pay.

"You OK over there?"

Jack's question startled Sam, and she realized she'd been impossibly rude in her silence. "I'm sorry. Guess I'm not great company tonight."

Jack gave her an understanding nod. The poor guy was probably bored to tears. He might even dock her pay—the contract called for her to "execute her duties to the best of her abilities and to the satisfaction of her employer."

Sam forced a smile. "I bet Lisa was a good dinner date."

"Her name is Tina. I did say Tina, didn't I?"

"Her, too."

Jack laughed gently, and she watched his face soften with something she hoped to God wasn't sympathy. "Who knows, Sam? After these six months are up, you and I could actually end up as friends. Stranger things have happened."

The warmth of that comment surprised her, and she fiddled with her wineglass for a moment before she smiled at him, this time for real. She looked at Jack Tolliver—that aristocratic nose and those dark lashes and the broad, charismatic grin—and she couldn't help it. Sam felt a hot rush spread from her chest down her arms and head right smack toward the crotch of her panties, which made two things painfully clear: she'd gone so long without sex that she didn't remember how to behave in the company of an attractive man, and she really should lay off the wine.

"A girl can never have too many friends," Sam said, hoping Jack couldn't tell how difficult it had been to come up with that stupid reply.

He speared a hunk of romaine lettuce and raised an eyebrow. "You actually think Monté will let you have auxiliary friends?"

She laughed. "I already have them. And I'd apologize for Monté, but that's just who she is. Though I suppose she could cut back on the play-by-play commentary."

Jack smiled. "How did you two get to be so close, if you don't mind my asking?"

"We started at Le Cirque the very same week. We were just babies back then, you know?" Sam shook her head, hardly recalling what it felt like to be twenty-two years old, madly in love, a new mother, and bursting with hope. "Everything we learned about hair and children and life we learned together—the wonderful and awful and the everyday stuff in-between. We became each other's family. She's always had my back and I've always had hers."

Their steaks arrived. Sam's was prepared to a perfect medium well and cost a whole lot more than thirty dollars and she didn't feel a speck of concern about the bill. Jack was fine company, and his relaxed demeanor helped her settle in. She laughed at his stories about football and politics and forgot that spending time with this man was her job.

At one point, Jack reached across the table and took her hand in his. He leaned close, and the devilish sparkle in his expression gave her another hot rush of awareness. Oh, this man was the stuff of which dreams were made. His words were smooth and his skin was warm and she didn't even have to be told that someone was watching.

She turned up the wattage on her own smile and squeezed his hand. In a whisper she asked, "What's the script call for tonight?"

"Hmm. How about you tell me you're going to the ladies' room and kiss me before you go? Stay there for about five minutes; then I'll introduce you."

Without taking her eyes from Jack's she asked, "Anyone famous?"

Jack laughed, picked up her hand, and put his lips on her fingertips. The kiss was gentle and he held her gaze as he held her hand. "I think we're being stalked by Brandon Miliewski."

Sam chuckled and pulled her hand from Jack's mouth as if he'd just said something highly amusing. The truth was, her knees were wobbling. When's the last time a man had kissed her fingertips? The only males she touched on a regular basis were three and thirteen years old. She reached for her purse and said, "I'll be right back, Jack."

As instructed, she bent to kiss his cheek on her way to the ladies' room. Jack turned his head just in time to catch her lips with his, and Sam didn't know if it was the wine or the delicious meal or just Jack, but she kissed him back, then slipped him a little taste of her tongue.

She shocked herself so much that she pulled away, blinked at Jack twice, then nearly ran to the bathroom. Once inside she stared in the mirror, steadying herself by gripping the edge of the sink with both hands. Who was this woman looking back at her? She didn't have the slightest idea. In fourteen years she'd barely had the time to ask.

She was a mom. She was a stylist. She was a friend and a daughter and an ex-wife. She was, thank God, a financially solvent person for the first time in her life.

But she was also just a woman—a woman who probably had needs that had nothing to do with potty training, speech therapy, or minimum monthly payments. She just didn't know what they were.

Samantha reached inside her purse and applied a fresh coat of lip gloss, then smacked her lips with finality. She was still decent looking. She'd been blessed with a functioning metabolism, good skin, and thick hair, and heaven knows that spending sixty hours a week listening to women bitch about the lack of those very things had made her appreciate her good fortune.

She might even still know how to use her . . . what had Jack called them? Her *aspects*. Sam sighed, recalling how she hadn't needed any special skills that night eighteen months ago when she went home with Bill Latham, the architect. Talk about less than magical. Ten minutes and it was all over, before she'd even gotten started. Sam went home knowing she'd have been better off spending a few quality moments with her B-O-B instead of Bill.

A woman entered the ladies' room to find Sam staring at herself and offered an awkward "hello" before fleeing to a stall.

"Hi," Sam said to the closed door, figuring she'd spent the required five minutes in the bathroom by then and could return to her date—no, her *job*.

She should slap some sense into herself. What

was wrong with her? Jack wasn't her boyfriend and he'd never be throwing her down on that luxurious guest bed and having his way with her and he would never be kissing her fingers because he treasured her . . . adored her . . . loved her.

The only reason Jack Tolliver was kissing her fingers or any other of her body parts was because she was dowdy. That's right—Jack was such a bad boy that he had to rent a boring mother of three to make him dull enough to be elected U.S. senator! Jack was too damn sexy for public consumption. And that's where Samantha Monroe had come in.

Sam laughed, throwing her lip gloss into her purse and putting a hand on a hip, staring back at her reflection.

There she was—dull woman. What had she selected to wear tonight? A dull pair of black slacks and a simple white collared blouse. Yes, the effect was dressy casual, but it was also just plain boring. She saw a bitter smile spread across her face. Yep, there she was, a woman so boring that she couldn't stop her husband from crossing to the other side!

Sam stopped breathing, the words hitting her chest like the painful insults they were. "Dull." "Dowdy." "Boring."

Undesirable.

Sam slammed open the ladies' room door and began the walk back to the table. When the hell had that happened to her? When had the joyous, alive creature she'd once been become downright matronly? Maybe it happened while Greg and Lily grew up and got pissed off. Maybe it happened during those first four months after Dakota was born, when Sam lived on two hours' sleep a night. Maybe it was the result of going too many years without picking up a paintbrush.

She caught Jack's eye from across the darkened dining room. He had an elbow propped on the back of his chair, gray tweed legs crossed, nonchalantly commanding the attention of the men now clustered by the table. He tilted his head and produced a sweet smile she knew was not for her as much as it was for his audience. All the men turned to look at her.

And something in Sam snapped.

She was supposed to be the embodiment of the Hoosier everywoman? She was so gifted at being drab that she was earning more per week than the president of the United States? Well, fuck dowdy. Fuck the everywoman crap.

Sam slung her purse strap over a shoulder. As casually as she could, she swept her hand across the front of her blouse, popping open an extra top button. She put one foot in front of the other, sliding her palms along the fitted waist of her blouse and down the slacks that hugged her hips. She'd be damned if she'd walk toward that incredibly handsome man like a dowdy everywoman.

She was only thirty-six years old and merely a little worn-out, not dead.

With the men still watching, Sam decided to add some *oomph* to her stride. She tried to remember how to produce a sexy smirk and hoped that what she came up with didn't make her look like the woman in one of those sinus headache commercials. And she sauntered right on up to that group of men in suits and enjoyed the way they parted so she could reach her target.

"Miss me, baby?" She leaned down to kiss Jack right beneath his left earlobe. Every guy there had to have heard Jack's surprised intake of air, but Sam was the only one who knew that a tremble had coursed through his big body. She returned to her seat.

"Uh . . ." Jack stared at her with glassy eyes. He licked his lips. Eventually, he found the concentration required to speak. He stiffly gestured toward the group of men while staring at Samantha and said, "This is my fiancée, Samantha Monroe." Then he blinked, laughed at his own mistake, and gestured in Sam's direction instead. "I guess I got that a little mixed up, didn't I?"

Sam smiled with satisfaction at the sight of Jack Tolliver, undone. It seemed Mommy could still shake her aspects after all.

6

"How the hell did you get my home number, Miliewski?"

"I figured under the circumstances you wouldn't mind that I give you a call."

"Mind?" Christy sat up and reached over for the bedside light, thinking it had to be at least 2:00 A.M. OK—the clock read 10:00 P.M., but she'd had a long day. "Of course I mind! If I'd wanted to spend time with you I would have accepted your dinner invitation. If I wanted you to call me at home I would have given you my number! But I didn't—therefore, I suppose you could say I mind!"

Miliewski was quiet for a beat, then said, "They're engaged."

Christy rubbed her forehead. "Who's engaged? What are you talking about?"

"Tolliver and Samantha Monroe. They were at St. Elmo tonight and he introduced her to our group as his *fee-ahn-say.* As in his future wife."

Christy's spine jerked straight. "Pardon me? I don't think I heard you right."

"Engaged. And you should have seen the way that little *mamacita* worked it tonight. I'm telling you, Jack is whipped in a way I didn't think was possible. He couldn't even introduce her without drooling on himself."

Christy laughed. This was so ridiculous she'd almost fallen for it! But she was far too smart for Miliewski, and the doofus would pay.

"I'm being punked, aren't I?"

"Uh—"

"Brandon, I'm telling you, if you are doing this for the entertainment of the members of the state gaming commission or something let me assure you that you will live to regret the day you were even—"

"Oh, *shut up,* Christy. Why do you always have to be such a flaming bitch?"

She gasped.

"I'd never do anything like that to you. You're the most amazing woman I've ever known." Brandon's voice was crisp enough to convey hurt and a touch of moral superiority. "I am simply passing on the facts as I've come to learn them—which is what you journo types call a *tip* the last time I checked—but hey, if you'd rather I talk to Al Gilligan over at Channel 3, no *problemo.*"

Then Brandon Miliewski hung up, leaving Christy to gape incredulously at the now-silent phone. She slammed it down in its cradle and put her fingertips on the pulse below her jaw—it was hammering faster than at the end of her Thursday night hip-hop cardio class.

There was no longer any doubt that Jack Tolliver was scamming the public.

Because there wasn't a woman on earth who could get that man to agree to a trip down the aisle, especially that fast. If Christy herself hadn't been able to do it, then it couldn't be done.

She checked to make sure Brandon's number showed up on her caller ID—just in case she needed to reach him. At some point in the future. For verification. Or a quote. Not that she welcomed the idea of ever having to speak to the sweaty-faced lobbyist again in her life, even if he did think she was amazing.

The car ride back to Sunset Lane was more awkward than the date itself. As they drove north along Meridian Street, Sam looked out at the old mansions that lined the city's primary north–south boulevard. She must have driven past these gracious homes a thousand times in the years she'd lived here but had never really given much thought to what the lives inside those homes were like. Well, now she lived in a home even grander than the ones passing by her window. At least temporarily. And as surreal as it seemed, she was living one of those lives.

"That's the governor's mansion, right over there." Jack pointed out the driver's side window toward a sprawling brick home on a lot at least three times as large as its neighbor's. "I basically grew up there."

Sam nodded. "Kind of big place for one kid."

Jack laughed briefly, then turned to her. "Yeah, it

was. My mother had twins when I was seven, but they only lived for a few days."

Sam's mouth opened in surprise; then she laid a hand on his shoulder. "Jack, I'm so sorry."

He gave a soft shrug, keeping his eyes trained on the road. "Two girls. I would have had actual siblings. Maybe I wouldn't have turned out to be such a selfish bastard."

Sam blinked, hearing the pain in his voice, intrigued by the small window he'd just provided into the way he thought about things. "That's very sad." She squeezed his shoulder a last time and returned her hand to her lap.

Jack nodded. "Real sad."

Sam watched him swallow hard, the rigid lump of his Adam's apple moving down and then up his throat, and it was all she could do not to reach out and stroke his head, the way she'd often done for Greg when he struggled with feelings that threatened to be too big for him to handle.

Jack pulled up to the traffic light. "I think having other kids might have mellowed Marguerite out somewhat, too. Losing the twins was very hard on her, and she disappeared on me for a few years."

"Disappeared?" Sam frowned. "You mean she left?"

"Not that anyone else would notice, but there wasn't anybody inside her for a long time. She wasn't all that interested in me. But, eventually, she did bounce back and held on to me tighter than ever. Jackie Chan's got nothing on MDT's grip, let me tell you."

Sam smiled politely, hoping he'd keep talking, well aware that this was the first time Jack had volunteered anything even remotely personal about his life.

"How do you get along with your mother these days?" she asked.

He made a soft clicking sound of disappointment, then tightened his mouth. "I'd like to tell you that we're estranged, but she won't let me be."

Sam laughed at that. She was fascinated by the tongue-in-cheek attitude he seemed to have toward his own life. She was starting to think that Jack Tolliver didn't take himself very seriously.

When Sam didn't say anything right away, Jack gave her a friendly pat on her left knee. "You're missing your cue, Miss Monroe. This is where my date usually points out that my distant and cold relationship with my mother is at the root of my commitment phobia."

Sam shrugged. "Ah. There you go. I didn't even know you had one of those. Besides, I'm not your date—I'm your employee—and it's not my place to say."

A smirk of appreciation spread over Jack's face as he turned left onto Fifty-sixth Street and drove up the hill toward Sunset Lane. "We may not be dating, but you're damn sure the only woman I've ever been engaged to." He turned onto the densely wooded drive, and the headlights of his Lexus lit up thousands of pale, bare tree branches that hovered over the road. "And I've been sitting here thinking that Kara is going to flip when she hears I blurted that out tonight, ahead of schedule."

"Talk about missing your cue," Sam said, smiling to herself.

"I think you have a sadistic streak in you, Samantha, like all females."

Sam coughed. "Say what?"

"Back there at St. Elmo. The man-eater walk and the *'Miss me, baby?'* routine. That was cruel. I was so floored I could have easily revealed national security secrets had I known any. Maybe I shouldn't be a senator."

It was Sam's turn to give him a friendly pat on the knee. "You'll be a great senator and I'm sorry I did that. It wasn't anything personal—I was feeling a little sorry for myself and had to make sure I still had it."

Jack retrieved the remote control from the storage compartment between the seats. He stared at her while he pressed the button that opened the iron gates at the end of the circular drive. "Make sure you still had what, Sam?"

She shrugged, gathering up her purse and making sure her coat was buttoned before she got out of the car and said good night. "Oh, nothing. It's stupid."

Jack turned off the car engine and unlatched his seat belt, then turned to face her. He had one of those little lopsided smiles on his face. Clearly, he was enjoying her embarrassment.

"Exactly what are you insecure about?"

She put her hand on the door handle. "Forget it. I'm sorry I did that—you're right; it was mean. I'll tell Kara about what happened. I'll explain to her that it was my fault. Good night Jack."

Click. All the doors locked.

Sam laughed, shaking her head. "You're funny."

"Still had what, Sam?"

"Oh, stop. Seriously. This is silly. I've apologized. Now I've got to go in so Monté can go home."

Jack's eyes darted toward the house, where only a few rooms were lit. "I'm sure Monté won't mind staying a minute. I'm waiting to hear about those things you need to make sure you still have."

Sam's heart was racing. What was going on here? He was teasing her, but the look in his eye and the heat she felt pouring off of him was no joke. Jack Tolliver was dangerous. He was a sexual predator—albeit a really cute one.

"Look, Jack—this job has made a huge difference in my life and the lives of my kids. It's a miracle, really, and I just want to do it right, help get you elected, then disappear into the background again. I don't want to screw this up."

Jack touched her again, and this time it wasn't a platonic pat. He kept his big hand spread over her knee and a good part of her thigh and he squeezed just enough that she got the message—he was big and male and she was small and female.

There wasn't enough air in that Lexus.

"Talk to me, Sam." The heat of Jack's palm went straight through the fabric of her slacks and singed her flesh. "Nothing will ever get screwed up just because you talk to me. I like you. I'm just curious what was going on in your head the moment you opened that can of female whup-ass on all us poor guys tonight."

Sam leaned her head against the seat and let go

with a big laugh. Then she pressed her fingers into her temples. "Oh, boy," she whispered.

"I'm all ears."

Sam looked over at Jack and felt empathy for every woman who'd ever found herself in this exact position—alone with Jack Tolliver in the semidark, those evergreen eyes alive with a sexy playfulness. Any woman would be dead meat in these circumstances. And a woman who hadn't had male attention for what seemed like an eternity? She could fuckin' forget it. "Well . . ."

Jack stirred, and Sam was treated to the vision of his profile in the dim light. He was beautiful—the pleasing planes and ridges of his cheeks and jaw, the thoroughbred line of his nose, those sinfully wide lips, the slight upward tilt of his eyes. She wanted to paint him.

She needed to paint him, and she hadn't needed to paint anything in a very long time.

He tilted his head and smiled at her. "Tell me, sweet Sam."

She tried to hold it in. She failed, and she felt something crack open inside her heart. "Oh God! It's like I'm waking up after being in a coma or something, Jack!"

His hand began to stroke her leg.

"It's like I've been sleepwalking through my life, getting through the day and not realizing how fast those days were piling up, not asking myself what I really want or need because I'm afraid if I know then I'll see how empty I am. My kids are everything to me—but I don't think I've been a very good mom, because I just shut the rest of myself off in order to survive. I have been so damn tired for so long—" Sam stopped only because Jack's hand had ceased moving and its rhythm had apparently lulled her into a stupor of self-pity. "You must think I'm a crazy woman."

Then his hand was in her hair, and it was the strangest sensation. She spent her days massaging clients' heads, seeing their eyes close in bliss as she worked her magic. But when was the last time a man had touched her head like this? When was the last time she'd felt this kind of magic? She closed her eyes. Jack's long, strong fingers were gentle and warm and Sam couldn't help it: she felt herself weaken. She felt her head fall back and relax into the support he'd offered her.

"You're not crazy, Samantha. You're spectacular."

Sam's eyes flew open at the sound of his words, because his voice sounded blatantly sexual and real close. He'd moved his face to within an inch of hers. His hot breath brushed against her cheek. She inhaled him and was rewarded with a scent that was rich and warm and reminded her of sugar cookies just out of the oven, or anything else she'd never been unable to resist.

"Oh, Jack, wait—"

He didn't. That gentle hand guided her head close enough that his mouth covered hers, and he held her there, and between the heat of his open lips and his slick tongue and the unmistakable command of that hand behind her head she had no option but to surrender to it, let herself drown in it, because Jack Tolliver was kissing her like she'd never been kissed in her life.

It felt great.

Then it pissed her off.

Why hadn't anyone ever kissed her like this before? Why hadn't she ever been with a man who knew how to kiss like this? What had she been doing with her life?

The kiss got rougher and hotter and Jack very nonchalantly unsnapped her seat belt and pulled her body close to his. He leaned into her and continued the kissing and the pressing, and she heard herself make the oddest little noises of surprise and need. When he moved his lips to her throat, slid his tongue down to her collarbone and up to the tender spot under her earlobe, she realized he was giving her the same treatment she'd dished out at the restaurant.

Talk about cruel.

He nuzzled into the crook of her neck. "You are so soft."

"Jack—"

He sucked at her delicate flesh. "You taste so good."

"You'd better stop."

"I don't want to stop."

"Oh God!" Sam groaned. "If you don't stop right this second—"

"Yes?"

"It's just that I'm a little frustrated."

"That makes two of us."

"Oh, never mind!" Sam's cry thudded to a stop inside the tightly sealed luxury car. "Just hurry up and do it, then! I'm so hot right now I'm going to combust. Take me right this second. Please! *Fuck me now!*"

Jack went still. He pulled back from her, straightening his arms so he could study her carefully. Sam dared look at him, and the expression on his face was wide-eyed shock.

"Holy fucking shit," Jack whispered.

Sam closed her eyes in mortification. Had there been a rejection in that curse? Did she really just beg, out loud, for her boss to have sex with her?

How did a person go about recovering from such a faux pas?

"I am so sorry," she whispered, trying to turn her face away from Jack's scrutiny. He cupped her cheeks in his big hands and turned her toward him.

"Sam? Hello? Is that you?"

She kept her eyes shut tight and tried to pull his hands away from her face, but he wasn't budging.

"Look at me, Sam."

"I'd rather not."

"Open up your eyes and look at me."

She opened one eye enough to see Jack smiling at her, his shock now reduced to just garden-variety surprise.

"As you can see, I really am a crazy woman—a sex-starved crazy woman. I guess that's another thing you should have looked into before you asked me to marry you. Pretend marry, I mean. I really should be going now."

Jack smiled at her. His hands softened their grip on her face, but they did not let her go, and she felt one of his fingers stroke up and down her cheek. The stroke swept higher and then lower, until his fingertips were brushing all along the side of her hair, her cheek, her neck, and moving down into the opening of her coat and her blouse.

Sam let out a little humming sound from the back of her throat and closed her eyes again. She was tingling all over.

"You are not crazy, Sam." He gingerly kissed the tip of her nose. "You've been going to waste is all, baby."

He unbuttoned her coat. She let him. He unbuttoned her blouse and she let him. She felt the cold air on her skin and knew it was working its puckering magic on her nipples, and she didn't care. She opened her eyes to watch him rake his fingers across their hard points, which looked sharp enough to slice through the lace of her bra.

Jack sucked in a breath. "All this gorgeous, wonderful woman has been going to waste and I don't know how the hell you ended up here in my car and in my house and in my life, but *damn*—let's make the most of it."

The porch light flicked on, flooding the car with a beam as intense as an FBI searchlight. They both shielded their eyes.

Monté's voice rang out into the night. "You two can come on in the house like grown folks!"

Dale began to bark, and then the little dog bolted out the front door, yipping all the way to the car.

This rude interruption, plus the sight of Jack rebuttoning her blouse with lightening-fast competence, brought Sam to her senses. She began to wonder how many blouses he'd undone and redone over the years, how many nipples he'd grazed with his fingers. She figured that since most women had two nipples, the number could be well into the thousands.

The car doors unlocked, sounding to Sam like a starting gun. She decided to race to the house before things got any worse.

"Sam?" Jack called after her. As she ran, she heard the distinct sound of little doggy nails scraping down the side of a really expensive car.

Monté leaned against the door frame with her arms crossed over her chest and an I-told-you-so look on her face.

"Hard day at the office?" she asked, holding the door open as Sam scurried toward the stairs. "Uh-huh. Well, the kids are asleep. They told me I could let Dale inside, but the damn dog pooped on that little Oriental rug by the kitchen sink. Simon's staying over, so I figured I would, too, and I picked one of the guest rooms down the hall, if that's all right. This place has more rooms than a Motel 6."

Sam reached the top of the landing, skidded on the marble floors as she rounded the corner, and headed up the steps leading to the north wing of the house.

Monté called after her, "I'll expect a full report in the morning, and I ain't referring to how your steak was prepared!"

"Good night, Monté!" Sam couldn't wait to get behind the closed doors of her suite, where she could ask herself the same question over and over and over: *What in the world do I think I'm doing?*

OK. That was definitely something different.

Jack plopped his bare feet up on the ottoman and collapsed into his favorite leather chair, managing to keep every drop inside his full bottle of Corona.

He reached for the TV remote and flipped through 107 channels of nothing and clicked it off. He let his head sink into the supple cushion as he closed his eyes.

How could this be happening? How was it that the guy who could reliably have any woman he wanted found himself in a situation where he shouldn't have any woman at all? Worse, the one woman he found appealing—spectacularly appealing—was the one who was most thoroughly verboten.

Jack pinched the bridge of his nose between his thumb and index finger, then took a swig of beer.

He'd been rock hard for nearly three hours now, since the moment Samantha Monroe sauntered toward him from the women's room, a determined gleam in her eye and a nice sexy sway in those compact, rounded hips. He'd stopped talking in midsentence and stared, his jaw falling open in disbelief. A quick blink or two to ensure he wasn't imagining this vision, and it was *on*. Jack never thought he'd be capable of getting a boner in Brandon Miliewski's presence, but he had. Thank God for St. Elmo's generous white linen napkins.

And thanks to Sam's nuclear sex meltdown in his

car, his damn dick would not go soft. He might never go soft again as long as he lived.

With another draw on his cold beer, Jack focused on finding something to think about that didn't involve Samantha Monroe or her soulful blue eyes, saucy smile, soft hair, hard nipples, or the way her voice dropped an octave when she begged him to fuck her.

His mother. That should do it. He'd think about MDT and her last unanswered phone message and the frightening possibility of her showing up here for Christmas. If that didn't make him go limp, nothing would.

Jack finished the rest of the Corona and jumped up to toss the bottle in the kitchen recycle bin. But he must have landed on his feet wrong, because a searing hot agony shot up from his shin through his hip. This was perfect—the combination of his mother and the painful reminder of the lowest day in his life was a guaranteed hard-on deflator.

His phone started to ring.

"Why the hell would you go do a stupid thing like that?" It was Kara. "I haven't even nailed down the Goldman Steinam people yet! And you know how skittish Whitcombe Industries is! This was not our plan, Jack. You were supposed to tell the world about Sam at the same moment you declared. This stunt could put nearly a hundred grand in corporate contributions at risk."

"Sam called you already?"

"I called her. She told me. I asked her who happened to be present when you had your little senior moment and when she said it was a lobbyist she'd met once before named Brandon somebody I nearly peed my pajamas! Brandon Miliewski is such a needy weasel that he's already gone to somebody with this, I'm sure! He'd do anything to have a reporter owe him one. The only question is which one did he pick? Somebody who covers legislative issues, probably, but no one's called me at home yet for a quote."

Jack heard Kara pause to take a much-needed breath before she went on.

"Who does he know?"

"He knows every State House reporter in Indiana, I suppose. How did Sam sound when she called you? Is she all right?"

"Does Miliewski know Christy?"

"I have no idea. Did she sound good to you?"

"Who, Christy?"

"No, Sam."

"Sam? She sounded fine. Why wouldn't she? She said her steak was wonderful."

Jack nodded to himself, relieved. Of course she wouldn't have told Kara what happened in the car. That was a good thing, but he was dying to know if the too-short episode of hot groping had left Sam as disheveled as he was.

"Did she sound tired?"

Kara remained silent for a moment. "What is with you tonight, Jack? I thought we were clear on the timing. Now we're going to have to do damage con-

trol and maybe even throw together a press conference for tomorrow. I've called Stuart and we'll be
there in a half hour to go over this."

Jack sighed. "I'm at my condo."

"I know where you are! Jesus, Jack! I called you
on your home phone and you answered it, so obviously you're at your condo. What is your problem?"

He didn't know what to say.

"Jaaaack?"

"MDT says she wants to come to Indy for Christmas. I think I'm breaking out in hives."

Kara snorted. "Yeah, she called me today to bitch
about you. I didn't tell her what was going on, because I think that little conversation needs to happen
face-to-face and I think Stu and I should be there to
back you up."

Jack rolled his eyes. "You'd better. This was your
idea."

"She needs to see this as something you are absolutely convinced will work; otherwise she'll blow."

"No shit." Jack opened the fridge and found another Corona, twisted off the cap, and took a sip.
"It's pretty sad when a grown man needs to take his
posse along for a visit with Mother."

"She's not exactly Mrs. June Cleaver."

"Mrs. Meat Cleaver, maybe."

Kara laughed. "I know I don't have to tell you, but
the Divine Ms. M needs to be your vocal ally in this
campaign. She still carries a lot of weight with the
AARP crowd, and if she doesn't stump on your behalf you bet people would notice. We need her up
there at your side. And she needs to look like she's

thrilled out of her mind that you've finally settled down."

"Oh, she'll be out of her mind, all right."

"Sam told me about the car, Jack. I hope you're not too pissed."

Jack was about to take another sip of beer, but the bottle jerked in midair, just shy of his lips, and cold beer streamed down the front of his dress shirt. "She *told* you?" He grabbed a wad of paper towels and gave the front of his shirt a pat-down.

"Yes. She feels awful about what happened. She offered to take it out of next month's stipend, but I told her you probably wouldn't be that anal about it."

Jack stared blankly at the buttons on his kitchen microwave. Then he looked aimlessly at the pot rack, then out the window toward the pink floodlights of the Eiteljorg Museum down the street. What a bizarre reaction for Sam to have, as if the price of coitus interruptus could be taken out of a stipend! "Kara? I'm not sure I follow."

"She said Monté saw the whole thing happen."

"Oh great."

"So how much damage was done?"

Jack put down the beer and rubbed the back of his neck. "No permanent damage, Kara. It was a mistake, and it won't happen again. Sam and I are adults and we are entirely capable of moving on from this."

"Hmm," Kara said. "That's a pretty philosophical way to look at a few scratches on a car door, but I'm glad you're taking it so well, because the dog also crapped on a rug in the house."

It was all he could do not to guffaw. Jack felt dizzy with relief. "Man, that's good news," he said.

"You don't have to get all sarcastic about it."

Kara and Stu showed up a half hour later, as threatened, and the three of them sat around Jack's dining room table until two in the morning, coming up with a way to make the most out of his misstep at St. Elmo. It was agreed that he and Sam would rev things up a bit with their public appearances but stick with the original plan for him to announce both his candidacy and his engagement at the dolphin aquarium dedication.

"It's just too good not to use to full advantage," Kara said, closing up her laptop. "I mean, kids and a zoo? You can't get any more wholesome than that."

In the meantime, Kara suggested that Jack and Sam be seen together as often as possible, starting with next Saturday's symphony Christmas charity ball. Her instructions were to avoid answering any questions about the engagement directly but not deny anything, either.

"Let's tease the hell out of 'em," Stu said.

"The idea sounds better than it actually feels," Jack snipped.

"Like you've ever been on the receiving end of teasing," Kara said.

After Jack saw them to the door, he smiled to himself. That's exactly what had happened earlier that night in the car with Sam—she'd teased him mercilessly. Maybe she didn't intend to, but the result was that she'd left him panting, unsatisfied, and curious as hell. The truth was, he found her fine sense of humor and simple beauty bewitching. The fact that she was a vixen-on-the-down-low didn't hurt, either.

Jack turned off a living room lamp and the kitchen lights. Sure, he'd feasted from the female menu over the years. He'd piled his plate with stunningly beautiful women who had as much *oomph* as a stalk of celery. He'd nibbled on smart women who couldn't stop analyzing long enough to enjoy sex. He'd munched on his share of party girls, and, like junk food, they could be quick and easy but left him hungry for something substantial soon after.

What he'd tasted in Samantha Monroe was something he'd never encountered anywhere else, and he had to admit there was something incredibly sexy about a woman who looked like Wonderbread but burned his tongue like a bowl of five-fuckin'-alarm chili.

And as Jack walked down the hall and into his bedroom, he realized that out of all the women he'd dated in the last decade he couldn't think of a single one he could turn to, right now, for a little comfort. There wasn't one female who'd offer him some loving and be willing to keep her mouth shut about it. There wasn't anyone he could trust. So it looked like he'd be living the life of a de facto monk until this primary was done.

What in the world had he done to himself?

7

The hum of music and laughter flowed over Sam, and she looked around at the D & D Night crowd with great pleasure. Tonight they welcomed two members back into the fold—Candy McGaughy, absent since her baby girl was born three months before (her third), and Olivia Petrakis, who was rebounding from a divorce (her second). Denny and Wanda were there, along with Kara, Monté, Marcia, and their newest member, Brigid Larson, a wholesome-faced divorced mom with two kids who owned a popular breakfast place over on Massachusetts Avenue, tucked in between the art galleries, New Age bookstores, and boutiques.

It was Brigid who brought it up. "My God, Sam! Everyone knows what a hottie Jack Tolliver is! How did you meet him? How long have you known him? How long have you been dating? I read all those articles—are you really engaged?"

Sam batted her eyelashes and didn't dare look over at Monté. She let her gaze wander toward Kara instead, who nodded almost imperceptibly in Sam's direction, as if to give her the go-ahead. Since Christy had reported on Jack's "alleged" engagement and the papers followed suit, they'd been playing a game of hide-and-seek with the facts.

"Kara introduced us a while back. I haven't been dating him very long at all, and as far as being engaged goes . . ." Sam paused to steady her breath. "I don't want to jinx anything. My plan is to just see where it goes."

Candy's mouth hung ajar. "So you really are engaged to the most eligible bachelor in Indiana? I give birth to one measly child and this is what I miss?"

"You'll note the lack of a ring," Monté said, drawing everyone's attention to Sam's naked finger.

"Rings are nothing but medieval patriarchical symbols of male oppression of female power," Denny said with an impatient wave of her hand.

"I love rings," Wanda said. "Do you know what kind you'd like? Are you going with gold, white gold, or platinum?"

"Platinum for sure," Monté's said.

Kara laughed and Sam rolled her eyes.

"We haven't talked about it all that much," she said, smiling. "Believe me, the day I walk out into the world with an engagement ring on my finger, you-all will be the first to know."

As everyone nodded their approval, Sam took a moment to review the tangled web to herself: Kara, Monté, and Denny knew she was a hired gun; Marcia, Wanda, Candy, Olivia, and Brigid thought she was Jack's real girlfriend; and no one at all knew she'd done her best to get laid in his Lexus the other night.

For Sam, this ordeal already required a sharp memory and a decent output of energy just to keep all the details straight, and Jack hadn't even announced he was running. She wondered how difficult it would be to avoid making a slip in the coming months.

"I'm going to be her maid of honor," Monté said, acknowledging the coos and congratulations from those who didn't know any better. Sometimes it seemed Monté was enjoying this ruse more than Sam was.

"I've decided my colors will be pea green and mustard yellow," Sam said, making Monté work for her fun.

"You know green doesn't do a thing for my complexion," Monté said, giving her braids a haughty shake. "I was thinking some kind of neon orange might be better."

Olivia let go with an exasperated sigh. "Green, yellow, construction-cone orange, it doesn't matter. Everything ends up an amorphous smear of blackness and regret in the end anyway."

After a moment of silence, Candy said, "Thanks, girls. This party is doing wonders for my postpartum depression. I think I'll go home and flush all my Zoloft down the toilet. Who needs it?"

"That would be a sin," Marcia said. "Give it to me and I'll put it in the candy dish at my station."

"Anyway," Kara pointed out, "it's called Drinks &

Depression Night, not Drinks & Delight Night, or something upbeat like that."

"Decadence & Diversion Night," Brigid said.

"Delicious Drama Night," Olivia said.

"Deliver me some Dick Night," Monté said.

The evening had degenerated into one of those occasions that should have made Sam downright mortified. They were making a racket—snorting and wailing and hands banging on the tabletop—but Sam herself was laughing too hard to remember to be embarrassed.

On the way out of the Lizard Lounge an hour later, Kara pulled Sam aside. "Can I talk to you alone for a minute?"

Monté hung nearby, just outside the door to the bar. Sam gave her a hand signal that she'd be right out and joined Kara at two end bar stools. The look on Kara's face was sheepish, like she was about to say something awkward.

Had Jack told her?

"Look, I know that this whole thing was my idea, and I really have no right to ask you this—"

Here it comes. . . .

"I didn't want to mention this in front of Monté or Marcia because I figured they'd try to jump in and say that they were just as talented as you are and could do it just as well as you, though I'm not convinced that's the case. I guess I'm selfish."

Huh?

"Jack said he didn't care if we did it at the Sunset Lane house, as long as we cleaned up afterward—"

What?

"He said he might even want to watch us, if you were OK with it. I told him I didn't care."

Sam's mind went blank as Kara leaned in close. "You've got to do my roots. Nobody but you has touched my hair for nine years, and if something went wrong, I . . . I . . . I can't even think about it. I'd become a shut-in."

Sam blinked. "You want me to do your hair?"

"Yeah. What in the world did you think I was talking about?"

Sam smiled. "I'll gather up some supplies and we can meet at the house Sunday afternoon. Will that work?"

Kara hugged Sam tight. "Thank you!"

"But don't let anyone else know I'm doing this, or I'll have cars lined up on Sunset Lane, and I can't see Jack being too thrilled with that."

Kara patted her hand. "I wouldn't worry too much about him. It's funny, but I think Jack really likes you, Sam. Something about you seems to chill him out."

Chill him out? Sam said good night to Kara and joined Monté on the sidewalk, thinking to herself that Jack had the exact opposite effect on her.

She and Monté walked the three blocks to the parking garage, their breath hanging in the lights that illuminated the cold downtown night.

"How did shopping go today?" Monté asked. "Did you find a dress for the symphony thing you gotta go to Saturday?"

"Uh, not exactly." Sam shoved her hands deep into the pockets of her peacoat.

"Where did you go? You probably didn't shop at the right place, is all."

Sam had to agree with that statement, since it was awfully hard to find a formal gown at an art supply store.

"I had to run a few errands first, but I eventually ended up at the Fashion Mall up at Keystone and then Castleton Mall. I just didn't see anything I liked."

Monté sent her a doubtful look. "Did you try anything on?"

"No."

Monté shook her head. "Girl, if I had your body and your checking account, you couldn't drag my ass out of the dressing room. I think you need a fashion intervention, and I'm just the woman to do it."

Sam chuckled at the idea that Monté assumed she'd denied herself a shopping splurge when the opposite was true. Her first stop of the day had been Bates Art & Drafting Supplies, where, with Dakota's help, she'd selected 650 dollars' worth of pure pigment oils, Escoda sable brushes, linseed oil, thinners, gesso, and huge rolls of canvas the Bates staff was now custom stretching into three panels, each three feet by six feet. She'd been feeling the urge to paint big lately—she didn't know what yet, but she knew she was headed in a new direction. In her mind's eye she saw a huge triptych showing the evolution of something, a concept or a point of view. She knew it would come to her.

"I did go a little nuts with the Christmas shopping, though," Sam said.

Monté laughed. "That's understandable. It probably felt like biting into an éclair after years of dieting. I can't say I blame you."

Sam hugged her arms tighter to her sides in an effort to stay warm. "I told myself I wouldn't go completely overboard with the kids' gifts this year, especially because I'm saving for a hefty down payment on a house, as you know. But I just couldn't help it, Monté—it was too much fun. You won't believe what I got each of them."

Monté smiled. "Can't wait to hear."

"I got all three of them iPods, plus a laptop computer and printer."

Monté jerked her head back in confusion. "How's a child who don't know how to wipe himself supposed to surf the 'Net?"

Sam laughed and hooked her arm around Monté's elbow. "That stuff's for Simon, silly. I got Dakota a Wiggles' balloon bounce."

Monté stopped in her tracks and removed her arm from Sam's. "You got my boy a computer and an iPod?"

"Of course I did."

"Now why would you do that?"

Sam smiled. True, she'd briefly wondered if Monté would consider the gifts overkill but decided to risk it.

"Because I can. Because I love Simon like he was my own kid and it brings me joy to do this for him. I know you'd do the same for my kids if the luck were reversed, and don't try to deny it."

Monté pursed her lips for a moment, looked

around at the downtown lights, then nodded at Sam. Tears welled up in her large brown eyes. "You know that's right," she said, slipping her arm into Sam's again.

The two women grinned in silence as they made their way up the parking garage elevator. They got into Sam's van and she started the engine. Monté looked over at her, one eyebrow arched high. "I'm damn-near afraid to ask what you're getting *me* for Christmas."

Sam laughed. "As you should be."

Jack straightened the black tie at his throat and clipped on a pair of cuff links. Tonight he'd chosen his grandfather's vintage set that featured the likeness of Marilyn Monroe depicted in platinum and diamonds, the cuff links his father said proved that the old guy had gone through a midlife crisis back when they didn't even know men had them. Jack gave a quick yank on the sleeves of his tuxedo shirt to make sure he could move his arms freely, wondering what Sam would be wearing tonight and whether thirty-eight was too young to be having a midlife crisis of his own. Then he hooked a finger in the shirt collar and tugged, making sure he could breathe. On any occasion, five hours in a tuxedo would be an ordeal. At a symphony charity event with sexpot Sam pretending to be his chaste date, five hours was going to feel like the eternity of the damned.

Jack slipped into the classically cut Armani jacket, hoping for both their sakes that Sam would find a way to relax tonight and forgive herself for her outburst in the car. He'd forgotten the whole episode!

Jack buttoned the jacket and ran a hand through his hair, hoping that Sam would come to see her outburst for what it was—a perfectly normal and healthy response from a perfectly normal and healthy woman who'd been abnormally neglected for an unhealthy period of time. That's all.

Jack grabbed his wallet and car keys and took one last glance at himself in the floor-to-ceiling mirror of his dressing room, thinking that it would be nice if Sam would wear something red and slinky tonight, with a long slit up the side of her leg—a leg he'd never actually seen. Every time they'd been in the same room together, Sam had worn pants or jeans. Nicely fitted pants or jeans, make no mistake about it, but pants nonetheless.

It was true that Samantha Monroe wasn't the tallest woman he'd ever known. In fact, she was much shorter than the type he usually found attractive. She had to be a foot shorter than he was and a hundred pounds lighter.

But Sam Monroe was an interesting woman. A levelheaded mom. One sexy little female.

And he could only imagine what lay beneath those pants. Taut, peach-hued flesh. Toned muscle. Freckles. A hard knee, a sharp shin, sweet little pink toes that would look good being slipped out of a pair of high-heeled sandals and into his mouth . . .

Jack grabbed his black cashmere coat from the closet and headed down the elevator to the underground parking garage. Yes, he'd forgotten all about Samantha's hot sex explosion in his car and the way she smelled and the way he nearly erupted when she'd begged him to . . .

Who was he kidding? Jack knew he'd be lucky to finish the night alive.

The evening had an odd feel of déjà vu to it, and Sam realized it reminded her of the night Dave Schindler picked her up for the Valparaiso High School junior prom. The only things missing were a white gardenia corsage on her wrist and a nervous mother taking Polaroids of the couple in front of the fireplace.

"You look r-r-really pretty, Mom," Greg said, a bag of Doritos hanging from one hand and Dakota's fingers gripped in the other. "What time should we expect you home?"

Sam smiled at the protective tone in Greg's voice, a voice that seemed to be starting to creak and crack its way from child to man. "I'm not exactly sure. What would you say, Jack?"

Sam turned toward her date for the evening, quite possibly the most handsome man who'd ever lived, dark and mysterious in a sinfully expensive tuxedo, a coat tossed casually over one arm. He looked as if he should be wearing one of those sticky name tags emblazoned with the words: *HELLO! I'm God's Gift to Women.*

"Jack?"

He snapped to attention, and Sam felt her cheeks go hot. Jack had been staring at her exposed leg as if in a trance. She never should have allowed Monté to talk her into this Vanna White getup. It was way too red and way too open-down-the-front and slit-up-the-side. But she had to admit it wasn't dull, boring, or dowdy, and that's why she'd bought it.

Jack swallowed hard, then gave Greg a man-to-man nod. "I'd say by midnight. The concert goes until about ten thirty, then there's a reception."

Lily put her hands on her hips. "And so you're the designated driver?"

"I am." Jack grinned at Lily with appreciation. "How about I give you my cell phone number, in case you need to reach us?"

"Knock yourself out," Lily said, immediately smoothing over her rudeness before Sam could. "That would be thoughtful, thank you."

With a chuckle, Jack left the great room off the kitchen and headed toward his office, probably to get a piece of paper. Sam turned to Lily.

"You know, if I didn't love you so much, I'd have to wring your skinny little neck."

Greg laughed. "Not if I beat you to it," he said.

"Don't go, Mama! Stay wif me—!" Before Sam could protect herself, Dakota had a hunk of her dress gripped in his Dorito-hued fingers.

"No, baby. Mommy has to go to work. I'll be home in a little bit." She tried to pry his digits off the fabric but only succeeded in helping him tear off a few tiny red beads sewn into the material. Sam gripped his wrist. "No, Dakota. Please don't rip Mommy's dress. I need to go somewhere fancy tonight and this is the only thing I have to wear."

"No, no, no, no, no!" He pulled harder, and Sam was at least grateful that the Dorito smear would blend into the deep red of the dress. She cringed, remembering how close she'd come to buying a white crepe pantsuit for the occasion.

"Hey, Dakota Benjamin."

Jack's voice was calm and low, but the sound of it seemed to startle Dakota. His blue eyes flashed to Jack hovering over him. His chubby fingers relaxed. A shower of minuscule beads fell to the wide plank floors.

"Hey, Mr. Jack!"

Jack held out a pencil to Dakota. "Listen, champ, how about you give me a hand and write down my cell phone number?"

Dakota scrunched up his nose and frowned, then licked some bright orange dust off his fingers and his palm. "I'm only *free*," he said, sporting an attitude Sam knew her youngest could have acquired from any number of people in his life. "I don't know my numbers yet. I know some letters, like *D*, 'cause that's my name letter. Greg and Lily know all their numbers, though."

"Right." Jack looked deflated, and Sam couldn't help but smile. He'd had the right instincts, just the wrong details, and that was impressive coming from a man who had little or no experience with children.

"Let's do it together." Lily took the pad of paper and pencil from Jack, then knelt down next to her brother. Jack gave her the numbers slowly, and Dakota repeated each one with enthusiasm while Lily wrote.

When they were done, Dakota smiled at Jack and gave him a big, orange thumbs-up. "I'll call you later, Mr. Jack," he said.

• • •

Sometimes, Christy thought she had the gift of extrasensory perception when it came to Jack Tolliver, and occasionally, especially if she'd had a couple of lemon drop martinis, she'd allow herself to ponder the greater meanderings of the universe and just sit back and be awestruck by it all. Maybe she could sense his presence because he was her soul mate. Maybe she could feel his energy in a crowded room because they had been tragic lovers in another lifetime and she and Jack were destined to dance the dance of fate and sorrow and missed opportunities into infinity.

Christy turned, seeing Jack just as she knew she would. But there was an unexpected twist: her soul mate was bending toward a redhead in a red dress, smiling at the woman as he stroked her bare upper arm. Christy's thoughts became decidedly less poignant—she thought maybe Jack could just go to hell like the scum-sucking pig he was!

"Happy holidays, Christy!"

"Happy holidays to you!"

She engaged in conversation for several minutes with the symphony's director of public relations—covering everything from Handel to Hanukkah—but her eyes and her attention were focused on Jack and Miss Firecracker Red over there. That dress looked ridiculous on Samantha Monroe. She obviously needed an image consultation, a little crash course in what women who venture out into society wore to things like symphony benefit concerts. Red sequins with a slit up the side? Not hardly, and not ever in Indianapolis, even at Christmas. The woman looked like she was auditioning for a job as one of Santa's slut elves.

Apparently, the public relations woman had wandered off without so much as a good-bye, because Christy suddenly found herself alone. She shrugged, taking another small sip of her martini, noting that her teeth were really bugging her again and giving herself kudos for what she'd selected to wear for this event—basic black that looked anything but basic on her. The contrast of the severe dark lines of the Calvin Klein sleeveless gown and the pale gleam of her skin and hair was just the effect she was looking for. Elegant. Reserved. Utterly ladylike.

"What the fuck?"

Oh God, she hadn't meant to say that aloud, but Jack had just kissed the slutty elf with one hand at the nape of her neck and another hand so low on her back it was nearly on her ass! Three old biddies just swiveled their heads and stared at Christy, lipsticked mouths agape at her outburst, but there was nothing she could say, really. The damage had been done. So Christy gave them a bug-eyed look and slugged down the rest of her cocktail. Besides, Kara DeMarinis was approaching from her left, and Christy knew she needed to look slightly bored, which would be difficult to do after what she'd just witnessed.

"Ah, Christy. Just the woman I was hoping to run into."

Christy sighed. "And why is that?"

"It's always a pleasure to see you, of course, but I

also wanted to apologize again for not being able to make tomorrow's show."

Christy placed her empty glass on a waiter's tray as he sashayed by. Maybe it was the lighting in the Hilbert Circle Theatre's promenade, but it sure looked like Kara DeMarinis was going gray, big-time.

"Your roots need a touch-up, dear."

Kara stiffened almost imperceptibly, but Christy was plenty perceptive.

"I can recommend a good stylist. Her name is Marcia Fishbacher, a few doors down from here, at Le Cirque. But I think you may already know her, seeing that your candidate's temporary tart used to work for her."

Kara's eyes narrowed, but Christy had to admire the fact that the hand holding that Merlot was steady as could be. Kara was a decent sort, and if she wasn't part of Jack's entourage, she and Christy very well might have been friends.

"I see you've done your homework," Kara said.

Christy laughed. "Oh, I've just skimmed the syllabus, sweetness. But I am planning on doing some extra-credit research. I'm going to get way, way down into the dirty truth of the subject matter. What do you think of that?"

A corner of Kara's mouth curled up. "It just kills you that he's happy, doesn't it?"

It was Christy's turn to smile, and she relished it, taking her time to carefully plan what she'd say. "Jack Tolliver isn't interested in being happy, Kara. He's interested in booty, fame, and keeping his mother off his back. But most importantly, he's interested in expending the least amount of energy possible in his effort to get those things."

It shocked Christy to feel Kara's cool hand touch her shoulder. "You poor thing," Kara said, feigning concern. "After all this time and all you've done to get your revenge, you're still in love with him." Kara gave a gentle nod toward Jack and the slut elf. "How hurt you must be."

"Oh, shut up, Kara." This was getting boring. "I'm not sure what you're up to yet, but I'll figure it out. You can count on it." Christy turned to go, knowing her evening was about as done as it could get. She left with a parting shot. "And Kara? Don't waste your bullshit on me. Save it for the campaign, where it belongs."

Jack wasn't sure what he'd done to deserve this night, but he'd take it as the gift it clearly was.

She'd worn red. Red with a slit! Red with *cleavage.* There was a God.

Sam had been funny and sweet and comfortable with everyone he'd introduced her to. She was, in a word, charming. When people asked what she did, she told them she was a hairstylist on sabbatical. When they'd asked how long she'd known Jack, she'd answered with a smile, "It's only been a short while, but it feels like I've known him forever." She truly enjoyed the musical program, a hell of a lot more than Jack did, that's for sure, since *The Messiah* made his knee ache. Sam ate a plateful of hors d'oeuvres, and it thrilled him to see she wasn't embarrassed to consume actual food in public, unlike many women he'd dated. She'd laughed and snuggled up to him when he'd pulled her close. Sam Monroe had been a dream date.

Until just a few minutes ago.

People had already started talking about the weather's bad turn before he and Sam prepared to leave the reception. Rumors running through the crowd claimed that two inches of ice was expected to fall over the Circle City overnight, that state troopers had already shut down parts of I-65 and I-70, and that power was out on the North Side due to downed wires. But Jack had dismissed most of the talk as the kind of exaggerated gossip that routinely caused bread, milk, and toilet paper to disappear from grocery store shelves. Hoosiers could go goofy over a little bad weather.

But then he and Sam stepped outside onto the Circle to find the sidewalks already coated in ice and frozen rain coming down from the sky like miniature daggers.

Sam asked to use his cell phone to call the kids, and there was no answer. She panicked, worried about how frightened Dakota would be if the power was out and how Lily and Greg didn't know where to find flashlights or candles. She began muttering to herself about how the kids were unsafe stumbling around in the huge, strange house in the dark and how much better it would be if they were still in the old place on Arsenal Street, which they knew like the backs of their hands.

Jack wondered if all moms got this psycho when

something a little out of the ordinary happened and they couldn't reach their kids.

"This is awful. I'm freaking out." Sam now sat in the passenger seat of the car, one hand gripping the door handle and the other slapped onto the leather dashboard.

"We'll get there," Jack said, trying to time his words between the intermittent rasps of the windshield wipers scraping over ice. "They are going to be fine, Sam."

"Can't you drive any faster?"

Jack smiled and reached over to caress her tense shoulder. "I could, but then there'd be a hundred percent chance we'd end up in a ditch versus the eighty percent we're now dealing with."

"Put both hands on the wheel, please."

"You got it."

They made it to Thirty-eighth Street, only to be greeted by a wall of flashing red lights. The intersection was blocked by ambulances, dozens of police cars, and a few tow trucks.

Jack snaked his way around stopped traffic and tried to turn west to avoid the accident scene. A police officer held up a gloved hand and motioned for Jack to stop. It was a good thing he was going about three miles an hour, because he could barely bring the car to a halt in time to avoid running the policeman over.

Jack lowered his window and greeted the officer, shielding his eyes from the glare of the emergency lights.

"You'll have to pull over and remain in your vehicle, sir." The officer who gave the flat command had a plastic rain cover on his hat and was wearing a bright yellow slicker. "We're not letting anyone through."

Jack nodded, hearing Sam begin to make pathetic little groans of frustration from the passenger seat. "I understand, Officer, but is there any possibility that I can just—?"

"Jack Tolliver?" The cop leaned into the window, his wet face lit up with a grin. "Man, I haven't seen you in ages! It's me—Ed Kitzmiller, Hoosier football, offensive line."

"Ed! Hey, man!" Jack reached across his body and gripped Ed's hand with gusto. "Great to see you!"

"No kidding. Wonderful!" Ed peered inside the car and noticed Sam. He nodded respectfully. "Ma'am."

"Oh, hey, Ed, this is Samantha Monroe. Sam, this is Ed Kitzmiller, the best lineman I ever had the pleasure to work with."

Ed leaned forward, placing both hands on the open window ledge, shaking his head. "That's such a crock, Tolliver. You worked with some of the greats when you played for the Colts, man."

"I did indeed. How long have you been with the IPD?"

"Going on sixteen years, man. I got three kids. Jared's a junior up at Lawrence High, running back. He's got his mama's build, not mine." Ed gave his gut a pat through the rain gear.

"Now who did you marry again?"

"Cynthia Perryman. Remember her? Cute little—"

"Hello?" Sam's shout sounded fairly desperate. Jack looked over to find her gesturing wildly.

"Oh. Right. Hey, Ed?" Jack leaned toward the open window, feeling a blast of frozen rain on his cheek. "We have a problem here. I need your help."

"You got it," Ed said without hesitation.

"I need to get up to Sunset Lane off Fifty-sixth Street. The power's out and Sam's kids are in the house alone and she's . . ." Jack looked over at her to see a tear streaming down her cheek. "It's OK, Sam." He touched the sleeve of her coat, then looked back at Ed. "We really need to get up there. Can you let us by?"

Ed gave a swift nod of understanding. "I'll do better than that. Hold a second."

Ed carefully made his way toward the center of the busy intersection, where he had a few words with someone who seemed to be in charge. While they waited, Jack took Sam's hand in his, and she didn't resist. She stared out the passenger side window, but at least she didn't take her hand away.

"Pull around here and then follow me," Ed said. "I'll escort you."

Jack grinned. "Ah, man, you're great. Saving my ass like you did for four straight years in Bloomington."

Ed apparently liked that, and tilted his head back into the icy rain and laughed. "As long as you're aware that's exactly what I did," he said with a grin. The grin began to fade, and he cocked his head slightly. "Your injury. Jesus, Jack. I puked when I saw it happen. Every guy I know said it was the nastiest thing they'd ever seen in professional sports. My God, I've been thinking about you all these years."

A lump rose in Jack's throat. Though his attention was on Ed, he sensed Sam turn toward him. Then he felt her other hand cover his protectively. The lump in his throat got tighter. "Thanks, man," he said. "Thank you."

Ed slapped him on the shoulder. "Well, you look damn good now—for a politician." He laughed. "I'll get you and your girlfriend home."

Jack wasn't normally a sentimental guy, but he was overwhelmed by a sudden rush of . . . what was it? Tenderness? Here was his old friend Ed Kitzmiller cutting him a break. Here was beautiful Sam Monroe sitting right next to him, holding his hand in concern. He felt plugged into the world. He felt damn good. And he heard himself call out, "She's my fiancée, Kitz! Can you believe that shit?"

Ed stopped so abruptly he nearly lost his balance on the ice. He looked back toward the car with a silly smile plastered across his face. "I'll be damned," he said.

It took another forty minutes, but they made it to the house in one piece. Jack tried to convince Ed to come in for coffee, but Ed pointed out there was no electricity and, besides, he needed to get back to work. He then offered to pitch in with Jack's campaign for Senate if he'd like his help. Jack gave Ed a quick hug and said he'd take him up on it, then made sure he got safely out of the drive and back onto the lane. He parked the Lexus in the garage and went in to find Sam and the kids.

"Lily? Greg?" Sam's voice sounded so small in the cavernous and dark house. She didn't want to yell too loud, in case Dakota was sleeping, but she was nearly shaking with worry.

"Lily?" Sam poked her head into the empty formal living room. There was just enough ambient light that she could make it across the main foyer and stumble through the dining room, parlor, library, great room, and butler's pantry, calling for Lily and Greg at each turn.

Nothing.

Sam took a deep breath, insisting to herself that there was no reason to be worried. The house might be dark, but it was dry and warm and there was food and water and, frankly, abject luxury all around. Her children were fine.

If only she could find them.

She felt her way down the long hallway that connected the main house to the pool house. It was eerily silent and dark and she was trying her best not to cry.

"Sam?"

She nearly jumped out of her skin at the sound of her name. A strong hand steadied her at her lower back.

"Let's check upstairs, OK?" Jack turned her by the shoulders and guided her through the dim kitchen to the back stairwell. The passageway was narrower and far less formal than the grand staircase at the front of the house, and Jack's arm stayed tight around her as he led her up the dark steps and to the north wing. "Maybe they fell asleep before the power went out. They might not even know there's a storm."

Sam nodded. Jack was right, of course. And for a brief moment, she wondered why she'd reacted with such panic to something as simple as an early ice storm.

Maybe deep down, she was afraid of the good fortune that had come her way, that it wasn't possible for her to have escaped the grim situation she was in. Maybe she felt it was all too good to be true and that something extremely bad was bound to happen that would wipe out all the good.

That had to be it. And she clung to that understanding of her own insecurity even when they didn't find anyone in Lily's bedroom, or Dakota's or Greg's. As they reached the double doors to Sam's suite, she heard giggles and the unmistakable sound of Dale's bark, and it had to be the sweetest music she'd ever heard in her life. She threw open the doors.

"Mom!" Greg leaped up from where he sat next to Lily, on the floor near the fireplace. "We were so w-w-worried!"

Lily jumped up, too, and Sam's two older kids were suddenly in her arms. She squeezed them tight and felt the relief rush through her so hard that tears came to her eyes.

"Don't get all psycho on us, Mother," Lily said. Then she kissed Sam's cheek. "But we're real glad to see you."

Sam peered around Greg and Lily at the small form of Dakota under the comforter in her bed. She watched with wonder as Jack pulled aside the covers and scooped up her baby in his arms. He winked as he turned to carry Dakota down the hall to his own room.

Sam snuggled with Lily and Greg on one of the room's two couches, taking comfort in their smiling faces in the warm glow of the gas flames. Dale jumped in her lap.

Her family was all right. Everything was all right.

". . . and then all the sudden, the TV just zapped off and the whole house went black!" Lily swept hair off her face and Sam loved the sense of wonder she saw in her daughter's eyes. "This place is like a tomb without lights, Mom! I'm telling you—total Scooby Doo haunted mansion stuff. We were completely freaked because we couldn't see our way around!"

"Did Dakota cry?"

"No!" Lily began to laugh. "Mom, he just loved it. He ran all over the place like a crazy man and we had to catch him and lock him up in here."

Sam shook her head. "That kid."

"We had n-n-no idea where to look for f-f-flashlights."

"The butler's pantry," Jack said to Greg as he strolled back into Sam's room. He relaxed into the couch across from them. "For future reference, that's where you can find most anything you would need in an emergency—matches, candles, batteries, flash-lights, first-aid supplies, duct tape, chocolate, and booze to restock any of the bars."

Sam frowned at him.

"Not that you ever would want to restock any bars or anything."

Lily laughed. "I guess every palace has to have a secret hiding place, right?"

Jack smiled, and the sight took Sam's breath away. Those deep green eyes of his glowed in the firelight and his white teeth gleamed, and Sam wondered what it would feel like to be Jack Tolliver's woman for real, what it would feel like to be loved by such a male specimen. Sam sighed. If only outside beauty were a measure of a man's heart. But she'd learned the hard way that that wasn't the case, and a man's heart was the only thing that mattered in the end.

She gazed upon all that sexual beauty—packed into a tuxedo, no less—and had to smile. Yes, Jack was art on legs. But she wanted a good man, not a perfect-looking one. And a good man was a balance of passion and levelheadedness. A good man would put the woman he loved before all else, including his job and his ego.

Sam wondered just how many women had been rolled flat as Jack's ego took a turn around their block.

"There's an honest-to-God secret room in this house," Jack told the kids, leaning forward to rest his elbows on his knees. "My grandfather had it built into the wall of his office when he designed this house about eighty years ago. I'll show it to you sometime. It's pretty cool, I've gotta say. I loved it when I was a kid. I used to hang out in there and play army men."

"Whoa!" Greg sat up straight and leaned toward

Jack. "This house belonged to your grandfather the governor?"

"Yep. Then it belonged to my dad, who was a governor, too."

"I know! We read about them in history class. I think it's so cool that I'm living in the governor's old house. I'd really love to see that secret room someday."

It didn't escape Sam that all those words just came from her son's mouth without a single stutter, a sure sign that he was interested in the subject at hand. It seemed when Greg was fascinated by something it took him out of himself enough that his lips could keep pace with his thoughts just fine.

"So, you're a student of history, are you?"

"I love history," Greg said, nodding.

"The state of Indiana sort of requires that we study it in school," Lily added, with just a touch of annoyance.

Jack nodded. "Absolutely. I remember when I was lieutenant governor we used to sit around and brainstorm about how we could torture the youth of our great state. We always came back to history and, of course, math."

Both Sam's kids were silent for a moment, until they figured out he was kidding. Sam watched the realization spread across Greg's face just as he started to laugh. She watched her daughter roll her eyes.

"I'm thinking once I get to Washington, I'll whip up some teenage torture legislation, like no driver's licenses until you're twenty-one or something."

"No way!" Greg said, sitting up straight.

"That would be major suckitude," Lily said, then narrowed her eyes. "Unless you're trying to be funny again or something."

Greg reached across Sam to smack his sister's arm. "I think he *is* funny, Bones."

Lily crossed her arms over her chest and stared at Jack for a second, and Sam was about to interfere on his behalf when she noticed the way his face had softened as he looked at Lily, how his eyes shone with amusement. Something was going on here between her kids and Jack, and Sam decided she'd let it play out.

"OK," Lily said. "You're pretty cool, Jack. But in the name of all that is good and holy, don't mess with that law until I've got my learner's permit."

8

This was the kind of context in which Jack usually did his finest work. He was alone with a beautiful woman in her boudoir, in the dark, in front of the fireplace, and they'd already decided that he'd be spending the night.

In his playbook of love, this was the moment when the ball was delivered into his waiting hands via a flawless snap. This was when he'd reach back with grace and steadiness and rocket that sucker in a perfect spiral down the field, a direct hit into the breadbasket of his intended.

Touchdown. Every fucking time.

Jack loosened his black tie, crossed his right leg over his bad knee, and laughed a little to himself. Of course, this was no ordinary entry from his little black playbook. This was Sam, and the boudoir was the one his mother's cronies preferred when they came to visit, which was a little strange, and the lights were off not as a part of an overall plan of seduction but because of a power outage. Jack was spending the night not because the woman had invited him but because the roads were iced up.

In his rational brain, Jack knew that all this meant that the usual rules did not apply, but his heart and his dick weren't listening. All he wanted—the *only* thing he wanted—was the feel of Samantha's body against his, his hands on her flesh, his mouth on her skin, that little moan escaping from the back of her throat as he buried himself inside her.

"Would you like to go downstairs and have a glass of wine?" she asked him.

Jack was up off the couch. "Red or white?"

"Uh . . ."

He was at the door. There was no way he could risk a change in venue. He wanted Sam in this bedroom, not in the damn kitchen. "Your preference, madame?"

He watched a nervous little smile spread across Sam's lips and marveled at how sweet and sexy she was. He marveled at the way that red dress shimmered in the firelight and how her skin glowed and how he wanted to lick her from her navel to her temples and then all the way back down to the soles of her pretty little feet.

"Red is good."

Hell, yes, it was, Jack thought to himself as he raced down the back stairs, mentally reviewing which wines might be stashed in the butler's pantry, because he sure wasn't going to risk the five minutes it would take to run down to the wine cellar. Red was great. Red hair and red dresses and tiny red-painted toenails and the red lights that were pulsing behind his eyelids—these were all good things.

Jack first rooted around for a flashlight, then snagged the first Cabernet he found, along with two red wine goblets and a corkscrew. Then he made a snap decision to provide whatever else might be needed up there, took off his tux jacket, spread it out on a marble counter, and began to pile things in the center of the satin lining: a lighter, six white tapered candles, six ceramic candleholders, and two additional flashlights. He bundled up the whole mess, stashed the corkscrew in his pocket, stuck the wine bottle under his arm, and cradled the goblets in his free hand.

"Wow." Sam blinked in surprise. "That was quick."

Jack smiled. His knee would never again be strong enough to withstand a direct hit from a three-hundred-pound defensive lineman or even go more than two miles around the high school track, but he could still make quick work of a set of stairs—as long as it wasn't first thing in the morning.

"I live to serve," he said, placing the bottle down on the coffee table, enjoying the slow chuckle his falsehood had elicited from Sam.

"Did you steal your mother's silver or something?" Sam nodded at the sack he'd tossed on the sofa.

He smiled at Sam as he uncorked the bottle, trying not to dwell too much on what he was doing, because, clearly, he was trying to seduce her.

Clearly, he wanted her.

And if he got her—and when did he not get what he wanted?—things could get a little dicey around here.

Kara and Stu would go ballistic. They'd accuse him of all sorts of nastiness, none of which was true. The only truth was that he really liked Sam Monroe. He thought she was sweet and beautiful and smart. He thought they could have a hell of a lot of fun with the five months and two weeks that lay ahead.

He untied the bundle and began placing items on the coffee table. "I figured we could give each kid a flashlight and we could use the candles."

"That was nice of you."

"No problem."

"Tell me about your knee, Jack."

Great. He lowered himself into the sofa across from Sam and gave himself—and the wine—a few minutes to breathe. "Let's see. I got hit so hard I saw angels. That's pretty much the whole story."

Sam tilted her head and ran a hand through those tempting red curls of hers. He knew her hair felt like the finest silk. He knew it smelled like heaven.

"I think you might have left out a few details."

Jack sighed. "My NFL career was over before it really got started. I'd spent two seasons on the bench as second-string quarterback, then our starter retired, and I got my chance. We went all the way to the Super Bowl my first season out."

Jack untied the black satin of his bow tie and took out the top stud of his tuxedo shirt, stuffing it in his pants pocket. He noted how Sam watched every move of his hands, swallowing hard and blinking while she stared.

She was halfway to the end zone, if he could only get her to change the subject.

"So what exactly happened to your knee? And how did it happen?"

Jack tried not to laugh. He couldn't possibly give her the honest answer and make progress toward his goal, which was getting into the elastic band of her panties. In his experience, women were not exactly turned on at the mention of muscle separating from bone.

"It's pretty gruesome, Sam."

She nodded, tucking her legs up tight against her butt. He wished he were one of her legs.

"That's what Greg told me, and that's what your friend Ed said tonight, so that's why I'm asking." Sam's gaze strayed toward his knee. "It's the left one, right?"

"Right. The left one." He uncrossed his legs and poured two glasses. "Here. Drink up. If I'm going to tell you about my knee, you may need to be slightly tanked."

Sam held out her hand and Jack reached over the coffee table and placed the goblet in her hand. He intentionally let his fingers brush against the inside of her wrist as he retreated, and he was rewarded with a big-eyed stare of surprise.

"Cheers," he said, reaching for his own wineglass and clinking his crystal against hers.

"Bottoms up," Sam said.

Jack closed his eyes in a valiant effort to dismiss the lustful image that just flashed in his brain. That's the thing that amazed him about being with Sam—he thoroughly enjoyed her company yet couldn't seem to shake the lustful brain flashes, one after the next, all involving her naked and offering herself with abandon, this time with her bottom up in the air.

"Tell me how you got hurt."

Jack took a long drink of the Cabernet, wondering what the hell he'd pulled out of the pantry in the near dark, because it tasted a little musty, in his opinion. He frowned and began reading the label on the wine bottle.

"You don't want to tell me, do you?"

He set the bottle down and looked her in the eye. "It was supposed to be a pass play. We were down by three with fourteen seconds on the clock and it was third and ten." Jack noted the blank look on Sam's face. "It was our last chance to score in the third quarter. We were losing."

"Oh." She nodded and took a sip of wine.

"I couldn't find an open target, and I tried to bolt from the pocket, and I saw him coming. . . ." Jack shook his head and took a deep breath. He really hated remembering this moment, and if it had been anyone but Sam asking, he would have told them to drop the subject.

"Wait." Sam untucked her legs and sat up straight. She put her glass down. "You don't have to tell me, Jack. I'm sorry for intruding."

He glanced up, shocked by the look of concern on Sam's face. She smiled softly at him. "I can read about it online, I guess. I can see that it's hard to have to relive all that. I guess I didn't realize how awful it would be for you."

Jack thought this was a good time to make his

move and switched from his couch over to Sam's. He relaxed next to her and draped an arm over the back of the sofa, looking down into her face. "You mind if I come over here to tell you? It'll be easier for me if I can whisper."

Sam nodded.

This might not be so bad after all.

"Of course, when it was happening, it was just a blur. I only learned the details six months later, when I finally got the courage to watch the film."

"OK."

"Apparently, before I could get any momentum going, a Cleveland defensive end bounced off a block and used every bit of his six-foot-six, two-hundred-and-seventy-five-pound body to slam me to the AstroTurf. Have you ever played Whack-A-Mole at the State Fair? You know that game where you use a sledgehammer to slam down the little gopher head every time it pops up?"

Sam nodded, her eyes wide. "Sure. I love that game. Stress relief through violence."

"Exactly." Jack laughed softly as he brushed a curl from the side of Sam's face. "I was the mole, babe. And as I thudded to the ground I felt stuff tear apart inside my body. From inside my helmet, I swear it sounded like somebody was smashing a big old party-sized bag of potato chips right in my ear. The pain was so intense I blacked out, and when I woke up . . ." Jack shook his head slowly. "When I woke up, I wished I were dead."

"Oh my God, Jack."

"The docs at Methodist Hospital called it a

cluster-fuck injury. I'd dislocated my knee, damaged a bunch of nerves and some arteries, torn three ligaments, and ripped the calf and hamstring muscles right off my bones."

Sam gasped. *"Holy crap."*

"I was told that if the initial surgery didn't go right, they'd have to amputate."

"Please stop." Sam closed her eyes and put a hand to her chest. "No wonder you didn't want to tell me. This is just awful."

"But it worked out all right, if you consider six surgeries and five years of rehab all right. I survived. Both legs are still attached. I can walk and even run a little, which is a hell of a lot better than the docs hoped for me. So I came out smelling like a rose."

Jack didn't expect this, but Sam threw one arm over his shoulder and the other around his waist and she hugged him. Hard. And she just stayed there, breathing against him, holding him close.

The feel of her warm little female body pressed so tight against him, the soothing, spicy scent of her hair, the soft pressure of her breasts against his chest—all these things caused him to feel the strangest rush of warmth. This felt so good. Just having her here like this. With him.

"I am so sorry, sweetie," Sam whispered in his ear. He felt her delicate lips brush his cheek and couldn't decide what it was that had bothered him about what she just said, and then he realized it reminded him of the day they first met. He'd made a fool of himself falling out of his chair, then looked across the conference table to see Sam's concern and desire to help.

She was mothering him. Not exactly what he was looking for.

Jack took hold of her upper arms and gently peeled her off his chest. He tried to smile at her politely. "I'm perfectly fine, Sam. You don't have to comfort me."

A deep frown appeared between her auburn brows. Sam leaned away from him and studied his face so carefully it was unnerving. It was like she was summing him up, examining every line and pore and wrinkle and making some kind of silent decision about him.

"I disagree," she said. "We all need comforting. But I get the feeling that you never really let anyone comfort you about this. How many years ago did this happen?"

"That's ridiculous, Sam. My hospital room was filled with people. I still get letters from Colts fans every time ESPN airs a 'most gruesome injuries in professional sports' retrospective."

"How many years ago?"

"Thirteen. And I sure don't need you to mother me."

Sam's eyes widened in surprise; then she let loose with the kind of laugh Jack hadn't heard from a woman in ages. It was raucous and deep and she slapped a hand down on one of her sparkly red thighs. "Oh, my," she finally said, blinking and using a dainty finger to wipe away a tear. "That's a good one."

"What's so funny?"

Jack noticed a subtle change in Sam's expression and the way she held her body. She raised her chin and relaxed her shoulders, allowing a slow, sensual smile to spread across her lips. "Hey, Jack?" she whispered.

"Yeah?" His heart was doing the Whack-A-Mole thump in his chest.

"Everything I'm thinking and feeling about you is so unmotherly you wouldn't believe it."

He licked his lips. "Really?"

"Definitely." Sam reached down and slowly removed the sling-back high heels she was wearing. Jack watched them plop to the floor one by one, and the dainty black shoes on the white carpet looked alarmingly carnal to him.

"Like those nonmotherly things you said to me in the car?" His hands went to the Marilyn Monroe cuff links at his wrists, and he stowed them in his pocket with the shirt stud. He had a feeling that his pockets were going to be loaded with studs in just a few minutes.

"Just like in the car—only more so." Sam hopped up so that she knelt on the cushions. She balanced herself with one hand on the back of the sofa and the other on Jack's thigh, her face close to his. She wiggled an eyebrow.

Jack looked down the front of her dress and was treated to a spectacular view of cleavage, creamy mounds of flesh, scattered freckles, and the barest hint of pink areola. "I see," he said.

"I'll be right back."

He watched Sam grab the three flashlights and pad

across the carpet in bare feet, loving the view of her cute little round ass in that red dress. He wanted to bite it so bad his teeth ached.

Sam looked over her nearly bare shoulder. "I'm going to check and make sure the kids are asleep and leave these by their beds. Don't move."

Don't move? He couldn't fucking breathe, but he sure wasn't going to sit there and twiddle his thumbs in her absence. He planned to light some candles and get real naked real fast, then jump in her bed. Jack was beginning to think that Sam was a woman who appreciated the no-nonsense approach.

"I won't move a muscle," he said as she walked out the door, wondering what exactly "more so" could mean coming from a woman who'd already said the best three words in the English language: *"Fuck me now!"*

"Ohmigod, ohmigod, ohmigod."

Before she reached Dakota's bedroom door, Sam leaned an unsteady hand against the wall and tried to catch her breath, nearly knocking a small gilt-framed expressionist reproduction to the floor in the process. Unless she took immediate action to stop it, she was about to have sex with Indiana's most notorious millionaire politician playboy. There were so many surprising things about that development that she hardly knew where to begin. She barely knew the man! She was his employee. And let's face it—she had no experience handling a player like Jack. She was way out of her league.

Sam put her other hand to her chest, feeling her

heart dance around in a panic. This was all Monté's fault. It was the dress—a dress that made Sam feel far more vampish than she had a right to. The dress gave her a false sense of daring. The dress made her too big for her britches. At that thought, she pressed her thighs together, finding that her britches were so wet she was in danger of dripping on the expensive Persian carpet runner under her feet.

She hadn't had sex in eighteen months, for crying out loud! This was no way to ease back into things. Having sex with Jack Tolliver would take some serious balls. She couldn't go through with this—could she?

Sam straightened, pointed the flashlight into Dakota's door, and made sure he was asleep. Apparently, Jack had done a decent job of tucking him in, as Dakota was snuggled down into the comforter, thumb in mouth, thoroughly in dreamland. She laid the flashlight on top of the covers, kissed his curly head, and whispered good night.

She left a second flashlight with Greg and the last with Lily, who were both sleeping soundly, and returned to the dark hallway, realizing she'd need to walk back to her suite with only the slightest hint of firelight to show her the way. With each step of her bare foot on the carpet, she engaged in an inner debate. *I can/I can't. I want to/I shouldn't. I can have sex with Jack and stay sane/I'm just torturing myself. I am perfectly capable of keeping a one-night stand in perspective/I'm not cut out for casual sex.*

She stood outside the half-open door and peeked inside. She didn't see Jack on the couch, but she did note the arrival of three white candles on the coffee table, their flames adding to the glow in the room. After a big, fortifying breath, she pushed open the door all the way and dared to look at the bed.

This couldn't be happening. In a few short weeks she'd gone from sleeping alone on Kmart sheets to being invited to lie down in that decadent collection of smooth satin and fine cotton under a diaphanous white canopy, in this elegant room, with that exceptional naked man at her side.

"Are you really naked?" Sam took a tentative step into the room and shut the door behind her. She heard her own breath coming hard.

"Come over here and find out." Jack clasped his hands behind his head and sank back into pillows. It was a move that displayed an arrogant sexuality, not to mention a pair of killer biceps. Patches of dark hair appeared under his arms and over the finely sculpted chest now coming into view as the sheet slipped down his body. Jack flashed a white grin at her. "I highly recommend it."

"Oh God." Sam froze, her hand still clutching the doorknob behind her.

Jack bent his good knee—the right one—and it caused the sheet to slide farther down his body, exposing a hard waist, a solidly muscled hip, and a bit of upper thigh. Sam hadn't been in the same room with a body like this since figure-drawing classes at Hanover, and those models weren't as defined as Jack. Her fingers itched. She needed a brush and a canvas. She wanted to capture that sleek rope of muscle where it attached at his hip. She wanted to shade in the contours of his six-pack using violets and browns and blues. She wanted a vista of skin in peaches and shadows, blue-blacks for his hair, a stormy mix of green, blue, and black for those erotic cat eyes of his.

The eyes that bored into hers at that very moment.

"Get in here, Samantha."

"I . . ." She let her hand fall from the doorknob. She cleared her throat. "It's just that—"

"Come to me."

She swallowed. Jack's voice was commanding and confident, and she had a sudden physical memory of what it felt like when he kissed her, his hand at the back of her head. His voice sounded like that—sure and steady and in control.

"Or I'll come to you." His smile broadened. "And when I get there, I'll get rid of that dress of yours and carry you over here and toss you on the bed like you've always needed."

Sam blinked. How did he know that's what she'd always needed? He was right, of course, but how did he know? "That could work."

The covers went flying. Jack was on his feet, and the first thing she got a glimpse of was a Michelangelo-quality butt and her eyes nearly popped from her head. Unbelievable. Then he turned around and she gasped. Talk about seeing angels.

His body was poetry. It was song. It was nature at its masculine best. And she let her eyes travel down from those golden, cut shoulders to that tapered waist and tight hips, down those big thighs and sculpted calves right back up to the heavenly zenith between his legs—dark and rigid and swaying in a way that was mesmerizing.

She let her eyes wander back to his face, which was now quite close to hers.

Zzzzzip.

His hands were at her spaghetti straps, then her elbows, and then her hips. She felt the cool air of the room brush against her breasts and belly and back. The dress slithered to the carpet with a soft hiss of fabric.

She stood before him in nothing but a pair of beige bikini panties.

"Say it," Jack said, his gaze sweeping down her body and back up again. His fingers snaked into her hair. Sam tried to get her lips to move, but she couldn't, which seemed fine, because she had no idea what he wanted her to say anyway.

Jack took the pad of his thumb and stroked her bottom lip, none too gently. Sam's knees began to shake.

"Say what you said in the car, Samantha."

"Uh . . ." Sam tried to recall what it was she might have said that he'd liked so much, but truly, her mind was not functioning. The only things that seemed to be functioning were her female parts, where all sensation and need seemed to be focused.

"Keep both hands on the wheel?" she offered tentatively.

Jack laughed. He slapped both hands on her ass and pulled her close. "You know what I want to hear."

Sam nodded, the fog lifting from her head. Jack

apparently liked her unladylike explosion of pent-up lust. She was a little uncomfortable with it, herself. Maybe she was just out of practice. But for this incredibly sexy man with those hands and these eyes and that heat and the carnal way he was smiling down at her—she could do that one small thing to make him happy.

"Fuck me now," she said.

Sam was up off the floor, Jack's hard forearm under her knees and his other arm around her waist. Instantly she felt herself get spun around and tossed through the air. She landed on the bed with an "*oomph.*"

Jack grabbed her legs and pulled until her butt hovered at the edge. He propped her feet on his shoulders and grinned down at her.

"I like it when you say that."

"I can tell." Sam's heart thudded. This was not the normal kiss–fondle–insert pattern she was used to. This was not the way it was with Mitch, and certainly not the way it was with that architect guy, whose name she didn't remember and who clearly didn't matter anymore.

"I like a whole lot of things about you, Sam."

"Really?"

Jack stroked his hands up and down Sam's legs, which she was terribly glad she'd shaved that evening, because his fingers slid along the smooth skin, bringing tingles to her spine.

"I like the way you smell. I like your smile because it's genuine and warm and pulls me in." His hands cupped her butt. "I like your cute little ass."

Sam moaned.

Jack's fingers brushed across the swell of her breasts and flicked at her nipples, which were alarmingly hard. "I just love your breasts, Sam."

She sighed, the pleasure so intense it was almost pain. It *was* pain—the pain of deprivation. She felt tears sting her eyes.

Jack wasn't done. He traced his fingers down the center of her belly, then slid them up her sides to her hair. "You have beautiful curls and such a pretty little neck." Jack leaned forward, pressing her legs back toward her shoulders, as he licked her throat. "I like the way you taste, baby. I want to taste you everywhere. Would that be all right?"

"Oh *God*!"

Jack let up on the pressure and straightened again, and Sam felt his hands slide down the whole length of her body to her feet. He grasped them. He studied them intensely. Sam watched, amused, as Jack began to delicately lick at each toe on her left foot, then her right. It tickled, and she giggled.

Sam squirmed when Jack began to slowly suck at each toe, but he held her tight as he took his time. Each toe was slurped into his wet and hot mouth and his tongue swirled as he sucked, one toe after the next, with great attention and concentration. She was wondering if maybe Jack had a foot fetish when he suddenly stopped.

"I have a thing for your feet," he said, looking down at her sheepishly just before he dragged his tongue along the length of each sole. "I hope you don't mind."

Sam shook her head rapidly. "I can live with that."

Jack then pushed her legs together, knees straight. He nibbled and licked his way down each Achilles tendon and each calf and the ticklish back of each knee and both thighs until he ended at the crotch of her panties.

Sam tensed a little, all the blood rushing to her head and all the moisture collecting in her underwear. This was the part that scared her a little—the actual sex. This was what she craved and missed and needed and this was what she wasn't sure would be a smart thing to do.

How in the world could she look Jack in the eye as they strutted around town pretending to be a couple after she'd coupled with him? How was a woman supposed to collect her paycheck after that?

Then Jack began sucking at her swollen lips through her panties and Sam howled with pleasure. "Oh, oh, oh *yeah!*"

He laughed, the sound muffled by the silky underwear. He began to push his tongue gently into the fabric-covered hollow between her lips; then he kissed the tender inside of her thighs and nibbled at her belly, all while she moaned and sighed and squealed.

"I also really like the noises you make, Sam," Jack said, taking a breath. "You make some very sexy little noises."

"Oooh. Oh. Yes."

"And you know what?" Jack curled his hand inside the crotch of her panties and slid his fingers up and down her slit, then gently pushed inside her. "I can't wait to hear how you sound when you're coming all over me."

Sam began to pant. She felt his fingers push farther into her body and his thumb seek out her excruciatingly sensitive clit and she could feel herself tremble. Her hips began to push back at him.

"I have a feeling that's going to be soon, Sam. Am I right?" He intensified his probing and increased the pressure with his thumb. He put his lips on her left nipple and bit gently, and Sam gasped at the unfairness of his expertise. She was going to come right then, ten seconds after he'd put his hands on her. How embarrassing.

"Oooh God *yesssss* right *now!*"

Jack slammed his lips onto hers and murmured to her as the pleasure rolled in an ebb and flow that caused her fingers to go numb and her ears to roar, and then she exploded, but he kept kissing her, stroking her, whispering to her as she wallowed in the rich, dark pull of the best non-solo orgasm she could ever recall having.

Jack dragged his lips from her mouth and down her neck, across her breasts, down her belly, all while he gently removed his hand from inside her, swept her panties up and off her legs, and ripped open a condom. She had to laugh, even in her orgasmic haze, because Jack was so smooth it was entertaining. Where he'd stashed the condom she had no idea, but before she could catch her breath he was covered up and smiling down at her.

Sam's throat suddenly tightened. He was so beautiful and she had her legs spread open and she felt the hot tears spill down her cheeks. "It's been a long time for me, Jack," she said.

He stopped. He frowned. He dropped to his elbows and cradled her head in his hands. Jack kissed her wet cheeks and stroked the hair from her forehead.

"I want you bad, Sam. But if this is too much for you, I understand. We don't have to do this, sweetheart."

"What? Are you nuts?" Sam smacked both hands down on that perfect butt and guided him toward her. "Yes we do! There's no way I can stop now. That's the first decent orgasm I've had in the new millennium."

Jack laughed softly and flexed his hips a bit, and Sam felt her body begin to give way to his ample erection. He was tentative at first, stroking her face and kissing her and easing himself into her. Sam could hardly believe the sensation—she didn't remember ever feeling this full in her life. Maybe she never had been, not like this. And she wrapped her arms around Jack's muscular back and hooked her heels onto those rock-hard thighs and did what she apparently did best in his company—she begged for it.

"Please. God yes, take me," she whispered, learning in a hurry why Jack had a reputation as a ladies' man. He knew what he was doing. No doubt about it.

Jack moved his hips in a slow grind, with a gentle determination, until he had every bit of himself inside her. He cooed to her, kissed her, cupped her ass in his hands while he leaned into her and gave her the best fucking she'd had in her life. Then it got even better.

He raised himself up to a standing position and adjusted Sam so that she was once again at the very edge of the bed. He opened her legs wide, kissed her feet and toes, and began to give it to her.

"I don't want to hurt you, but—*fuck*—I can't hold back."

Sam gulped down air. "Then don't. Just give it to me, Jack."

"Oh God yes! This is incredible. You are so—" Jack opened his eyes and looked right into Sam's face. A huge smile lit up his eyes and he laughed. "Damn! You've still got it!"

"I still got it!" Sam laughed with him. "This is amazing!"

"You're amazing. Baby, just look at you. . . ." Jack's eyes were filled with wonder. "You are so beautiful, Sam. You look perfect with me in you, do you know that? This is incredible. I'm not going to be able to get enough of this."

Sam felt a hot rush spike deep in her belly. She was going to come again. Unbelievable. "Don't stop!"

"I won't."

"Don't ever stop! I mean it!" Sam grabbed his upper arms and held on tight, her eyes locked on his. "I'm coming again. Don't you dare stop!"

"I'm never going to stop. Ever—" Jack dropped her feet and gripped her upper thighs and pulled her even closer. "Oh God, I lie." Jack laughed at himself. "We'll do this again, I promise. But right now . . . I'm sorry, but you feel so damn good I can't . . ."

Sam's shoulders rose from the bed and she felt her

entire body begin to spasm as she cried out. Jack just continued pummeling her harder, faster, his eyes glazed over with lust and locked on hers, and he began to come with her. She gripped his shoulders and stared at him in wonder as she felt him swell and throb inside her, drops of sweat falling from his face onto her breasts.

"God, Sam!" Jack gripped her harder and gave one last push, remaining deep inside her as he began to shake and groan. "Oh shit, yes! My God!"

He collapsed on top of her and she threw her arms around him and squeezed, feeling his body tremble from head to toe. Jack had his face buried in the crook of her neck and his breath was hard and fast. All she could do was close her eyes and hold on tight as the heat continued to spread through her limbs, followed by a bone-deep peace. She didn't know how much time had gone by when Jack finally spoke.

"Sam?"

"Mmm?"

"I'm having this mental picture." Jack slowed his breathing. "I lift you up from the bed right now, carry you in my arms, tuck you in, and snuggle up with you until we fall asleep together."

Sam smiled underneath him. "That's a nice mental picture."

"Unfortunately, I can't move."

"I figured."

"You nearly killed me."

She laughed and stroked his big back. "You'll live."

As he chuckled, his body rubbed against hers. She

knew he was keeping most of his weight off her by propping himself on his forearms. Sam took the opportunity to caress the taut muscles of his upper arms, sighing at the substantial feel of him. She could definitely get used to this.

She pushed the thought out of her head.

Jack managed to shift his weight to his feet and separate himself from her. He lowered her legs and scooted her body up on the bed. It wasn't as romantic as carrying her, but it got the job done, and in an instant he was in bed next to her, pulling the covers over them both.

"Come here, Samantha." He drew her close, gently pushing her head down to his chest. He kept his hand on the back of her head, as if to make sure she didn't move.

Like she'd want to.

Sam let her fingers play in Jack's sparse chest hair, enjoying the thick, coarse quality of each strand, feeling her pulse return to normal and the tingling subside. She'd never been with a man as in charge as Jack. Or as big as Jack. Or as physically powerful. It had felt extremely erotic to be underneath him, so small in comparison, dragged around the bed like that.

She loved the fact that the dowdy hairstylist had the bad-boy player so excited he couldn't control himself. Sam smiled, her cheek pressing against a firm pectoral.

"How you doing down there?" Jack stroked her hair and kissed the top of her head.

"I'm great. You?"

"Better than great."

Jack was big and solid and steady against her. He was so different from Mitch. Her ex-husband always seemed to be in motion, at his glass studio and at home, and much of it had been nervous, undirected bursts of energy. Mitch was a pale man with blond hair and a slim build and an intensely handsome face. Her favorite times with him had been whenever she got to watch him blow glass. She'd always be entranced by the complicated dance steps of his work, how he would pace and circle as he'd spin the glass, thrusting the long metal pole into the fiery oven and pulling it out again. It used to turn her on seeing him like that, at his most passionate. She'd always leave the studio with a wistful hope that Mitch could summon the same intensity for her someday. But he never really did. His glass always got what passion he could muster, and she'd always gotten the leftovers.

"That was sure different," Sam said, her thoughts finding their way into words.

"Hmm. Not exactly a hall of fame nomination." The amusement was clear in Jack's voice.

"You know what I meant."

"Maybe."

"You're a wonderful lover, Jack, but you surprised me."

She felt Jack's chest move with silent laughter. "I surprised myself."

"How's that?"

"Oh well, you know, I wasn't exactly suave. You felt too good for me to manage suave. And it's been a while for me, too."

That made her laugh. "Oh?"

"It'll be three weeks on Tuesday."

"My God, how have you survived?"

He patted her shoulder. "I ask myself the same thing every day."

Sam blew out a breath of air and shook her head. "It's been eighteen months for me, Jack."

Jack's hand stilled on her shoulder. His whisper came out rough. "That's a very long time, sweetie."

"You're telling me. And that was a onetime shot. So I've had sex a grand total of once in close to four years."

Jack rose to a sitting position and propped several pillows behind his head, pulling Sam with him. He hugged her tight but didn't say anything.

"And really," Sam continued, "those last few years before I got pregnant with Dakota were mighty dry. That was when Mitch hit on the pea-pod theme with his work and decided he was gay. I think of it as his pea-pod-to-penis period."

"I see."

"Yeah, so he had his sexual crisis and took me along for the ride. I wasn't getting any sex! That's a crisis." Sam peered up at him. "You knew my husband decided he was gay, right?"

"Kara mentioned it."

"Yeah, well, he reverted to heterosexuality one last time for the road. Then he was outta there."

Jack's big hand came to rest on her hip, and he cupped her, pulling her closer. "I'm sorry, Sam."

"Me, too."

"You deserve so much more than that."

She laughed, then nodded gently against his chest. He was right. She did deserve more—all around. And that was why this job had been a godsend for her. "I was hoping that after the primary I could start dating again, you know? Invest some time and energy into finding a man I can at least do things with. I'm ready for that."

"I'm sure you are," Jack said.

"But he has to like my kids. I know Monté has dated some potentially interesting men who couldn't handle the fact that she had Simon. She sent them packing."

"I just bet."

"She's tried Internet dating. She told me it's like a gambling addiction—you're absolutely sure the next one is going to be the big payoff, but he never is."

"Sounds pretty grim."

"But I have no idea what's out there for me. I haven't had time to pay attention to what's swimming around in the pool of thirty-something single men of Indianapolis. What if there's not much to choose from?"

"Probably just sharks and bottom-feeders, huh?"

"Maybe you could introduce me to someone nice."

Jack cleared his throat. "Samantha? You are the first woman I've ever slept with who used pillow talk time to ask me to find her a date."

Sam giggled and removed her head from Jack's chest, sitting up next to him. "We both know that *this*—" She gestured at the two of them in bed, then gave his comforter-covered thigh a pat. "This is going nowhere."

Jack had no response, which was what Sam expected. What was there to say? They both knew they'd succumbed to a momentary lapse of good judgment and that was that. As the seconds ticked by, Sam smiled to herself and looked around the room at the firelight, the candles, and thought how silly it all was. This was about as romantic a setting as she could imagine, but what had happened here hadn't been romance. It had been just sex. Incredible sex. Oustanding sex. But just sex.

"I'd like to date you, Sam." Jack's soft words sounded like a cannon going off about an inch from her ear.

"Excuse me?" She stared at him. Jack relaxed his head back against the pillows and looked at her through half-closed eyelids. The smallest smile played on those lips of his.

"I'd like to date you." He crossed his beefy arms over his chest. "I'm pretty sure I meet all your requirements. I'm a man. I like to do things. I'm still in my thirties. I think your kids are pretty cool. I'd like to date you."

Sam's mouth fell open, and she saw Jack's smile widen at her reaction. "That's not possible."

"And why's that?"

"Because we're *engaged,* Jack. Well, fake engaged anyway, and you can't date someone you're pretending to be engaged to."

"Who says?"

"I'm sure it's against somebody's code of ethics."

Jack shook his head back and forth slowly, looking like he was scanning through a cache of ethical trivia he stored in his brain. "Nope. I think we're good."

Sam clutched the covers to her chest. "Are you serious?"

"Serious as a heart attack."

"You want to date me?"

Jack smiled at Sam, then grabbed her hand. "You say that like it's the strangest thing you ever heard. Why wouldn't I want to date you? You're fun and sweet and beautiful and smart, and as I just found out, you're great in the sack."

"So are you." Sam swallowed hard and continued staring at him.

"Thanks. But maybe you don't want to date me. Is that it?" Jack sat upright and crossed his legs, leaning closer to her. "If that's the case, I understand completely."

Sam let out a shocked breath of air. "Not to worry."

Jack lowered his gaze and chuckled before he raised his eyes to her again. "Then we're on?"

Sam's head spun. Who wouldn't want to date Jack? But this was just too complicated. "Let's say we date. What happens in three months when you decide you're ready to move on to Courtney or Brittany? Because we'll still have a business arrangement. You and I will still have to parade around town like the happy couple, and that doesn't sound all that fun to me."

Jack nodded. "OK. Then I won't get sick of you in three months. But who are Courtney and Brittany? Do I know them?"

"See? I'll be lucky to last three weeks." Sam wanted to put some distance between herself and Jack, but she knew she had precisely nothing on, and even though Jack had already seen her naked, walking nude around a room in front of a man was different. It implied a level of comfort she didn't have.

She could hardly believe any of this was even *real*.

"Look at it this way, Sam. At the very least I can be your warm-up, get you ready for all those single thirty-something Indianapolis men who'll be waiting for you to break up with me."

"Right." Sam really needed to get out of the bed. "Please close your eyes, because I have to use the restroom."

Jack laughed and shook his head. "The electricity is out, Sam. And I've already seen you. You're gorgeous."

Sam realized she'd been picking at a toss pillow's hand-tied tassel and a bunch of satin strings now puddled on the bed. She threw the pillow behind her. "Yeah, well, do it anyway, please."

"I'll try my best."

Sam looked sideways at Jack but didn't have it in her to chide him further. He was gut-wrenchingly handsome. Rumpled and relaxed in a post-sex sort of way. He looked so lovable. But she knew better, didn't she? This was Jack Tolliver, the guy who'd made that incredibly rude remark about a teacher's ass. She wracked her brain to remember one of the *Star* headlines she'd found on the Internet: *"Sexist Slip" Ends Tolliver's Campaign; Congressional Candidate "Ashamed" of Self.*

Sam studied Jack. That's what women were to

him—pieces of ass. Why should she think she was any different? That would be nuts.

In a flash, Sam flipped the comforter over Jack's head and ran to the suite's bathroom, catching a glimpse of his grin as she shut the door behind her, which turned out to be a huge mistake, because there wasn't even a smidgeon of light in that room. She fumbled around to her left, where she knew an ornate white wrought-iron shelf held a stack of towels. She grabbed the first thing her fingers landed on and spread it over the front of her body. Unfortunately, she'd grabbed a washcloth.

"Nice robe. A little short, though." Jack had been waiting on the other side of the bathroom door when she opened it, and when he offered her a candle, his eyes scanned her from head to toe. "Thought maybe you could use a little light."

"Thanks." Sam grabbed the candle, turned, and flicked the towel over her bottom as she headed for the enclosed commode at the opposite end of the room. She heard his laughter as she ran.

Once inside the enclosure, Sam leaned against the door and groaned. This was completely unfair. Jack had turned out to be funny and kind and nothing like she'd expected him to be—and he wanted to *date* her. It was hard to reconcile the player reputation with the sweet playfulness she'd just encountered. Who was Jack Tolliver? Could he be trusted? Was he for real? Or was she just asking to have her heart broken?

Sam set the candle down on the back of the toilet and took a seat. Maybe she was looking at this all wrong, which would be understandable, since she hadn't exactly become a seasoned dating veteran in the last couple decades. Maybe this wasn't about her heart. Maybe this was about pleasure, enjoyment, diversion—sex. Maybe she could date Jack and keep it all in perspective. How many women would kill for this arrangement—a handsome former NFL quarterback had asked to date her, and he'd be paying for the privilege? She'd wanted to be a kept woman, after all, and this was pretty much the definition. In a way, Jack would be a kept man, too, because she'd be keeping him entertained and happy for the six months they were obligated to spend in each other's company. It was a no-brainer. A snap. Sam flushed the toilet, washed her hands, and opened the door.

A big hand grabbed her wrist. Before she could scream, a pair of hot, skilled lips covered hers. Without a doubt, Jack was the best kisser she'd ever encountered. He was completely in charge, firm but tender, and not stuck on one approach. Jack could really mix it up with those lips of his, with a little help from his teeth and tongue. Sam's knees began to buckle.

"Come with me."

Jack opened the large glass door to the shower, and Sam stepped into a wonderland. Apparently, while she'd been sitting on the toilet plotting how she would use Jack for her own selfish pleasure, he'd been in here creating a wet, warm love nest. Sam smiled at how he'd lined the candles high up on the shower ledge, away from the spray of the six water jets.

"This is really nice, but—"

"The tank in this place is huge. We could go days without power and the water would stay hot."

Sam grinned up at him, letting her eyes take in the full impact of what was displayed before her in the misty candlelight. She started at his head and that very serviceable cut someone had given him, a cut that accentuated the slight wave in his thick dark hair but gave it room to move. It was a rakish cut, with enough length to give him a groomed-but-casual look. He definitely needed something more conservative if he was going to win the election.

"You're too sexy for your own good," Sam said, reaching up and combing her fingers through his damp hair.

"You say that like it's a bad thing."

Sam laughed. "I meant your haircut, specifically. You need to go shorter on top. You need to de-emphasize the trendy bad-boy thing you have going."

Jack brought put her palm up to his lips and kissed, then dragged his mouth along the inside of Sam's wet wrist. She trembled. "That's the nicest thing you've ever said to me, Samantha."

"Oh?"

"Except for that other thing I like to hear."

Sam's heart skipped a beat. "We'll always have that."

"I think that would be nice." Jack pulled her up against his chest and hugged her. "Really. It would be nice to be in a relationship with someone you liked as a person in the real world, who you could take back to your private lair and have great sex with."

"Mmm. It does sound nice. I've never really had that before; have you?"

Jack chuckled and set Samantha before him, rubbing her back. "Seems it's always been one or the other, but never both at once. I'm not sure why that is." He gave her a devilish grin. "Unless we're counting tonight, because I definitely had a great time with you at the concert and I sure as hell had fun with you in that big bed out there."

Sam swallowed hard. "Me, too." She reached up to stroke Jack's face, feeling just a touch of raspy beard. "Do you really think we can date? Can we pull this off?"

"I don't see why not."

"I don't think Kara and Stuart would appreciate the fact that we've been . . ." Sam shrugged, looking for the right way to say it. "You know. . . ."

"Going at it like rabbits?"

She laughed.

"You know what they're going to appreciate even less? That I really do like you. That I'm interested in you as a person and a woman. Because that makes things even messier. If it was just sex—"

"It's not just sex?"

Jack cocked his head, and a stream of water coursed down his neck. "Not for me, sweetheart."

"OK."

"How about for you?"

"I don't know what it is for me, honestly." She brought her hand down to his hip and stroked him there, noting the way his hip bone just barely showed under his taut skin. "You are, by far, the sexiest man I've ever known."

He smiled at that.

"But I'm not sure I want to invest any emotion in you. I'm not exactly looking to get my heart stomped on right now. And I think maybe you only like me because I'm here and I'm convenient and I'm the only woman you're even allowed to hang around with for the time being."

"Not by a long shot."

"Well, it's hard to know for sure."

Jack nodded thoughtfully, pulling her close again and cupping his big hands on her bottom. He kissed the top of her head. "You fit very nicely against me, Samantha. Have you noticed?"

"I sure have."

"I fit pretty good in you. Did you notice that?"

She giggled, hugging him hard. "I thought I felt something unusual going on down there."

Jack laughed, letting his hands roam all over her back and shoulders and butt and upper thighs. Sam felt him push her backward a little, until they were both fully under the spray of the water jets. "I want to get you wet," he said.

"That shouldn't be a problem."

He lifted Sam's chin with a finger and looked into her eyes. Jack's gaze was earnest and warm, and it sliced right down into the most vulnerable place in Sam's heart. She really had to keep her head on straight with Jack. She couldn't—absolutely could not—do something stupid. She would not fall in love with him.

"I want to eat you up," Jack murmured inside her ear, just as his hands began to spread her thighs apart. Sam gasped as she saw him sink to his knees in the shower. He looked up at her from his kneeling position and gave her a wicked grin. "Open up for me, Sam."

"Oh God." She was already shaking and he hadn't even done anything but talk to her and touch her legs. She was a sitting duck. She was no match for Indiana's answer to Casanova. And when his fingers grazed the tender juncture of her inner thigh and pubic hair, she gasped.

"I won't hurt you, baby."

Sam felt his mouth land on her swollen outer lips and she nearly shot through the ceiling. How could she tell him that she'd only experienced this particular sensation one other time in her life and Mitch couldn't stand to do it for more than a few minutes? What kind of pitiful existence had she been leading?

"Easy, baby," he whispered, just as he adjusted his angle and touched the tip of his hot tongue on her clitoris. It was out-of-this-world. Sam braced one hand against the shower wall for support because she feared she would collapse. The hot water streamed down her back and rolled down her body. His hot tongue slurped at her, his lips kissed her, his teeth gave her little love bites, each touch producing its own unique spike of pleasure, and the pleasure was gaining velocity, gaining strength, welling up inside her belly. . . .

Jack suddenly drove a finger inside her and hooked it, stroking the inner walls of her vagina, and all she could think was, *It's not fair. It's not fair. It's not fair.* . . .

She detonated, grabbing on to his head for dear
life, amazed at the brilliance of the orgasm as it
slammed against her shut eyelids. She was seeing
stars! A single flash of light! The heavens opened up
with such sudden brightness that she momentarily
feared that she had come so hard she had crossed
over into the other dimension, which she didn't
know was even possible.

"That was one powerful orgasm," Jack said, leaving kisses all over the front of her wet thighs, her
stomach, her hips. "You could have lit up New York
City with that one."

Sam moaned, opening her eyes reluctantly, still
holding on to Jack's head. She blinked in surprise at
how bright it was in the shower, then looked down to
see a fully illuminated naked man kneeling before
her, his cheeks squished by her palms. "The lights
are on!"

Jack tried to nod the best he could.

"Oh God. Sorry."

"Mommy, change me now!"

Jack and Sam went still. Jack looked horrified.
Sam mouthed a curse and put her finger over her lips
to urge Jack to remain silent, then motioned for him
to get up and move to the end of the shower stall,
where he had the best chance at remaining hidden.

Jack grunted slightly as he pushed himself up, and
it was at that moment that Sam saw his left knee for
the first time. She gasped.

"Now, Mommy!"

Sam opened the frosted glass door, still reeling
from the sight of Jack's scars and aware she could not

possibly let her child know they'd been in the shower together. What kind of mother was she? Dakota peered up at her and frowned, and Sam saw he was wearing his usual attire—a Bob the Builder T-shirt and not much else.

"Please wait for me in the bedroom while I dry off, OK, pumpkin?" She reached around to turn off the water and a loud crash reverberated through the room. She cringed. "Sorry," Jack whispered, staring at the candlestick lying near the shower drain. *I bumped the wall,* he mouthed at Sam, but it was too late.

"Mr. Jack is in there?" Dakota's eyes widened in excitement. "Hey! Mr. Jack!"

"Please hand Mommy a towel, OK?" Dakota reached behind him and pulled a large towel from the shelf, which came unfolded as he dragged it across the floor. Sam grabbed it and tossed it to Jack behind her back. "Thank you, pumpkin. Can I have one more, please?"

Dakota narrowed his eyes at Sam and reached for a second towel, and she could see his little toddler brain working in overdrive. Sam hastily covered herself and was about to sweep Dakota into her arms and whisk him into the other room when he ducked under her reach and flung open the shower door.

"Mr. Jack?" Dakota presented his nighttime pull-up, soaked to capacity, and Sam stared in disbelief as a big, male hand appeared from behind the chrome edge of the shower door. The thumb and index finger accepted the diaper by the tiniest pinch possible. "Change me now, Mr. Jack, and don't forget to use the wipes."

9

"Looking good, Ms. DeMarinis." Sam parted Kara's heavy, stick-straight hair with a comb, inspecting her work. "You should be set for another four weeks or so."

Kara turned her head to look at Sam, panic in her eyes. "And I can come back here, right? You'll do this next month, too, right?"

Sam smiled. Clients were understandably picky when it came to their hair, but Kara was downright paranoid. She was so worried that her gray would show or, worse yet, someone would figure out she dyed it that she always double-checked the concoction Sam whipped up in her little plastic bowl before she'd allow her to paint it on her roots—Aveda No. 5 in ash and No. 5 in gold, with 20 volume developer. Maybe that was just the lawyer in Kara. Or the control freak in her. Or both.

"I'll be happy to do your hair here at the house as long as it's OK with Jack."

"Don't mind at all." Jack appeared in the doorway to the butler's pantry, his face sporting a wicked smile, still wearing the rumpled tuxedo shirt and pants from the night before. He leaned against the door frame and crossed his arms over his chest.

It took all Sam's concentration not to make little whimpering noises at the sight of him. She hadn't seen him since they'd said good night at her bedroom door, both agreeing it was too risky for him to sleep in her room. Jack said more than once that they'd been lucky that it was Dakota who busted them and not Greg or Lily. "Do you think Dakota will say something?" he'd asked her.

"It's anyone's guess," she'd answered.

Sam busied herself cleaning up the mess and putting away her tools of the trade, sensing Jack's eyes on her the whole time. She avoided making eye contact with him, worried that if Kara happened to be watching, the jig would be up.

Kara rose from the straight-backed chair and removed the plastic cape that covered her sweater, chatting with Jack. "Sam says the lights came on about two in the morning up here. Downtown didn't have power until a couple hours ago."

"Yeah, we got lucky last night," Jack said. Sam's head snapped up and she glared at him. He had the gall to wink at her. Unbelievable.

"That's good," Kara said, inspecting her roots in a hand mirror.

"Sam says I need a different haircut if I expect to be elected senator. She said I need something less sexy. Do you agree?"

Kara frowned in his direction and put down the mirror. She studied his hair.

"You really think so?" she asked Sam.

She shrugged, thinking back on what Jack had looked like standing in that shower the night before, his muscles glistening in the candlelight, his eyes shining down on her, that tousled hair framing his handsome face. The man was a sex god. "He could use a trim, I guess."

Jack immediately fished out his wallet, keys, and cell phone from his trouser pockets and took a seat in the vacated chair. He folded his hands in his lap. "I'm all yours."

Sam looked to Kara for guidance, but Kara gave her a "don't-ask-me" shrug. "Sure. Just no buzz cuts. Makes voters think of Oliver North."

Jack laughed. "Kara, you're a treasure trove of political wisdom. Where would I be without you?"

"God only knows." Kara retrieved another chair from the adjoining breakfast room and settled to Sam's left. "So how did he do last night?" Kara asked Sam. "Did he make us proud?"

Sam was about to reach for the scissors, but her hand froze. Then it occurred to her that Kara was referring to the symphony event. "No slips of the tongue that I noticed."

Jack snorted.

Kara went on, oblivious. "Well, there wasn't anything in the paper about you two this morning—the ice storm dominated the news." She fluffed her hair and reached for the mug of coffee she'd left on the counter. "So what do you say, Jack? Think it's time you whipped out the family jewels?"

Jack's big laugh was the only thing that hid the fact that Sam had just choked on her own breath.

They all heard the front door open and slam shut and Monté's voice traveled through the foyer. "Good morning, sunshine!" she called out, the sound of her heels tap-tapping across the parquet floors as Simon attacked the front staircase at least two steps at a time. "Yoo-hoo! What's shakin' in the big house to-*day*?"

"We're in here!" Sam yelled out.

"What's everyone doing?" Monté arrived in the butler's pantry door, sporting a pair of red stretch pants and a green knit sweater. Earrings shaped like miniature gold Christmas ornaments dangled from her ears. She frowned at Jack in the chair. "I don't think the man needs a makeover."

Kara sat up straighter. "Absolutely not! We hired an image consultant and ran a series of focus groups, and he was perfectly within the range of positive voter response we were hoping for."

"Just giving him a trim," Sam said to Monté. "Number two guard on the clippers. Leaving the sideburns at ear level."

Monté dragged in a second breakfast room chair and made herself comfortable on the other side of Sam. "Yeah, well, it's a good idea. The length makes me think of a surfer dude, not a senator."

"My concern exactly," Sam said.

"But don't go too short or I'll be thinkin' Marine Corps or some damn thing."

Kara smiled. "See? I told you."

"Mmmm . . . mmm," Monté said, checking out

Jack's rumpled tuxedo trousers. "He's a sharp dresser, I'll give him that."

They all giggled, except Jack, who cleared his throat. "You know, there's something demeaning about three women talking about me like I'm not even in the room. I feel so cheap."

"At least we're talking about you. Political death is when they don't talk about you." Kara took a sip of her coffee. "Like this morning. I am not at all pleased that you two lovebirds weren't mentioned in the Style section. That's why I think it's time for jewelry."

"It's always time for jewelry," Monté said. "I've been trying to tell the man this for weeks now."

"Days," Sam muttered.

"You're absolutely sure it's all right to borrow something?" Kara asked Jack.

"There's so much old crap in there, she wouldn't notice anything missing."

Kara laughed. "Are you nuts? That woman remembers it all—little tiny details from your father's first gubernatorial campaign, what Allen Ditto's wife wore to his first swearing-in, way back in 1972. She's amazing."

"Who's amazing?"

"My mother," Jack explained to Monté. "I decided I'd use one of the family's old pieces as an engagement ring. Thought it would be unique."

"Just so long as it's uniquely large."

"And all this time I thought size doesn't really matter to women," Jack said, clearly enjoying the exchange with Monté.

"That's a damn lie all around," she said. "You

been spending too much time with women who don't have the nerve to speak the truth, is all."

Jack nodded and said, "You may be right, Ms. McQueen."

"Please keep your head still or your hair won't be in anybody's range of positive response," Sam said.

"Maybe Christy will mention you two on *Capitol Update* this afternoon," Kara said, brightening. "I ran into her last night at the symphony—crankier than ever, I swear."

"Yeah, that girl was in the salon the other day, yakking it up with Marcia," Monté said. "I never did like her."

"I never even met her," Sam said.

"Me, either," Monté said. "But she never struck me as somebody I'd like to get to know."

Kara nodded. "She was probably at Le Cirque digging for dirt on Sam. Christy told me she thinks we're up to no good."

"Well, we are," Jack offered.

"Is she going after me? Is that what you're saying?" Sam had been running her fingers through Jack's hair to test the evenness but stopped suddenly. She looked to Kara. "That's kind of scary."

"You're squeaky clean, Sam, so don't worry. Christy's just another one of Jack's scorned women and the only thing she wants is what she's always wanted—his nuts on a skewer."

"Ouch," Jack hissed.

"Did I cut you?"

"No, sweetheart. Just reacting to the comment about my nuts."

The room went silent, and Kara and Monté sent puzzled stares Sam's way. She was about to ask them what the problem was when it dawned on her that Jack just called her sweetheart. She needed to cover for him.

"Well, darling, I won't let that awful woman near your nuts." Sam waved her scissors in the air with élan, then gave the blades a wicked snap. *"En garde!"*

Kara and Monté laughed.

"You two are getting pretty good at this," Kara said. "Now let's make it official."

The smell of his father's office always did a job on Jack's psyche. It was the smell of old books and old money, of leather and linseed oil. It was the smell of his childhood, his loneliness, and the knowledge that he was never quite important enough to drag his dad's attention away from his work. The fact that the shrine was now Jack's office never felt right to him. It was as if the ghosts of his father and grandfather hovered there among the old law texts and the gleaming mahogany, checking on him from the great beyond, fully aware that Jack's heart wasn't in it, and not at all pleased with that fact.

As Jack fiddled with the lock on the family safe, he acknowledged that was the one thing that had always eluded him about politics—a sincere zest for it, a consuming passion like he once had for football. His mind could grapple with the key issues facing the state and the nation. It wasn't that he presumed to have all the answers, but he did have carefully considered opinions, and he understood the nature of the most serious challenges facing all Americans—national security and foreign policy, the deficit, education, jobs and trade, crime, the environment, Social Security, health care.

He never minded studying the reams of reports and analysis Kara and Stuart sent his way or meeting with key lawmakers on all levels to hash out issues. He didn't mind the public speaking or the constant parade of events and appearances.

What he minded was the nagging realization that he didn't know why he bothered to do any of it. He understood on an academic level how his work as a politician affected real people, but for some reason he often felt apart from those people—detached. He knew it was more than simply growing up wealthy. His lack of connection embarrassed him. It was his biggest secret. And he hadn't noticed it until the day he got his leg mangled. Sometimes he wondered if his soul didn't get mangled right along with it.

"Do you remember the combination?" Kara stood so close that he could feel her breath on his neck.

"Of course. Why don't you have a seat and relax?" He motioned for Kara to sit on the sofa and glared at her to stay put.

It amused Jack how the three women were now poised on the edge of the ancient leather sofa like eager schoolgirls, hands folded in anticipation. They were such an odd trio of females lined up together like that—Kara and her long, sleek, cool demeanor; Monté with her in-your-face honesty, joyous self-confidence, and loyalty to Sam; and Samantha—

petite and sweet and hardworking but so much more that he suspected it would take a lifetime to get to the bottom of that woman and even then the job might not be done.

"Are you *sure* you know the combination? I think it's been years since you've opened that safe, hasn't it?"

Jack chuckled to himself. Kara had been a part of his life for so long she was like a sister to him—a demanding, scheming, wickedly brilliant sister. She had been his friend for nearly twenty years. She drove him nuts and he adored her. He knew her moods and her sore spots. He knew how her brain worked. He knew he wouldn't be running for Senate if it weren't for her—this was as much her race as it was his. Sometimes he thought they should just cut back on the middleman and let her be the senator.

"I'm all over it, boss," he said to Kara, telling himself that he hadn't lied when he told her he knew the numbers. Technically, he did. It was the order of the numbers that escaped him, and at that point he'd nearly exhausted all his options.

"I say we just blow it sky-high," was Monté's contribution.

Jack glanced over his shoulder and smiled. Every time he thought about how Sam and Monté and their offspring just showed up in his life one day, it made him chuckle. He didn't know how bored he'd been until they arrived. And to think—if he'd told Kara absolutely "no" on her scheme, he'd never have met Sam, a possibility he didn't want to contemplate.

Though he'd only known Samantha Monroe for a few weeks, he'd become attached to her. He didn't like going a day without seeing her.

It was a mystery how that had happened.

"Got it!" The internal workings of the safe clicked into place and Jack pulled the handle, opening the heavy antique door. The safe was no more than four feet high and three feet wide, but it was crammed with the flotsam and jetsam of Tolliver history, those treasures MDT had chosen, for whatever reason, not to put in the Bank One safe-deposit box. Jack lifted out a black velvet chest about the size of a hardback dictionary. He placed it on the desk.

"I've only seen inside once," Kara said in a reverent whisper.

Jack turned the box and opened the lid, and all three women rose from the couch like they'd been hypnotized. They walked wide-eyed to the big desk and bowed down.

"Holy f—" Sam slapped a hand to her mouth.

"You know you're going to have to let us try this shit on," Monté said, looking up from her stooped position. "Every girl's gotta know what it feels like to be a princess at least once in her life."

Jack grinned. "Have at it, ladies, but pick something we can use as an engagement ring. That's the whole point, right?"

"My God, look at this!" Kara held up a three-strand pearl necklace accented with a diamond-framed cameo.

"I hope you have all this stuff insured," Monté

said, running her fingers over the necklaces, bracelets, earrings, pendants, pins, and whatever else MDT kept in there.

"We do," he said. "Excuse me for just a few minutes, ladies."

Jack sat down at the desk and called Stuart, the whole time watching the women laugh, gasp, help one another with old clasps that didn't work so well, and shout in delight. Kara ran back to the butler's pantry to retrieve the hand mirror so they could admire themselves. Jack had to admit the black onyx bracelet looked really nice on Kara and that Monté looked like a diva in those diamond drop earrings that he thought may have belonged to one of MDT's aunts. When Sam reached behind her slim neck and snapped on a ruby and diamond choker and tossed her curls, the sight took Jack's breath away.

"Damn, Sammy! You sure you weren't accidentally swapped at birth or something? That looks like it was made for you!"

"It really does look perfect on you," Kara said, then shook her head. "Just not with jeans."

"The dressy casual dilemma again," Monté mumbled, making Sam laugh.

Jack held the phone to his ear as Stuart discussed the finer points of his aquarium speech, but he was unable to take his eyes from Sam. Another of those lurid mental flashes hit him, again featuring Sam in the red lingerie, but this time she was wearing that ruby red choker around her neck, and it was all he could do not to jump up and kiss her until she begged him to stop.

With real disappointment, he watched Sam remove the choker and return it to the jewelry box. Suddenly her eyes lit up with wonder.

"Wow. This is so pretty." Sam's slender left hand emerged from the black velvet chest. She held her hand out in front of her, fingers spread wide, to the admiration of Kara and Monté. He couldn't see what she'd selected, only a thin gold band that circled the back of her finger.

"Whoa," Monté said. "That's nice and big, but not Lil' Kim big."

"That ring is gorgeous," Kara said, holding up Sam's hand for closer inspection. "It looks Victorian." She twisted Sam's hand a bit so Jack could see.

He nodded his approval, still listening to Stuart ramble on about the pros and cons of linking Jack's campaign too closely to Allen Ditto's record. *Very pretty,* Jack mouthed to Sam, studying a diamond and emerald ring he was fairly sure he'd never seen before. *Perfect.*

Jack watched Sam smile at the ring, wiggle her fingers, and laugh. For some reason, it truly pleased him to see Sam with a ring on her finger. It pleased him down to his bones.

He abruptly ended the call with Stuart and joined the women on the other side of the desk. "May I interrupt for a moment?" He pushed his way in between Kara and Sam and slipped the ring off Sam's finger.

"Shortest engagement in history," Monté said, with a shake of her head.

"I just want to do this right." Jack stood in front of Sam, who looked up at him with her blue eyes narrowed in curiosity. He slipped the ring back on her finger, saying, "Samantha Monroe, will you pretend that you plan to marry me?

"Yes, Jack." Sam smiled. "I would love to pretend that I plan to marry you."

"How romantic," Kara said.

"Hey," Sam said with a laugh. "This is way more romantic than my first time around, trust me."

"That's sad," Jack said.

"It was. I shoved the EPT stick under Mitch's nose, we both stared at its two big, fat blue lines, and poof! We were engaged."

"Hell-ro?"

Jack whipped around at the sound of the voice, only to see little Dakota Benjamin standing in the opened pocket doors of the office, Jack's cell phone pressed to his ear.

"Hell-ro? Lady, are you there?" The kid scrunched up his face in concentration, listening to whoever might be on the other end.

Jack moved toward the child and held out his hand. "I'll take it, thank you, Ben."

"Mr. Jack gave me his phone number last night before he took the shower; did I tell you that?" The toddler smiled wide as he continued to talk into the phone. "By, lady." He shoved the phone at Jack.

With trepidation, Jack put the phone to his ear. "This is Jack Tolliver."

"And this is your mother. Have we been incommunicado for so long that you have sired children in the interim?"

Wonderful. "Not that I am aware."

"Who was that child? He or she sounded like a preschooler. Where in the world are you?"

"At the Sunset Lane house." A pang of horror shot through Jack—MDT could be calling for a ride from the Indianapolis airport, for all he knew! "Where are you, Marguerite?"

"Naples."

Jack could breathe again.

"But not for long."

So much for breathing. "I see. What are your holiday plans, then?"

"That depends entirely on you. I thought I would spend a few days at the house to celebrate with you before you gear up for the primary. You are declaring, aren't you? Kara told me you'd obtained the required signatures from the voting districts and that your focus group results were good. So you do plan to declare, is that correct?"

"That's the plan." His eyes shot to Kara, who hissed out a few select curses.

His mother continued. "I hate to revisit this issue, but I don't believe we established why a preschooler is at Sunset Lane, answering your cell phone."

"The preschooler?" Jack looked to Sam, who mouthed, *I'm sorry.* He gave her a shrug—there was nothing to do now. It was his fault for leaving the phone in the butler's pantry unattended. The kid didn't do anything wrong by answering it. "His name is Benjamin Monroe—"

"His last name is Bergen," Sam promptly corrected him.

"I mean Benjamin Bergen," Jack said, noting Sam's deepening scowl. "OK, actually, it's *Dakota* Benjamin Bergen, but I thought calling him by his middle name might increase the chances of him getting potty trained before he grows a mustache."

MDT paused for a moment, then sked, "Exactly to whom does this Dakota person belong?"

"He's Samantha Monroe's youngest."

A blessed silence graced his ear, and for once Jack prayed his cell reception had tanked without warning. That or the earth had just opened up and swallowed him whole. He'd take either one.

"The waitress with whom you've been photographed?"

"She's a hairstylist on sabbatical, Marguerite."

"An unemployed hairstylist who doesn't have the same last name as her youngest child? How many children are there? How many last names, Jack? This is the woman you've chosen to display around town on the eve of your campaign?"

Jack shook his head in amazement. He'd long known that his mother had earned her black belt from the Marie Antoinette School of Public Policy, but her snootiness never ceased to amaze him.

"All three of Sam's children have her ex-husband's last name."

"I see. An unemployed, divorced mother of three."

"That's not entirely—"

"Is Kara aware of this?"

Jack laughed. "That's an excellent question. Let me check." Without putting his hand over the tiny receiver, he yelled to Kara, "Sam Monroe has three children? Gadzooks! Were you aware of this fact?"

"What in the name of God is going on up there, Jack?" MDT had ceased pretending to be calm. "I demand you tell me the truth, and I demand you tell me now."

Jack was nearly bursting with the warm fuzzy feeling he usually got mid-conversation with his mother. "All right, Marguerite. The truth is, we've hired Sam Monroe to pretend to be my fiancée through the primary. And the two of us are cavorting around town on purpose so that when I declare next month it won't surprise anyone that Sam and her kids are at my side." Jack ignored the openmouthed stares offered by Monté, Sam, and Kara and charged right ahead. "Basically, Mother, we're betting that their presence will soften my reputation for being a pretentious, self-centered, misogynistic jerk, not that those personality traits have ever been incompatible with the U.S. Senate, or any elected office for that matter."

The blissful silence returned. Unfortunately, it was brief.

"You are joking," Marguerite said.

"I am not."

"Expect me in four days." She hung up.

She'd *found* him. That's all Christy could think as she scurried down the tiled hallways in the bowels of the Channel 10 TV studios, clipboard in hand. She'd done what the prosecutor's office and their team of

investigators had failed to do for three long years—
she'd found one Mitchell J. Bergen, former husband
of the slut elf. She'd found him in about two hours. A
quick bit of background research on Bergen revealed
that the *Star* had done a feature story on him six
years earlier, complete with photos of the man and a
whole array of bizarre pea-pod-shaped glass sculp-
tures. She then went to eBay and tracked sales of
three similarly strange pea-pod creations, tracing
them back to a shop in Wetumpka, Alabama, of all
places, run by a glassblower by the name of Michael
Bouvier. She called the phone number listed and
asked to speak to Mitchell Bergen, and *voilà*! One
deadbeat dad on a stick!

Of course, Bergen insisted she had the wrong
number and hung up, but Christy had talked to
enough unwilling sources over the years to recognize
the heavy breathing of a trapped animal when she
heard it. Now all she had to do was figure out a way
to coax the vermin out of hiding and lure him back to
Indianapolis, somehow making it worth his while.

If she could guarantee the prosecutor's office
wouldn't scoop him up off the street, she knew she
could bait him with his kids. There wasn't a man on
earth so coldhearted that he wouldn't want to see his
kids after a three-year separation. Bergen had to be
filled with remorse about what he did. How could he
not be?

"Five minutes, Christy."

She gave a pleasant nod to the assistant producer
and told him she'd be right there. Today marked the
150th *Capitol Update* show with Christy as host. She

felt quite proud of the three years she'd spearheaded such a quality forum for political debate. She felt proud that the show not only was aired live on Sunday but also was taped for release in three additional weekday time slots, on two channels. She remembered the communications professor at Purdue who once told her she was too much of an airhead to make it in broadcast journalism, adding, "And that's saying something." Well, just last year good ole Professor Shit-for-Brains sent her a congratulatory note on her success. She responded with the form letter she sent all her fans, along with an autographed color glossy eight-by-ten.

"Two minutes!"

Christy clipped on her microphone and chatted briefly with her guests for the afternoon—a few regulars plus Brandon Miliewski in his debut appearance. It was the least she could do for him, considering the way he'd been so helpful and the fact that she'd needed a last-minute replacement for Kara DeMarinis, who decided to play coy with Jack's campaign. That was fine with Christy. Besides, she planned to take advantage of Brandon's goofy devotion at some point in the near future, and this would grease the skids. Everything happened for a reason.

Today's topics would include the school-funding crisis, statewide disaster preparedness, and the video poker legislation now stalled in committee. Of course they'd get around to the Senate race scuttlebutt, and that was when she could cast her first doubt on whether Jack's very public tryst was the real deal rather than a political ploy. It was going to be a good show.

Christy crossed her shapely legs and yanked down on the back of her suit jacket, tucking it under her butt so her shoulders formed a straight and tidy line onscreen. Her mind was spinning, pondering just how she'd use Mitchell Bergen to extract the real story from the slut elf and how Brandon Miliewski might come in handy as her man in the field. It would all come together if she let it stew. Some of her most fortuitous flashes of brilliance had come when she simply relaxed and let things happen.

Out of the corner of her eye she saw Brandon gazing at her adoringly. She offered him a small smile, noting that even though his eyes bugged out momentarily, he had the wherewithal to recover just as they went live.

That man was really beginning to show promise.

Mitchell peered into the pockmarked mirror in the bathroom of his glass studio, a two-room storefront that doubled as his home. He hardly remembered how he'd ended up in this nowhere southern town or how long he'd been here. The last few years had been a fun-house ride of the highest highs and the lowest lows, and his last low had sent him here, to hide. Again.

Mitch knew in his heart that one day he'd be found, but it had been a shock nonetheless. He didn't even know which agency that woman worked for— she didn't say. Was it the police? The prosecutor's office? A private detective agency? He wondered just how many avenues Sam had used to try to track down his sorry ass and whether she felt any sense of victory now that she had him.

He wished he had money. If he had money, he could go back to Indianapolis with his pride intact, pay the back child support he owed, and beg his kids to forgive him. He wouldn't bother to ask the same of Sam. There was no point.

Mitch rubbed at the dark circles under his eyes and scratched at his scraggly chin and knew there was no way he could go back like this.

He had two options, and neither of them was very appealing—he could turn himself in and go to jail or move again and start over somewhere new. That was it. And the truth was, he was too exhausted to even think about going through the hassle of borrowing somebody's truck and scamming for help moving his ovens and supplies one more time, in search of a smaller town in an even less obvious state, where he could feign to be the eccentric artist who just wanted to be left alone. That was such a lie. He didn't want to be left alone. He wanted to see his kids and he wanted to go home, but he'd made too many mistakes to do either. It was as simple as that.

Mitch lay down on the old single bed at the back of the building and crossed his arms over his eyes. Three years ago, he had been living a lie and it was strangling him. He left Sam to pursue his grand adventure, but he did it all wrong. He hurt a lot of people. And now, five states and six not-so-grand lovers later, he had about seventy bucks to his name, a pay-as-you-go cell phone, access to a public library computer, and nothing to live for. At least the cocaine wasn't an issue anymore—it's amazing how no money and no access can cure a drug habit.

He almost wished the mystery woman with the blocked caller ID would call back. At least he'd know what fate held for him. With a sigh, Mitch figured it wouldn't hurt to stay put and prepare himself for that knock on the door, no matter who, and what, might be waiting on the other side.

10

The group was celebrating the first day of Christmas vacation with a visit to one of their old neighborhood's favorite restaurants, and Dakota was clearly the only one thrilled with the mariachi band now serenading their table. But that was part of the ambience of El Sol Restaurant—good food cheap, and bad music for free. The toddler bounced around in his chair and clapped his hands with abandon as the three-piece ensemble broke into their rendition of "La Cucaracha."

"I'm telling you, I think your fiancée has a real crush on you," Monté said, leaning in to whisper over the music. "You'd better be careful around him. I don't think you're in any shape to be fighting off advances from a man like that."

Sam nearly choked on her iced tea. "What's that supposed to mean?" She checked to make sure Greg, Lily, and Simon weren't paying any attention, then whispered, "Are you implying that I don't have the willpower to resist Jack Tolliver?"

Monté leaned back into her cheerfully painted wooden chair and blinked, saying nothing with her lips and everything with her eyes.

"Really, Monté. Is that what you're saying?"

"Damn straight that's what I'm saying. Watch yourself."

Sam took another long gulp of iced tea, stalling for time. She'd never kept a secret from her best friend in all the years she'd known her. Monté knew everything about her life, even the snooze-a-thon one-night stand with Bill the architect. It pained Sam to not be able to tell Monté what kind of rush she was experiencing with Jack, that courtesy of her new boss she'd had the first spectacular kiss and the first cataclysmic sex of her life—all at the ripe old age of thirty-six! But she and Jack had discussed at length how to handle this, and they'd agreed to keep their tryst to themselves. That way, they could just enjoy each other and see what developed, without worrying about who knew what, who said what in front of whom, and who approved or disapproved. Besides, she didn't want the kids thinking something real and possibly permanent might be developing between her and Jack. The last thing they needed was further disappointment.

So Sam and Jack had agreed to let the world at large think their love was true, let their inner circle think it was a ruse, and enjoy the adult playground that lay somewhere in between.

"I can handle Jack Tolliver," Sam said, trying to smile with confidence over her outrageous fib. Monté was right, of course—Sam was in no shape to resist the likes of that man, and frankly, she hadn't even bothered to try.

He was funny, charming, sexy, and interested. He was *there* and came with a six-month written guarantee that he'd stay put. That was an offer any lonely woman would jump at.

"I just don't want you to get hurt is all, Sammy, and that man has 'heartbreaker' written all over him in permanent marker."

"Thank you."

Monté changed the subject, apparently satisfied she'd saved Sam from doom. "So what's the plan for when the dragon lady arrives? You all going to stay put in the house?"

Greg and Simon laughed, and Sam realized the kids had just tuned into the adult conversation. Sam gave the guitar player a crisp five-dollar bill and wished the band a merry Christmas, hoping they'd take the hint.

"Did you just call Jack's mother a dragon lady?" Lily asked, looking impressed.

"Seems to me she and Jack aren't all that close," Monté said.

"I don't think he even likes her," Simon said. "And I can't see how a man can hate his mama, even if she drives him crazy."

"I've raised you right," Monté said.

After lunch, everyone piled in the van and Sam drove to a Christmas tree lot near the Lafayette Square shopping mall. They picked out a seven-foot-tall blue spruce, had it bundled up with twine and lashed to the luggage rack. When they returned to

Sunset Lane, they found that Jack had left a tree stand in the great room, just as promised. It took everyone working together to get the thing secured and straight, and while no one had been paying any attention to Dakota he opened each box of holiday decorations and removed the wire hanger from every ornament he found. "I'm helping, Mommy! See?" he said proudly.

They spent the afternoon swimming, listening to Christmas music, wrapping gifts in secret, and setting them under the tree. Monté made her famous chicken and dumplings and a chocolate cake for dessert, and they lit a fire in the huge great room fireplace afterward. The day had filled Sam with a deep sense of peace and security, and she looked at the faces of the kids in festive light, Dale twitching with a doggie dream as he lay in front of the fire, and she wanted to paint what she saw.

"I'm going to start painting again after the holidays," she said out loud. "As soon as I find a place to set up."

Monté sipped her decaf and smiled. "I was wondering when you'd get back to that."

"And that means you have to start singing again," Sam teased.

"Mmm, well, I don't know how much demand there is for lead singers with carpal tunnel syndrome and the beginning of varicose veins."

They both laughed, knowing too well what thirteen years behind a styling chair could do to a person.

"Just be glad you can take a break from the shop for a while, Sammy."

"Oh, I am glad." Sam looked at Monté with concern and love and then smiled. "I can't wait for you to open your gift tomorrow night."

Jack's deep voice penetrated the stillness of the room. "Oh yeah? Did you get me something good?"

Sam's pulse immediately spiked and her whole body went on alert.

"Mr. Jack!" Dakota jumped up and ran toward Jack. Before Sam could stop him, he jumped into Jack's arms, assuming he'd be caught. Jack did catch him, gave him a quick hug, and promptly sat him back down. "Hey, Ben. What's happening?"

Monté frowned at her and Sam shrugged. It was funny that Jack was determined to prove that Dakota's name was linked to his refusal to use the potty. But the child didn't seem to mind being called Benjamin, so where was the harm?

Dale began barking at the new arrival and Sam leaped from the sofa to return the dog to the Florida room, his official prison. As she ran by Jack, he winked at her. "Hi, sweetness," he whispered.

Jack stayed for most of the evening, playing Trivial Pursuit with the older kids. He mentioned to Sam that he'd be working on a project much of the next day, in the upstairs of the south wing. Sam assumed it had something to do with Marguerite's arrival.

"You sure your mother won't mind us celebrating here tomorrow night?"

Jack shook his head and smiled at Sam. "She'll probably just make a brief appearance, put her two cents in, and then leave. She usually goes to services at First Presbyterian on Christmas Eve, then heads to the mayor's house for a little holiday cheer."

"I just don't want to intrude."

"This place is yours to enjoy until May. Nothing has changed, Sam."

A half hour later, Sam saw Monté and Simon to the door, put Dakota to bed, and sent Lily and Greg upstairs for the night. When she returned to the great room, she found Jack munching on a piece of chocolate cake. "You can bake, too? My God, will you marry me?"

Sam smiled, plopping down right next to him on the sofa. "Monté made the cake. And I'll pass your offer on to her."

"I've missed you," Jack said simply. He placed the dessert plate on the glass coffee table. "I haven't felt right without you these last few days."

Sam knew what he meant. She'd felt the same way, and she nodded her understanding.

"I would really like to date you tonight," Jack said, grinning. "I've been thinking all day about how I need to date the hell out of you."

Sam laughed and reached out to stroke his forearm. He was wearing jeans with a black cashmere crewneck over a white tee. He looked comfortable and irresistible.

"You have no idea how bad I need to be dated tonight," she whispered, keeping her eyes away from his face. "I can't stop thinking about the last date I had with you."

She was suddenly being pulled up and into his lap, and before Sam could figure out what was coming, he'd leaned her back into the crook of his arm and kissed her. Pleasure and heat coursed through her, and an overwhelming sense of being possessed settled deep into her being. Sam relaxed into his embrace, slid her arms around his neck, and kissed him back.

Jack's hands were in her hair and stroking her hip and running up her belly and to the buttons of her little blue cardigan. "I have a present I'd like you to open tonight if you don't mind."

Sam pulled back enough to look into his face. She blinked in surprise. It hadn't even occurred to her that Jack might get her something for Christmas. "But I didn't get—"

His mouth was back on hers, and when he'd settled her, he dragged his lips down her throat and bit softly into her shoulder. "This gift is really more for me than you."

With that, he reached behind one of the sofa pillows and pulled out a box elegantly wrapped in gold and silver filigree paper, tied up with a wide silver ribbon.

"Now?"

"If you don't mind. I was kind of hoping you'd wear it for that date we're about to have."

Sam put the box into her lap for a moment and studied him. She didn't know if it was wishful thinking or even downright delusion, but she couldn't see how anyone could think Jack was a jerk. He was sweet and generous with her. The way he looked at her right then did not convey that he saw her as simply a distraction. The way his head cocked a bit to the side, the way his lips curled into the barest hint of a smile, the way his gaze softened—it almost seemed like he was falling in love with her.

"Are you all right, Sam?"

"Huh? Oh, sure. I'll open this now."

The box weighed nothing, and she already had a fairly good idea what might be inside. She removed the wrapping paper, slid off the lid, and pulled open the tissue, revealing a burst of red satin and lace. She brushed her fingertips over each of the two wisps of fabric, discovering immediately that this was French stuff, expensive, and skimpy.

Jack's hand joined hers inside the box. "This will feel as good as it will look. See? There are no seams inside to irritate your skin." Sam watched, mesmerized, as Jack caressed the inside of the brassiere. "I wanted you to feel as beautiful as you are."

A small water spot suddenly appeared on the pantie, and Sam realized she was crying. No man had ever bought her lingerie before. Certainly no man had ever worried if the inside seams of her bra might be scratchy. This man was truly either God's gift to women or one sly operator. And who could she turn to for help deciding which it was? She should never have kept this from Monté, but it was too late now.

"You're a Ferrari that's been running on two cylinders, sweetheart." Jack's fingers wiped away her tears and he lifted her chin. "I can't wait to feel you cut loose on the curves for me. Please put these on."

Sam nodded. She got up and went to the powder room off the foyer, where she slipped off her jeans and sweater and plain underwear and put on Jack's selection. Once again, she had to hand it to him. The demi bra and thong fit perfectly, considering what they were designed to do, and her breasts were lifted high, nipples spilling over the top edge. The pantie triangle barely stretched over her mound, pulling high up on her hips. She turned around to look at herself in the mirror and saw nothing but a thin slice of red satin disappearing up the middle of her bottom.

With a satisfied sigh, Sam tousled her hair and walked back to the great room, smiling because she knew she was beautiful. She was a sexual goddess. The bomb. Or at least Jack Tolliver's temporary bomb-ass babe, and that was all she was going to worry about.

Sam sauntered her way back into the great room, and continued to slink toward him, her eyes locked on his as she moved close. Jack licked his lips in anticipation. When she arrived at the sofa, she straddled his lap and eased down on top of his thighs, raking her fingers through his shorter hair. She wiggled on him. She watched his head fall back against the pillows as his breath came in shallow puffs.

"You are so beautiful," he whispered.

"Thank you. I'm glad you like your gift."

Jack's gaze felt hot on her skin as he looked up and down the front of her body. When he raised a hand to squeeze a handful of breast and nipple, a streak of pleasure shot through Sam. She threw her head back and moaned.

"I must have been a very, very good boy this year," he said.

A loud thud caused them to whip their heads

around in surprise. It took Sam exactly one second to
jump off Jack's lap, dive behind the huge Christmas
tree, and come to grips with the fact that she'd just
shared the sexiest moment of her life with Jack's
mother.

Fuck, fuck, fuck.

This could not have happened. Jack squeezed his
eyes tight and opened them again, and there was
MDT, absolutely real, mink-covered shoulders
straight, face blank, mouth tight. Two large Louis
Vuitton bags lay where they had been dropped, at her
driver's feet.

Jack worried about Sam. He could see one bare
foot and ankle through the branches of the lush
Christmas tree, but the rest of her was hidden.
Maybe Marguerite would think she'd been seeing
things.

"Excuse me for interrupting."

"You were supposed to arrive tomorrow morning."

"I got an earlier flight."

He saw Sam's foot tap nervously and he realized
she was probably cold and most definitely mortified.
He stood up. "I'll see you to your room."

"That won't be necessary." Marguerite gestured
for her driver to follow her upstairs. Jack watched her
walk away like nothing had happened. Just once in
his life he'd like to see her veneer crack. He'd like to
see her break down and yell and cuss and call him
every name she could think of. Never—not even
when the twins died—had she ever cut loose. He'd
never been privy to her fury. Or grief. Certainly not

her love. All he'd ever known was this calm superiority, this bitter judgment. And he *hated* it.

"Tell Ms. Monroe I look forward to a more formal introduction in the morning," she said.

Sam successfully avoided Marguerite for all of Christmas Eve day. She got the kids up early and took them out to breakfast at City Market. Then they went to the mall and Lily and Greg did some last-minute shopping while Sam spent an eternity in the Santa Claus line with Dakota. Next she took everyone to the movies—Lily and Greg taking in an action flick while she and Dakota watched a Disney cartoon feature. Then she took them bowling and out to dinner.

"Uh, Mom?" Lily asked over Chinese food. "What time are Monté and Simon supposed to come over to the house? What if they get there before we're even home? Isn't Jack's mom supposed to show up sometime today?"

"She's already there," Sam said, trying to sound like she'd nearly forgotten that little fact. "She got in late last night."

"Oh?" Greg put down his fork. "So you've already met the dragon lady?"

Sam widened her eyes at Greg and inclined her head toward Dakota, who was munching on his fifth fortune cookie. "I haven't actually met Mrs. Tolliver. We caught a quick glimpse of each other before she got settled last night, but we haven't spoken."

"Ah, so that's why it's been family fun day," Lily said, with a knowing smile.

Sam's final stop was O'Malia's grocery store, which looked like it had been raided by a horde of Vikings. She grabbed the last remaining half gallon of eggnog and the least broken-looking pack of Christmas cookies and headed home. Monté's car was in the drive when they arrived, and Sam said a silent prayer that Marguerite had already left for church.

The group came through the garage entrance and made their way into the kitchen, finding only Monté, Jack, and Simon. Jack had the biggest smile on his face when he saw them. "Merry Christmas!" he said.

"I'm sorry we're a little late."

"We didn't want to see the dinosaur lady," Dakota said, at the very instant Mrs. Tolliver set foot in the kitchen. Sam wanted to roll up in a ball and die.

"I have the most unfortunate timing!" Marguerite said with a stiff smile. "It seems I always arrive right in the middle of the festivities."

Jack's mother turned her laser-beam gaze on Sam. Marguerite had Jack's green cat eyes, their shape accentuated by a few too many trips to the plastic surgeon. She had draped her rail-thin body in thousands of dollars of designer clothes, shoes, and accessories. Sam tried to remember what she'd worn that day—which jeans and which sweater—and stammered out her introductions, starting with the children, who all addressed Marguerite respectfully, thank God. But when Sam got to Monté and Simon she could barely keep a straight face. She knew exactly what was going through her friend's head. How many times had they laughed about this at Le Cirque?

Marguerite sported Monté's pet peeve white woman hairdo, which she gleefully referred to as the "Rich Bitch A-line Bob from Hell," a style cut higher in the back than the front, pulled back from the brow, and held in gravity-defying place with what looked like several coats of polyurethane. It never ceased to amaze Sam and Monté how even women with money could cling to one bad hairstyle and refuse to part with it until the day they died.

Marguerite's version of the hated coif was made all the more hideous because of the overprocessed condition of her hair. She was what Sam and Monté called a cotton-candy blonde, a woman whose hair had been bleached for so many years that it had the consistency of dryer lint. This woman needed an emergency hair resuscitation and she needed it *now.*

"So very nice to meet you," Monté said to Marguerite, keeping her eyes away from Sam.

The front door chimes echoed through the foyer and Marguerite said, "That would be my driver. It's been a pleasure meeting you all. Samantha, would you mind very much walking with me to the front door?"

"I'd be happy to do that," Jack quickly offered.

"No, no. I just want a private moment with Samantha before we enjoy our respective evenings." Marguerite returned her gaze to Sam. "Shall we?"

"Mother, there is really no need to—"

"I've got it, Jack," Sam said with a nod. "I'd love to see her out."

This wouldn't be good, Sam knew, and that's why Jack had tried to spare her. But she steeled herself and followed Marguerite to the mansion's huge arched front door, where Jack's mother assured the driver that she would be just a moment. She turned a frosty smile on Sam.

"So now, which is it, Miss Monroe? Are you Jack's paramour or are you his employee? I must admit I'm flummoxed about the entire business."

Sam opened her mouth to say something just as Marguerite glanced down at Sam's ring finger and flinched. The woman slowly raised her eyes again and gave Sam one hell of an intimidating glare.

"I have only one thing to say to you, Samantha, and please listen carefully. Do not get your empty little head full of dreams that you will somehow snare my son. This is a temporary upgrade for you. Do not get used to it. Are we understanding each other?"

Sam blinked, stupefied. She'd done hair on women like Marguerite, women who believed that money and status gave them the right to treat a stylist like a servant, but those chicks had clearly only been a warm-up for this encounter. Marguerite Dickinson Tolliver was a beast, and two things had just become very clear to Sam: it was no mystery why Jack had issues with women, and it was a miracle that the man had any redeeming qualities whatsoever.

"It is quite obvious you have something you'd like to say to me, Miss Monroe. By all means, let's hear it."

Sam cleared her throat. Sure, she had a few things she wanted to say. She wanted to apologize for how everything had started so awkwardly between them. She wanted to tell her that she had no right to be so condescending. She wanted to tell her to stay away from her children or she'd get her ass kicked. But most of all, she wanted to tell Marguerite that Jack and Sam's relationship was none of her damn business.

Instead, all Sam could manage was, "Whoever's been doing your hair should be doing hard time instead."

"You said what?"

Jack sat cross-legged on the great room rug in front of Sam, staring at her in wonder. He'd been right about her from the start. She was a survivor. Anyone who could go toe-to-toe with MDT should get hazardous duty pay. Or a medal.

"I know I could have been more mature about it, and that she's your mother and this is her house, but I couldn't help it. She made me mad."

Jack grinned. He was having the best Christmas Eve he could ever remember. It had been a hoot watching the kids open their gifts, sheer wonder in their eyes as they tore open the wrapping paper on computers, iPods, clothes, music, and toys. They'd all thanked Jack politely for his hefty gift certificates. Simon had shaken his hand and said, "That was nice of you, man. Thank you." Greg had given him a hearty pat on the shoulder. And Lily had smiled at him shyly. Both Benjamin and Monté had thanked him for his gifts with unabashed hugs followed by kisses on the cheek, though Benjamin's was a bit sloppier than Monté's.

The highlight of the evening was when Monté opened the gift she'd received from Sam. With a puzzled look on her face, she held up a recent copy of *Indianapolis Monthly* emblazoned with the headline *Where the Boys Are: The Top Ten Hangouts of the City's Sexiest Single Men!*

"You got me a two-month-old magazine for Christmas?" Monté asked incredulously. "Did you swipe this from the salon?" Sam had laughed and told her to open it to the marked page. They all watched as Monté read, then laughed, then opened an envelope that had been tucked inside. She wiped her eyes and sighed. "So what exactly are you inspiring me to do, girl? Finally take care of myself? Or use this exclusive fitness club gig to grab me one of them sexy single men?"

"All of the above, babe," Sam had answered, and the two women hugged each other and cried for what seemed like ten minutes. Jack used the time to help the older kids read their computer set-up guides.

Jack had saved Sam's gift for now, when everyone else had gone off to the north wing to sleep. Monté and the older kids had been instrumental in helping Jack decide what to get Sam and how to pull it together. He couldn't have done it without Monté's help yesterday. But everything was ready and he couldn't wait to see Sam's face the moment it was revealed.

"Are you ready for your gift?" he asked her.

A puzzled frown settled between her brows. "I thought I got my gift yesterday."

"Nope. That was just an appetizer, and besides,

that was more for me, like I said. This gift is all for you. Let's go see it." Jack stood up, stretched his knee for a second, and reached down for Sam. He pulled her up and took her hand, walking with her up the central staircase. When they reached the landing, he felt her automatically turn toward the guest wing, but he redirected her.

"Where are we going?" she asked, a surprised smile on her face.

"Close your eyes, Samantha," he said, once they were in the south wing's hallway. "I'll tell you when you can look."

The door groaned loudly when it opened, and Jack made a mental note to get back up here and oil the hinges. He flipped on the overhead light and looked around at his handiwork. He hoped she liked it. Monté had assured him she would. "Stay put just a second. No peeking."

Jack went ahead and turned on the two high-resolution lights he'd bought at the art supply store, then checked one last time to make sure everything was in its place. He returned to her side and held her hand.

"Merry Christmas, Sam. You can open now."

This was not the reaction he expected. Sam stood completely still, her face twisting in pain as the tears ran down her pretty cheeks. She shook her head and mumbled, "No, no, no. . . ."

"It won't work? I was hoping—"

"Oh my God, Jack." She walked into the center of the room, still shaking her head. He watched her touch the easels and the long worktable and walk over to the sink. Then she noticed how the floor was covered with pristine drop cloths. She glanced at the three six-foot-long sawhorses. Then she walked to each of the three bare, tall windows, finally stopping at the last window, leaning her hands on the sill, and looking out into the night.

Jack figured she was still crying, but he hoped they were tears of surprise and happiness. He hadn't wanted to offend her by this. He only wanted her to enjoy these coming months.

Sam finally turned toward him. She was scowling. She crossed her arms over her chest and walked up to him where he stood by the door.

"Why did you do this?"

"I—what do you mean?"

She waved her arms around her. "This! This is extravagant. Way over-the-top. I could have found a corner somewhere and—"

"Monté told me you were planning to work with some really big canvases, and I wanted to make sure you had enough room and light."

Sam's eyes got huge.

"I found those sawhorses out in the potting shed and thought they might come in handy for that. This room was my father's nursery and that's why there's a sink and bathroom in here. I thought it would make a perfect studio."

"Does Marguerite know you've done this?"

"Nope."

Sam laughed and shook her head some more. "You kind of like this, don't you? Waving me and the kids under her nose."

Jack took a deep breath and studied Sam. "Maybe you have a point. But I didn't put this studio together to piss off MDT. I did it for you. Please believe me."

Sam nodded. "It's just too much."

"No, it's not." Jack walked toward Sam and hugged her. He kissed her hair. "You deserve this, Sam. I can do it for you and it's something you have wanted for a long time. Please accept this gift."

She hugged him tight and buried her face in his chest. He just held her like that for several minutes, feeling her breathing slow.

"I am scared," she said, her voice muffled by his sweater.

"Of what, sweetheart?"

She pulled away from his embrace and looked into his eyes, all seriousness. "I'm scared of you, Jack. You're so good at this that you've managed to push all my buttons—outrageous sex, sweet thoughtfulness, attention, romance, concern for my happiness." Sam laughed and shook her head again. "I've known you less than two months and I'm going under, Jack. If you keep this up, we're going to have a really big problem. I'll fall in love with you."

Jack felt his heart stop. He'd been here too many times, and it was always the cue for him to go. He'd never wanted a woman to love him. He'd never trusted the ones who'd claimed they did. He'd never wanted love and commitment and the risk that went along with it. But for some reason, his feet weren't itching this time. There was no instinct to bolt with Sam Monroe. He was OK with this. Better than OK.

Jack smiled down at her, realizing he was immensely pleased by what she'd just said.

Yet another mystery.

"You don't have to be afraid, Sam. And you're not getting all those things from me because I'm 'good' at this. I'm crazy about you. And I don't know how I got so lucky to have found you."

He kissed her. It felt so right to have Sam settle into his arms the way she just did, pressing up against him as her mouth yielded to his. She felt perfect. And he had the sudden realization that something changed in him when he was with her like this. He felt like a whole person, a person who was connected to something real. And he was overcome with the desire to do whatever it took to make this woman happy and to make this woman his.

"Come to my bed with me, Jack," Sam whispered into his ear. "Let me thank you properly for your gift."

They turned off the lights, shut the door, and made their way in silence to Sam's suite. He locked the double doors, flipped on the fireplace, and left the lights off, re-creating the night of the ice storm, the night his heart had begun to melt.

He managed to carry Sam to the bed this time, the way he'd always envisioned, and then slowly began to remove her clothes, the tiny buttons not as difficult to open as he'd imagined. He gasped. Beneath that simple sweater, Samantha had been wearing his gift, and the sight of her beautiful breasts spilling out from the red satin was more than he could take. He ripped off her jeans and his own clothes and he went

to the foot of the bed and stared at her in wonder as
his vision came to life. Sam raised one knee, threw
her arms over her head, and smiled at him, her
auburn curls spilling out on a sea of pillows. He felt
something foreign and powerful well up inside him
and he had to admit it was not completely welcome,
but he went with it anyway. Jack crawled up the bed
and covered her body with his, knowing that his
tears were impossible to hide because they were running down Sam's neck more than his own.

"I didn't get you a gift," Sam said, crying, too.

"Oh, sweetie. Yes, you did."

Christy lay in bed reliving the night's surprises, waiting for the ibuprofen to kick in—her wisdom teeth
were really starting to annoy her.

Of all the people to run into at the mayor's Christmas Eve shindig! Marguerite Tolliver! Oh, that
woman was smooth. But a lifetime as a politician's
wife had made her that way, and, as everyone knew,
it was often the wife who ran the show anyway. It
had probably been that way during Gordon Tolliver's
reign as well.

She was there with Allen Ditto! To someone who
didn't know that the oldies had been lifelong friends
it would almost have appeared that they were on a
date. Ditto leaned in to catch her every word. He
fetched her drinks at an event where there were
plenty of catering people on hand to take care of that
chore. He stayed at her side through the night.

Of course, it was too much to resist. Christy
couldn't stop herself from bringing up business, even

if it meant she might never again be welcome at one of the mayor's invite-only gatherings. There was an unspoken rule at these elite functions to steer clear of the nasty side of politics, at least for a night, but Christy believed a person would never get anywhere in life if she didn't take full advantage of every opportunity that came her way.

Marguerite seemed a bit chilly. It was almost as if it took her a few moments to remember who Christy was and that she'd once invited her on a girls-only shopping trip to Chicago. Allen was his usual self, pleasant in an earnest sort of way, talking in generalities, not saying much of anything quotable. She supposed that's how he'd lasted so long in the Senate.

Eventually, she'd gotten around to asking Marguerite what she thought of her future daughter-in-law. That moment right there was worth the price of admission. Even frequent-flier Botox injections couldn't mask the very real reaction that little question got. Marguerite's face went rigid, and Christy could see her pulse pound against the paper-thin skin at her throat.

After a too-long silence, in which Allen had cleared his throat at least twice, Marguerite smiled at Christy and replied, "Tolliver men have always had excellent judgment when it comes to women."

They walked away after that, leaving Christy to wonder if that was a compliment to her, since, after all, Jack had once chosen her, or an insult because he'd eventually dumped her.

Christy pulled the covers under her chin and closed her eyes, smiling to herself in the dark, knowing that the real important bit was that Marguerite was clearly uncomfortable talking about Jack's alleged fiancée and Marguerite Tolliver never let it show she was uncomfortable about anything.

There was definitely a story here, and Christy would get it if it was the last thing she ever did.

11

The day had arrived, and Samantha was more nervous than she thought she'd be. The kids were doing great. Jack had taken Greg to his tailor and bought him his first suit, and he looked so grown-up and sure of himself standing there next to Sam. Lily had agreed to wear what she referred to as "normal people clothes" for the press conference, even volunteering to lay off the kohl for a day. Sam had taken Dakota to the bathroom three times in the last half hour, praying that they could avoid any kind of pants removal in the time it took for this thing to be over with. She had Dakota swear to her that he would tell her when he had to go potty so they could leave the stage.

"No pwobwem, Mommy," he'd assured her, giving her a thumbs-up.

Kara had warned them that reporters would try to corner them at every turn, even if they went to get a drink of water or use the bathroom, and that's exactly what happened. They said nothing, just as they'd been instructed. Sam and the kids knew the whole idea was to make it look like Jack brought them just to see the dolphins, and when the media hounded him about his political ambitions as a matter of course he would happen to admit that he'd decided to run for Senate and then find a way to get Sam and the kids to join him onstage.

They stood on the floor next to the raised dais, not on display but not exactly hidden. Marguerite sat in the front row, and Sam would occasionally feel her evil eye descend upon her. They had successfully avoided each other these last two weeks, as Marguerite had moved into a hotel Christmas Day and never returned to Sunset Lane, much to everyone's relief.

Sam glanced at Greg and Lily and knew they were starting to get nervous. She couldn't blame them and wished this were already over. The whole thing had been a zoo in more ways than one, the kind of production Sam had only seen on TV. When Jack had cut the ribbon on the new dolphin exhibit a few moments ago, the spectacle of all those video camera lights, reporters, and big shots was overwhelming. Jack was now up onstage using his politician's voice to describe what an asset the zoo was to Indiana and how the new exhibit was an example of how private and public partnerships could be the bedrock of economic development.

It unfolded just the way Kara said, and she watched Jack handle the barrage of questions with grace and humor. He didn't seem to mind the camera flashes and the occasional impolite shout. He looked the part up there at the podium, in a simply cut black suit, white dress shirt, and beautiful tie in abstract blues and greens, a choice Kara had spent days agonizing over. It had seemed silly to Sam at the time, but she guessed the genius was in the details.

Eventually, Jack made his announcement, and that's when things got hairy. Reporters started shouting, and Jack answered a few basic questions, then reminded them that the day was about the zoo and not about his campaign and told them to all enjoy themselves. He turned to go and someone shouted, "At least introduce us to your fiancée!" Jack laughed and motioned for Sam and the kids to join him. He reached for Sam's hand as she walked up the steps.

"This is Samantha Monroe and her children, Greg, Lily, and Dakota Benjamin."

Sam's head started to spin. Her knees shook. She smiled as naturally as she could, but she hadn't been on a stage since Valpo High's production of *Bye Bye Birdie* her sophomore year, an experience that made her so queasy she decided to stick to set design. As the reporters continued to shout, Sam was so preoccupied with preventing herself from fainting that she hardly noticed Dakota pulling on her hand.

She felt Jack's arm come around her shoulders and she was grateful for the support. She continued to smile.

"The rumors are true. We are engaged."

The questions spiraled out of control. *How did they meet? When was the wedding? Did he plan to adopt her children?* Sam was seriously beginning to question her sanity in ever agreeing to this when

Greg whispered into her ear with urgency, "Mom! Get D-d-dakota!"

The crowd burst into laughter as Sam handled the calamity as quickly and efficiently as possible. In one motion, she yanked up Dakota's pants and tucked the wet diaper under her arm, whisking him down the stairs and to the bathroom.

Jack's next comment echoed throughout the dolphin pavilion and was received with warm laughter.

"It's potty-training time, and we're fighting the good fight, something I'm sure all of you parents out there can relate to."

"My God, that was pure genius! Are you sure I can't get you to do a soft bio spot with Jack?"

"Soft *what*?"

Kara laughed. She'd been laughing a lot that night, on the ride back from the zoo, while the kids swam, and now over pizza in the kitchen. Kara claimed Sam and her brood had "charmed the shit" out of Indiana's voting public. Sam had to shake her head—and she'd thought working in a hair salon was a bizarre way to make a living!

"Is that anything like soft porn?" Monté asked.

"Sort of. Soft bio spots are usually thirty-second TV ads that don't get to the nitty-gritty on issues, just kind of give you a look at the candidate as a person, you know, touchy-feely drivel." Kara dug into her pizza with abandon and continued talking with her mouth full. "We've already spent close to a million on his issue spots, but we could always do another soft one and run the living hell out of it right before the primary."

"A million dollars?" Sam asked, astonished.

"What I'm picturing here is Jack taking the kids sledding. Or maybe throwing the Frisbee for Dale, hiking with you in Eagle Creek, or antiquing in Brown County."

Monté said, "Why don't you just videotape Jack changing one of Dakota's big ole stinky diapers?"

"My God! That's brilliant!" Kara swigged down some of her Diet Coke. "You should go into politics."

Monté shook her head slowly. "You're damn crazy."

After they'd stopped laughing and the kids had come and gone, grabbing more pizza to take back to the great room, Sam decided to make certain that Kara had heard her. "I'm serious. No kids in the ads. It's bad enough that they were on TV today. I think now that everybody knows we exist, they don't have to be paraded around in front of the cameras ever again."

"But *you'd* consider doing it, right?"

Sam sighed. She knew her contract called for her to participate in campaign advertisements as needed. "I will. But I'd like to have some say in the finished product, because you know they'll run it on TV after we break up, and if it's too mushy it will make all of us look ridiculous."

"I've considered that, too," Kara admitted, nodding thoughtfully. "So, it'll be low-key but high-impact. We'll start shooting in the next few weeks."

The natural light was remarkable in this room, and sometimes Sam would imagine what the space must

have looked like back in the 1930s, when Jack's dad
was a baby. It had probably been decorated with in-
tricate wallpaper and heavy drapes and filled with ornate wood furniture. It would have been the exact
opposite of the room now, with its white walls, un-
adorned windows, and tarp-covered floors. But the
room felt like pure extravagance to Sam. It was her
space and filled with her things. It was where she
went to think and feel and dream and paint. Sam
didn't know if the room had a generous vibe all its
own or if it just reflected her own reawakened enthusiasm, but the result was the same—her studio was a
heavenly retreat, where she escaped every afternoon
during Dakota's nap and every other chance she got,
to reacquaint herself with herself.

Sam had been working on several simple paintings since Christmas, and it felt like she was hearing
her native tongue spoken after years of silence.
Some days, Sam would enjoy the process so much
that she'd cry with relief, thrilled to see something
come alive under her hand again. Other days, she'd
get so frustrated with her lack of finesse that she'd
stomp her feet and scream and yell at the canvas.
Once, she'd given the anger a name—*Mitch*—and
she looked at what she'd been working on and realized she'd been painting his face. Sam knew all the
pent-up sadness had to come out somehow, and this
was as good a way as any.

Many days, Sam would paint while her mind
picked at the concerns that swirled in her head. Lily
had settled in fine at Park Tudor and had found some
nice, nonconformist friends, and she was blossoming

with her advanced placement classes. Sam had always known Lily was smart but hadn't expected her to dive into academics the way she had. It was a joy to watch.

Greg was having a rougher time, which surprised Sam. His private speech therapy was progressing extremely well and he was excelling at his classes, especially history. The problem was he missed Simon terribly—Greg only saw him a couple times a week now—and had retreated into himself, reading for hours on end in his room. Sam and Monté had discussed getting Simon into Park Tudor for his high school years, even if it meant splitting the tuition.

And then there was Dakota. He needed to get out of diapers and it needed to happen *yesterday*. Sam knew he was on the edge of a breakthrough and all her hard work was about to pay off, but it couldn't happen fast enough. Sam also needed to really start looking for a house. She needed to get more life insurance. She needed to talk to Marcia about working part-time when she went back to the salon instead of full-time, a request she might not like. Sam had been seriously thinking about hiring a competent private investigator to find Mitch. She could afford it. She had unfinished business with her ex and she wanted it over and done with. She was ready to move on.

Of course, Jack was on her mind all the time. He'd taken up residence in her head and her heart and sometimes she could even feel him and smell him when he wasn't anywhere near. And things just seemed to get better—and more complicated—as time went on. The weeks of fake-but-actually-real dates, campaign events, and excellent sex were moving along at a fast clip, and with each day she found she craved him more, laughed with him more, and knew him better. She was in love, no doubt about it, but she'd never bring it up. It was as if the two of them had an unspoken agreement to never mention life after May, so there she was, headed to her own execution and liking it.

On that Wednesday afternoon in mid-February, Sam was working in her studio while Dakota slept. She was swimming in calm waves of ideas and form, at peace with what she was sketching. She thought maybe she was getting somewhere with her plans for the three large canvases, still stacked up against the far wall of the studio waiting for her inspiration. Sam knew it would be silly to push herself to start the triptych before the primary when she'd only have to pack up and move everything. She'd give herself time with this. She deserved to.

A faint knock on the door brought her out of her sketch, and she assumed it was Mrs. Dyson, the housekeeper, who often chatted with Sam for a few minutes before she left for the evening. But it was Jack, who poked his dark head into Sam's studio and smiled at her. From behind his back he pulled out a potted hydrangea, and Sam felt her stomach drop.

She loved him so much.

"Hey, Senator." Sam put down her sketchbook and pencil and smiled. She enjoyed watching him walk across a room—any room, but it was especially erotic to see his graceful and strong body saunter through her space, just like he did her heart.

Jack set the pot down on a windowsill and leaned in to kiss her.

"How's my sweet Sam?"

"Good."

"May I?" Jack waited for her OK and he picked up the sketch pad. "Wow." She watched him frown. "What the hell is it?"

Sam laughed. "It's an abstraction. It's supposed to convey a feeling rather than an actual thing. Like one of your thirty-second soft bio spots."

"Got it. Come here, Samantha." He sat on the sturdy worktable and motioned for her to join him. She climbed up on his lap and wrapped her arms around his neck.

"We get to see the video this week; did Kara tell you?"

"Yeah," Sam said. "I'm a little scared."

Jack chuckled. "It can't be too bad. It's just the two of us walking down the street in Bean Blossom while it snows. I know we were there for hours and hours, but they'll probably use about three seconds of it."

"I know."

"And no one will ever suspect you were wearing that white lace bustier under your down jacket."

"No one but you." She kissed his cheek and laughed with him, and it took just a few seconds for everything to change, as it often did with them. Jack tightened his grip and pulled her close.

"It's been four days, Sam."

"Five. I counted."

"God, I need you so bad."

Sam began ripping off her clothes and shucking her boots. Jack was naked and gleaming in the golden afternoon light and Sam moaned at the sight.

"I have to paint you."

His eyes went panicky. "Now?"

Sam laughed and climbed back up on the table with him, spreading her legs to sit on his lap, facing him. "Not right this second, silly, but sometime soon. I've wanted to paint you every since I met you."

"Yeah? I've wanted to do certain things with you from the very beginning, too."

Sam put her hands on his big, solid upper arms, getting that same thrill she felt every time she touched his body. She smiled down at that impossibly handsome face and asked, "What kind of things?"

"I wanted to kiss you, for one." And he did. Jack kissed her so hard and hot and good that she could feel a tingle of need start in the core of her body and spread outward, warm and luscious as it coursed through her. It still amazed her, what Jack was able to accomplish with a single kiss.

"And I wanted to touch every inch of you. I wanted to hold you tight." His arms went around her and then his hands slowly explored her bare flesh— her shoulders, back, butt, and thighs—leaving little electrical flashes of pleasure wherever his fingertips landed.

Then Jack grabbed her by the waist and raised her up just enough to position her above his hard cock. He looked her in the eye and said, "Sam, sweetheart, I wanted to take you the second I laid eyes on you."

He pushed her down just enough that his cock head parted her pussy lips, and he stayed there, moving in small circles.

"You're such a tease." Sam kept her gaze locked on his, his torture making her wet, the pressure not enough, and she watched as those lively green eyes suddenly went dark and serious. She could see his chin tremble.

"Are you OK?"

He closed his eyes for a second, then looked at her once more. "I've wanted to love you. Do you know that?" He pushed farther into her, and she gasped in surprise and gratitude, immediately feeling her muscles clamp down on his erection.

"I've wanted to know everything about you so that I would know how to make you happy."

He grabbed her hips and slid all the way inside her, impaling her, not letting her go.

"Sweetie, I've wanted you to be mine. For real, for always."

"When did you decide that?"

Jack laughed. "Just now. I want you to stay with me. Don't go after May. Please."

"But Jack—*oh my God*!"

He bit down gently on one nipple, then the other, while moving deep inside her. "Come for me, sweet Sam. Come all over me. I've never felt this way about a woman—*ever.* God, Sam, I want—"

"Whatever you want, it's yours."

"I want you to have my baby."

Jack stopped moving for an instant, then laughed,

regaining his rhythm inside her. "Holy hell! I want you to have my baby!"

The alarm ringing in Sam's brain was drowned out by the pleasure as she clutched down in a hot and liquid orgasm that shot her into a swirling, dark place where nothing mattered but Jack, that he was inside her and fucking her, holding her tight and calling her name.

Jack exploded right along with her. And in the time it took for both of them to stop gasping for air, Sam had counted backward and forward through her menstrual cycle—twice—and come to the conclusion that this was the worst possible time for her to have unprotected sex. Unless, of course, she was desperately trying to get pregnant. Then today would have been perfect.

"I'm sorry. I know I should have used a condom."

"Yep. That would have been the wise thing to do."

"I'm sure it will be all right."

"Of course."

After a few minutes of quiet hugging, Sam kissed Jack's cheek and climbed off the worktable, scrambling to find her clothes and boots. "Dakota will be getting up in a few minutes."

In silence, Jack picked up his clothes and put them back on, smoothing out the wrinkles the best he could. Finally he said, "You're angry with me."

"No." Sam suddenly felt exhausted, and she collapsed into her drawing chair, hanging her head and staring at her boots. "Not angry, just confused. Totally confused about what you just said and what we just did and what we're doing. What are we *doing,*

Jack? I'm starting to think maybe we're both nuts."
Sam raised her eyes to see Jack staring at her with
concern. "You're trying to get elected, not fall in love
and have babies."

A wry smile appeared on Jack's lips. "I knew
there was something I'd overlooked."

Sam tried not to laugh but did anyway. "You're
amazing, Jack Tolliver. Sometimes I think you don't
even *want* to get elected!" She waited for his come-
back, but he didn't have one. "So? Do you?"

"I don't know."

Sam stood up from her chair, her jaw slack.
"Huh?"

"I said I don't know. And that's the truth."

Jack walked over to the middle window and
clasped his hands behind his back, staring out into
the winter afternoon. "Won't the Park Tudor car pool
be dropping off Greg and Lily soon?"

"In about a half hour. Now tell me what's going
on. Tell me why you're putting yourself through this
and, I might add, spending millions of dollars to get
somewhere you're not even sure you want to go."

"I'll do a serviceable job in the Senate."

"Only if you truly want to be there. If you don't,
you shouldn't run."

Jack turned to her and leaned back against the
windowsill, nodding. "All I ever really wanted was
football, Sam. I wish you could have known me back
then. I was fully alive, truly happy." He stopped suddenly, like that was the end of the conversation.

"Stay right here and talk to me, Jack."

He nodded and took a deep breath. "I don't know

why I'm saying all this. I've never told anyone what I think I'm about to tell you. Not even Kara or Stu."

"Maybe it's time you let it out."

He looked at her, tears welling in his eyes, and nodded. "The thing is, one day I had it all—I was breaking every fucking record there was—and the next day, I was dog food. Simple as that, Sam. Everything I'd ever done was instantly blown to hell by the fact that I'd been hit harder and hurt worse than just about anyone who'd ever played the game. And that's . . . that's not—" His voice began to crack and he used the back of his hand to take a quick swipe at his eyes. "That's not what I deserved to be remembered for."

Sam took a step toward him. It killed her to see Jack like this.

He held up his palm. "No, sweetheart. Let me finish this." Jack's beautiful mouth became pulled and thin. "The day we met, I told you that the only things Tolliver men did well were football and politics—do you remember that?"

"I remember."

"Well, that's what I'd always been told. From the time I was a kid, I'd been informed that I'd do football and then I'd do politics, like my dad and his dad. But football was stolen from me—fuckin' ripped away like my muscle from my bone and I never fuckin' got over it!"

He looked away toward the back wall of the studio and took several deep breaths. Sam watched him swallow hard before he could talk. "I missed out on the joy and went right to the obligation and never let that bitterness go. I think I went dead inside. All I wanted after the injury was distraction—anything to keep my mind off how fuckin' angry I was. Politics was just something to do. Women were a game. I behaved like a real dick."

Sam raised an eyebrow but said nothing.

He looked up at her and produced a sheepish smile. "So basically, the day you met me in Stuart's office, not only was I a dick, but I was a dead man."

Sam inched closer still and stroked his shoulder lightly. "You looked pretty good for a dickhead dead guy."

Jack cracked a smile, pushed himself from the windowsill, and walked by Sam, letting his hand brush across her cheek as he went. He walked to the far window and gazed out. "I've been going through the motions, you know? Doing what MDT expected of me just to get her off my back. Never feeling any real passion for what I was doing with my life or anyone in it. Never getting close enough to a woman to risk getting slammed to the ground and having it hurt as bad as my knee."

Sam cocked her head to the side and studied his wide, strong back. "Excuse me for asking, but when were you ever hurt by a woman? I must have missed that story."

Jack looked over his shoulder. "Oh, you know. The first woman in my life—my mother. Not exactly the warmest female on earth."

"So I've seen."

Jack turned back to face Sam and crossed his arms over his chest. "You know about the twins, right?

Well, when they died, that was the end of everything. I never felt like I had a mom after that. She was empty. Colder than ever. And all she cared about was my dad, and I seemed to always be in the way, never what she really wanted, which was the twins. So, yeah. Marguerite slammed me to the ground real good. And I never forgot it."

Sam reached out and touched his hard forearm. He uncrossed his arms and grabbed her hand in his.

"But you took the risk with me. Why, Jack?"

He laughed. "Maybe because you're such a little pipsqueak that I know you can't do shit to me."

Sam smiled at that. "How sweet."

"Or maybe it's just that you're the most loving, warm, normal, real, hardworking woman I've ever met. I see you with your kids and Simon, and with Monté, and I'm in awe of you. I think your warmth has thawed me out."

"You're not so dead anymore."

"I have a pulse these days."

"I can attest to that."

"And I'm not such a dick."

"I never thought you were."

"It's all because of you, Sam. You know that?"

She shook her head. "It's because of *you*. You decided it was more fun to be alive than dead. You decided to let down your guard and let someone see your heart. I'm glad you chose me, Jack, because I really love that heart of yours."

He squeezed her hand tighter.

"So are you going to stay in the race or not?"

"I think I am."

"Why? What are you doing it for?"

Jack laced his fingers with Sam's and stared at their joined hands for several long moments. When he looked up, he had a pensive smile on his face. "I think my motivation would be a who, not a what. I'd do it for you and Lily and Greg and Ben, if that would be OK with you. For Monté and Simon and for everyone who needs someone to speak up for them."

"Now that sounds like a man running for office."

"Do I have your vote?"

"You can have my vote and anything else you want."

The door opened with a creak, and Sam had just enough time to pull her hand away from Jack's before a half-asleep Dakota stumbled into the room. He was still wearing his pajama bottoms, which was never a good omen.

"Change me now, Mommy."

Jack straightened up and gave Sam a chaste kiss on the cheek. "Let me handle this one."

The man had no idea what he was volunteering for, and Sam did her best to convince him that now was not the time to broaden his horizons. But Jack wouldn't listen.

"I can handle one wet diaper, Sam. I was an NFL quarterback, the former lieutenant governor of Indiana. I'm going to be a U.S. Senator. You just stay in here and sketch and I'll let you know when the mission is accomplished."

Sam shrugged. "Go for it, big guy." She watched Dakota take Jack's hand and follow him out of the studio, walking like a cowboy packin' some serious heat. Sam shook her head, figuring that a man who'd been in politics as long as Jack had was probably better equipped for the job than most.

Jack looked down at the kid, happily scanning a little plastic book while yet another gullible grown-up tended to his unpleasant personal hygiene. Jack laughed to himself. This went way beyond the toddler equivalent of reading *Sports Illustrated* in the john—this kid looked like a king who couldn't be bothered with wiping himself.

"This is no way to live, boy," Jack announced, throwing the disgusting wad of plastic and wipes in the diaper pail, deciding he would use the toddler's basic male nature to get him out of this rut once and for all. "Hey, Ben? You want to play a game with me?"

The child blinked and looked askance at Jack over his Thomas the Tank Engine picture book. "Hide-and-seek?"

"Nope."

"Catch?"

"Not exactly."

"What?"

"I'm going to show you how to do something only men can do—girls can never do this no matter how hard they try. You interested?"

The child put the book aside and looked down the length of his belly to judge how well Jack completed his assignment. He pulled on the diaper tabs to make sure they'd hold. "Did you 'member to use the wipes, Mr. Jack?"

"I remembered, champ."

"OK, let's play."

Jack helped the kid off the changing table and headed to the bathroom across the hall. The child stopped in his tracks and shook his head. "No. No, no, no, no, no."

Jack had to admire Ben's resolve. It would definitely come in handy in his future, if only he could harness it for good and not this kind of pure evil.

He glanced over his shoulder. "Hey, man, not to worry. I'm just washing my hands. Stay out in the hall and wait for me, please, because there's nothing to see in here."

As he hoped, Ben immediately entered the bathroom with an expectant look on his face. He glanced nervously at the toilet, then averted his eyes.

Jack knew he had to move fast. He needed something that would float. Something colorful would be best. Something that could be flushed without destroying the whole plumbing system.

He wracked his brain for anything that might be upstairs in the guest wing of the house. "Hey, Ben, would you do me a favor? Do you know what sticky notes are?"

Ben frowned. "No."

"The tiny square notes you stick on things? Sometimes they come in colors like yellow or pink or blue. I bet Greg might have some on his desk."

"Oh, sure. I like those."

"Can you get some? We'll meet back here and play our game."

"OK, Mr. Jack."

After more than five minutes, Jack's hands were pruning, but the child did return with a little robin's-egg blue pack of sticky notes.

"Why are you still in the bathroom, Mr. Jack?"

"My hands were real dirty. Hey, thanks, man!" Jack toweled off quickly, raised the toilet seat, and threw a few tiny pieces of blue paper into the water.

"Uh-oh," Ben said.

"Check this out. Girls can't do this."

"Really?"

"I'm totally serious." Jack unzipped his fly and set his sights on the paper, dunking it and sending it spinning. "Hey, would you look at that! I got one!"

Ben walked a step closer and peered into the toilet, his eyes growing big with interest. He pointed a little chubby finger. "Get that one!"

"No problem, kid. They can run, but they can't hide!"

Ben was already wrestling with his pants, and Jack was impressed with how quickly the kid could drop trou. He stood next to the toilet and tried to shoot, but his aim was a bit off and he struck the back of the toilet.

"Uh-oh."

"No problem, pal. Happens to the best of us. Girls can't do that, either."

"Really?"

"At least I don't think so. Need a better angle?"

Ben nodded and Jack lifted him up a bit so he could shoot down into the bowl. "I got 'em!" Ben cried.

"You did!"

"I got that guy, too!"

"Nice work, ace."

"Die, die, die!"

OK, maybe that was enough. Jack put the kid down and zipped up his own pants just as he noticed Sam standing in the hallway outside the bathroom door, her mouth and eyes wide open. Jack put a finger to his lips, then helped Ben with his pants.

"Think you might want to play again?" Jack asked, flushing.

"Yeah! When?"

"Well, let's see. Maybe the next time you think you might have to pee. Or whenever. We don't have to do it right away. How about sometime next week?"

The child's eyes narrowed and his mouth tightened. He stared a long moment at Jack before he let go with a deep sigh. "OK, Mr. Jack. I will tell you the next time I think I have to pee-pee, but my name is Dakota, not Ben."

Jack and Sam locked eyes for a moment and it was all Jack could do not to bust loose with laughter. This kid was a born diplomat, or car salesman. He smiled down at the little bugger. "You got it, Dakota."

About an hour later they were playing "Drown the Bad Guys" again. Jack was awfully proud when, a week later, Sam told him the kid was finally, officially, thoroughly, potty-trained.

Jack found it ironic how the tables had turned. They no longer lived in fear of Ben—no, Dakota—

taking off his pants in public, while Jack, on the other hand, was taking off his pants in private and on a regular basis, thanks to the little guy's grateful mother.

12

This adventure was either the start of a whole new life for Mitch or one whopper of a stupid decision, and as he looked over at his first-class travel companion Mitch couldn't be sure which it was. The man's name was Brandon Mikluski or McMurtry or something, and he looked a little shady, like a preppy hatchet man. He was well dressed, educated, and nerdy. He didn't say much. So far, he'd only given Mitch the bare facts.

An anonymous benefactor had been kind enough to pay off all of Mitch's back child support, plus find him an apartment and a job and a used car. All that was in exchange for a little information about his ex-wife. When Mitch had first heard this proposition over the phone two weeks ago, he thought for sure it was the police pulling a sting on him. He'd read about stuff like that—a whole slew of deadbeat dads were once rounded up when they'd received invitations to a free prime-rib buffet and a vacation time-share presentation. They all showed up expecting a free meal and a slide show and got handcuffed instead. So Mitch told the guy on the phone not to bother with the under-cover crap—he was ready to turn himself in. But this Brandon fellow, who was the dude on the phone, as it turned out, just laughed and laughed. He assured Mitch he wasn't the police, and it turned out he wasn't lying.

So now Mitch found himself in a pale gray tufted leather seat sipping a Bloody Mary on a Delta Airlines flight from Atlanta to Indianapolis. He could hardly believe that in a few days, if everything went like this Brandon guy told him it would, he'd be able to see his kids again. All he had to do was go talk to Sam and get her to admit the truth about something on tape. When-ever he asked Brandon exactly what truth he was sup-posed to weasel out of Sam, his response was, "We'll get to that." When Mitch asked who was so hot for this tidbit of information Brandon said, "It's not necessary that you know."

Mitch wasn't stupid. He knew that what he was being asked to do was definitely sleazy and maybe even illegal. But how else was he ever going to pay the child support he owed? And how could he ever see his kids again unless he did?

"Is Samantha in some kind of trouble?" Mitch asked again.

"I told you, no. She and the children are doing fine, apparently."

"How do you know her?"

"I don't. It's more of a friend of a friend kind of arrangement."

"I don't want her to get hurt."

With that, Brandon turned his round, red face to Mitch and smiled big. "Of course you don't. Clearly, you've always had her best interests at heart."

That stung. "You don't know anything."

"Sure I do," Brandon said, looking out the plane window as if he was bored with the conversation. "She supported you and your goofy glass pods for over a decade and then you knocked her up one last time, decided you preferred boys, and hit the road. I'm sure all those support checks just got lost in the mail."

Mitch took a long chug of his Bloody Mary and crunched on the celery stick, hating that even a part of what that chubby little ass-wipe just said about him was true. He really had been selfish, but he'd been suffocating trying to live a lie with Sam. He could never go back to that existence. But maybe this was a chance to return his life to some kind of order and make it up to the kids the best he could.

"It's none of your business, but I really did make the best decision I could at the time I had to make it." Mitch had read that line in some kind of self-help book a few years back and it had resonated with him.

"Whatever." Brandon stared out at the apparently fascinating view of empty sky at cruising altitude.

"I'm only doing this because I want to see my children again."

Brandon sighed with impatience. "Fine. Here." He reached between his fat legs and retrieved his laptop computer and hit the power switch. "You can see them again right now if you want."

Within a few moments, Mitch was staring, incredulous, at a videotape of Samantha and the children at some kind of political rally. Was that Dakota? It couldn't be! And Lily was so grown-up and beautiful! And Greg? Greg was almost a man! Mitch felt a ripping sensation in his belly. There was no way so much time had gone by, that he'd missed so much. He scrubbed at his eyes with his palms, knowing how they all must hate him. He felt like he might throw up.

". . . allegedly got engaged right before Tolliver announced his run for U.S. Senate. We thought that was a little too much of a coincidence."

Mitch raised his head and stared at the videotape again. Sam looked scared but lovely in a stunning maroon wrap dress, glancing up at a major hunk Mitch recognized as a former football star. He didn't know who was more beautiful—his ex-wife or the athlete. They made a gorgeous couple. "What did you just say?" Mitch asked, his head clearing in alarm. "What the hell is this? Who's 'we'? Is this some kind of dirty politics?"

"Samantha Monroe and Jack Tolliver claim to be engaged. We simply want to be know if it's a real relationship or a campaign ploy."

Mitch took another swig of vodka-laced tomato juice and tried to wrap his brain around what was going on. "Do you work for the mob?"

Brandon's eyes flashed in alarm before he shook his head. "Uh, no."

"So you're a flunky for his opponent and I'm just a dirty politician's errand boy?"

Brandon looked offended. "Absolutely not."

"Then what? Who would spend all this money to make me an honest man and bring me to Indianapolis on the off chance that I could get Sam to tell me what's going on? Who hates this Tolliver guy that much?"

"This isn't about revenge, Mr. Bergen. It's about truth, democracy, and—"

Mitch's laughter cut him off. "Whoever you work for, he's got to have exhausted all other options, because Sam probably won't give me the time of day, let alone reveal any of her secrets. I'm sure she fucking *hates* me."

"We figured you'd have the best shot of leveraging the truth out of her. Ex-husbands always know which buttons to push."

Mitch froze with a thought so horrible he couldn't believe it hadn't dawned on him until that moment. He swallowed hard. "Hey, Brandon, do you know if Monté McQueen is still in town, by any chance?"

Brandon frowned. "Who's that? Someone else you owe money to?"

"No. No." Mitch laughed uncomfortably, waiting for relief to settle over him. It didn't. "It's nothing. Never mind." Oh God, the idea of facing Sam's wrath was bad enough, but there was no way he'd survive an encounter with Monté. She'd warned him three years ago that if she ever saw him again she'd slice off his balls with her straight razor. Monté had always intimidated him.

Mitch noticed Brandon smiling, nodding for him to return his attention to the computer. It looked like a campaign ad, with some generic bluegrass music in the background and a voice-over going on about all Jack Tolliver's accomplishments. Then there was Sam! Mitch stared in stunned silence as his ex-wife held hands with the candidate while walking down some snowy small-town street, window-shopping for antiques and snuggling up to the politician. Sam looked so happy. And *damn,* her boyfriend was a hottie. For her sake, Mitch really hoped it wasn't a stunt.

The voice said, *"Jack Tolliver—a new partnership for a new Indiana,"* and the camera zoomed in on Sam's and the man's hands clasped tightly together.

It was so touching, Mitch thought he might cry.

Then he looked over to see a smarmy smile growing on Brandon's face, and Mitch knew with certainty that, oh yeah, he was making a huge mistake coming back to Indianapolis. This arrangement smelled bad from every angle. But hey—fifty-seven thousand dollars didn't fall from the sky every day.

Mitch reached between his legs to make sure his equipment was still intact, at least for the time being.

The Ball State auditorium was a mob scene, and Sam did her best to keep smiling, shake hands, and pretend to be comfortable. It was the first of three debates scheduled among the party's four declared candidates, and the hall was packed with students, university staff, press from every town in the state, and Joe Blows off the street.

Sam was standing near her second-row seat, surrounded by a clump of campaign staff and volunteers, many of whom she'd never met before tonight.

Of course there was Stuart, Jack's chief of staff, and Kara, his campaign manager and press secretary. There was also Jack's political director, deputy political director, constituent outreach director, research director, chief financial officer, county coordinator, and volunteer coordinator and a slew of college student volunteers all quite pumped up for the event, wearing *Tolliver for Senate* campaign buttons.

Everyone seemed to be excited about the endorsements Jack had been raking in from business and industry groups, farming groups, and labor organizations. It all sounded like good news and Kara couldn't stop smiling, so Sam smiled, too, and fanned herself.

She was perspiring, and she wondered if it was because the auditorium was warm, or because she was nervous, or because she wasn't used to wearing a thousand-dollar suit. She looked down at herself and shook her head. She was channeling the spirit of Jackie Kennedy tonight, courtesy of Kara, who'd taken her shopping just for this appearance. They'd settled on a beautiful designer suit in a chocolate brown wool and silk blend, with burgundy velvet embroidery on the cuffs, waist, and flared hem of the slim-style skirt. It was a very 1940s Hollywood starlet look with a modern twist, complimented by a pair of Alberta Ferretti pumps they'd found on sale and a burgundy suede cloche bag.

Jack had told her on the trip up from Indianapolis that he wouldn't be able to concentrate up onstage with her looking that stunning. He was always so good with the compliments.

The debate began, and Sam watched dutifully, rooting for Jack and smiling with every small victory he seemed to have against his opponents. He blew them all out of the water as far as looking senatorial went. He was cool and handsome and charming, while Congressman Manheimer was sweating bullets and had to wipe his brow with a handkerchief. Sam could have sworn that at one point, while Manheimer was going on about family values, Jack winked at her. He was such a bad boy, and she loved that about him.

The audience had been instructed to stay in their seats during commercial breaks and to wait until the intermission to use the restrooms. But Sam couldn't hold out. She really had to go and whispered to Kara that she'd be right back.

With great relief, she made it to the women's room and nearly tap-danced her way into an empty stall. She tried to shut the door, but it jammed, and Sam gasped when a hand crept in, then an arm pushed its way through. The door flew open, pinning Sam against the side wall.

"Sorry. But you and I need some private time." The woman slammed the door shut behind her.

"Being alone in here felt pretty private to me."

"You know what I mean."

"You're Christy Schoen."

The blonde's smile was very practiced. "I am. And you're Samantha Monroe, soon to be Samantha Tolliver."

"I was told you'd hunt me down eventually."

She appeared shocked. "That's an awfully harsh way of putting it, Ms. Monroe. I'm just doing my job."

Sam laughed. "So you do some of your best work in public bathrooms? Have you cornered Jack in the men's room yet?"

Christy chuckled, then steeled her eyes at Sam. "I'm giving you a chance to come clean—you get one chance to give me your side of the story before things get really messy."

Sam felt her pulse quicken and she was suddenly, unpleasantly, reminded why she came in here in the first place. "I really do have to use the restroom."

Christy didn't flinch. "Don't let me stop you."

"Whatever you say." Sam hitched up her skirt and pulled down the red satin thong over her stocking tops and began to squat. Christy's mouth fell open, and she turned to face the door while Sam did her business.

"I know what you're doing, Ms. Monroe."

"I'm peeing."

"I mean with Jack."

"All rightee, then." Sam flushed and pulled up her panties and straightened her skirt. "Would you please excuse me while I wash my hands?"

Christy turned around again, clearly furious. "We are on the record. Whatever you say to me is fair game."

"I would prefer you talk to Jack directly."

"He won't return my calls."

"Gee, I wonder why?"

"Besides, these questions are for you."

"Well, go ahead then. I'm missing the debate. What is it you'd like to ask me?"

Sam was suddenly grateful that Kara had prepared her so well. She felt surprisingly calm for someone being held hostage in a bathroom stall. Maybe that's what an exquisitely made suit could do for a woman's confidence.

"How did you meet Jack?"

"Kara DeMarinis has been a longtime client of mine at Le Cirque. She introduced me to him."

"How long have you known him?"

"Not long. We met in November."

"How in the world could you have been engaged by Christmas?"

"When something's right, you know it immediately."

Christy laughed. "Uh-huh. So, tell me all the things you know are just so *right* about your fiancé—some of the little things about Jack Tolliver that you just *love*."

Sam's spine tightened. Kara hadn't gone over these kinds of questions. Maybe because even Kara hadn't expected such a personal assault from Christy. So Sam relied on what her mother had always told her when she was a kid: "*When in doubt, tell the truth.*"

"He's a terrific kisser," Sam said, smiling. "I mean, *whew*! That man can kiss."

Christy snorted with impatience.

"He's opened his family estate to me and the kids. He's made us feel welcome and cared for."

"Yes. The entire Western Hemisphere has heard."

"He pays attention to the details. He'll surprise me sometimes by following up on little things that I've forgotten I even mentioned." Sam cocked her head and grinned at Christy. "He turned the old Sunset Lane nursery into a painting studio for me."

Christy frowned.

"And he makes me laugh. Jack's got a such a wonderful self-deprecating sense of humor."

Christy nearly choked. "I do believe that's the first time anyone's ever used that phrase in conjunction with Jack. Did you forget to take your medication today or something?"

Sam ignored her. "And ironically, even though he's a politician, he's a private person. I think it's because he's been through so much with his injury and rehabilitation. But he's opened up to me. He's shown me his pain and his hopes and I love him for that. I'm honored to have him as my friend and my future husband."

Christy nodded slowly, taking it all in. "Kara's sure trained you well. Please let her know that I'd be impressed if I weren't so nauseated." She crossed her arms over her chest. "And to think—on top of all that, Mr. Sensitivity just happens to be loaded. Or maybe you hadn't noticed?"

"I noticed."

"How convenient for you and your children."

"I would have loved Jack if he were a car mechanic."

"Or a poor glassblower?"

Sam felt a bolt of rage run through her limbs. She didn't like this woman. Not at all. And Sam was getting the feeling that this little bathroom stall get-together was more than an ambush—it was a direct threat of some kind.

"I'm not sure what you're looking for, Christy, but I'm afraid you're not going to find it here."

"Oh. Now that's where you're wrong. I'm going to find exactly what I'm looking for and you're going to give it to me, whether you realize you're doing it or not."

Sam frowned. "I don't think I understand."

Christy leaned in, her tiny pink nose just inches from Sam's face. "You and your kids materializing at Jack's side right after Ditto bowed out was a ridiculously obvious move, Ms. Monroe. I would have thought Jack was smarter than that, but I suspect it was Kara's idea."

"I have nothing to say to you."

"I know you two are not really engaged." Christy yanked Sam's left hand up to inspect the ring, which shut her up for a moment. "Nice touch."

"It's very beautiful, isn't it?"

Christy narrowed her eyes. "I know this is all for the benefit of his campaign and I suspect he's paying you. I mean, really—you're *so* not his type! He'd never marry a divorced woman your age who had kids! A hairstylist? It's ridiculous! And I'm going to prove it." She leaned away, apparently satisfied with herself, and Sam noticed that Christy's jaw seemed a little puffy. "That man won't be able to run for the zoning commission when I get this story. You can pass that on."

"Thanks. I will. Now, if you'll excuse me." Sam reached for the door latch, but unbelievably, Christy knocked her hand away.

"Don't touch me," Sam said, all sense of play gone from her voice. "I will file charges."

"Actually, I envision charges being filed against you and Jack both when the truth comes out."

Sam shook her head. "You know, I haven't been in a fight in the girls' bathroom since ninth grade and I'm way overdressed for one today, but I swear, if you don't move your blond highlights away from that door, you're going to regret it."

Christy didn't budge. "This is your last chance, Ms. Monroe. You tell me what the real story is with Jack and things will go much easier for you in the long run."

"Get away from the door."

"I have ways to find out the truth whether you co-operate or not."

"You're crazy."

"All right—so tell me what his scar looks like, then. If you know him so well, then tell me what his bad knee looks like. He's psycho about not letting anyone see how screwed up it is."

That was news to Sam, since he'd never tried to hide it from her. She shrugged. "Well, there's a scar about six inches long that runs up the center of his kneecap and one about four inches that runs up the back of his knee. He's lost most sensation there, so when I kiss him behind his knee he can't feel it."

Christy snarled.

"He has two deep incisions on the outside of his thigh. There are several smaller marks where he had arthroscopic surgery later on. And his left calf looks a little misshapen from being reattached." Sam smiled generously. "And by the way, he has the cutest little mole on the inside of his left leg, about an inch from his penis."

Christy's mouth fell open.

Sam took advantage of her surprise by grabbing the latch and pulling the door open, trapping Christy against the wall as she made her escape.

It was another three hours before Sam could tell anyone about her restroom rendezvous, because once the debate was over, Jack dropped in on four network mobile news sets and then made appearances at the local Muncie station's eleven o'clock news. It was past one in the morning when Sam sat with Kara in the backseat of Stuart's BMW, while Jack sat in the front. Kara and Stuart had been drinking so much coffee throughout the evening that they couldn't stop talking.

"As we've always known, Charlie Manheimer is your only threat. The rest of those schmoes are background noise."

"Yeah," was Jack's one-word response to Stuart's comment.

"He seemed very nice," Sam said, recalling her brief introduction to Manheimer that night, a handsome gentleman in his late sixties with clear blue eyes and stark white hair.

"Of course he *seems* nice," Kara said. "He's a three-term congressman. He's got the act down by now."

Sam frowned and looked out at Highway 69 passing by in a dark blur. "Are there any just plain good folks in politics? Who actually care about people more than power and ego?" No one answered her.

"OK, maybe that was a naïve question but I was just curious."

"Basically, *hell* no," Stuart said with a laugh.

"I think there are many politicians who earnestly care about their constituents," Kara corrected him, then turned to Sam. "But earnestness doesn't get you into national office—money does."

"And it's a damn shame," Jack said, turning around.

Stuart caught Sam's eye in the rearview mirror. "Am I dropping you off at Sunset Lane, Sam?"

Before Sam could respond, Jack said, "Since you and Kara live downtown, just drop Sam at my place and I'll drive her home."

"You sure you don't mind?"

"It's no problem."

Sam felt Kara's keen stare on the side of her face. It was the perfect time to tell everyone about her ladies' room assault.

"She did *what*?" Kara nearly jumped out of her seat belt.

"Oh, man," Stu said.

Jack had turned all the way around to study Sam, his mouth tight. "Did she hurt you?"

"Of course not. I could take her out if I had to."

"Can I watch?" Stuart said.

Jack laughed.

Kara didn't. "She said she knows Jack is paying you?"

Sam hadn't often seen Kara that worried.

"She said she suspects he's paying me, because I'm so not Jack's type."

One of Jack's dark eyebrows arched high on his forehead. "Oh, really?"

"Yes." Sam looked down at her hands folded in her lap and fought back tears. She'd been over-the-top emotional the last few days, and it was annoying. She took a breath and looked up again. "Christy said you'd never marry someone my age who was divorced and had three kids, especially someone who was a hairstylist. She said it was obvious we were brought in just for the election."

"Damn," Stu said.

"The contract is a private matter," Kara said, reassuring herself as much as Sam, it seemed. "Christy has no access to your banking records, Sam. She's not a cop and even then it takes a court order. She's just trying to intimidate you."

"We all know she's jealous," Stu said, turning down the car's heat. "She's pissed that she's not the woman at Jack's side right now."

"Oh," Sam said quietly. "I guess I didn't realize they were that serious."

"We weren't," Jack said.

"That woman would do anything for a story this big," Kara said. "She's convinced she's national network material and just needs one big break. Well, she's not getting her big break here, that's for damn sure."

The rest of the way back to the city, Sam kept her eyes closed as if she were asleep. She wasn't. She was exhausted and felt incredibly sad, too hot, and a little dizzy, but there was no way she could sleep. She wondered how Jack could have ever been interested in someone like Christy Schoen, even casually. She knew that there had been many women in his life, but she'd always convinced herself that there was something exceptional about each one. Christy was pretty, in a high school cheerleader kind of way, but she was plastic and mean and selfish. How could the same man who was attracted to *that* be attracted to her?

"Every time I saw you out there in the audience, I wanted to rip that beautiful suit off your body and molest you."

"Was this before or after Manheimer's family values speech?"

Jack chuckled and continued to push Sam through his living room, past the kitchen and dining room, and back toward his bedroom.

"Is this the grand tour of your condo? Because it's hard to see much walking backward like this."

"This is the grand tour of my sheets, baby."

Jack was so turned on he couldn't believe it. Samantha was an irresistible combination of traits all squeezed inside one petite, sweet, steady woman. It seemed even being trapped in a bathroom stall with Christy Schoen hadn't fazed her. Sam was a marvel. A warrior princess. And sexy as hell.

"I love you, Samantha."

The shock in Samantha's eyes was compounded by the unceremonious way he'd just dumped her on his unmade bed. He threw his body over hers.

"I love you so much. I want you and the kids to

move in with me after the primary. Seriously. I don't give a damn who thinks what. Be mine, Sam. Please."

Her sweet little red mouth opened in awe and Jack didn't wait for an answer. He just attacked her, covered her mouth and chin and face and throat in kisses, moved her hands up over her head, and showed her what she meant to him.

She was a treasure. He unbuttoned the front of her suit jacket and spread his fingers wide to grasp her smooth, pale waist. He reached around and undid the side zipper on her skirt, pulling until it cleared her hips. He kissed her navel, roamed his hands over her little round belly, slipped his tongue under the band of what had obviously become Sam's special occasion panties—the infamous red thong. He was going to buy her dozens more.

It took him only a few moments to get the thong and skirt completely off her body, followed by her jacket and bra, Sam's moans urging him on. Soon she was dressed only in a pair of chocolate brown hold-up stockings and a pair of sexy high heels, her little pussy open and swollen for him already.

"I love you, Sam. Please, God, tell me you love me, too."

Her delicate arms went around his body and she gripped him tight. Her lips felt so good on his face and he marveled at the urgent way her hands pulled at his clothes. "I love you, Jack. I've loved you right from the start. I couldn't defend myself."

He helped her struggle with his tie and dress shirt,

then ripped his undershirt over his head. "Defend yourself? From little ole me?"

Sam laughed just as he raised and separated her thighs, licking along the length of her slit. She tasted salty and sweet and potent, and Jack wanted to drown in that damp heaven.

"You're just too good at this," she groaned. "I couldn't resist you."

Jack stopped long enough to correct her. "No baby, you're the one who's good. You're the one who's irresistible."

"Maybe we're just good together," she whispered, digging her nails into his shoulders. "And maybe there's no reason to try to resist each other anymore."

"I can't think of a single one."

Jack dragged his lips up the front of her body and kissed her hard, giving her a taste of herself. He felt her hips start to undulate beneath him and he felt certain he would die if he couldn't get inside her.

"Fuck me now, Sam," he said, rolling over on his back, pulling her with him. He watched in wonder as she spread her thighs and slowly lowered herself on his erection. There was no condom and no time to worry about that fact. She was around him, gripping him, milking him with her body, those gorgeous blue eyes looking right into his soul.

He put his hands on her hips to guide her, making sure her movements were slow and encompassed him along his entire length, from balls deep to the very tip and back again.

"You like that, Jack?"

"It's the most amazing thing I've ever felt. It's always like this with you. Why didn't I meet you years ago?"

"Because you were a football star and I was a hairdresser with a husband and kids."

"Right." Jack reached up and wrapped his arms around Sam's delicate frame, pulling her down so that her breasts were crushed against his chest. "I'm so in love with you, sweetie. Do you know that?"

He felt Sam's head nodding up and down against his shoulder. He stroked her back.

"I am in love with you, too, Jack."

He rolled Sam over onto her back again and propped himself up on his hands. He loved looking down at her whole body, so creamy and small and female. It felt like everything he'd ever done with any other woman had only been a dry run. Nothing ever felt this complete, this right.

Sam screamed out when he bit her nipple, and he could feel her coming all over him. "Yes, Sam, let it go. Give me everything, sweetheart." It was astounding how hot she felt to his touch, so full and sweet, with her scent rich and heavy in the air.

Sam pulled his mouth to hers roughly, and they kissed each other hard, sealing in his love for her and her love for him as his body roared and erupted inside her.

Jack let himself swim in the warm comfort of Sam's arms, still inside her, his heart and soul at rest, and he suddenly needed her to understand something. Jack rolled to the side and pulled her tight into his arms.

"You really are my type, Sam." He stroked her curls while she snuggled closer, her breath warm on his chest. "You are what I have always wanted, and I was about to give up that I'd ever find you."

"We found each other."

"We did."

"It was just an unorthodox way of meeting."

"Highly unorthodox." Jack kissed the top of her head. "You've just got to tell me—what perfume do you wear? I swear I've never smelled anything like it. I have dreams about the way you smell."

She chuckled softly. "It's not perfume. It's a combination of essential oils I mix myself—jasmine, rose, and a little ylang-ylang."

"Isn't that a rap group?"

Samantha squeezed him tight. "I'm glad you like it. All those oils together are called 'fire nature.' "

"It fits you, my little fiery one."

She kissed his cheek. "Am I really what you've been looking for?"

"Absolutely. And I wonder sometimes if I even knew what I wanted before I met you. All I know is I saw you, and I started to buzz all over, and a very loud voice in my head said, *This one*. I guess some things in life are just a mystery."

"The best things usually are."

"So when did you know about me? Was it at our first meeting?"

"Hmm." Sam adjusted her position so that she was lying directly on top of him, stretched out from head to toe. God, he loved that arrangement. He stroked the firm globes of her butt and breathed her in.

"As you may recall, you fell on the floor at our first meeting."

"Ah, yes."

"I thought you were kind of goofy. Then I just planned to use you for sex."

He laughed so hard that he nearly knocked Sam off her perch. "Oh, how the tables turn, baby."

She kissed him sweetly and laughed with him. "But you know, that didn't last long, and I found myself falling a little bit every day. By Christmas, it was a done deal."

"Or just starting."

"True."

"Sam? What have you been looking for?"

Her body stilled and her breathing slowed, and Jack knew she was weighing her answer. He wasn't sure if he liked that idea—he wanted her to be free to say what was on her mind, no matter what it was. He expected candor from his advisers, and if Sam was going to be his woman, for real, he'd want the same from her. He'd need it. "Please tell me, Sam."

She sat up, straddled his body, and placed her hands on his chest. He wasn't sure he could carry on a conversation with her like this, displayed in all her glory in front of him, his very own little fiery vixen of love.

"I've always wanted to be part of a real couple, Jack. A man and a woman who are passionate about each other, but treat each other with respect and kindness. I've never had that. Mitch was . . . well, he wasn't passionate about me, for one, and I guess we all found out why that was." Sam tried to smile and it broke Jack's heart.

"It wasn't your fault that he was gay, sweetheart."

"I know that." When she nodded, her curls spilled into her face. He reached up and brushed them away from her cheek.

"He was pretending," Jack said. "It was never real for him, and frankly, I am very glad he figured that out. What I can't understand is that he left his children. That was despicable."

Sam tilted her head and looked at him seriously. "Mitch basically used me, Jack. Once I got pregnant and we decided to get married, I supported him—he never turned a profit with his glass. It wasn't a partnership and it sure wasn't kind, and that's what was missing in our marriage—passion, respect, and kindness—and that's what I want now, with you."

"Let me give that to you."

"Let's give that to each other."

"I would do anything in the world for you, Samantha."

"Then love me. Just love me and let me love you back and everything else will find its place."

Jack sat up and grabbed Sam tight, rolled with her again and again, and after some intense kissing, some laughing, and after she rubbed all over him in a way that made him glad he was alive, he found his place. His place was inside her, loving her, for real.

13

"You sure you're OK, Sammy? You look a little thin."

"Ha! I'm thin? Look at you! You look absolutely stunning!" Sam glanced up from the stack of mail she was sorting and smiled at Monté. A couple months at the gym had done wonders for her friend.

"Yeah, I got no complaints. I'm still managing to lose me some and get me some all in the same place."

The two women laughed while the kids swam. It was a pleasure to hear Greg giving Lily hell so flawlessly.

"Maybe your suit wouldn't keep falling down if you grew some boobs," he was saying to his sister, in between splashes. "We sure don't want to see anything you got, so don't blame us."

Sam smiled. No, her kids' manners hadn't improved much, but Greg's speech therapy was going gangbusters.

She continued to sort through the mail, feeling a

solid peace at her core. She was in love with Jack. The campaign was going extremely well. They would find a way to break it to everyone after the primary that they really were a couple and planned to stay that way. For the first time in many years, Sam felt real joy when she imagined her future.

Sam's gaze fell to the plain white envelope in her hand, and she began to tremble. Her heart nearly stopped. She studied the return address, written in handwriting familiar and alien at the same time. Her head began to spin. This couldn't be.

"Oh my God," Sam whispered.

"What's that?" Monté asked. "The bank telling you they've run out of storage room for your money?"

Sam slowly raised her eyes from the envelope and tried to focus on Monte's face, which was now quite concerned.

"Sammy? What the hell—?"

"It's a letter from Mitchell."

Monté blinked and wobbled her head on her neck a few times. "Say what?"

"I . . . I . . . can't open this. Here." She shoved the letter in Monté's hand and leaned back in the lounge chair, hugging herself.

"You want me to open this? What if it has anthrax in it?"

"I'm sure the only thing in there is a load of bullshit," Sam said.

Monté stared at the envelope, frowning. "This is an Indianapolis address. Now how in the world is that possible? I feel the need to load up my razor and go for a drive."

"Just read it to me, please."

Monté shook her head slowly several times as she ripped open the flap and pulled out a piece of lined paper torn from a spiral notebook. "Well, let's see now. . . ." Monté checked to make sure all the kids were busy in the pool and then she began to read in a quiet voice:

> " '*Dear Sam:*
>
> " '*I know you must be shocked to get this letter from me. Believe me, I'm shocked to be mailing it. First, please let me apologize to you for leaving the way I did and not living up to my responsibilities to the children. I have done a lot of soul-searching lately, and I know I was wrong. I won't ask you to forgive me. I think that would be asking too much.*' "

"You know that's right," Monté said. "Keep going."

> " '*I've finally gotten my life together after a long, unhappy time. I've made a lot of poor decisions and I got myself into trouble, financially and in my personal life. But things are looking up.*
>
> " '*I've attached a copy of a cashier's check that was delivered to the county on Thursday. I have paid all the child support I owe and hope to fulfill my obligations from here on out. All you have to do is go to the prosecutor's office and pick up the check or make arrangements for automatic deposit. I have a hearing in court in a couple months, where I will probably receive probation for skipping out, but I am willing to face up to my mistakes.*' "

Monté glanced up at Sam with her eyes wide. Then she held up the letter and showed Sam the copy of the check, to the amount of fifty-seven thousand dollars. "When it rains, it pours, I guess."

Sam was having trouble breathing. "Is there anything else?"

Monté cleared her throat and finished reading.

> " 'The only thing I would ask of you is that you meet me sometime soon so that I can talk to you in person, apologize to you in person, and discuss with you how I might go about seeing the kids.' "

Monté pursed her lips and took a long moment to mull that over. "The man must be on crack," she said.

"Don't joke. He just might be."

> " 'So please call me at the number below and let me know where and when it would be convenient to meet. I look forward to seeing you, and I thank you for taking such good care of the kids while I was away.' "

Monté folded the letter and placed it back in the envelope, handing it to Sam without further comment. Sam doubled the envelope and shoved it in her pants pocket, realizing her fingers were numb.

"I can't believe this." Sam covered her face in her hands and tried to stop breathing so hard. Eventually, she looked up and stared at Monté, who stared back at her. "I never imagined he'd pay up and ask to see the kids. It will kill them. Dakota doesn't know that man from Adam!"

Monté reached over and held her hand. "Sam, you need to talk to Denny about this, ask her what you are legally obligated to do here. Mitch may not even have a right to see them. I don't know."

Sam nodded, feeling a little bit better, but it occurred to her that her sense of hard-won peace had just been shattered, all because of Mitch. The irony was that Sam would have killed to have that check six months before, but now it was meaningless. She didn't even want the money if it meant she had to deal with him—she'd just give it to some kind of victims' fund or a children's charity.

Why had Mitch chosen to play nice right *now*?

"I've got a very bad feeling about this," Sam said to Monté.

"You, too, huh? Well, just promise me one thing—you will not go see that man without me."

"That's a promise. Don't forget to bring your razor."

This was a monumental waste of time, and Christy was going to be late for her hair appointment with Marcia, which would then make her late for her lunch date with Brandon. But her dentist had practically begged her to go see this oral surgeon fellow, so there she was, sitting in a waiting room as the precious minutes ticked by, alternating her glances between the latest *Cosmo* magazine and her watch. It struck Christy as proof that the apocalypse was indeed near when a mainstream woman's magazine devoted a trio of articles to how to perform oral sex on a man. Where had the charm gone? Where was the genteel romance? What had become of basic human decency?

Besides, her jaw had been so sore lately that giving anyone a blow job was the last thing on her to-do list.

"Ms. Schoen?"

Finally! Christy followed the nurse back to the examination room and waited. It was a pleasant shock to see a very attractive young doctor enter the room and smile down at her. He had dark hair and smoky gray eyes that reminded her a little of Jack Tolliver. That was unfortunate. She'd never be able to have a relationship with him, then.

"I don't think you can wait much longer on the extraction, Ms. Schoen," he said, examining her chart and X-rays. "I know you've been putting this off for almost a year, and my concern is that you'll develop a systemic infection." He smiled down at her. "I've always said that an impacted wisdom tooth is like infidelity—it's got to come out sooner or later—and you have four of those little gems."

Christy wasn't sure if he was joking, but she knew she didn't want a jokester slicing open her gums.

"I understand that you are quite skittish about this procedure. Many patients are, but most everyone is pleasantly surprised that the discomfort is less than they feared. You will receive general anesthesia and a prescription for pain relief. We recommend that you take off a couple days to recuperate and heal. Speaking and chewing will not be comfortable activities for at least twenty-four hours."

Well, that certainly sealed the deal. "I can't possibly do this until after the primary election, which is May 9."

The doctor scowled and looked over at a wall calendar. "That's five weeks from now."

"I realize that."

"I'm not sure you can hang on that long."

"I have no choice."

"Are you involved in the mayoral campaign or something?"

Christy gasped. "There is no mayoral campaign this year. I am the political reporter for Channel Ten News and the host of *Capitol Update with Christy Schoen*. It's aired Sundays at two P.M. and in three time slots later in the week."

The doctor shrugged, jotting down some notes in Christy's chart. "I'm sorry. I don't watch much television."

Christy left the office with an appointment card for May 11 at 8:00 A.M., wondering if she could trust a man who didn't watch TV. She was sure she could find some other competent oral surgeon between now and then.

Her appointment with Marcia whizzed by without much to show for it except that her hair was up to snuff. Marcia had seemed hesitant to discuss anything having to do with Samantha Monroe, and that Monté woman dished out looks that would have scared the crap out of a weaker individual, so Christy just played it cool. The last thing she wanted was to tip anyone off that she was overly interested in Samantha Monroe.

Only Brandon knew. And sitting across from him at Michael Pi's Chinese restaurant, Christy had to say she had been wise to enlist his help. He'd carried out everything flawlessly to this point. He'd convinced Mitch Bergen to come on board and dragged him back to town; he'd managed to remain anonymous while paying Mitch's child support debt with a cashier's check; he'd found a cheap place for Mitch to live and a cheap secondhand car for him to drive; he'd even gotten Mitch a job in the mail room at an insurance company. Brandon was turning out to be a brilliant assistant.

Sure, there were times when Christy cringed at how much this was costing her. But the way she figured it, it was an investment in her future. She had cashed out some of the Microsoft stock her daddy gave her as a high school graduation present (something that pissed her off back then) to meet Mitch's expenses. When this story broke and when the network offers started pouring in, she knew she could recoup her loss in a matter of months.

"So, when do you think you'll have time to let me make you that quiet dinner for two?"

Christy realized she would have to be quite careful with this part of the arrangement. She was leading Brandon on until the story broke, and she needed to keep him an ally forever afterward. She had to admit that his savvy had impressed her. And sometimes she liked his smile. But she wasn't ready for any quiet dinner for two at his place.

"Let's plan on celebrating after the story breaks."

"I can't wait that long. I love you, Christy. I've always loved you."

She reached out and stroked Brandon's soft hand.

"We're going to be having so much fun in the next few weeks that the time will fly by."

A few moments later, Brandon asked Christy why she'd barely touched her General Tso's chicken.

"My wisdom teeth have been bothering me. I need to have them removed after the primary."

Brandon stopped chewing and shook his head, quickly wiping his mouth with a napkin. "You better plan on taking a week off. I'll come to your place to take care of you."

Christy felt a shock course through her. "A week?"

"Oh God, yes. Three of my four were impacted, and I was a wreck for a week. I really pissed off my roommate at the time because the anesthesia made me nutso. Apparently, I just rambled on about everything and I told him what an asshole I thought he was. He moved out three days later and stuck me with the utilities."

This was very disturbing news. Christy took a sip of ice water and cursed herself for not taking care of this a year ago, when it first became a problem. She swore to herself right then that she'd never again put off for tomorrow what she could do today.

"We need to get Mitch Bergen wired and send him in."

"Sam Monroe hasn't even indicated she got his letter."

"That's not good."

"She hasn't picked up the check, either. I looked into it."

"Damn. This has got to work."

Brandon smiled at her. "It will. Give it a little time. You really are a genius, you know."

Christy smiled at him and allowed him to hold her hand across the table. "I know," she said.

Marguerite Tolliver was thoroughly displeased. She'd been back in Naples since mid-January and couldn't seem to shake the sense of impending doom she'd brought with her from Indianapolis. Jack wouldn't listen to her. He was acting like a hormonal college boy. He was absolutely smitten with that middle-aged lingerie model he had squirreled away at Sunset Lane. He'd even given that woman his Great-grandmother Tolliver's wedding ring to wear around town as a lark! It was despicable, but no matter how Marguerite tried to approach Jack, he shut her down. Just recalling the specifics of their last conversation made her feel unwell.

"I thought you wanted me to be a U.S. Senator," Jack had said, sitting next to her on Gordon's old office sofa. It had disturbed her that her son's voice seemed devoid of emotion.

"Of course I do! You will do splendidly on Capitol Hill!"

"Then let me handle my personal life and my campaign. I know what I'm doing."

"But Jack—I don't think you do. This was a misguided idea from the start. If anyone finds out what you've been up to, your political fortunes will be ruined forever. I don't want to see you hurt like that."

"You mean you don't want to see the Tolliver name hurt like that."

"It's more than that."

"I don't know that it's ever been more than that for you, Marguerite. I don't know if you've ever seen me as more than someone to carry on the name."

Oh, how that had hurt her! She knew she'd never been the world's most touchy-feely mother, but she'd always been proud of Jack and had encouraged him every step of the way. He couldn't have become the man he was without her having done something right. *Right?*

As Marguerite sat at her outdoor breakfast table watching Nestor tidy up the flower beds, she allowed her mind wander to the twins. She so often pondered how her life and Jack's life would have been different if those two precious angels had survived. But they hadn't. And after they died, she threw herself into Gordon's career with twice the passion. She was aware that Jack felt a bit ignored during that period, but that's what she needed to do to survive. No growing boy needs a mother insane with grief. Jack had seemed to handle it all fine.

Of course she wanted Jack to find a woman to love, settle down, and start a family. In fact, Marguerite sometimes felt silly that she placed so much of her own deliverance on the shoulders of babies who did not yet draw breath and perhaps never would. But she wanted those grandchildren. She wanted them *now,* before she grew too old and frail to hold them in her arms, to rock them, to cuddle them.

She wanted those grandchildren before she died. She needed proof that the family would continue on.

It broke her heart to watch Jack squander his most

vital years and his astounding gifts on cheap women and an aimless political career. She would be happy to see him in love, she truly would, no matter *who* the woman was.

But Samantha Monroe?

Dear God, he was bedding a woman he'd paid to pose as his fiancée! That made her nothing but a call girl! A call girl with three children! The concept made Marguerite so sick with worry for her son that she temporarily considered spilling the beans to Kara and Stu in the hopes that they'd make Jack end the tryst. But why would they? A real love affair only made their twisted charade that much more believable. And Marguerite wasn't exactly proud to announce just how severely Jack had lowered his standards.

Marguerite took a sip of her coffee and sighed. The election was just over a month away and she was supposed to be returning to Indiana next week in support of Jack's final campaign push. Her schedule of appearances included a women's club luncheon and a mental health association banquet, one radio and two print interviews, and, of course, Christy Schoen had been hounding her to appear on *Capitol Update* to answer a series of questions on live TV about how thrilled she was to welcome her future daughter-in-law into the Tolliver clan.

No, thank you.

But what Marguerite just couldn't forgive was how Samantha Monroe had the audacity to tell her that her hairstyle was a crime. How dare she! Marguerite loved her hair and had loved it for nearly thirty years just as it was.

"You want the hibiscus cut back, Mrs. Tolliver?"

Marguerite turned toward Nestor's voice, staring at him blankly, thinking that there was absolutely nothing wrong with her hair . . . was there?

"Mrs. Tolliver? Do you want it trimmed?"

"What? Oh, cut it all off for all I care."

That Friday's D & D Night was a departure from the norm. Nine women descended on the Sunset Lane house for a swim party and indoor picnic. The downstairs was invaded by laughing, wine-sipping women, alternating between the Florida room, where manicure and pedicure stations were set up, the butler's pantry, where hair was being done, and the kitchen, where they found the sustenance required to continue on—guacamole and blue corn tortilla chips, brownies with macadamia nuts, crispy rice treats, Chex mix, artichoke dip, bruschetta, and a fruit tray with fat-free, sugar-free dip.

Kara had her usual root touch-up and trim. Denny wanted her blond spikes sharpened. Wanda wanted to see what she'd look like with auburn highlights. Candy McGaughy said she needed to go shorter because with the baby she had no time to style her hair. Olivia Petrakis just wanted a pedicure, and Brigid Larson decided she wanted to go full-on-drama with big romantic curls.

Monté gave Sam her usual no-fuss trim and then pulled her hair up in a cute clip, a few curls falling around her face. Sam touched up Monté's braids and gave her a manicure. Marcia settled for a simple trim and sat back and enjoyed Candy's serviceable pedicure.

"You're pretty good with nails," Marcia told her.

"I have to be pretty good at everything," Candy said. "I'm a mom."

At some point, Brigid got the idea to bathe Dale in the butler pantry's sink, an event she enjoyed far more than the dog did. When Brigid began to pour conditioner on his frizzy coat, Monté said, "You know, that shit is five bucks an ounce retail."

Brigid grabbed the clueless dog and stood him up on his hind legs. "I'm worth it," she said, gesturing with the dog's front paws. Everyone laughed.

"So, Monté, Sam says you met a man at the gym," Olivia said, munching on a brownie. "What stage is the relationship in? The 'I'm happier than I've ever been in my life' stage? The 'I'm starting to wonder about this man' stage? Or the 'Hello, Officer—how do I file for a protective order' stage?"

Denny snorted. "You should date more women, Olivia."

Monté waved them all away. "He's a nice man, y'all. Divorced, with two kids in college, and he treats me like a queen. He's the first man I've really liked in years, so give a sista a break."

"Wow. This sounds like love," Kara said.

"And he's cute, too," Marcia added with an eyebrow wiggle. "He came into the shop the other day and all business came to a standstill."

"That happens when any straight man walks into Le Cirque," Sam said.

"What about your legendary romance, Sam?" Wanda plopped up on the countertop with her glass of wine. "Have you set a date?"

"Not yet," Sam said, helping to dry off Dale. "We're not going to stress about that until after the general election in November."

Kara caught her eye and gave her a look that said, *Quick thinking.*

"Well, the two of you look so happy together whenever I see you on TV or in the papers," Candy said. "He always seems so sweet to you."

"He is," Sam said, putting away hair dye supplies in a bottom cupboard. "I've never known a man like Jack before. I feel completely free to be myself with him. I never realized a relationship could be so fun and feel so right."

"Ooh, and I bet he's one hell of a kisser. You can just tell," Wanda said.

"Mmm-hmm. I bet he can do it all," Marcia said.

"You got that right," Sam said, washing her hands in the sink.

When she turned around, Sam was greeted by alarmed stares from Monté, Denny, and Kara. She was saved when Jack chose that moment to check in on the party.

"Careful, ladies," he said, grabbing a slice of bruschetta. "I got in big trouble once for making sexist remarks like that."

"Lord have mercy," Monté said.

"I was just—" Olivia looked like she was going to pass out. "I'm—"

"He's just messing with you," Kara said. "Jack loves that women adore him."

"Especially a certain woman." He walked over to Sam and kissed her cheek. To everyone in the room, it looked innocent enough. Only Sam knew that he'd managed to flick his tongue against her skin, and she couldn't help but giggle.

Jack introduced himself to a starstruck Brigid, a slack-jawed Olivia, a nervous Wanda, a grinning Candy, and a gushing Marcia.

"It's so wonderful to finally meet you!" Marcia said, shaking his hand. "We are all so thrilled about you and Sam!"

"Uh-huh," Monté said.

"Is there room in the schedule for a quick trim?" Jack asked.

"Yes," everyone said in unison.

Sam trimmed his hair while he chatted with Brigid and Wanda about how to volunteer for his campaign. Greg and Lily popped their heads into the butler's pantry.

"Hey, Jack!" Greg said, smiling. "Getting a pedicure, too?"

"Naw. I'm holding out for a bikini wax."

"I can do that for you," Marcia said.

Greg told Sam that they were heading upstairs for the night, just as Dakota ran into the butler's pantry.

"Mr. Jack!" He did a headfirst dive into Jack's lap. Sam watched the tiny snippets of Jack's dark hair attach themselves all over Dakota's shirt and pants. She leaned down to kiss her youngest.

"Sleep well, little man," she said.

"'K, Mommy. 'Night, Mr. Jack." Dakota reached up and grabbed Jack's cheeks between his hands and planted one right on his lips.

Jack laughed and roughed up Dakota's curls. "Good night, Dakota."

"Lily, would you remember to take him to the potty one last time before he goes to bed?"

"Gee, Mom? How could I forget? How could *any-one* forget? Our lives revolve around Dakota's bath-room habits."

"Anything's better than those diapers," Simon said, looking around Greg into the crowded pantry. "'Night, Mama. 'Night, everyone."

After Sam had finished Jack's trim, he stole a few brownies for the road, said his good-byes, and headed home. It took Sam nearly a half hour at the front door to see her friends out, making sure no one forgot their swimsuits or platters.

"Oh, Sam," Marcia said, hugging her. "It must be wonderful for you to see that your children are get-ting such a positive male influence in their lives."

"It really is," Sam replied.

Monté was finished straightening up the mess in the kitchen when Sam found her. She watched her best friend slap the dishrag over the faucet with high drama.

"Have a seat, Sammy."

Sam sighed and pulled up one of the stools to the counter. She figured this would happen. So far, she'd managed to juggle the deception pretty well, but she knew Monté would see through it eventually. In all honesty, Sam wanted Monté to know, so that she could confide in her.

"You're in love with him," Monté whispered harshly.

Sam said nothing, twirling the antique emerald and diamond ring around her finger.

"Damn, girl! Are you completely insane?"

Sam met Monté's agitated gaze with a peaceful resolve but remained silent.

Monté waved her hands through the air. "The man's been practically living in this house! I see the way you look at him. And the way Dakota was with him tonight? *Hello?* Your little boy is getting way too attached to your boss. Know what I'm saying?"

"You've got to trust me on this."

Monté bugged her eyes out and put her hands on her noticeably slimmer hips. "How long you been sleeping with him?"

"A long while."

Monté stomped her foot on the hardwood floor. "How could you have kept this from me?"

"I'm so sorry, Monté!" Sam let her head drop and pressed the heels of her hands into her eyes. Eventually, she dared look up. Monté had pulled a stool up to the counter and was shaking her head. "I am so sorry, Monté. I should have told you, but by the time I figured out my mistake it was too late. I knew you'd be really pissed."

"How long *exactly* have you been sleeping with him?"

"Since the night of the ice storm."

Monté's mouth fell open, then snapped shut. "You sure didn't waste any time, did you?"

"It was a mutual sexual meltdown."

"Mmm-hmm. Except that for Jack, sex doesn't carry the same weight as it does for you. You don't play by the same rules he does, Sammy. I doubt you're even playing the same *game*. And you sure as hell know better than to give a man any before the third date."

"I think the ice storm was my fourth or fifth date. And I know what I'm doing. Jack loves me."

Monté reached for Sam's hand. She looked worried. "No, girl. *I* love you, and that's why I'm going to say what I'm about to say." Monté sighed before she went on. "Jack's great. I really like him. I do. And he sure is fine. But Sam, his track record with women is not exactly the—"

"He's changed."

Monté rolled her eyes heavenward. "Do you hear yourself? How many busted-up women do we listen to—all day, every day—who say that very same thing?"

"Jack and I have something special, Monté. It just happened—neither of us planned on it. Jack makes me feel respected and treasured and desired all at the same time. It's so unlike anything I've ever experienced before that it's not even funny."

"OK, Sam. So has he told you he loves you?"

"Yes." Sam couldn't stop herself from beaming. "He says it often and I say it right back."

"And have the two of you discussed your plans for the future? Has he asked you to marry him?"

Sam shrugged, smiling. "Not in those words, exactly. But I know he's open to that."

Monté leaned away from Sam to glare at her properly. "I don't know what to say. It's like I've been shut out of your life or something. I tell you damn near everything, Sam! I told you all about Roy Harrison from the health club, and that's not even anything serious. Well, not yet, anyway. And here you are having this outrageous love affair and you didn't bother to fill me in?"

"I'm sorry," Sam said. And she was—she felt like a jerk and hated the idea that she'd hurt Monté in any way. "I'd feel the same way if you shut me out of something like this."

"I'd never do that."

"OK, but please understand that this isn't just a love affair. I work for Jack. My kids' future is linked to whether I can pull off this very public deception I've got going. I'm being followed into toilet stalls by reporters hell-bent on finding the tiniest crack in our story, for crying out loud! And for a while, I wasn't sure what Jack and I had. I thought maybe it was just a fling that wouldn't last." Sam took a breath, seeing that her rationale wasn't impressing Monté. "I was going to tell you."

"Mmm-hmm."

"I'm sorry for shutting you out."

Monté nodded. "Well, I'm guessing this is another secret I'm supposed to keep?"

"If you wouldn't mind." Sam hugged her friend. "And you really do look wonderful, Monté."

"Don't you try to distract me by telling me I got it goin' on, even though I know I do."

Sam laughed.

"You know Kara's going to suspect sooner or later," Monté said, frowning.

"I disagree," Sam said. "People see what they want to see, and I think Kara sees what's happening with Jack and me as a well-orchestrated performance, a reflection of her own genius. I don't think she has a clue."

Monté got up from the stool and reached for Sam's hand, pulling her up. "Come on. Let's get some sleep. I think I'll take the Lincoln Bedroom tonight."

"You're nuts," Sam said with a snicker. She turned off the lights as they moved toward the foyer and the front stairway.

Monté stopped halfway up the white marble steps and glared at Sam. "If Jack Tolliver does anything to hurt you, I swear I'll—"

"No." Sam squeezed Monté's arm and encouraged her to keep moving. "No sharp objects are coming near that man."

It was hours later when the phone woke Sam from deep sleep. She struggled with the light and reached for the phone by her bed. Not many people had this number and she couldn't even begin to imagine who'd be calling at this hour. The caller ID said "number not available."

"Hello?"

"Sam, it's Mitch. You have no idea how good it is to hear your voice."

14

Sam shot up in bed and pulled the covers close to her chest, as if a layer of luxury goose down could protect her heart. "I have nothing to say to you, Mitch."

"Don't hang up. Please."

She didn't, and as she held the phone to her ear, Sam wondered why—was it the familiar sound of his voice? A perverse curiosity about why he'd chosen now to appear in her life? Or was it the fact that for the first time in three years she had a chance to hold Mitch over the fires of hell for what he'd done to Lily, Greg, and Dakota?

"I just want to see the kids, Sam. I need to see them."

Sam's spine went rigid. Denny had told Sam that Mitch would probably do this and told her how to handle it. "You currently have no visitation rights. Talk to your lawyer. I am not legally obligated to have this discussion with you."

"Just meet me. Talk to me. You can't be so cruel as to deny me a chance just to see them."

Sam suddenly felt quite cold. "Where did you get the money to pay off your child support debt, Mitch?"

"You say that like I robbed a bank or something, Sam. I earned it, of course."

"Glass pods must really be coming back into style."

"I knew you'd be bitter."

"Bitter?" Sam heard herself laugh so loud she was afraid she'd wake Dakota in the next room. "Listen up, Mitch. I'm glad you left. As angry as I was that you abandoned me with three kids to raise and as hard as these years have been, it was a blessing in disguise. I am far better off without you."

"Please, just meet me. We can go somewhere quiet to talk, somewhere we can—"

"Talk to your lawyer. Do not call me again." Sam hung up and didn't sleep the rest of the night. The worries swarmed in her mind like hornets, angry and ready to sting. What was Mitch up to? She knew she couldn't trust him. It would devastate the kids if their father suddenly reappeared in their lives only to leave again.

She would do whatever it took to make sure that didn't happen.

"I'm still very curious who hired you." Mitch was trying to make small talk while Brandon secured the microphone wire with one last strip of medical tape. Mitch hoped it wouldn't rip off his skin when he went to remove the ridiculous contraption. "I mean, really, how did you find out that Sam had an appointment this morning at the prosecutor's office? How does a person get that kind of information?"

"It doesn't matter." Brandon never seemed to have much patience with Mitch. "All that matters is that you get Samantha Monroe on tape saying the engagement is a publicity stunt. We don't care how you do it; just do it. And if you don't, you're on your own—no car, no apartment, no job. Got it?"

Mitch despised this guy. He'd always hated dweebs like him, who'd somehow found themselves in positions of authority and then milked it for all it was worth. Brandon What's-his-name clearly thought he was too good for this assignment.

"You told me I could see my kids again. That's the only reason I'm doing your dirty work."

"I told you that you'd at least have a *chance* of seeing your kids again. Your debt is paid. You'll have to discuss the legal technicalities with your attorney."

"I don't have one. Are you a lawyer?"

Brandon pulled Mitch's shirt down over the wire and stared at him in discomfort. "Uh, yes. But I don't do custody."

Mitch was getting more hacked off by the second. He was pissed at this Brandon jerk and whatever politician he worked for. He was pissed at Sam for treating him like he was a waste of her time. But most of all, he was pissed at himself for getting into this mess.

He wanted to see his kids. That's all he wanted.

"How does that feel?" Brandon asked, zipping up the ugly forest green fleece-lined jacket he'd made Mitch wear. It was so not his style.

"Fabulous! The fabric has so much movement. And the color is to die for!"

Brandon scowled at him and took a few steps back, and Mitch laughed. He so loved to play with homophobes.

"Remember, don't touch the recorder afterward. Call me and tell me you're done and we'll meet at the City Market men's room, where I'll take all this off of you."

"You're such a tease."

"Ugh. I can't wait for this to be over." Brandon headed for the door of Mitch's apartment.

"You and me both." After the door shut, Mitch stood still for a moment, overcome with a sudden flash of creative brilliance. He went around the apartment and gathered up what little stuff he had worth keeping and threw it in the trunk of his beater Pontiac. All it would take was some research at the library—after all, he hadn't exactly had his finger on the pulse of Hoosier politics the last few years—and he'd never have to lay eyes on this place again. He was thinking California this time.

Maybe he'd make it big out there. Maybe the kids would want to come out for a visit.

Sam hadn't been inside the City-County Building in years, and walking the halls of the sterile concrete box of a building gave her the willies. The last time she was here it was to finalize her divorce.

She pushed open the glass door of the Marion County Prosecutor's office and spoke to the receptionist. Sam waited a few minutes past her appointment time, fascinated by the frenetic pace of busy people rushing in and out of the suite of rooms, case files clutched to their sides. It reminded her of a typical day at Le Cirque, and Sam realized she didn't miss it one damn bit.

Maybe she wouldn't go back to part-time. Maybe she wouldn't go back at all.

"Ms. Monroe?" A harried-looking young woman in a blue suit stood in front of her in the waiting area. "Let's come on back."

The process took only about fifteen minutes, and Sam left holding a county check for every last penny Mitch had ever owed her children. The deputy prosecutor had asked Sam the same question she had—where did Mitch get the money? Sam told the lawyer she had no idea.

She'd barely exited the office when a hand landed on her upper arm. Sam spun around to see Mitch hovering close, those familiar eyes shadowed with something she'd never seen in all the years she'd known him—desperation.

Sam was stunned. Nothing came out of her mouth. She pulled her arm from his touch and headed into the crowded main hallway of the third floor, knowing he was right behind her.

"We have to talk," Mitch called after her. "Sam, please! You've got to talk to me."

"Leave me alone." Sam took one look at the crowd waiting for the next elevator and felt nauseated. She decided to hit the stairs. Sam cursed herself for the stupid move as soon as she heard Mitch's footsteps right behind her.

"Sam! Please!"

She whipped around and stopped on the landing between the second and third floors. She held on to the painted metal railing to steady herself, because she was suddenly very dizzy.

"I have nothing to say to you, Mitch. You fucked up. You can't see your kids because you fucked up, do you understand?"

Mitch now stood two steps above the landing and looked down into Sam's eyes. He appeared so much older than he had just three years ago and was dressed like a guy ready to play eighteen holes. The Mitch she knew was more of a black jeans, black T-shirt, and black leather jacket kind of guy.

"You look so beautiful, Sam. You were always such a beautiful woman."

"Oh jeez. I think I'm going to throw up."

"And I know I messed up bad. Please give me another chance."

Sam laughed in his face. "Mitch? *Hello?* This is not about me. It's about your children. And it's my job to do what is best for them, a concept you apparently never fully grasped."

"Don't be such a bitch."

"Forget it." Sam turned to continue down the stairs and almost fell. She braced a hand against the concrete block wall.

"Wait! I'm sorry!" Mitch tromped down after her. "It's just that I saw you with Jack Tolliver and I knew that if I didn't come forward right now he'd probably adopt them and then I'd *never* have a chance to tell them how sorry I am for hurting them. I just want to be their father again!"

Sam slowly turned around, only to see tears streaking down Mitch's face. Her immediate instinct was to soothe him, the emotional remnant of a ten-year marriage, no doubt, but she didn't have the energy.

"I hate myself for what I've done to them, Sam. You have no idea what I've been through these last few years and how I've kicked myself for leaving the way I did."

"Uh-huh. And you have no idea what I've been through."

"I'm sorry, Sam."

"Right. Well, this is not a conversation I want to be having, Mitch. I'm not feeling too good at the moment. Besides, you should be discussing this with your lawyer, not me."

"Fine. But I'm telling you that I won't stand for Tolliver adopting the kids when you get married, do you hear me? They're my children and they are the only things that matter to me in this life!"

Sam frowned, her mind racing in an attempt to figure out how to end this rapidly disintegrating encounter and make it down the next two flights of stairs. "I feel dizzy." She plopped down on the last step and Mitch followed her.

"I have a right to re-establish a relationship with them." He peered down at her. "The idea that some other man would adopt them makes me crazy."

"Pardon me if I don't quite trust your sudden love for your children."

Mitch's shoulders shook, and before she knew it, he'd sat down right next to her, put his face in his hands, and cried like a baby.

The gray concrete stairwell walls felt like they were closing in on her. She felt clammy. On the edge of being sick. She needed to go.

Mitch's voice was strangled when he spoke again. "Please don't let him take my kids! They are the only thing I ever did right in my life! Oh God! I'm begging you!"

Sam pushed herself up to her feet and fought off nausea. "Stop it, Mitch. Just stop." She grabbed her purse. "He's not going to adopt them. Look, we're not really engaged to be married, OK? Jack Tolliver hired me to pretend to be his fiancée until the primary. That's all. It's a business deal. I need to go."

Mitch slowly raised his face, and Sam watched, horrified, as her ex-husband's eyes flashed with something that looked almost like glee. How did he go from devastation to glee in a heartbeat?

"Thank you, Sam. That's all I needed to know." Mitch stood up and wiped off his jeans. "So long as they're still my kids. I guess I'll talk to my lawyer."

Mitch bent down to kiss her cheek and Sam backed away. He gave her a smirk and walked past, and as Sam watched the green windbreaker disappear around the stairway's next bend, she wrapped her arms around herself as tight as she could, feeling dizzy and tired and sick with the thought that she'd just made a horrible mistake.

• • •

"What do you mean he's gone?" Christy stared at Brandon in disbelief, noting that he was sweating like a boxer.

"What I mean is he didn't show up at our designated meeting place to hand over the tape. He didn't go back to the apartment and he hasn't shown up at work for two days."

Christy's jaw fell open in shock, and that movement sent sharp streaks of pain all along her chin and up to her temples and into her shoulders. It hurt so bad she wanted to cry.

"I can tell you're upset and I'm sorry, baby, but we'll find him."

Brandon opened his arms and Christy stared at him in disbelief. Could he want to hold her? Had it developed to the point where he thought she'd want that? And what was with the *baby* crap? Christy silently thanked God that the primary would be over in just a few weeks so she could extract these wisdom teeth from her aching jaw and Brandon from her life!

She eased into his arms, gritting her teeth as he hugged her and rubbed her back. If anyone walked into her office at this moment she'd die. Christy pushed him off her and smiled.

"Well, you'll just have to track him down, then," she said, trying to sound casual when she was panicking inside. She'd spent a fortune to drag Mitch Bergen back here. He was her only shot. She needed three independent verifications of the information before she could take it on air, and she knew no one would comment unless she could play the tape for them.

Samantha Monroe's family in Valparaiso said they hadn't heard from Sam in more than a year. Jack ignored Christy, referring all questions to Kara. Of course, she warned Christy to stop harassing Samantha and gave her just enough information so that she couldn't claim Kara had shut her out entirely. Stuart said nothing, as usual. Marguerite Tolliver wouldn't answer Christy's calls. That left Sam's two teenagers, now enrolled at Park Tudor. Christy could try to catch them after school, she supposed, but she'd never used kids as sources and didn't know how reliable they would be. Or if it was even ethical.

All Christy knew was that failure was not an option. If she was going to break into a national network slot, this was the time to do it and this was the story. She could *not* let it slip from her grasp.

"Maybe we should call the police," Brandon suggested.

"And tell them what? We've lost track of the snitch we paid to get the audio I need for my award-winning story? I don't think so."

Brandon cleared his throat. "Technically, Christy, you're the one who hired him. I just volunteered to help you out."

Oh really? Christy thought to herself. *Technically, I feel like telling you to fuck yourself.* She didn't know how much longer she could take all this stress. Her jaw throbbed, and she feared she was gobbling so much ibuprofen that she'd blow a hole through her stomach before she could get the stupid molars out.

"Are you all right, Christy? You look kind of pale."

"Fine—just my wisdom teeth."

Brandon opened his arms again and Christy made a beeline to her office door, which she opened wide. "I've got to work on my piece for the noon news, Brandon, but call me the second you track him down."

"I just hope he's not out getting high somewhere," Brandon said, walking past her.

"Find him, *now.*"

"You've been so quiet tonight. Are you OK, sweetheart?"

Sam squeezed Jack's hand as she kept her eyes focused on the colorful production of *La Traviata*, well aware that in this opera box she and Jack were displayed for the crowd almost as conspicuously as the performers onstage. "I'm fine," she said, giving him a brief smile and kissing his cheek.

"Whatever's bothering you, I'm looking forward to making you forget all about it later."

Jack released Sam's hand and let his fingers do a discreet dance up her bare forearm to her elbow, against the curve of her waist, down her hip . . . Sam gasped . . . then Jack gripped her upper thigh.

He leaned in to whisper in her ear over the music and his breath felt hot against her face. "I look forward to sucking on your luscious lips, Sam—both sets. I look forward to nibbling on your toes and your earlobes and your sweet pink nipples. I just love the way your nipples get rock hard at the slightest touch; have I ever told you that?"

Sam swallowed. "Uh, not at the opera."

Jack chuckled while twirling his tongue along the sensitive skin behind her ear, and Sam giggled, too. It still amused her how she once felt suspicious of Jack because he had no creative outlet that she could see. Oh, how wrong she'd been! Jack's creativity was of the sexual variety—the words he used, the tension he built, the desires he had—and she'd take that over glass pea pods any day.

Sam suddenly stiffened at the thought of Mitch. She'd not been able to shake the bad vibe she'd carried away from that encounter in the stairway. Monté flipped out when Sam admitted she'd told him about her arrangement with Jack.

"You know you can't trust that man," Monté had said. "Just pray he doesn't figure out how he can use that against you. This is not good."

No, it wasn't. And Sam wanted to tell Jack about it, but she knew he had enough on his mind in these last weeks of campaigning. Her ex-husband's antics were the last things Jack needed to be concerned about.

In the coming weeks, Sam would be traveling with Jack to all corners of the state, visiting high school auditoriums, standing outside factory gates, throwing out the first pitch at a Little League season opener, and accompanying him to countless dinners and town hall meetings.

She would deal with Mitch quietly and efficiently.

"Something's wrong," Jack said, pulling away from Sam. "Why won't you tell me what it is?"

Sam snuggled up against Jack and felt his arm wrap around her shoulders. What she loved most about Jack was that he gave her a sense of being taken care of yet didn't smother her.

"I'm a little tired, is all." That wasn't a lie. Sam couldn't remember the last time she'd been this exhausted. It had probably been while she was pregnant with Dakota and cutting hair sixty hours a week. Campaigning was damn hard work.

"Sam?"

She looked into his face and was struck by the tender concern she saw in his eyes. It was difficult to believe that Jack had ever been a stranger to her, that she'd ever doubted him.

"I want you to know how much I appreciate what you're doing. I mean that."

She nodded at him.

"You're a trouper. You've done an amazing job with the press and Kara and Stu—trust me, I know they can be obnoxious—and even Marguerite. I don't think I could have done this without you."

Sam smiled. "I'm glad I could help."

Jack leaned down and kissed her, deep and sweet and slow, and neither noticed it was intermission until the house lights went up.

The next morning, Sam opened her eyes, bolted from the bed, ran into the luxurious all-white marble bathroom, and threw up.

Well, she knew what this was. She'd been here before, three times to be exact. She was *so* pregnant.

◆ ◆ ◆

Jack was shocked to hear that Allen Ditto was calling him at his campaign headquarters, since he hadn't spoken to the man in years. But as Jack picked up his phone he thought this could be a good thing—maybe the retiring senator was ready to endorse him after all.

"Hello, Allen! It's so nice to hear from you."

The voice on the telephone wasn't Allen Ditto's. It was Sam's or a tape recording of Sam's voice, and Jack was so shocked at what he was hearing that the meaning of her words hardly registered.

"You like?" a man's voice asked.

"Who is this? Because you're sure as hell not Allen Ditto."

"No shit, Sherlock. Have another listen."

The recording ran again. *"Look, we're not really engaged to be married, OK? Jack Tolliver hired me to pretend to be his fiancée until the primary. That's all. It's a business deal."*

"Who are you and what do you want?"

"I'm nothing but an anonymous offshore banking account number. You'll be sending one million dollars to me within the next twenty-four hours or I'll give this tape to the press."

Jack leaned back in his swivel chair and tried to comprehend what was happening. He didn't have a clue who this bastard was. He'd never heard his voice before. And how did he get that recording? Was it legit or spliced together? And who would have been able to record Sam's voice without her knowledge?

Of course it was Christy.

"Tell your boss lady that I don't negotiate with terrorists or blackmailers. Good-bye."

"Wait!"

Jack hung up and buzzed his secretary. "Get Christy Schoen on the line, now."

"Christy Schoen, *Channel Ten Action News,* how may I help you?"

"I'm on my way over to your office. You better be there."

As he started up the Lexus and headed toward Media Row, he decided this was one little errand he would be pleased to take care of himself. He'd tell Stuart and Kara all about it later.

"Mom? You OK?"

Lily was checking on her again, and Sam didn't know how much longer she could stay locked up in the bathroom like this, hiding from the world.

"I brought you some tea. Do you want it? I got my midterms back today. Wanna see?"

"I'll be out in just a second, sweet pea." Sam splashed cold water on her face and grabbed some lip gloss out of the medicine cabinet. She pinched her cheeks, wishing she could get them to look as pink as the whites of her eyes did—she'd been sick so much in the last twelve hours that she'd ruptured a few capillaries. Sam blinked at herself, and decided she looked like a pregnant, redheaded Queen of the Undead.

Sam exited the bathroom and took the tea gratefully. Lily guided her over to one of the two sofas and handed Sam the computer printout of her midterm grades, which were straight A's.

"Lily, you are an incredible young woman. I am so proud of you!" Sam hugged her oldest with all her might, the printout clutched in her hand, and was suddenly overcome with a vivid memory of holding this same person in the first seconds of her life, her precious, tiny, brand-new life. Sam began to sob.

"Mom?" Lily patted and soothed her back. "Mom? What's wrong? Do you have a brain tumor or something? You're really scaring me."

Sam shook her head but couldn't speak. She just kept holding her daughter and crying. Dale began clawing at the carpet at Sam's feet, looking for the ideal place to lie down for a nap.

Sam pulled away from Lily and began to wail. "That dog is supposed to be in the Florida room! I promised Jack he'd stay on the porch! What have I done? I've screwed up so bad!"

Lily squinted her eyes and patted her mother's hand. "Yo, Mom. News flash. Dale hasn't set foot on that porch for months. He has the run of the place. He was in the pool the other day. He sleeps on the couch in Jack's office. Nobody cares."

Sam put her face in her hands and howled. Dale offered up a series of sharp yips as harmony. Lily sighed. "OK. It's Auntie Monté time."

Sam nodded.

"Is she working today?"

She nodded again.

"Here. Drink your tea and don't move, Mom."

Lily got the cordless phone from its perch by the bed and had Monté on the line in seconds.

"Hey," Lily said. "We are in full crisis mode here at the palace. I think Mom's losing her shit—I mean—no, wait, that's exactly what I mean. Mom is losing her shit and you better get up here quick."

"I have no idea what you're talking about."

Christy looked all puffy around her throat and jaw, and she sounded like Brando in *The Godfather.* Jack studied her carefully.

"The tape. I'm asking you who the creep was who taped Samantha without her knowledge and then spliced together that little gem of a sound bite."

Christy's eyes got huge.

"Here's the situation as I see it. Whoever you hired went gonzo on you, Christy. He just called me and told me to pay him a million dollars or he'd give the tape to the press."

Jack had to give her credit. Christy Schoen had a steel rod for a spine and a steel trap for a brain. He'd eventually discovered that her heart was made of the same substance, and sometimes he couldn't believe he had lasted three months with her, at Marguerite's behest.

God, was he glad he found Sam.

"Answer me. Is he an intern? One of your hangers-on? A guy from studio engineering who's been in love with you for years?"

"I want you to leave my office, Jack. I think you're making all this up just to upset me."

"Upset you?" Jack laughed hard. "You barrel

through this town not giving a damn who you upset or destroy or misrepresent. You follow people into toilets, for God's sake! Christy, you are the only person in the world who hates me enough to try to orchestrate something like this. It's your mess to clean up."

"I don't hate you, Jack."

"Sure you do."

"All right, I do hate you, but so do hundreds of other women you've unceremoniously dumped."

"I don't think the number is that high, but thanks for reminding me that I need to apologize to every single one of them. Anyway, none are as conniving as you are. You're the only suspect."

"Come on, Jack! It could be anyone! Maybe this is Charleton Manheimer's doing. Did you even consider that possibility? You know, I could probably help you with this if I knew exactly what the tape said."

Jack laughed again and got up out of his chair. He headed toward the door, his back to Christy.

"At least you could have found someone more suitable for your little game. I mean, Samantha Monroe? Puh-leeze!"

Jack turned very slowly, walked back to Christy's desk, and leaned his fists on it. "More suitable? What do you mean?"

Christy swallowed hard, and at this close a range, Jack could definitely tell she had a problem with her teeth.

"I just meant someone more your type," she whispered, leaning away from Jack.

"I'll tell you what my type is, Christy. She's a

woman who appreciates the little things in life, who has an adventurous spirit, who likes to be silly and laugh, who is as beautiful in her soul as she is in her swimsuit. My type of woman is the kind who is loving, brave, and responsible, but can still let loose where it counts. Samantha Monroe is my type, and you can quote me directly on that."

A thoroughly puzzled expression crossed Christy's face, and Jack realized it was the first time he'd ever seen her doubt herself, even for a second.

"What the hell is wrong with your jaw, Christy?"

She rolled her eyes. "Four impacted wisdom teeth."

"Ouch." Jack straightened up. "Don't listen to what the oral surgeon tells you—it hurts like a mutha and you'll walk around like a zombie for a week."

"Thanks for the heads-up."

"Don't fuck with my fiancée, Christy." Jack stared into her widening eyes to make sure she got the point. "Sam Monroe is the best thing that ever walked into my life, and I'll be damned if you'll hurt her."

Jack reached for the door once more but stopped. He looked over his shoulder at her. "I apologize for my behavior that night at the awards dinner. What I did was inexcusable. You didn't deserve it. And I'm sorry it's taken me so long to tell you that."

Jack slammed the office door shut behind him, savoring the look of utter bewilderment he'd just seen on Christy's face.

"She's indisposed at the moment."

"You told me that two hours ago. What's going on up there? I want to talk to Sam."

Monté paced back and forth in Sam's suite, holding the cordless phone up to her ear with one hand as the positive pregnancy test stick dangled from the other.

He really wants to talk to you, Monté mouthed to Sam, who then reached out for the phone.

"Hey, Jack! How's everything at headquarters?"

When Monté rolled her eyes, Sam realized she'd overdone the perkiness a little.

"It's been an interesting day, to say the least. We have another labor dinner tonight, this time the state and local government employees. Is it OK if I pick you up a few minutes early? There's something I want to talk to you about privately, and we sure don't seem to have much private time these days."

Sam took a big gulp of air, wondering if he had somehow guessed she was pregnant. "That sounds fine. I have something to talk to you about, too."

Jack went silent. Finally he said, "I've known for a while that something's on your mind and I think I may even know what it is. We'll talk about it tonight. I'll pick you up at six, OK? I do love you, you know that, right?"

"Yes," she said.

Jack hung up and Sam weakly clicked the phone off, letting it drop to the comforter.

"I think he's going to dump me," Sam whispered.

"What? Why in the world do you say that?"

Sam shrugged. "He said he had something he wanted to talk to me about—that's never good. Plus, you've got to remember that the last time I was pregnant, Mitch told me he'd decided he was gay."

"Don't think that's much of a risk this time around."

Sam gave her a feeble smile.

"Besides, he told you he loved you. You told him you loved him. Have a little faith." Monté put the phone back in the cradle. "I'll go down into the kitchen and rustle you up some chicken soup. Just rest for a bit."

Sam closed her eyes and concentrated on her breathing, trying to recall what it felt like to be pregnant with Dakota and when it was that she'd felt the first flutter of life inside her. She spread her hands across her belly, trying to calculate exactly how far along she might be.

There were two distinct possibilities—one that would put her at almost three months and another that would put her at about six weeks. Knowing how her body worked, it could be either, because she'd continued to have scant periods for the first four months she was pregnant with Greg. This could easily be a repeat of that. Sam had begun counting backward week by week when the phone rang. She picked it up from the bed, assuming it was Jack again.

"Hi."

"Look, we're not really engaged to be married, OK? Jack Tolliver hired me to pretend to be his fiancée until the primary. That's all. It's a business deal."

Sam froze at the sound of her own voice coming through the phone.

"I want a hundred thousand or I'm giving this to the press."

It took several long seconds for Sam to get her lips to move. *"Mitchell?"*

"I taped our little conversation the other day. I was wired for sound, baby."

"Oh God, no. . . ."

"Hey, maybe I'll give it to that congressman he's running against. Manheimer? I bet he'll cream his jeans when he gets ahold of this."

Sam's stomach lurched. She recognized the lilt in his voice. He was on something. "Please, please don't do this, Mitch."

"Wire the money by the end of the business day tomorrow and I won't."

Sam pulled herself up and swung her legs over the edge of the bed, fighting back a wave of nausea. She had to think fast, find a way to reason with him. "Any money I give you will come out of your children's future, do you realize that? Is this how you show your love for them?"

"Shut up, Sam."

"I've saved nearly all my stipend, except for what I spent on Christmas gifts, and I was going to use it as a down payment on a house for us. The rest has gone into trust funds for their education and I couldn't get my hands on it even if I wanted to."

"Trust funds?" Mitch laughed. "My kids got fuckin' trust funds? Woo hoo!"

"Is it coke? Is that what you're on?"

"Got a pen for that account number?"

"I won't do it."

"Fine. Then I'm going public with this, you're out of a job, and Jack Tolliver is done for."

"Mitch!" Sam stood up, breathing deep to clear her head. "I've got about seventy-five thousand dollars to my name and that's it."

"What the fuck?" It sounded like Mitch dropped the phone. He picked it up amid a torrent of cursing. "I thought you'd be good for more than that. The Tollivers are rich!"

"That's all the cash I have."

"I'll take it."

Sam rocked back and forth and gripped herself tight. "This is blackmail, Mitch. I can go to the police."

"By the time they find me, if they ever find me, the damage will be done, so go ahead."

Sam heard herself laugh. It came out sounding cartoonish, maybe because this was finally it—the moment she finally cracked. Maybe Lily was right—she was losing her shit. She'd been fighting for three years to keep it together, and now, just when everything seemed to be perfect, she finds out she's pregnant and gets blackmailed, all in the same day!

She laughed again. "This is hilarious, do you know why?"

"No, but I'm afraid you're gonna tell me."

"Because I really am Jack's girlfriend. I finally found a man I can love and trust, who loves me the way I've always dreamed, and if that tape gets out, it won't even be the truth. That's what I find so hilarious."

Mitch was quiet for a moment and Sam heard him breathing fast. "You told me he hired you."

"He did. We fell in love after."

"Are you engaged for real?"

"No."

"OK. I'm revising my request."

Sam's heart leaped.

"I want you to break up with Jack Tolliver and *then* wire me the money."

"What?"

"I don't want him adopting my fucking kids! Don't you get it? I told you that already! No judge in the world would give me my kids back, and if you stay with him *he'll* get them!"

"This is crazy talk, Mitch. You're high. You need to think about what—"

"You need to wire the money to this account. Got that pen yet?"

Sam scrambled to the bedside table for a pen and piece of paper and wrote down the fourteen-digit number, repeating it to make sure she had it right.

"Don't let that jock get his hands on my kids. Break it off with him or I'll release this tape. Simple as that. And I'll find out if you don't do it, Sam. I'll be watching you."

That was enough. "You never cared about your kids and you don't now, so don't you *dare* use them as an excuse for any of your fucked-up scheming. Jack has been more of a father to them in just a few months than you *ever* were!"

Mitch's laugh was low and ugly. "Just break it off with him now, Sam. You wouldn't be able to keep him anyway. You know I'm right. A man like Jack Tolliver could never be satisfied with you. You turned me off women altogether and you'll do the same to him."

Sam's chin began to tremble. She would not let

him do this to her. "I am not responsible for your sexual identity issues."

"Think whatever you want."

"You will never see the children again as long as you live. Go to hell, Mitch." Sam clicked off the phone and threw it with all her might at the closed double doors of the suite, just as Monté came in carrying a tray. Monté ducked as the phone whizzed over her head, then blinked at Sam in surprise.

"Damn, girl." She walked across the room and placed the tray on the table. "If you're gonna be throwing shit at somebody, I think it should be Jack."

15

Sam tried to smile as Jack held open the limo door for her and then slid in beside her. The moment the driver put the car in gear, Jack put his arms around Sam, drawing her close.

"I can't wait for the primary to be over. There are a million things I want to talk to you about." Jack's lips skimmed across Sam's hair and down the side of her face and her throat. She realized this might her last encounter with one of Jack's miracle kisses, and she reveled in one last feel of those infamous lips on her skin. She leaned her head back in bliss, knowing she would remember this moment as long as she lived.

Sam had agonized over this all afternoon, and she realized she had to go along with Mitch's insane request. If the tape ever got out, Jack's career would be over, and it would be all her fault. She's the one who opened her big mouth! Mitch was her crazy ex-husband! And if the tape was released before the primary, not only would she ruin Jack's reputation, but she'd screw up her children's future as well! Her contract specified that if she revealed the arrangement publicly, she'd lose the trust funds and would have to pay back every penny of the almost eighty-five thousand dollars she'd earned, a feat that would surely take the rest of her life.

Sam was the world's biggest fuckup. The world's biggest *pregnant-yet-again* fuckup. What was it with her and sperm, anyway?

"I have something I need to tell you," Jack said. "I'm afraid it's not very pleasant news."

Maybe her instincts had been right. Maybe Jack really was breaking up with her. She would survive. She could make it through this conversation. She focused on his face and nodded.

"I've already told Stu and Kara about what happened and how I've decided to handle it," Jack said, stroking her hand.

They knew she and Jack had been a real couple? Did they know she was pregnant? Did Jack? "I see. When did you tell them?"

"Uh, today." Jack frowned at her and got ready to say something, but she interrupted him.

"I know this has to be hard for you, so don't even bother saying it. I understand. I'd give you back your ring, but I'm supposed to wear it until the primary, right?" Sam tried to produce a little laugh. It came out as a sob.

"Baby, what are you talking about?"

"I think this is for the best; I really do. Recent developments have led me to believe it would be best for us—the real us—to break up."

Jack lowered his chin and raised his eyebrows. "Come again?"

"Break up. You and me. Something has happened on my end, too, and trust me when I tell you it would be best for everyone if we stopped seeing each other." Silently, Sam sent him mental telepathy messages to forgive her when she came back to him after the election in November, with his baby in tow, and told him the truth about Mitch, the blackmail, the threats, the pregnancy. . . .

"You're breaking up with me?"

"I am."

Jack turned to look out the dark window of the limousine. He said nothing for a very long time but eventually turned back to Sam. His face now exhibited that politician's mask she hadn't seen in months. It was like he'd shut a door in her face.

"Answer one question for me, Sam."

She nodded. *Please don't ask me if I love you. Yes, I love you. Of course I love you. Please don't make me lie about that!*

"Why?"

Sam felt her eyes well with tears. Her body began to tremble. She had no idea how to lie to Jack. It wasn't in her. "It's very complicated, but I just don't think I'm ready for this kind of commitment. I'm so sorry."

The hurt Jack felt was so intense that it showed through his mask for just an instant. He scooted away from her slightly and looked out the window again. He didn't say a word to her for the rest of the drive.

Jack gave the most lackluster speech Sam had

ever heard. He couldn't seem to muster enthusiasm for much of anything, except getting out of there and heading home. Half the audience of state and municipal employees left before he stopped talking. When he was walking off the stage, Sam heard him tell the moderator that he was "trying to fight off something."

"The flu?" she'd asked.

"A real bad case," he'd said.

Sam found herself solo in the limo for the ride back. She had no idea how Jack planned to get home. Sam couldn't remember when she'd been this sad and had trouble separating what was nausea from what was heartache. It all roiled together in a mess of emptiness, agitation, exhaustion, and deep loneliness.

She dragged herself up the stairs and fell into bed in her dress. The next morning she awoke to find Dakota playing trucks in the bed next to her, and she had just enough time to throw up and take a shower before Monté arrived to drive her to her doctor's appointment.

The same obstetrician had delivered all three of Sam's children and was shocked to see how Dakota had grown. But the real shock came later, when Sam lay on an ultrasound table in a cool, dark room and the monitor showed two beating hearts instead of one.

"What am I going to do?" she cried, yanking at her hair. "Everything is falling apart! All my plans are ruined! Don't you understand how this could destroy my life?"

"Oh, shut up, Christy," Brandon said, crossing his legs and putting an arm over the back of her couch. "You can be such a drama queen sometimes. Why don't you come over here and sit down?"

It suddenly occurred to Christy that inviting Brandon to her home wasn't exactly the smartest thing she'd ever done. But where else were they going to have this conversation? Yes, Brandon had a legitimate reason to visit her at work, but Christy had taken a couple days off. All the stress had given her a zit right on the tip of her nose. And besides, the fewer times Brandon was seen going into her office, the better.

"I can't sit down. I'm too pumped up on coffee. I even smoked a cigarette this morning out on my balcony. I'm a wreck. If we don't find Mitch Bergen in the next week, my life is over."

"You still look beautiful to me."

Christy stopped pacing her living room and glanced down at Brandon's wide, congenial face staring up at her. Then she scurried over to the large mirror over the breakfront and stared at herself. She looked like hell. Her hair was tangled and she had dark circles under her eyes and that zit was now roughly the size of Krakatoa. Brandon must be off his nut.

In the mirror, she watched him come up behind her. Then she felt his arms go around her waist and he pulled her tight. She knew she must truly be at the nadir of her existence if this felt good to her. Christy closed her eyes and leaned back against his sturdy body. She sighed.

"Where's your bedroom?" Brandon whispered roughly.

She straightened her left arm and pointed down the hall. Maybe if she didn't use actual words she could pretend she'd misunderstood him, that she thought he was asking for directions to the bathroom.

Christy allowed him to pull her down the hallway and into her bedroom. She allowed him to back her up until she fell onto the bed. She allowed him to climb on top of her and kiss her.

God help her, but Brandon Miliewski was a really good kisser. She felt a hot rush of need spread through her body.

"Mind if I get my handcuffs out of the car?" Brandon asked her.

"Maybe some other time," Christy said. She closed her eyes, kept her hands to herself, and pretended it was Jack who was making love to her. That was the only thing that ever got her off.

"I'm having a stroke. An embolism. A coronary. Maybe all three. I need a break."

Stuart stumbled out of the racquetball court and chugged from his bottled water, and Jack took the time alone to adjust his knee brace, lean back against the battered wall of the racquetball court, and slide all the way down to the hardwood floor. He draped his forearms over his knees and breathed deep.

This had been the worst couple of weeks of his life. The pain he'd experienced after his injury had been of the physical variety, and it was easy for him to understand. All he had to do was survive the initial slam, have surgery, do rehab, and take pain medication, then repeat the cycle until it was done. Sure it was a bitch to live through, but it was simple to understand.

The kind of pain he was feeling now was much harder to get a grip on. It was elusive. It wasn't confined to one part of his body. It originated in his heart and spread everywhere. Even his toenails ached. He couldn't sleep. He was losing his lead in the polls because he'd been barely functioning. Every time he saw Sam or had to stand next to her and smile for a photo, he felt like he was dying inside. She looked sad, too. More than sad. She looked ashamed. She looked exhausted.

Whenever he tried to talk to her, she said the same thing. *"I'm doing what I know is best for both of us,"* and not a whole lot more. She'd done a bang-up job avoiding him while still managing to be present for every appearance or event at which she was needed. Jack knew she wasn't telling him something. It just didn't feel right. She'd shut herself off to him, and without that light—that radiance he'd discovered in her—he couldn't see well enough to put one foot in front of the other.

At first, Jack wondered if some of his misery was just due to the fact that before Sam no woman in his life had ever dumped him. He'd always been the dumper and never the dumpee. But he knew all this agony couldn't come from a battered ego. His whole fucking heart was broken. For the first time in his life, Jack understood what that expression meant.

The emptiness reminded him of the disappearing act Marguerite pulled on him when he was a kid.

Back then, Jack would spend hours in the secret room of his dad's Sunset Lane office, playing army men with a flashlight, while his dad conducted business. No one ever knew Jack was back there.

Where was he supposed to hide now? He was winding down the primary phase of a $3 million campaign for the U.S. Senate. He was stuck. He was in this. There was nowhere to go.

Jack laughed softly to himself, spinning the handle of his racquet in his hand. It amused him to recall how he'd explained to Sam that he'd just been going through the motions before he met her, that he felt dead inside before she came into his life. Well, it was ten times worse now that he'd lost her. He'd once joked that she was such a pipsqueak that she could never hurt him. How wrong he'd been. Sam's love had become so crucial to his existence that when she took it back Jack took a hit harder than anything the angriest three-hundred-pound lineman on earth could dish out.

"You all right? Am I being too hard on you with my serve?" Stuart laughed at his own joke and Jack tried to smile. "Seriously, Jack. What the hell is wrong with you lately? Whoever tried to blackmail you hasn't resurfaced and he probably won't, so I hope it's not that."

"It's not."

"You do realize Kara's tripping, right? She says you won't talk to her about anything, either. The whole staff is worried you're losing your edge."

Jack shrugged. "Could be."

"You've got to get it back."

"Don't know if I can, Stu."

Stuart slid down the wall right next to Jack. "Look. I'm going to ask you something and it may piss you off, but hear me out, OK?"

Jack nodded.

"Remember when I told you back in November that getting involved with Sam Monroe would be the stupidest thing you ever did? Well, listen, if that's what's bumming you out, forget I ever said that. She's really a fabulous woman and, truth be told, I think you two make a great couple. I've seen you look at her sometimes like you were in love. I've never seen you like that before, Jack—ever. And hey, you can tell me to go to hell if you want, but I'm just giving it to you straight."

"I appreciate that."

Stuart grinned. "So, did I hit on something? Are you and Sam . . . you know . . . involved for real?"

"Nope," Jack said, standing up. "When's Marguerite supposed to get into town?"

"Thursday." Stuart frowned at him, well aware that Jack had changed the subject for a reason, and scrambled to a stand as well. "I've booked her into the Ritz until the Wednesday after election night. She said she's ready to do whatever you need her to."

Jack nodded. "Let's wrap up this game, then. We've got to go over my notes for the last debate."

He saw Stuart give him a sideways glance and prepare to ask him something else, only to think better of it at the last second.

Smart, smart man.

◆ ◆ ◆

"We're almost done, gang. Tonight is the last debate. Then tomorrow is the election, and remember, Kara wants you guys at the big victory celebration. Have you picked out what you'd like to wear so I can double-check it?"

Sam set out a plate of homemade peanut butter cookies, determined to get her children through the next two days with a cheerful heart even if it killed her.

Sam still had so much to do. She had to find a rental house for them to move into in about two weeks, because buying a house was now out of reach. Both Lily and Greg wanted to continue at Park Tudor next year, so she'd like to stay in the Meridian Kessler or Broad Ripple neighborhoods, and that was going to be pricey. And the place had to be big enough for a total of five children plus a dog. Yeah, right. The market was flooded with those.

She also had to set up her work schedule with Marcia so that she could start booking clients. The dream of not going back to the salon was a joke now. She still hadn't decided what to do with Dakota and even considered slinking back to Mrs. Brashears with the new, potty-friendly version of her child, in the hopes that a combination of trust fund cash and begging would get him back into the Wee Ones Academy.

She found it ironic that since Mitch had stolen her stipend, his fifty-thousand-dollar check was the only thing that would keep them afloat. And, not for the first time, she wondered why a man desperate enough to steal from his own children would have bothered to make that payment in the first place. There was only one answer, of course—Mitch didn't make the payment. Someone else did. And when Sam started going in that direction, her imagination went wild.

After the polls closed tomorrow night, she'd get to the bottom of it. If she could somehow get ahold of that tape and destroy it, she could tell Jack everything long before the November election, improving the odds that he'd find it in his heart to forgive her.

Greg munched on a cookie. "So everybody's still pretty confident he'll win?"

Lily shook her head. "I heard Kara say Jack was losing momentum, that it looked like he didn't give a shit anymore about anything. You know his poll numbers are way down."

"Yeah," Greg said, nodding. "I've been worried about that. I wonder what's going on with him. Maybe we should have a talk with him."

"No!" Sam said, too abruptly. "I mean, he's swamped the next couple days. Let's give him some space and then we can all chat after the election."

Lily snapped a cookie in half and carefully studied her mother. "Why haven't you told me why you were so upset a couple weeks ago? Does this have anything to do with Jack? Because . . ." Lily shot a quick glance toward Greg. "We kind of figured the two of you were getting it on by now."

"Oh my God," Sam muttered.

"Eeew," Greg said, cramming another cookie into his mouth.

"Well, we did!" Lily said defensively. "I mean,

what we're saying is that would be OK with us, Mom. We wouldn't be skeeved out or anything if you and Jack wanted to be a couple. I just figured you were waiting to get through the primary before you told us, is all."

Sam closed her eyes and chuckled to herself. It seemed whenever she convinced herself that she was successfully hiding something from her kids they saw through the bullshit. It was that way when she and Mitch fought, when she got pregnant with Dakota, when Mitch left, and all the while she struggled to keep disaster at bay in the years that followed. Yes, she could always limit what information she gave them, but they saw the big picture anyway.

"You're partially right, Lily," Sam said. "We need to sit down and talk about a lot of things after the election, and my relationship with Jack is one of them. But the most important thing right now is that we fulfill the terms of our contract. Do you guys understand how crucial that is?"

They both nodded.

"Good. We're not bringing anything up right now that will cause the slightest ripple. We can't let anything or anybody screw this up."

"OoooK, Mom," Greg said, putting his milk glass in the sink and looking at Sam like she was unbalanced.

Greg and Lily grabbed their book bags, kissed Sam's cheek, and headed upstairs. As they were leaving the kitchen, Sam heard Lily whisper, "It's probably PMS."

Sam let her forehead drop to the cool wood of the breakfast table and rolled it back and forth. Yes indeed. She had one hell of a case of PMS—*Pregnant Mommy Syndrome*—and she knew it would surely get worse before it got better.

The debate was painful to watch. Jack wasn't able to focus. When it was his turn to answer a question from the three-person panel of journalists, he hardly ever used his allotted three minutes. Rebuttals were short if they came at all. Jack looked bored, like he would've preferred to be anywhere else in the world than up on that stage at Murat Theatre, and Charlton Manheimer pounded Jack to the ground at every opportunity. There were lots of them.

Sam glanced to her left and saw two rigid female faces. Kara seemed near tears, and Sam could imagine how distraught she must be after all she'd done to get Jack to this point, only to watch him choke in the eleventh hour. Marguerite, who had refused to acknowledge Sam's existence despite the close proximity, looked furious. She looked like she was ready to spring from her first-row seat and wring her son's neck.

This was a mess, and Sam was responsible, and part of her wanted to run up on that stage and tell Jack she loved him, she was pregnant with his twins, and she didn't care who the hell knew about any of this. Sam bit the inside of her mouth. But that wasn't her call to make. It wasn't *her* career and reputation that would be ruined when the tape came out. It was

Jack's. As twisted as it had gotten, the truth was, she was doing this for him. Because she loved him.

And watching him suffer made it painfully clear that he loved her, too.

Christy held the ice pack to her jaw and read the morning paper. She felt sick about Jack. True, it was sort of entertaining to see him crash and burn like this, but it was a slow burn, nothing sexy, and nothing that was her doing. So where was the rush in that? Yes, he'd probably lose tomorrow's election. But there'd be no blockbuster story. Who cared if a candidate just kind of lost his "oomph" at the end of a campaign? Interns could handle that angle, and she'd let them.

Christy was in an ugly mood. She had three zits, her cheeks were now so swollen that she looked like a chipmunk, and today marked the last daily news cycle in which she could air Mitch's tape and have it mean anything. With her luck, Mitch would show up in August, when Jack was no longer in the race, and give her a tape that would, at best, be a postscript on a former political figure. Sure, they'd gossip about it at the State House, but no one else in Indiana would give a rat's ass, and neither would the networks.

So, fuck it. *Fuck it all.* Christy called the oral surgeon's office and begged to be squeezed into the schedule that day. The receptionist said she was in luck—they had a cancellation at one o'clock.

Well, at least she'd been lucky in one way today. Maybe it was a sign of things to come.

• • •

Brandon needed some solace, and the one place he knew he could find it was out on West Sixteenth Street, at Long's Bakery. When things got really bad, like today, a dozen of their warm, melt-in-your mouth yeast doughnuts could make him happy again. Not that he'd eat the entire dozen. Not every time, anyway. At least not in the car on the way home. Someone had told him Long's doughnuts were so good because they used pure lard in their recipe. He'd rather not think of what was in the doughnuts. He just wanted to eat them.

Things were a mess. Mitch Bergen had vaporized. Christy still wouldn't let him in her pants. That night in her apartment had been a disaster—she pushed him off her and pushed him out the door before he could close the deal. Brandon was confident that if she'd only give him a chance, he'd prove he had what it took to keep her happy. But he couldn't help but feel that he'd blown the only chance he'd ever get.

He parked his car right on Sixteenth Street, where he could keep an eye it, since this was not the best of neighborhoods. He went through the front door that was decorated with a *Welcome Race Fans* banner and got in line. Even at two o'clock on a Monday afternoon, the place was rocking, the few scattered tables filled with a clientele in everything from business suits to the rags of homelessness, all there for the simple pleasure of strong, hot coffee and orgasmic pastries.

Something about the man sitting at the corner table next to the Shriners' gumball machine caught Brandon's attention. Maybe it was the color of the hair, which was probably blond when it was washed. Or maybe it was the stoop in the shoulders. No—it was the hands. The hands wrapped around a Styrofoam cup. Holy shit! That was Mitchell Bergen over there!

Brandon's turn at the front of the line came at the exact instant he spotted Mitch, and he was torn. Did he have time to place his order? If he spoke out loud would his voice carry over to where Mitch sat? Would Mitch recognize his voice and look up?

"What do you want, mister?" The lady behind the counter was not interested in his dilemma.

Brandon whispered, "A dozen yeast and a medium decaf."

She raised her eyebrows. "You a spy or something?" she asked, ringing him up and chuckling.

Brandon paid his money and waited, trying not to stare at Mitch. He got his order, ran out to the car, placed the doughnuts in the passenger seat and the coffee in the beverage holder, all the while studying the bakery door. Mitch was still in there.

Brandon opened his trunk and rooted around in and around his gym bag until he found the things he needed and tucked them inside his jacket pocket. He went back through that bakery door, thoughts of glory and Christy—naked—swirling through his brain. He reached the table, pulled Mitch to his feet, and immediately stuck the ice scraper into his side. "I will shoot you if you make a sound," he whispered. Then Brandon whipped out a pair of handcuffs and snagged Mitch's wrists, leading the stunned man from the bakery. Brandon winked at the lady behind the counter on his way out.

He threw Mitch in the back, tied his ankles together with the red paisley power tie he preferred for televised committee hearings, and drove off. He found a dead-end residential street in Speedway and pulled over at the cul-de-sac. Brandon got in the backseat with Mitch, who had done nothing but moan and mumble during the short ride. Whatever he was tripping on had done the job a little too well, Brandon feared.

He took a deep breath and patted Mitch down. There it was—the wire, the microphone, the miniature tape recorder, all stuffed into the inside zip compartment of his windbreaker. He had it! He had it!

Brandon dumped an unshackled Mitch at the Wishard Hospital emergency room, where he told the triage nurse that he'd found the man on the side of the road and brought him in as an act of mercy. She asked for Brandon's name, but he declined to give it. The instant he was back in his car, he called Christy's cell phone. She wasn't answering. He called her office. She hadn't come in that day at all. He called her home and got her machine.

He looked at his watch: it was 3:45 P.M. Christy could get this on the air for the six o'clock news if he could find her. Still sitting in the Wishard emergency drop-off lane, Brandon hit the play button and listened to the conversation between Mitch and Sam Monroe. This was gold. Pure fucking gold.

Christy would love him forever.

◆ ◆ ◆

"Dear God, Jack, you cannot be serious."

"I love Sam and she dumped me—totally out of the blue. She said she wasn't ready for a commitment, can you believe it? That's always been my line!"

Marguerite blinked, not sure what to say. She was astonished that Jack was pouring out his heart to her. He'd never done this, not even when he was a small child.

"I'm nothing without her. She won't even talk to me anymore."

She pursed her lips. Marguerite didn't care for Samantha Monroe, of course, but she couldn't abide by the idea that the woman could have been so cruel to Jack. As far as Marguerite knew, no one had ever broken up with her son.

"So this . . . this sudden lack of interest in the election is because of a broken heart?"

"Yes." Jack rested his elbows on his knees and hung his head. "I was going to ask her to marry me after the primary." He looked up and there were tears in his eyes. "Marry me for real."

"Where is she right now?"

"Upstairs. She stays in her studio or the guest wing when she knows I'm using the office."

"Studio?"

"I turned the old nursery into her painting studio."

"I see."

"I got so used to having her in my life. Every time I imagined my future, Sam was there. Now that she's gone, I . . . oh, man, I miss her so much." Jack buried his face in his hands and cried.

Marguerite sat down next to him on the couch and said, "There, now." After making that motherly comment, she wasn't sure what to do next. She folded her hands in her lap and glanced around the room, thinking how ironic it was that Jack had finally decided to confide in her, after all this time, and she was at a loss as to what to do. She returned her gaze to her son. He might be broken at the moment, but she saw him for who he was. He was brilliant, strong, and charming. He was a Tolliver through and through.

Marguerite reached out and placed her hand on her son's shoulder. Jack's head snapped up and he stared at her in wonder. It then occurred to her that she couldn't recall the last time she'd touched Jack, except for the requisite buss on the cheek upon arrival or departure. The last time she recalled hugging him was at his high school graduation. That couldn't be right, could it? That was over twenty years ago.

Jack blinked, and a tear made its way down his handsome cheek. The sight of her son reduced to tears like this—the harsh pain she saw in his eyes— this was unprecedented. Jack hadn't reacted like this even when doctors informed him he might lose his leg. In fact, he'd been stoic in comparison. And all this over a woman! Marguerite felt helpless.

"Would you like a hug, Jack?"

He stared at her like she had sprouted a second head. "I'm sorry. For a second I thought you asked me if I wanted a hug."

Marguerite removed her hand from his shoulder and stiffened. Even dealing with his own hurt, Jack was willing and able to hurt her. She rose from the couch.

He rose, too, and hovered above her. "I'm sorry. That was rotten of me. You surprised me, is all."

Marguerite nodded. "I surprised myself."

"You've never been a hugger."

"I suppose that's true."

"You hurt me a lot when I was little, Mother, do you realize that? You left me to figure out life on my own. Dad was too busy for me. You were so busted up over the twins that it was like you couldn't bear to look at me."

She felt her heart thud in her chest. "I believe that's somewhat of an exaggeration."

He smiled sadly. "Maybe. But that's what it felt like to me."

She looked away, staring out the floor-to-ceiling windows. "I'm sorry, Jack," she whispered.

He said nothing for a moment. Finally, she heard him sigh. "Thank you, Mother. You still up for that hug?"

Marguerite didn't move. She couldn't remember how she ever managed to get her arms high enough or wide enough to embrace her son.

"I'll hug you, then." Jack leaned down and wrapped his arms around her thin frame and gathered her close. It was, at once, delightful for her and awkward. It was certainly too much. Marguerite raised her arms briefly and patted his back, then pulled away. "That was nice," she said, smiling up at him. "Feeling better?"

"I guess," Jack said, laughing a little. "Thanks, Mom."

"So what's next? Is there time to get back on track, do you think?"

Jack shoved his hands in his chino pockets and shrugged. "I have an election eve thing scheduled at seven at the Marriott ballroom. I'm supposed to give a speech and rally the troops for precinct work tomorrow, plus do a few last-minute interviews for the eleven o'clock slots. Kara has me going hard until the very end."

"As any good campaign manager would. I'll be there tonight for you if you wish."

Jack nodded. "Thanks."

Marguerite headed toward the door of Gordon's office and was about to wish Jack well tonight. But when she turned toward her son she saw Gordon instead—handsome, cunning, strong Gordon, who, though certainly capable, never would have accomplished what he had without her love. It dawned on her that Jack must have found that in Samantha Monroe, as odd as it seemed.

"I want you to know that I am so very proud of you, son." Marguerite knew she needed to be quick about this because her voice was faltering. "You are a good man. And whatever happens tomorrow, I want you to know I'm proud."

She exited, determined that he wouldn't see her cry.

"Where are you right now? Right this instant?"

"Hoo-iz-schish?"

"Christy? I've been calling you for an hour. What the hell's wrong with you?"

"I jush had my roral surshery. Whash up, Big B? Wanna go to my playsh? Bring yer hancuffsh."

Brandon pulled his cell phone away from his ear and stared at it. *No. No fucking way did she just get her wisdom teeth out.*

"Where are you, Christy? Answer me."

"I jush love it when you get all bosshy like that."

"Where are you?"

"In my car."

"Don't tell me you're driving."

" 'K, I won't tell you."

"Pull over. Where are you? I'll come get you."

"Ooooh God, yessh. We gonna do it in your car?"

"Give me an address."

"Four score and scheven years ago . . ." Christy began laughing hysterically and Brandon heard brakes squealing in the background, followed by slurred curses.

"I got the tape, Christy. Focus on what I'm saying, here. I found Mitch. I have the tape in my hand and it really does have Samantha saying she was hired to pose as Jack's fiancée. You were right. Do you understand me?"

"No waaaaay. I gotta get to the schtashun."

"Yes, you do. I'm going to ask one more time. Where the *fuck* are you?"

"Well, I think I took Tenth Schtreet over to College Avenue, but I took out my contactsch for the schurshery, so I'm not really sure, but I'm just now turning left."

"Stop! College is one-way going right."

"Scheriously?"

"Get out of the car. Wait on the sidewalk. I'll come get you."

" 'K. Bring the hancuffshs."

Brandon cut through town as fast as he could manage, and just as he was reaching the intersection of Ohio and Pennsylvania he saw the strangest thing—a little red Nissan 350Z convertible moving north on the southbound street. It was Christy, and she drove right on up on the sidewalk in front of *The Indianapolis Star,* scattering screaming pedestrians and taking out three newspaper boxes and two parking meters before she thumped to a stop, the front end of her sports car kissing the red brick exterior of the newspaper building.

Brandon did a U-turn. He took advantage of the mayhem and left his car in the middle of the street for a quick getaway. He ran to the sidewalk, just in time to see Christy emerge from the wreckage. She seemed unhurt but was drooling, laughing, and pointing at the newspapers strewn everywhere. Brandon grabbed her by the hand and tried to get her to come with him, just as two photographers burst through the *Star*'s front door. Talk about a photo opportunity!

"Let's go." He made eye contact with her. "Now."

"Isn't that Christy Schoen, the TV chick?" One of the photographers lowered his camera and stared in disbelief. "Hey, man, is that Christy Schoen? Is she wasted?"

"No." Brandon shoved Christy in his car and drove off, knowing he could be charged as an accessory to whatever plethora of felonies and misdemeanors Christy would soon face. It was now 4:40

P.M. She still had time to get this on the air if she could stay out of police custody for a while longer. "When's your deadline for the six o'clock news?"

Christy face was turned away from him.

"How much time do you have?"

"When did the trees get so tiny?" she asked. "Is my car OK?"

"Christy. You need to focus."

She turned toward him, her eyes half-open. "Sho what exshactly did the that schlut elf bitch say on the tape?"

Nothing looked right on her. The doctor said she was about eleven weeks along, but her belly had already popped. Sam looked like this when she was about five months pregnant with Lily. She didn't even want to picture herself with two full-term babies living in her abdomen. She'd be as wide as she was tall.

"How about this?" Monté said, holding out a black skirt and a white lace blouse.

"Too severe."

Monté grabbed the hanger that displayed the expensive brown suit with burgundy velvet piping.

"I wore that at Jack's first debate."

"Nobody will remember."

"Kara said never to repeat wardrobe at public events. And besides, it's too hot for May and I'm pregnant, remember? An unwed mother? A homeless, unwed mother of five?"

Monté stared at her blankly. "How about this one?"

"Who cares what I wear tonight, anyway?" Sam grabbed the moss green sheath dress. "I won't be on

TV. Jack's just giving a speech. This is old, but it's fine."

Sam stepped into the dress and a pair of taupe pumps. Monté zipped her up the back. Sam added some little dangly earrings with green beads. She found a simple beige purse and held it over her bulging belly. "Will this work?"

Monté nodded. "You look fine, Sam. Just fine."

"Mom! Mom!" It was Greg, and he was calling for her all the way down in the foyer. He sounded panicked. "Turn on Channel Ten! Now!"

Sam's heart beat wildly. Had Jack been in an accident? Monté ran to the entertainment armoire and flung open the doors, grabbing the remote, just at Lily, Greg, and Dakota burst into the suite.

They all stared, in silence, as the anchor introduced that night's top story.

"We are so busted," Lily said.

It was almost too painful for Brandon to watch. The makeup people had begged Christy to remove the gauze packing before she went on camera, but she'd refused. She'd asked them, "Whicsh is worsh for our viewersh? A little gausheze or blood dripping down my schin like I'm Mrs. Dracula?"

At least she'd sobered up some. She couldn't drink coffee, but she'd put off taking any pain medication and the anesthesia was wearing off. Christy and the producer had worked like fiends throwing together the segment, while the news director hovered over Christy and repeatedly asked her, "Are you sure about the authenticity of this? Are you absolutely sure?"

Just as she was racing down the hall and into makeup, the police arrived. The four officers assigned to bring her in agreed to wait until the commercial break before they took her to the station for a little chat about property damage, reckless endangerment, and driving while intoxicated.

So there she was. Christy was getting her moment of glory. She was breaking the story she was convinced would be the crowning achievement of her career. But damn, Brandon had sure seen her look better. Her speech was noticeably slurred. She'd just drooled a little. She had at least three zits. And the police were getting restless.

He wasn't so sure this would end up the way Christy had envisioned.

Kara stood in the center of the Sunset Lane office, remarkably calm and clearly in charge.

Stuart, Jack, and Marguerite were instructed to stand behind the big mahogany desk. Sam and Monté were invited to sit on the couch. Kara stood in the middle, her feet planted wide, remote control in hand.

"All right, people. Jack's speech is scheduled to start in an hour. It's a twenty-minute car ride to the hotel. That means we have forty minutes to find out what exactly happened here and what we plan to do about it. Everyone turn off your cell phones and pagers. Any questions so far?"

No one moved.

"Happy viewing." With one click, Christy Schoen's segment played. Sam had already seen it, so she looked at Jack instead. He must have felt her, because he caught her eye. What Sam wouldn't give to know what was going on behind that mask. Did he think she had betrayed him? Did he hate her? Would he believe her when she told him the truth?

"Is Christy drooling?" Stuart asked in disbelief. "What the—"

"Her wisdom teeth," Jack muttered.

Sam looked to Marguerite, who stared back at her with disdain.

"Lord have mercy," Monté whispered to Sam. "This is sure gonna be an interesting little get-together."

Christy's voice was so slurred and the room was so full of tension that Sam had to fight back laughter when the segment began. "In a schocking development on the political front, *Channel Ten Action Newsch at Six* hash learned that U.S. Schenate candidate Jack Tolliver paid a woman to posche ash hish fianshay in order to win votesch."

Christy went on to explain the arrangement in a mostly accurate, but slurred, way, then played the audiotape of Sam talking in the City-County stairwell. They ran her words along the bottom of the screen for dramatic effect. Of course, Christy failed to mention who taped the conversation, how she got it, or whom Sam was talking to.

Christy ended her report with, "Neither Tolliver nor any of his campaign offishcialsh could be reached for comment on this excschlushive report."

Kara clicked it off, then looked at each person in the room for one second. "We're going to do this Q and A style. I want your answers to be quick and I want them to be honest."

Kara looked at Sam, suddenly at a loss for words. Sam launched right into it.

"Mitch—my ex-husband, Mitchell Bergen— came back to town, paid off all the money he owed in child support, then was waiting for me in the City-County Building when I went to pick up the check. He became hysterical at the idea of Jack—" Sam raised her eyes to see Jack listening intently. "Well, he didn't like the idea that I was engaged to Jack because he could possibly adopt the kids if we got married. I told Mitch the truth to get him to calm down. Turns out he was taping it the whole time. He trapped me. I know I violated the terms of my contract when I told him and—"

"I don't give a damn about the contract," Jack said, his entire body tensed. "Did he lay a finger on you? Did he threaten you?"

"He blackmailed me. He said the only way he wouldn't release the tape to the media was if I paid him all the money I'd earned from my stipends. I wired it to an account number he gave me."

"Oh no, Sam—" Jack bolted around the desk, but Kara stiff-armed him.

"Go on. Hurry," Kara said.

"I know I should have told you, Jack, but Mitch is crazy and obviously on drugs again and I did what he said because I thought it was the only way I could protect you."

"Dear God," Marguerite said.

"Then Mitch told me . . . well, he threatened me that—" Sam couldn't help it. She started crying, and

Monté squeezed her hand and told her to get it out. "OK." Sam took a deep breath. "Mitch threatened me that he'd release the tape unless I broke it off with Jack in real life—unless I told Jack it was over between us. For real. Not the contract, but our real relationship."

It was silent for several seconds. "I knew it," Stuart whispered.

Kara looked at each person in the room and surmised the situation instantly. "You mean to tell me that I am the only one in here who was in the dark about this?"

Monté chimed in. "Like the night of the ice storm. No lights. Bumping into shit everywhere."

"There's more." Sam took a deep breath and looked past Kara to Jack. "It gets worse, or better, or worse, however you want to look at it, but I think it's great."

"We have five minutes," Kara said. "So, how about we look at it real fast."

"I'm pregnant."

Jack used his quarterback experience to slide around Kara. He gathered Sam up in his arms and kissed her. Sam was trying to beg him to forgive her, but he wouldn't stop kissing her long enough so that she could get the words out.

"I want a raise," Kara said.

Marguerite lowered herself into the desk chair.

"I love you so much, Sam," Jack cried, twirling her around. "My God! This is a mess and I don't even care, because I love you and you're going to have my baby!"

"Jack, put me down a second." Sam straightened her dress. "That's not exactly true."

"Who's the father, then?" Stuart asked, apparently not getting enough drama.

"This is like *Days of Our Lives* meets *The West Wing*," Monté said.

Sam laughed, then noted the horror on Jack's face, which, thank God, was at least no longer covered in the politician mask. "Jack is most definitely the father, but it's not one baby. It's two. I'm having twins."

Jack laughed loud and put his hands on her tummy. "This is the happiest day of my life! This is all I want, Sam, your love and the children."

"Dear God in heaven," Marguerite said from the desk chair.

"But you're running for the Senate, Jack!" Kara cried.

"She's right," Sam said. "You can have me and the kids, but you're supposed to be a senator, too. It's what you've come to truly want and I won't take that away from you."

"But the voters will," Stuart said. "Unless we can convince them otherwise. Like right now."

"Everyone get in the limo," Kara said. "We'll finish this discussion on the way."

"There's nothing to discuss," Jack said, taking Sam by the hand. "I know exactly what I'm going to do."

Kara stood perfectly still, trepidation in her big brown eyes. "What's your plan?"

"I'm going to get up there on that stage and tell the truth—plain and simple."

"I haven't had a whole lot of experience with that," Kara said flatly.

"Neither have the voters," Stuart said.

"Then it will be a learning experience for everyone," Jack said. "Monté?"

Monté looked around the room to be sure there was no one else who could answer to that name. "Yes?"

"You take care of Sam. Help her get the kids ready and get her to the hotel. Don't leave her side. Would you do that for me?"

"Absolutely."

Jack turned toward Sam, taking her hands in his. "I need to jot down a few thoughts on the way to the hotel. I'll see you there, OK?"

Sam nodded, smiling at him.

"Answer me one question."

"Anything."

"Do you love me, Sam?"

"Oh, Jack. I love you. You will never have reason to doubt that ever again."

"Marguerite?" Jack turned toward his mother, who sat quietly at the desk. "Are you coming with us?"

"You-all go along. I'll have my driver take the rest of us." She rose from the chair and shooed Jack out the door. Then she set her sights on Sam and moved toward her. Marguerite stopped directly in front of Sam and opened her thin arms.

"Would you mind if I gave you a hug, Samantha?"

Sam let out a surprised laugh. "That would be nice."

Sam wrapped her arms around Marguerite. She kissed Jack's mother on the cheek and smiled at her.

Marguerite stared back at Sam, looking misty-eyed and a little lost.

"I have two favors to ask of you, if I may be so bold."

"Sure."

"I want you to do my hair. Cut it very short. I'll let my natural silver grow in. I've seen some older women who look quite stylish like that."

Sam nodded, not daring to look over at Monté. "It would be my honor."

"I wonder if you could do it now, before the news conference."

Monté was already out the door and Sam knew she was setting up in the butler's pantry. "We can do that."

"Wonderful. Thank you. And my second favor is, would you permit me to be a doting grandmother to the twins? I would understand if you turned me down. You'd have every right." Marguerite's face twisted with the effort not to cry. "But I'm asking anyway."

Sam smiled. "Absolutely, Marguerite. Of course you can."

Monté poked her head in the office. "The salon is open for business. I'll get the kids ready so we can go have ourselves a news conference that'll go down in history!"

The ballroom of the Marriott was packed with reporters, still and video photographers, and a sea of volunteers. Jack felt a light fluttering in his chest and a spring in his step as he climbed the stairs leading to the stage. He headed toward the podium, thinking that he'd had some great moments behind podiums and some truly awful ones and he wasn't quite sure which this would turn out to be. It didn't matter—the only things that mattered to Jack weren't things at all, and they were coming up the stairs behind him.

Sam held Dakota's hand. Behind them came Greg, Lily, and Marguerite. Kara and Stu were already seated in folding chairs to the back of the stage, and Jack gave a quick salute to Kara. She tried to smile bravely.

Jack placed his note cards on the podium and let the wave of questions hit him face-on. Some were kind, such as that of the woman radio reporter who shouted, "*Did you at least grow to like her?*" Channel 3's Ed Gilligan let it rip with, "*Is it true that Samantha Monroe was a kept woman?*"

Jack figured the quicker he did this the less Sam and the kids would have to face.

"Good evening and thank you, everyone, for coming on such short notice." In the split second required for Jack to take a breath, more questions were hurled toward the stage. "I think most of your questions will be answered if you allow me just a few minutes to tell you the truth," he said into the microphone. "I ask you to give me the courtesy of speaking uninterrupted."

An expectant hush spread over the crowd. In all his years in football and politics, Jack had always known that failure had a certain smell to it, and this room was packed with people sniffing for failure and/or blood. So many in this room would like to contribute to taking him down. But he planned to do their work for them.

"It's true. I paid Samantha Monroe to pose as my fiancée. We were never truly engaged to be married."

The crowd went crazy. Some of the reporters ran for the doors, more concerned with being first than with being accurate. Jack had no sympathy for them. He took a moment to glance behind him, and he saw Sam, strong and beautiful and smiling at him. Greg nodded his way. Lily produced a shy grin, and Jack was stunned by how lovely she looked that night sans the hiking boots and eyeliner. Dakota gave Jack a big thumbs-up, and he knew he had all the courage he would ever need and turned back to the mayhem.

"Do you think we can all act like adults in here?" Jack's question brought the ruckus to a halt. "This will be brief." He paused, looking down at his notes. "First, I am truly sorry for having lied to you, the citizens of Indiana. What I did was inexcusable. I take full responsibility for my actions and want it to be known that there is no one else that deserves criticism and blame. It was my campaign and my decision. I especially want it to be known that Samantha Monroe did nothing wrong. This was not her idea. I recruited her, negotiated the terms, and paid her to go along with my plan."

"How much did you pay her?"

"Did you have sex with her?"

Before he could respond to either question, he felt the dais vibrate under his feet and turned to see Lily hurrying Dakota offstage. Greg shook his head in disgust as he followed.

Jack's voice trembled with rage when he spoke again. "Modern politics has become a cesspool of the surreal. It's a game, ladies and gentlemen. And I thought the NFL was ugly—let me tell you, it's nothing compared to campaigning for national office. We are corrupted, each one of us. We've lost sight of what's important here, and that's the simple and profound privilege spelled out in our Constitution—we get to choose who represents us at every level of government. We're lucky sons of bitches."

Someone to the side of the stage—someone who sounded suspiciously like Monté—shouted, "Can somebody give me an amen?"

It was just enough to make Jack smile and catch his breath. "All I'm saying is we are supposed to elect people with brains, integrity, insight, patience, and—most important—heart. We need people in our towns and in Washington who actually care about those they represent, truly know them and care about them. We are not going to make it as a civilization if we focus more on who's got the better tie and which candidate's high-priced marketing consultant came up with the catchiest campaign slogan. We all need to clean up our act."

"So you're dropping out of the race?" That question was followed by a low rumble of laughter.

"No, I'm not. I'm running and I'll lose and I don't give a damn." He heard Kara clear her throat behind him. "I mean it. Starting right now, I'm running as Jack Tolliver, a very flawed—but honest—guy. I admit it! No man should be allowed to date as many beautiful women as I have and have such fun doing it. I was a child of privilege, and I've never known what it's like to be hungry or even have to save for a bike or a car or a ski trip. And back in college, honestly, I know damn well I inhaled every time I—"

"Jack!" Kara barked from behind him.

"Anyway, the whole point of this news conference is to respond to Channel Ten's news story, so here it is. Be sure your pencils are sharpened." Jack reached behind him for Sam's hand. She grabbed hold and stood at his side.

The cameras went crazy again and Jack waited a few moments for the noise to settle. He took that time to squeeze Sam's soft fingers in his, and he felt her warmth and love all the way to the soles of his feet.

He turned to Sam, smiled at that open, brave face, and kissed her—hard. He wrapped his arms around her and held her tight, pressing his lips to hers with such urgency that he feared he might be smothering her. He let her go enough to see the shock and delight in her eyes, then returned his attention to the hooting crowd, his arm still gripped around her waist.

"Life can be funny, ladies and gentlemen. Seems I hired this woman to be a stand-in for the real thing and that's exactly what she ended up being—the real thing. She's determined, courageous, fun, and a gifted artist. She's a great mom to her three kids, and I know she'll be just as wonderful with our twins on the way."

Jack heard a faint whimper escape his mother's lips, just before all hell broke loose. More reporters ran for the doors, and he laughed. "Might want to stick around a few more minutes, Ed!" he called out. "I'm not done yet!"

Jack leaned into the microphone and began to speak softly, realizing this was the most fun he'd had at a news conference in his entire fucking career. "I am still in this race, Indiana. Anyone out there listening, I'm telling you that you can vote for me if you want me in Washington, and I'll work hard for you if you send me, but I have to be honest—I love Sam and her kids more than any job, no matter how important. If I lose this Senate race, then so be it. I will dedicate my life to taking care of the people I love and making their world a better place, even if I do it on a school board or a zoning appeals board or in a neighborhood association. It's all the same work and it will all be for them, because they are what is precious to me."

Jack guided a stunned Sam to the center of the stage, away from the podium, and knelt down on his good knee before her. She'd already started to cry and her smile was shaky, but this was the most perfect moment Jack could imagine.

She touched his shoulder and whispered, "You sure you know what you're doing, Jack?"

He laughed, then pulled the old emerald and diamond ring off her finger. "I sure do," he whispered back. "I'm putting this Ferrari in sixth gear, baby."

Jack glanced over at Marguerite and loved that she'd managed to crack a smile. Well, good for her—maybe there was hope for Grandma yet. Her hair looked better, that was for damn sure.

He surveyed the audience, now a silent sea of openmouthed stares, and decided he'd reward all these patient people with the sound bite they'd been waiting for. Jack adjusted his kneeling pose to make it as Shakespearean as possible, slipped the beautiful old ring on his beautiful young love, and said, "Samantha Monroe, will you do me the honor of really, truly, being my wife?"

"Hell, yes!" Sam hooted with happiness, and threw herself into his arms.

Jack buried his nose in her spicy hair and cried some very public tears, feeling Sam's arms put the squeeze on him. Maybe it was poetic justice that this woman's tight grip was the only thing that had managed to set his heart free, but as he'd learned, some things in life were just a mystery.

Epilogue

Five years later

"You really should try to sex up your image a bit, Jack."

Kara heard him groan, and she knew it was pushy of her to insist they meet during the holiday break, but they needed to hash out the specifics of Jack's re-election campaign. The primary would be a cinch—Jack had the party's backing and his two opponents were nobody goofs with no funding. It was the general election next November that had Kara nervous. Jack's likely opponent was so youthful, gorgeous, brilliant, and rich that Kara had trouble sleeping at night.

"Give it a rest, Kara, babes." Jack raked his long fingers through his dark hair, now tinged with gray that seemed especially noticeable under the breakfast nook chandelier. "I'm a forty-four-year-old father of five, which includes a pair of preschool divas, and I'm afraid this is as sexy as it gets."

Monté shook her closely cropped head and her earrings jingled. "The chicks still dig you, Senator."

After the laughter subsided, Kara listened to what Monté had to say, hardly recalling that there was a time Kara questioned Jack's naming her his press secretary. Monté had gone back to night school to finish her degree while working full-time as Jack's constituent outreach director in his Indianapolis office. She'd learned the ropes and done such an amazing job that Jack had brought her to Washington two years ago, where her nerve and plain-speaking genius seemed to work magic. Kara had to admit that Jack had made a perfect choice.

"Now," Monté went on, "I'm not necessarily sayin' that women are going to sweep you into office with the same tidal wave of support they gave you six years ago, but all our focus groups indicate you're still hot with the ladies."

"I can attest to that." Sam placed a steaming teapot on the table and bent down to kiss Jack's head. He gave her a playful smack on the rear. Kara smiled, knowing that Jack and Sam's real romance— the entire life they'd built together—had turned out better than anything she could have manufactured.

Sam owned a successful Georgetown modern art gallery and had been commissioned by private collectors and corporations to paint several major pieces. She'd been a huge influence on Jack's political life, encouraging him to sponsor domestic violence legislation and a bill to increase federal day-care funding. The irony didn't escape Kara that because Jack was now known as a champion of working women and families, he'd lost some of that dangerous bad-boy edge that got him elected in the first place.

"And I don't care what marketing research says; I'm not dyeing my hair. That would be ridiculous, and, I might add, pathetic." Jack poured himself a fresh cup of tea. "Voters elect people to office, not hairdos."

"But Ryan Watson is—"

"A kid! What can he possibly know about life at thirty-two?" Jack took a sip of his tea. "I was clueless at that age. I didn't learn what life was about until I got married, adopted three children, and had two of my own."

"Watson is married and has a baby," Stuart quietly noted.

"He's a baby himself."

Kara sighed. Jack had taken the "honest-but-flawed-guy" concept and run with it, becoming a standout freshman senator known for his simple talk and passion for his job. Jack split his time between Indiana and Washington and really got out there to mix with constituents. He'd served Indiana well, and Kara was determined to see him stay put, Ryan Watson or no.

Kara heard footsteps and voices nearing the kitchen doorway and turned to watch Lily, Greg, and Simon saunter in. It had been a year since she'd seen what Monté called the Mod Squad, all together in the same room, and it was startling how they'd matured.

Simon was nineteen, a sophomore at Howard University in Maryland, where he was majoring in industrial engineering. He had to be at least six-two, but he still had the same baby face, soft, warm eyes, and sly sense of humor. Monté often said that Simon's happiness was her greatest achievement.

Lily was twenty-year-old and a senior at New York University. She'd studied graphic design and fashion, and she planned to stay in the big, bad city after graduating a year early in the spring, much to Sam and Jack's chagrin. Lily had shot up to five-ten, had a chic, shorter haircut, and was a lot more sparing in her use of eye pencil these days.

Greg was eighteen, a freshman at Northwestern University, where he was a member of their nationally ranked debate team, an especially sweet success for a kid who once had stuttered as bad as Greg had. He planned to attend law school.

Next came Dakota. He was almost nine, a musical prodigy on the electric bass guitar, of all things. He'd been invited to sit in with a few famous rock groups when they came through Washington, and the *Post* had done a feature on Dakota and his own prepubescent garage band, with perhaps the most unfortunate name Kara had ever heard: Sphincter Management. Dakota's red curls were so long they nearly covered his eyes, but not the sparkle in them.

The last—and loudest—addition to the crowd was the Terrible Tolliver Twins. With their arrival, Kara knew for sure this meeting was over.

"She stole my tiara!" Maggie stomped up to the table, glaring at her father. "She's a mean stealer!"

"This is my crown, not hers!" Ana clomped in right behind, attired in a pair of sneakers and one of

Lily's old cut-off formals. "Her left hers in the car! It's got gummi bears stuck in the diamonds! I saw it! This one's mine!"

"It's 'she,' not 'her,' " Maggie informed her sister. "You're talking wrong again."

"Lord have mercy," Monté said to Sam. "I thought you'd stockpiled this place with tiaras as a precaution."

"Guess you can never have too many," Sam said, smiling at Monté and then her raven-haired identical twins.

"Shall we discuss this, ladies?" Jack scooted his chair back from the table and opened his arms. Kara sat back, prepared to watch Jack work his daddy voodoo on his high-maintenance daughters, Marguerite and Indiana Dickinson Tolliver. As always, Kara was impressed to see how Jack relied on a combination of tact and charm, this time to get them to agree to share the one non-gummi-bear-encrusted crown in ten-minute intervals.

"Did everyone hear about Christy and Brandon?" Stuart asked.

"Hey! I was going to tell them!" Kara was truly pissed that Stuart beat her to the punch, because they hadn't had any interesting developments in the Christy Schoen fiasco in ages. At first, it seemed there was always a new twist—Christy got fired from Channel Ten for paying a source, a violation of the station's ethics policy; Mitch was charged with nonpayment of child support and narcotics possession and sentenced to probation, giving up his parental rights without a fight; Christy moved from job to job in small-town TV markets until she gave up and re-united with Brandon; Mitch disappeared again, never to be seen since.

Sam frowned, sitting down next to Jack. "I'm not sure I want to know the latest. The last I heard, Christy and Brandon got married and formed a lob-bying firm for nuclear power or something."

"It was the strip-mining industry, actually, and they're getting divorced," Stu said. "Apparently, Christy got an offer from a little TV station in Moline, Illinois, and she's taking it, leaving Brandon in D.C."

"Now that's a real shame," Monté said. "If ever two people were made for each other, it was that pair."

"Let's wrap this up, Kara." Jack stood, letting his two daughters slide down his legs like he was an amusement park ride. "We've got some celebrating to do around here. The pizzas should arrive any minute, and that's good, because I'm starved."

Jack began to walk away from the table with the two girls still attached to his ankles. They screamed with delight as he dragged them across the floor to-ward the great room. Stuart, Greg, Lily, Simon, and Dakota went with him, talking loud and laughing louder, moving at Jack's slow pace.

"I wish Marguerite were still alive to see this," Sam said, wrapping her arms around herself.

Monté touched her shoulder. "She got to see her son make it to the Senate and she got her grandkids, Sam."

Sam nodded. "And she turned out to more of a teddy bear than a dragon lady."

"Who'd've guessed?" Kara shook her head in

wonder. Five years ago, Kara was amazed at how Marguerite began to mellow, first when the twins were born and even more so after she married Allen Ditto, admitting that she'd had her eye on him for over a decade.

"Hey, you all know what tonight is, don't you?" Monté wiggled her eyebrows. Kara and Sam stared at her blankly.

"Pizza night?" Kara offered.

Monté scowled. "Friday? Last one of the month? Ring any bells?"

"It's D & D night!" Sam squealed. "Hold that thought!" She ran to the cabinet and got three teacups, poured a little into each, and passed them out. "It's not margaritas, but Jose Cuervo and I don't get along too well anymore."

"We got us some real men to comfort us these days," Monté said, laughing.

Kara knew that statement wasn't meant to hurt her, and it didn't. She'd come to understand that politics was the love of her life and always would be.

And as far as Monté went, everyone was thrilled for her and Roy, who would celebrate their second anniversary in February. Monté claimed Roy's work schedule of two weeks home followed by two weeks on the road made him the ideal husband. *"When he comes home I'm thrilled to see him, and at the end of the two weeks I'm thrilled to see his ass out the door. If this marriage doesn't work, then nobody's will."*

"I realize that none of us are the slightest bit depressed, but let's drink up anyway," Kara said, raising her teacup.

"To happiness," Monté said.

"To love," Sam said.

"To winning in November," Kara said.

The three clinked their cups together and in unison said, "To friends."